Resounding praise for Michael Scott Rohan's

THE WINTER
OF THE WORLD

"OUTSTANDING FANTASY FICTION"
Andre Norton, author of *The Mirror of Destiny*

"AMONG THE BEST OF THE CROP...
Rohan has an entertaining, engrossing style"
Science Fiction Chronicle

"BOLD...IMPRESSIVE...ORIGINAL"
Kirkus Reviews

"ENGAGING FANTASY...MARVELOUS...VIVID...
THOROUGHLY SATISFYING"
Publishers Weekly

"STARTLING...EXCITING...
HAUNTING...REMARKABLE...
Adept strokes of almost science and seeming reality,
and characters that live and breathe...
A gifted writer...Pages turn as if by magic."
Jean M. Auel, author of *Clan of the Cave Bear*

THE WINTER OF THE WORLD

VOLUME ONE

THE ANVIL OF ICE

MICHAEL SCOTT ROHAN

AVON BOOKS • NEW YORK

AVON BOOKS
A division of
The Hearst Corporation
1350 Avenue of the Americas
New York, New York 10019

First Avon Books Printing: February 1989

For Richard Evans

ACKNOWLEDGMENTS

To Deborah, as ever, for her intense involvement and support; to Richard, Toby, and Sarah and other staff members at Macdonald & Co. (Publishers) Ltd., for all they have contributed; and to Maggie Noach, agent extraordinary. Also for their ballads, to the shades of Aloys Schreiber and Carl Loewe.

Contents

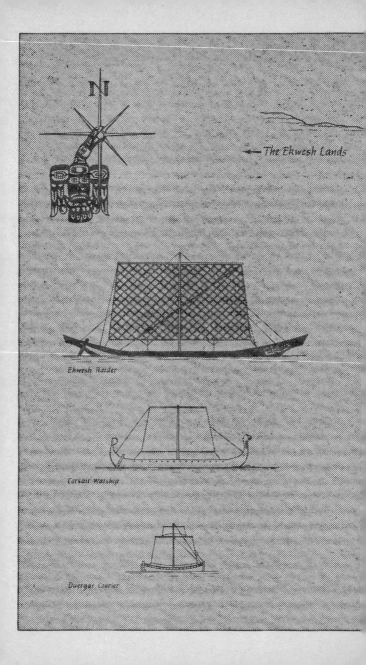

N

← The Ekwesh Lands

Ekwesh Raider

Corsair Warship

Duergar Courier

CHAPTER ONE

The Forging

It was the chill before dawn that woke him, and the snuffling and stamping of the great bull in its stall. The dawns were always cold then, whatever the season, in the Long Winter of the Old World, in the dominion of the Ice. So the chronicles record, and though copied and recopied by many hands, the voice of one who has seen, and felt, speaks still from their pages. But now, on this day, it was newly spring, and the keen air was making the great beast impatient to run free in the pastures among its cows. So the boy sprang out of his pile of skins, wincing at the air's bite, and began scrambling into those of them that were garments. If he let the bull begin bellowing here so early, it would mean a beating. He swung the moth-eaten fur cloak round his shoulders and seized the long goad off the wall, the strange shapes and characters in the icy metal branding his fingers with unknown wisdom. The bull's tossing head, with its horns as long as his body, was no more than a lighter patch in the blackness high above him, but with the ease of long practice he slipped along the stall wall, a slab split from a sandstone boulder, and quickly looped the goad through the carved ring in the bull's nostrils. Instantly the outswept horns ceased goring the air, the great head drooped, and the bull stood docile while the boy undid its tethers and urged it out of the stall. It waited placidly while he untied the rest of the herd and shooed and bustled the huge beasts, white as soiled ice, out into the pallid air, their breath billowing in clouds as they lowed and snorted, their hooves crushing the half-

1

frozen mud. Thus the day that was to change all days began, for him, like any other.

Nothing else was stirring in the little town called Asenby. The very houses seemed asleep, shuttered tight against the cold; even the wide-eyed faces painted in vivid red and black across their planks looked dazed and only half-awake. The boy scowled as they passed the Headman's great house with the painted whales framing its porch, leaping four stories to the rooftree. When he was a few strides further on he jerked the goad slightly; the bull snorted loudly in pained protest, awaking loud anxious lowings from the rest of the herd. But by the time the shutters slammed open he was already past, turning the corner toward the Landgate.

From the high old house on the corner light gleamed, warm and red as a breath of summer, running molten gold even into the cold puddles, and there came the low muttering of a chant. The boy scowled again, yet more darkly, and led the bull closer so he could peer in the open door as he passed. Yes, Hervar was there, his lean shadow dancing immense on the wall of the forge as he squatted over his anvil, crooning and tapping away at a flake of blackened metal. The new hoeheads that would be, new for the newmade virginity of the soil. In the working of the metal, in the quavering of the chant, lay potencies united by the power and craft of the smith to make the hoes potent in themselves—a virtue of fertility, for the fields and perhaps also the women who would till them. That much the boy knew, but no more, for all he wished to, for all he had tried to puzzle out the markings on the goad. The wizened old smith had always refused him knowledge, even the simplest instruction in signing and reading that he gave every child of the town. Now he was looking up, glaring through straggling sweat-plastered gray locks and waving the boy sharply away without missing a beat of the chant. His plump apprentice came bustling out, brandishing long iron tongs and shouting. "You keep off, Alv! Out to your work, or I'll scratch your pale hide for you where it itches! Tinker's brat!"

The boy sneered, twitched the goad around suddenly and set the wide horns tossing a foot's span from the apprentice's flattened nose. He retreated with a panic-stricken squeak, and the herd, moving close to the house, began to press against its walls and peer round-eyed and stupid into the smithy. Some beasts were actually scratching themselves against the timbers, till the house vibrated and the chant inside rose to a cracked screech. That might be too much. Hurriedly Alv called them off, back into the center of the street, slapping at their grimy flanks with his hands and leaving the goad securely in the ring.

The town wall was a massive affair, circling the little knot of streets and running straight out into the sea on either flank of the little harbor, acting as a breakwater. As long as Alv could remember they had been rebuilding and strengthening it, thickening the broad drystone base, shoring up the double rows of mighty pine trunks above and adding towers on the rampart that ran between them, so that constant watch could be maintained on both sea and land. The watchman in the gatetower ahead yawned when Alv hailed him, and made no haste about swinging the great bars up on their counterweights to open the narrow gate. The other herds weren't even stirring yet, though that would have been no defense for him if he'd been late. The cattle filed through in pairs, no more, and the gate swung to again behind. Alv dimly remembered it as wide, and always open in daylight, but these were troubled days; few traders' wagons ever rolled this way now. The cattle jostled and crowded on the uphill path, eager to get to their pastures, and when they reached the high meadows overlooking the town they broke and scattered, some clumsily skipping and bounding as if they were calves once more. Alv clambered up onto his favorite rock seat and deftly flipped the goad free from the ring. The bull stared at him an instant in baffled fury, then snorted violently and went lumbering away across the meadow. Alv settled down to eat the chunk of hard cornbread he had been given last night, and the strip of salt fish he had stolen to go with it. He looked out, far out across the sea to the horizon. Soon the sun would arise and bring him warmth; small birds were singing in the bushes, and the sky was filling with light that reddened the flanks of the cattle and the wisps of smoke that rose over the wood-tiled rooftops below, as kitchen fires were kindled. But the sight kindled other fires in him; how often he had sat there and prayed, to powers he did not know, that the calm gray sea beyond might leave its rolling and rise in wrath to sweep those rooftops away!

He shivered. The breeze off the sea was growing strong, sending ragged banks of cloud scudding landward; in the growing light they cast weird rippling shadows on the waves. For a few minutes he amused himself watching them—and then he sprang to his feet. In those shadows under the clouds other, deeper, darknesses were slipping across the waves, long sleek shapes lancing in toward the shore. Four of them, low in the water where a watchman nearer sea level might easily miss them in this dim, hazy light.

Without thinking he cupped his hands and yelled. Nothing happened. If he was wrong they'd flay him alive. He yelled again, and saw the Landgate watchman look up and wave casually. "No!" he screamed, so loud his voice cracked. "Out there, you fool! Out there!" Alv stabbed his arm out seaward again and again. The watchman turned and seemed to cock his head and squint into the low light. Then he sprang up, grabbed the huge steerhorn that hung above the gate and blew a loud bellowing blast. The bull in the meadow echoed it, stamping the turf in challenge. Confused shouts rose up from below, and the rumble of feet on the ramparts; an instant later another horn blew from the seawall, and a drum stuttered. All over the town shutters slammed open, voices squeaked and yammered, men and women charged half-dressed into the street, colliding with each other and tumbling down in the mud. Bright gleams moved more purposefully through the streets and up onto the ramparts, armored men of the town guard marching to their posts, staring as Alv was, out to sea.

He could see the ships more clearly now, sails furled on their low masts, foam rising along their flanks as long lines of oars dipped and rose in a fast, thrusting rhythm. For an instant, cresting a wave, a long outthrust prow stood out, with a wide flat platform just behind it. Along the black hull beneath the platform was painted an animal head with long sharp-toothed jaws agape. Above the hubbub below, a single name rose, almost like a sign. "The Ekwesh! Ekwesh raiders!"

For an instant Alv stood transfixed, staring. The Ekwesh, this far down the coast? But then he remembered his own peril. He went bounding down the slope, forgetting the path, arms flailing wildly to keep his balance as he skidded through the grass. But as he circled the hillside toward the Landgate a solid thudding sound came echoing up to him, and he saw the Landgate quiver and resound as heavy logs were piled against it.

"Wait!" he screamed at the top of his voice, hearing it absurdly thin and childish against the wind. "Let me in! Open the gate! Wait—"

On the rampart opposite, only a little below him now, a burly figure in helm and mail turned and gestured sharply. "No time now, boy!" bellowed the Headman. "Should've got back at once! Get away, hide yourself out there somewhere—and have a mind to those cattle!"

But I gave the alarm! I warned you! The boy stood there an instant with his eyes brimming at the unfairness of it, his fists clenched. But he knew well enough there was no use pleading; if the Headman wouldn't risk opening the gate for his own precious cattle, why risk it for one young thrall? So the Headman would reason, and so his town. Why had he ever bothered to warn them? Wasn't this the destruction he'd been praying for? Let them escape it if they could! As for himself—hide? Where, on these rolling hills? A little further up the slope, overlooking the seaward side of the town, was a clump of scrub. As well there as anywhere; at least he would have a good sight of the fun.

The ships were nearer now. They must have heard the alarm raised and were plowing directly inshore to the attack, knowing that they could not now hope to land and take the town open and undefended, not without a long siege, which was seldom their way. Archers massed on the rampart, but they were not yet within bowshot, not quite. Alv was staring wide-eyed; he had never seen so powerful a force. Each ship bore at least thirty oars on each side, and there looked to be more than just rowers on board; behind the low gunwales he could see other figures squatting and raising gaudy shields to protect the

rowers. Suddenly, obviously at command, every oar swung
upright in a great rippling movement like the flick of a
fish's fin. In that moment Alv saw three outlandish figures
step out onto the platforms. Then the oars swept down in
a new, even faster rhythm, and a harsh thudding sound
boomed across the water, like enormous drums. Harsh
voices sounded in time to it, the ships surged forward and
the figures whirled into a dance. Alv felt his mouth go
dry. Even he had heard of the shamans of the Ekwesh.
Garbed as the god-spirits of their clan they danced up war-
craft before battle, to set a fire in the hearts of their own
men and quench it in their adversaries. And if the rumors
were true, the mightiest of them could do more than that.

Then he heard the sharp rattle of a drum from the town.
Looking down to the harbor, he saw Hervar, draped in his
guild robes and bearing his iron staff, go hobbling across
the strip of shingle where the boats were drawn up. He
too was chanting, swaying, beckoning. Suddenly he broke
into a grotesque hopping, swaying dance that Alv had
never seen before, thudding his staff into the gravel,
splashing down into the shallows. Beyond him, at the gap
in the seawall, the incoming waves seemed to slow, collapse and break as they would around some underwater
reef or rock. Hervar danced faster, hopping back and forth
with little taut steps, working himself up into a frenzy of
concentration. The water boiled, bubbled and broke in a
hiss of spray over something that rose from the depths,
caked with weedy growths like the back of some kraken-
thing that had lain there for years uncounted. It was a
huge, metal-bound tree trunk, cut into the likeness of
a tall pillar, its capital a chunk of metalwork; from this a
network of chains dangled, swinging wildly in the boiling
sea. They drew taut suddenly, then slackened again as another pillar rose to left and right of them—a fourth, and
then a fifth, rising upward across the wide gap in the seaward wall and filling it with a many-stranded necklace of
chain, studded with fine spikes and hooks, lethal to any
ship that tried to pass it. Alv whistled with excitement;
this was the Seagate, pride of the town, creation of generations of smiths and shielded by their craft from the sea's
decaying. He had seen it only once before, as a very young

child, when it was used with great effect against a single corsair galley, dipping down to ensnare the hull and lift it out of the water, spilling out the crew.

From the Ekwesh ships a chorus of yells greeted this challenge, and for the first time Alv heard the sinister rasping song of spear against shield. Having missed their chance of surprise, the raiders would have to face the power of the Seagate, or go away emptyhanded. But that, he knew, was not their way. The ships were so near now he could see the shamans clearly, stamping and whirling on the narrow platforms. The leaping figure was the Bear, a suit of fur with huge clawed paws and a long-jawed mask that snapped and bit at invisible fish as the figure leaped. To the right the gaunt ugly likeness of the Wasp cavorted, jabbing its stinger down into fallen foes. But in the lead ship, racing ahead of the others, the strangest figure of all swept out wide wings, far wider than the platform, under a mask with a curved beak and crest that each stood out a full arm's length, matching the image painted on the boat's flank—the Thunderbird. Straight in toward the rising logs the sharp bows came, and the marksmen's arrows whined and skipped across the water. One plunged quivering into the side of the platform, but still the Thunderbird danced, faster and faster till the wings stood out and floated like an albatross's, white against the gray clouds rolling overhead. A shout came from the wall, then the flat snap of bowstrings and a swarm of arrows buzzed down around the raiders, pattering like rain into the sea. Alv, springing up in excitement, saw a ceiling of shields whip up to meet them, saw the Bear duck down and the Waspman, struck through body and throat, topple sideways into the sea. But the Thunderbird stopped dead, the wings flew up and back like a stooping hawk's, and the great mask split and fell away to reveal another, glittering hideous, distorted death's head in blue steel. There was a flash, a deafening crackle, and from the gray cloud overhead a streak of glaring blue light came hammering down into the town. Straight onto the beach it smote, onto the twisting figure with the iron staff. A groundshaking roll of thunder drowned out the drum. Light seared along the beach and was gone. A blackened, beardless image of the old smith stood frozen in his place, the staff glowing molten in the rigid fingers. Then they crumbled, and the staff fell sizzling into the surf. Hervar's body fell backward, like a leaf blown from a bonfire, and lay stiffened on the shingle.

From the harbor mouth came a sudden ominous creaking, and Alv saw the Seagate sway violently, its chains flailing and tangling. The defenders on the wall rushed to reach out pikes, spears, anything that might snag chains or pillars and somehow hold them upright. On one side they caught the chain to the nearest pillar and hauled on it; on the pillar at the other side they sank long poleaxes into the wood. But then a new wavecrest struck, the whole mass swayed once more, and with a relentless grinding of iron the central pillar went toppling forward and pulled the others with it. One fell straight downward, plucking the axemen down into the churning water; the other swung violently in the direction it was being pulled and came smashing down on the wall itself. The logs split, the rampart splintered, armored bodies fell thrashing into the gray waters; the pillar rolled down onto them as they struggled, and blotted them from sight. For an instant its weed-snared base reared up to the light, and then everything was gone. Over the frothing gap rode the leading ship, the Thunderbird dancer sprawled flat on the platform. The black and white bows ground into the harbor gravel, bounced once on the swell, and then the Ekwesh warriors were rising from beside the oars and spilling over into the shallows. But instead of rushing ahead, they stopped at the waterline and knelt down in the shelter of their shields. Then, as the defenders came clamoring down off the walls and from between the houses, the oarsmen rose from their benches with bows in their hands, and the long Ekwesh arrows went whistling out. The first townsmen fell, the others hesitated, and the kneeling warriors leaped up and charged as the other two ships came sailing in through the Seagate. The few remaining archers on the seaward wall died as they loosed their own shafts, and then it was hand-to-hand battle on the shingle. The black clouds opened and spilled dark rain over the scene.

To Alv, watching from the heights, everything seemed

to dwindle and retreat behind the rain-curtain, to become
a scurrying mass of figures through the winding streets.
Groups would meet and merge in violent action, but who
was who, and who had the upper hand, he could never
make out. Only when the groups fell away and the action
ceased he could see shapes that lay writhing or motionless
in the mud. But he quenched the horror of it with cold
laughter, telling himself he cared not who slew whom.
Tinker's brat, they'd called him! Well, maybe; as well be
child to one of those poor wandering wretches without
craft or art, as to any in Asenby town now. Why should
he care which of them lived or died there below? They
were no kin of his; his skin spared him that, and his brown
hair and lean hard features, wholly unlike their straight
black hair and rounded coppery complexions. He had
never seen anyone else who looked like him, though traders had said there were paler folk far in the south. A south-
erner let him be, then; he cared little for his unknown
parents since they'd abandoned him at the gate here—here,
where he was named Alv, the goblin, the changeling. The
Headman had taken him in and raised him, less from kindness than an eye for a cheap thrall; from his earliest memories he had labored, in the kitchen or the fields with the
women, and with the cattle since his ninth summer, some
three or four past. And yet all that time he had remained
an outsider, taunted and despised by other children, unable to forget what was embodied in his very name. *Alv!*
He slapped the goad down into his palm. It was no name
he called himself. And the malice in it rang true, for he
had learned to repay them with a hundred little irritations,
the only defense he had. Why should he suffer for them
now, or mourn? He watched, and did his best to laugh.
And when the cloudburst passed, and the sunlight sparkled
in clear clean air, it was all over.

Smoke rose from some of the rooftops, but not through
the chimneys, and no man moved to put it out. Three
Ekwesh ships were drawn up on the beach, and the tall
warriors went to and from them unhindered, unhurried,
carrying great bulky loads. He could see the paintings on
the black hulls clearly now, and they were very like the
ones on the walls that now seared and blackened in the

heat. The Ekwesh were close kin to the peoples of the north, the same cast of face and body, but save for a few words their tongues were different, and they were no simple farmers or traders. They came out of the west over sea, no man knew whence, they took and they returned. Rumor had it that their land matched their hearts—flinty, pitiless, blazing or chill with the changing seasons, the shifting passion. They were great sailors and great warriors, but they respected nothing that was not theirs, not land, property or life itself. And rumor whispered things darker yet—

Behind him the bush rustled. He half rose, turned and caught a glimpse of black armor, copper skin—then a great weight thumped down on him and ground his face into the earth. Winded, blinded, he was only half aware that his hands were being tied behind him. Then a hard hand twisted in his hair, hauled him upright and sent him staggering off down the path he could hardly see. He remembered, then, that there had been four ships; one must have landed down the coast, to cut off messengers or fugitives. By the time the mud cleared from his eyes he was in the town, stumbling along the streets he had left so short a time before.

A nightmare had settled on the place. The air was warm and hung with curtains of stinking smoke, and it was no sun that crimsoned the puddles. The painted walls were scorched or smashed, and the people who had lived behind them lay stark and cold in their shadow. At the first house a man in mail lay curled up below a window, embracing the arrow that transfixed him; on the step a woman sprawled with twisted limbs in a red-brown pool, and in the mud at the center of the street a young child lay with a single bootprint the length of its body, still twitching faintly. Alv was made to step over it, and almost stumbled. These were people he had known, had seen the day before; he remembered the child's birth, the feasting when even he had found a place and a full stomach. So it was throughout the streets, and each sight worse than the last, a vision that shook the boy with pity and horror beyond his understanding.

They came to the Headman's house, many of the household dead about it. The burly man lay there under the crackling rafters of his own proud porch, his body made a spilled shell by broad stabbing spears and his head half hewn from the trunk. Staring at the ruin, Alv grasped vainly at all the hatred he had once felt, but it fled from him now. A harsh, unkind man the Headman had been, there were few warmer moments to remember him by, but he had done no great evil, nothing worthy of such an end. What he was paled before what had been done to him. To Alv, staring at the ruin, the destruction he had once wished upon the place seemed a childish thing indeed, and he thrust it violently aside in his mind, bitterly regretting his laughter.

His captors dragged him to the square by the town's main well. To his surprise he saw that there were other townsfolk alive there, mostly younger women and children. Many of the Ekwesh were gathered there to guard them, and he had his first clear sight of them. They were tall men for the most part, and dressed much alike in rough leather kilts and stiff jerkins and helmets of heavier leather, studded with metal and painted with the same black and white designs as their boats—sailors' armor, light enough not to drag them down. Their arms and hair jingled with ornaments, often of amber and precious metals, but their faces belied the richness—set, scowling masks with cold eyes, and all seamed with great scars, even the youngest. In the center, near the well, stood a stooped figure in a long dark robe and broad-brimmed hat, leaning on a thick white stick and barking commands that sent the warriors scurrying left and right, occasionally with a crack of the stick on bare head or shoulder. Two Ekwesh were dragging a captive up to him, a middle-aged woman Alv recognized as wife of the town's sugarbaker. They flung her down on her knees before the man's feet; the hat bent over her an instant, then he gave a curt dismissive gesture. One of her captors dashed his spear-butt into the back of her head where it met the neck, the other flung her aside and passed his spear through her body, the broad blade eviscerating her; the huddled knot of captives set up a terrible wail. Then it was Alv's turn to be hurried forward, and the leathery hand clamped the back of his neck, forcing him to his knees. The face that bent over him, shadowed by the hat, was lean and hard, scarred like the rest but made even more terrible by its eyes, yellow and catlike under wrinkled brows, seeming to scan and weigh everything in their path.

The sight made him kick out in fury, afraid above all of being slaughtered like a goat where he knelt. The grip tore loose, the rawhide on his wrists snapped, and before he knew it he was on his feet, panting.

The old Ekwesh barked a word, and a spear stopped just short of Alv's throat. The man thrust his head forward like some ancient lizard, looked Alv up and down and smiled, revealing a row of carefully pointed and serrated teeth. "Strong," he said in a guttural accent, nodding to himself with satisfaction. "Sothran? Thrall here? So. Good thrall for us. You live."

Alv's anger boiled over onto his tongue. "Amicac swallow that!" he shouted, and spat mud onto the soiled robe. "Keep your mercy, eater of men's entrails! I know what comes of your thralls! Better dead I am than living a short life as your cattle—"

He was flung violently on his back, staring up at the spear that would tear out his belly. But there came a sharp command in another voice, and it did not fall.

Alv twisted round to see who had spoken. Over by the well, lowering the dipper from his lips, was another robed man. But he was no Ekwesh, though they fell back as he strode forward. He was the first man Alv had ever seen with skin much like his own. His robes were the color of ripe corn, with a rich pattern worked into them that shimmered in the clear light. He looked down at the boy for a moment, and then said "Get up!" in a brisk, neutral tone. Alv climbed awkwardly to his feet, uncomfortably aware of the spears still leveled at him. The newcomer looked him up and down, examined his hands as one might the hooves of an animal and then jerked the boy's head round and stared hard into his eyes. The man's own eyes were dark and piercing, though the sunlight seemed to strike a cold white light in them. "A strange thrall!" he said, in the same clear, colorless voice. "Your name? Your parents?"

"Alv. I was a foundling—"

"A well-spoken foundling." The stranger sniffed fastidiously. "A cowherd, that's obvious. Yet you were educated? Worked in the smithy?"

"Never! The old smith, he wouldn't—"

The man gave a cool laugh. "No. He would not favor someone he could sense might soon excel him. Well, boy, I am no maneater, and I keep no thralls. I am a man of your own land, a Master of the Guild of Smiths, one of those allowed by its rules to treat with the Ekwesh, to buy back goods they have looted. I have been away many long months; I go back now to my own new household, and I will need helpers in the years ahead—those who are like me, having no ties to family or folk to turn their hearts elsewhere. You have that in you that makes a smith, I can tell—but how much of one, only the tempering of time will show." He glanced lightly around. "Nothing remains for you here, if anything there ever was. If you will serve me, I will take you as one of my apprentices, for as long as you show promise. If that fails, you may find a place in my forge, or go your own way. Or shall I let these creatures do as they will?"

Alv blinked, unable to form words. He stared at this stranger who was offering him life, a new life, as casually as a drink from the dipper in his hand. He cut an impressive figure, though his face glistened with sweat as if he had lately run a race. His skin was like Alv's but swarthier; his long jet-black curls were plastered over his brow, but hung free around a face regular and unlined, betraying no particular age, with a long heavy nose over thin lips and a strong chin. It was an easy face to accept, to believe in—and what else was there, indeed, beyond the blades that quivered at the corner of his eye? "Yes!" he choked out. The man raised a sardonic eyebrow, and Alv realized what he had said. "I mean . . . yes, I will be your apprentice. I want to be—very, very much!"

The man nodded evenly, clapped him on the shoulder, and spoke a few words to the old Ekwesh. The old man took two short steps forward, robes rustling, the white stick whistled out before Alv could move and caught him hard across the cheek, splitting the skin open. Alv stag-

gered but did not fall; the old man spat copiously in his
bleeding face and turned away to bellow at his soldiers.

"A pleasant people," murmured the smith, and gestured at the bucket balanced on the well rim. "Wash yourself. I would as soon be spat on by a rattlesnake. When
you have done that, make your way down to the beach and
find my servant there—an old man, of our kind. Tell him
my things are to be loaded into the ships, and help him. I
fear we must endure the company of the Ekwesh for a day
or two longer, as by treaty they carry back what I have
recovered."

Alv looked at him a little dazedly, but he had long since
learned not to question openly. "Yes . . . master."

"Mastersmith. My name is Mylio, but I prefer the title." As Alv wiped his face on his cloak his eyes strayed
to the captive women, mostly slumped in apathy in the
mud. The Mastersmith caught his shoulder, "Leave them.
There is nothing you can do for them—and if I read you
aright, you owe them nothing. No particular sweetheart?"
He wiped his hand. "Hardly. We must find you some better garb. Go, then."

Alv nodded, "Yes—Mastersmith."

It was strange to walk through those gory streets unharmed, ignored by the slayers milling around him. Alv
felt as if he was somehow dead already, a ghost on his
journey to the River—not to cross it, perhaps, but to sail
away down it to another birth, another destiny, as the tales
told of some spirits great or terrible. Certainly he was
walking through death, for it lay all around him, and he
had to avert his eyes from what he trod in. When he came
to the beach and passed the long line of bodies, the townsmen who had fallen in that first volley, he kicked off his
soiled sandals and wrappings and left them where they lay,
though the shingle was bitter cold underfoot. At first there
only seemed to be Ekwesh about, but then he noticed a
small pile of boxes on its own near the last ship, and a
cloaked figure huddled in its lee. He stalked over toward
the pile, and an old pale-skinned graybeard picked himself
up slowly and peered at the newcomer with dull resentful
eyes.

Alv had met little else but forbidding looks; they no

longer affected him. "The Mastersmith sent me—Master Mylio. He has taken me as an apprentice, and says you are to load his gear into the ship, and I am to help you."

The old man considered slowly, chewing on nothing and gazing at Alv's ragged clothes. "An apprentice, eh? And what might your name be?"

"They call me Alv, here."

The old man blinked around. "None here will call you anything again unless they walk by night, Alv, eh? I am Ernan, the Master's only servant, save for my wife and a forgeboy. There is another apprentice, too, older than yourself and well schooled. But all are servants, even he, when and as the Mastersmith requires it. Do I speak clearly?" Alv nodded warily, and the old man picked up a bundle wrapped in skin. "Well, then. Remember that. Do you pick up one of those boxes, and follow."

Alv heaved the topmost box off the pile, a painted chest of bent cedar; it was the kind they made in many towns, he noticed—including here. It was heavy, and he staggered, but managed to hoist it onto his shoulder. Old Ernan was already striding around the side of the ship, canted sideways as it was beached; he walked right out into the shallow surf, and Alv followed, to where the steep curving gunwales were at their lowest. There a short slatted board had been lashed to make climbing up easier; it creaked and flexed and shifted underfoot, almost spilling Alv into the water. Ernan reached out, steadied him, then took the box and laid it down in a locker lined with oiled sealskin. "Now, sir apprentice," he grunted, "do you come down now and help me with the larger chest there. And this time have a care!"

Alv followed gingerly, and as he stepped down into the water his eye was caught by something a little way along the beach, black against the foam that washed around it. A few steps closer, and he saw with a shock that it was the old smith Hervar, left lying where he had fallen, scorched tongue protruding and charred arms thrust upward in a mute, meaningless gesture, as if to ward off the sky. *Someone who might soon excel him* . . . But he was past all enmities now. Alv turned at Ernan's angry growl,

and hurried to take the other end of the long black chest—
Ekwesh work, this, by the fierce bird designs around the
huge and heavy lock. It was less weighty than it looked,
though, and the two of them moved easily into the surf.
But as Ernan reached the ship's side, and Alv heaved the
chest up onto the gunwale, a fleck of color caught his eye,
a tuck of what the chest contained snagged in the throw
of the hinged lid. He was about to tell Ernan when the
color of the bright stuff awoke a memory in his mind, and
he peered more closely at that protruding piece. It was
soft and light like doeskin, but with a pattern painted on
it in stiff bright paints, blue and white. It was not something he would forget, that pattern of jagged feather shapes,
for he had seen it so recently, dancing and whirling upon
the prow of the leading warship till the very clouds opened
and the lightning came. What was the Mastersmith Mylio
doing with the Thunderbird dress of a shaman among the
Ekwesh? He remembered the dancer, collapsed as if in
exhaustion, and the sweat-soaked hair plastered to a high
pale brow. But then Ernan tugged impatiently on the chest,
and Alv folded his thoughts away in darkness, determined
not to leave even the slightest tuck of them for those dark
eyes to see. He had much to learn, and learn he would,
before asking rash questions. So when, toward midday,
the Ekwesh made ready to sail and the Mastersmith came
back on board, Alv kept his peace and greeted him with
respect.

As the laden craft slid through the shattered Seagate,
oars creaking on their pivots, he stood at the stern by the
massive tiller, drinking in the hundred stinks of salt and
tar and dried fish and finding none worse than that of the
Ekwesh themselves, and watched the flames mount over
the rooftops he had never called home. Suddenly the great
gilded windvane stirred; the towering steersman sniffed
the air sharply, and bellowed something to the chieftain
on the narrow foredeck. The oars were shipped, and the
deck vibrated under the crew's bare feet as they ran to
unfurl the sail from below the wide yardarm. The black
hempen square billowed and drummed taut, straining
against the web of tarred cords that strengthened it. A

strong wind arose from the south; it fanned the burning buildings to a furnace heat, but the boy named Alv it bore far from that place. Wide though his life's wanderings were, that brought him at last to the very heart of the world, he came there never again.

CHAPTER TWO

The Apprentice

The black ships ran northward on a following wind, and pursuit, if any there was, they left far behind them. The few small craft they sighted put about and ran for the shore, for there was now no power in this region strong enough to resist them. So it was for two days and nights, and throughout this time Alv was left on his own, for Ernan lay seasick in the stern and the Mastersmith was with the Ekwesh chieftains. Some boys his age might have been lonely, but Alv was well enough used to his own company, and content to huddle down among the cargo in its wrappings of greasy hide, think his thoughts, and stay out of sight. It was warmer there—and safer. He was in no real danger from the raiders; the Ekwesh treated the Mastersmith with awe, and left what he named his alone. A kick and a curse were the worst he got when he was in the way, like any stray animal on the decks; they treated their own no better. But from the other boats, where there were captives, he heard cries that haunted him. The Ekwesh were a fell folk, vain, proud, quarrelsome, and crueler than any other of that day. What he saw of them in the days after the raid only fed and swelled the hatred he felt, and it never left him.

But at last, after what seemed like an age, the bows of the chieftain's ship ground into the sand of a narrow beach between high cold cliffs. Then all the Mastersmith's goods were carried ashore with great care, and stacked high above the tide line, under his watchful eye. The moment this was done a sharp word was given and the warriors

18

who had carried the last cases ran to the bows and began to push them free. As they scrambled aboard on trailing cables the oars kicked up spray, backing water among the breakers, the rowers took up a chant and without sign or farewell the shark-sleek warship slid out to rejoin the others standing offshore. The watchers on the beach saw the black sails slacken as one and thresh in the breeze, while the great yardarms were canted round. Then the sails were reefed and the raiding ships swung about before the wind, gunwales dipping into the swell, and went racing out north and west toward the horizon, as if they fled the sunrise that was coming.

Alv shivered. The Mastersmith had given him a good cloak and fine fur-lined boots—no doubt from among the Ekwesh loot—but in this dawn he lacked the shelter of walls, or his pile of skins, however dirty, and the faint warmth of the cattle's bodies in the air. And the air in this new place did seem to carry some extra tang of cold. Beside him he could hear Ernan grumbling through chattering teeth. Only the Mastersmith, bare-headed and lightly robed, seemed not to feel the cold; he was looking up at the dark gap in the rock wall, idly caressing a bracelet on his wrist, and listening. After a moment Alv heard the light clopping of hooves, and an instant later saw a soft lantern-gleam in the dimness. A train of ponies was making its way down the path and onto the beach.

The rider on the lead pony sagged sleepily, but gasped and pulled up sharply when he saw the Mastersmith, and jumped down with a gush of apologies. The Mastersmith held up a hand. "You are early, my good Ingar. It is only that we were earlier, for the barbarians were in haste to be away. But on with loading, for so are we!" Alv watched the Mastersmith drift away, and fall into quiet conversation with Ernan, both men drawing strange numinous patterns on the sand. He had not missed the vast relief Ingar, whoever he was, had betrayed when he was welcomed kindly. It could be a bad thing, then, to fail this strange smith, even in a small way—that was worth remembering.

Ingar, as it turned out, was the master's other apprentice—a heavyset young man about four years older than Alv, with dark skin, straight features and blue eyes like Ernan's. He looked at Alv with something of the master's keenness, and nodded slowly. His speech was much like Alv's own. "You're welcome, boy. At the very least we can use another hand in our new forge—and a less clumsy one, I'll wager, than *Master* Roc here."

"Clumsy!" snorted a scornful voice from the darkness. It had a gruff tone to it, but its owner was obviously little older than Alv. "If you'd leave your old books and lift a finger in the forge once in a day, we might see how deft you are, *Master* Ingar!" The speaker came strutting forward into the lamplight, and for a minute Alv thought he was looking at a round cloth bundle with legs. Then one end of an enormous muffler was unwound, and a broad pale face glared out ferociously, "What're you gawking at, you? Not my fault I wasn't born with ice in my blood like all you ruddy northerners—'cept Ernan, and he's caught it with age. Three cloaks I'm wearing and I still crunch when I sit down—if ever I get to go on this little jaunt—"

"Listen," interrupted Ingar, "sitting down will not be your main concern for a while if you delay the master. Now come on, and you too, Alv; the ponies must be loaded at once. At least we'll have the sun soon."

When it rose it was bright, and Alv and Ingar grew quickly warm as they lugged the boxes up onto the patient beasts, who stolidly stood and cropped the few patches of dune-grass within reach. But hot as it was, Roc was slow even to throw back his hood; when he did Alv jumped, and exclaimed out loud. In the sun the boy's hair seemed to be a tousled mass of flame, a spectacular, impossible color—red. Beneath it his square, snub-nosed face was almost pure white, but spattered all over with flecks the same uncanny shade of red. Roc stared right back at him. "And just what're you yelping at now, may I be so bold? Never seen a body so handsome as me before?"

"He'll never have seen red hair, I'll be bound," chuckled Ingar. "Never been to the Southlands, then? They all look like that down there, you know. It's the sun makes their brains boil over."

"There's rubbish for you!" said Roc. "He's a sothran

himself, isn't he? Brown hair and green eyes—at least I
thought they were green . . .''

"No," said the Mastersmith, who had come up behind
them so quietly everybody jumped. "Alv is not a south-
erner such as yourself, though of the same kin. He has the
look of one of the old people of the north, before they
joined with the brown-skinned folk who came westward
across the Ice. And that is a very interesting thing to be.
So now, if you please, back to your work . . ."

The young men scurried to obey. "Old people of the
north, eh?" puffed Roc as they struggled to fix the carrying straps round an especially wide chest. "Well, kins-
man, you should be right at home where we're bound.
Further north than that men don't willingly go—except one
or two, maybe . . ."

"That's enough!" snapped Ingar. Roc pursed his lips
and was silent.

By the time the ponies were loaded it was full day, and
the Mastersmith stood up from the sand and swept a foot
carefully across all his drawings. Then he gestured casually to Ingar, now on foot, and the little party set off up
the rocky floor of the defile. It had many windings and
long steep slopes, and Roc and Alv, following behind,
often had to help and steady the beasts, and even haul
them on by their stiff scrubby manes over patches of scree
that slithered away beneath their hooves. At last they
emerged, some hundreds of paces from the cliff edge, and
found themselves in wide rolling country of the kind Alv
had always known. But as they crossed the top of the first
low hill, heading inland, it seemed to him that there was
a line of blue at the horizon too solid to be cloud, and that
in places it was crested like a wave, white caps glinting
against the sky and never folding, never breaking. He did
not understand what he was seeing, and he was too afraid
of looking foolish to ask Roc, but the sight stirred feelings
in him—of the immensity of the world, and what it might
contain, and of all the things he might find in it. The
shadow of the Ekwesh lifted from him; he felt like singing, but didn't know how the Mastersmith might react. He
hummed under his breath as he went, and at every rise in

what seemed to be a well-trodden path he watched eagerly
for that unchanging line, to see if it might look any nearer.

By and by the path led them to a road, and along this
they turned, with the Mastersmith strolling at their head.
He wore now the black robes of his guild and rank, and
at his side a short heavy sword. Ingar too was armed, and
casting watchful eyes around at every bank and copse they
passed. When the road cut through a wide area of woodland he dropped back to walk beside the younger boys.
"Got to be wide-awake here, the pair of you. The Mastersmith chose this road carefully, to judge by all the maps
he was drawing, but no path is safe hereabouts. Robbers
and outlaws gather near a big town, for they know what
road the merchants'll take."

"Are we near a town here?" asked Alv.

"That we are, and a big one, the last in these parts;
Harthaby they call it. We'll be there by early afternoon at
this rate. But we won't be staying long, we've a long way
ahead. And since we won't need all the ponies for carrying, at least we won't have to walk. Ever ridden a horse?"

"No," admitted Alv. "A bull, though, once or twice."

The others looked at him again. "A bull," muttered
Ingar, when he saw the boy was serious. "Well, a horse
shouldn't give you too much more trouble then."

Harthaby town was large indeed, some three or four
times the size of Asenby. Alv had never seen anywhere so
large; too wide for a single hill, its walls meandered out
around two or three, and each was crowned with a building larger than the Headman's house, larger even than
Asenby's granary. When they reached the main gate,
though, it was no wider than the Landgate, and well
guarded; there was a press of people waiting to pass. But
the Mastersmith simply spoke a few words to the guards,
and they passed his party through ahead of everyone, much
to Alv's embarrassment; nobody dared hiss or glare at so
great a smith, so they reserved it for the most ragged
member of his party. But he forgot that at once, the moment he was in the town, for so many streets and such a
throng of people were new to him, though the others said
there were many greater towns to the south. The huge
buildings, said Roc, were the Halls of Guild, where mem-

bers met and markets were held; it was to one they'd be
going now, though only for as long as unloading the boxes
and loading up some traveling gear would take. "And getting a bite to eat—if our noble master's not in one of his
fasting moods!"

"The Ekwesh gave me some food," Alv commented
ruefully, "but I never dared touch their meat . . ."

Roc shuddered. "Aye, the dirty brutes. Never know
whom you'd be eating, eh?"

Fortunately there was food enough at the Merchants'
Guildhall, though others at the servants' tables com-
plained bitterly about corn porridge and smoked fish, saying that they could get no decent delicacies anymore with
the corsairs terrorizing sea traffic from the south, and now
also the Ekwesh. To Alv it seemed like heaven to eat his
fill, and he even out-ate Roc. The Mastersmith and Ingar
dined with the Master Merchants, concluding their business over the chests brought from the ship. Watching them
go, Alv wondered how much of the recovered booty came
from his own town, and why Harthaby, so much richer,
had not yet been attacked. But he kept that thought to
himself. He was no less pleased when Ingar took him off
to find a bath and some new clothes. To his surprise they
were like Ingar's own, though less decorated—good woolen
shirts, jerkin and hose of black leather, and the black boots
and hooded cloak he already had. "The livery of an apprentice in our guild," said Ingar. "Our color is black—
probably," he added disdainfully, "because it hides the
dirt."

Alv looked down at himself doubtfully; the clothes felt
almost indecently soft and clean against his damp skin.
"Ernan and Roc don't wear it . . ."

Ingar raised an eyebrow. "Of course not. And count
yourself lucky that you do, so young and untried. The
Mastersmith has great confidence in you, that's obvious."

Just how much Alv only realized when they rejoined the
others, and he saw the look of shock on their faces. Ernan
sniffed disapprovingly, Roc whistled softly and nodded,
but said nothing. Indeed, from that moment a gulf opened
between him and Alv, and in many ways, though they
were to become fast friends, it never again closed. How-

ever, when they loaded the ponies with new supplies, apprentice and servant shared the work as before.

When they mounted up Roc did not spare himself a laugh at Alv's battle with the stirrups and frantic attempts to keep his balance, even by grabbing at his pony's stiff-bristled mane; nor did the girls and idlers in the streets, and more than once Alv burned with the same black anger of humiliation he had thought he left behind. He kept his eyes down or straight ahead and did not look around him. He did not know how long it would be before he saw this, or any other town, again. By copying Ingar, however, he managed to learn the rudiments of keeping his seat and managing the reins, and by the time they had reached the northern gate he already felt quite comfortable on horseback. And that was as well, for a long ride lay ahead.

For the first day they rode fast along well-made roads, and from time to time they would pass others, single travelers on wagon, horse or foot, or small trading parties serving outlying villages. That night they camped in a stone enclosure with a hearth and roofed sleeping area, obviously built as a way station for travelers; but it was very old and crumbling. When they woke in the morning it was Alv's turn to laugh at his fellows, because all but he and the Mastersmith were stiff and sore with the ride and sleeping on the ground. On the second and third nights they found other stations like it, though even more decrepit. All this time the road wound on between the low hills, unchanging, but it became more cracked and overgrown. Other travelers were few, rarely on foot, and always armed and distrustful. The station they came to late on the third night was a ruin, little better than a low wall with a firepit; on the fourth night, after a day of driving rain, they could not find the station, so overgrown was it. At last they settled in the shelter of a great cedar, wrapping themselves in all their blankets, skins and oiled cloth. In the morning they were all shivering and miserable again except Alv and the Mastersmith. "And this is the best of our journey so far!" the smith remarked, listening to coughs and curses as he led the party away on a narrow trail through the brush. "From here on the High road has not been maintained this last hundred years, and the land reclaims it. So instead we are setting off across the Starkenfells—a good week's ride over moorland."

"Is this where your house is, Mastersmith?" asked Alv, looking around dubiously as they neared the top of a slope. The trees were thinning out around them, and the underbrush also; ahead were wide patches of long grass, waving in the cool humid wind.

"No indeed—the climate is anything but healthy! It lies beyond the Fells—a day or two's travel through the forests, and then another two into the mountains—high above the cares of this world. But I imagine you have never seen a mountain?"

"I've heard of them," said Alv, a little casually. The Mastersmith smiled faintly, and stretched out a long hand northward. Alv followed his gaze as they crested the slope, and gasped aloud. The wave he had seen from afar seemed to tower over him now, a vast wall of gray-green glass sparkling in the clear air, flinging its jagged white crests up into the blue infinity like spray from the rocks. For a moment, such was the power and terror of the spectacle, he almost thought to see it come sweeping down across the land. And then it seemed a greater miracle that so immense and graceful a shape could remain frozen in that instant of motion.

"Mastersmith—"

"Yes?"

"How did mountains come to be? They have not always been there, surely? They look—as if they had been thrust up from somewhere."

The Mastersmith turned in his saddle to stare at Alv. "I was not mistaken, I see. There is perception in you, boy, true perception. Yes, they were thrust up, like a wave—and I believe not so long ago, in the life of the land, for the edges of the rock are sharp and little touched by the weather, and the fires under the Earth burn strong there—as you will see. But all the mountains are not the same age, I think, for some are more weathered than others and of different rock. That you will learn about in due time, boy, for a good smith must be able to find and mine his own new ore at times—to make it truly pure, and truly his. You will enjoy that, I think."

Indeed, Alv could hardly wait. In this alone he would surpass that old idiot Hervar, for the graybeard had not strayed beyond the village in all the years Alv could remember, let alone gone searching for ore. Small wonder he had got himself killed, if he was so little concerned with his art. It was not a mistake Alv intended to make.

Over the next few days it was increasingly he and not Ingar who rode and talked with the Mastersmith, plying him with questions and never failing to find an answer that fed the fires in his mind. He was wary of offending the senior apprentice at first, but for his part Ingar seemed glad of the rest. Hard as it was to believe, he seemed to find his master's company a strain, and was happier joking with Roc. Ernan rode in pinch-mouthed silence, which suited the others as much as it seemed to suit him.

So they journeyed across the moorland, a lonely, eerie place in which they saw no other traveler, and the only sounds of life were thin cool bird calls echoing through the damp air. At times the Mastersmith would point out the wheeling flight of a condor, high against the clouds, and once, as they drew nearer, a cloud of huge vultures rose from something—they could not see what, but it was large—trapped and decaying in a wide boggy patch. The taint of it seemed to cling to the wind long after they passed. It might have been that which drew the pack down upon them soon after.

They were hunting beasts, large but lean after the hard winter, and they crested the hill at speed, long tails stiffened and jaws set in wide fang-edged grins, breaking into harsh yipping cries as they saw the travelers. Catlike they were, carrion-eaters but just as ready to run down live prey; they were built for that, their limbs long, their brindled bodies light, flexing and stretching as they ran. But their shoulders were massive, to carry the heavy heads whose thick jaws could sever a pony's leg at a single bite. Alv, with his herdsman's eye, counted twelve of the brutes, and no chance of running to cover in this bare land. The Mastersmith whirled in his saddle; Alv expected him to draw a sword, but instead he sprang down and Ingar with him. They waved the others back; it seemed like madness, but Alv, acutely conscious of his new livery, seized a metal bar from the baggage and sprang down beside them. Ingar was calmly flicking an odd device, a flint and steel wheel with a thick loop of cord attached, till the brutes were almost on them. The cord sizzled suddenly, and flamed. The Mastersmith snatched it and drew back his arm as if to throw. Ingar swung away, covering his eyes, and Alv copied him, but an instant too late. A cloud of dazzling, searing light blossomed over the pack, as if the sun itself had come licking through the mists; flaming gobbets rained hissing down to lodge in their fur. Blinded, stung or afire, their onrush became a whirling confusion of yelps and snarls, burnt hair mingling with the carnivore stench. Only one huge beast, with gray streaks in its greenish fur, rose up on its hind legs and snapped viciously at the Mastersmith's face; Alv, still dazzled, heard a horrible bone-and-meat thud and saw the beast roll kicking at his feet. Another snarling shape loomed up before him, he struck at it and heard bones break, and as his sight cleared he saw Ingar stoop with a tinderbox in his hand. This time he closed his eyes, but the tongue of light raced scarlet across closed eyelids, and the pack turned and fled yelping, tails firmly between their legs.

"Good," said the Mastersmith calmly, wiping his sword on still-quivering fur. "Since nobody is hurt, let us be moving on at once, for if they regain their nerve and decide to stalk us, we shall have no peace by night. You have seen," he added, turning to Alv as they mounted up, "a useful alliance of subtlety with force. Never forget it. They were more afraid of the fire than our swords, though it could do them less harm. So are the weak in mind led or driven, be they beast or man. The art of the true smith can be turned to great ends in this world, and often by applying its simplest skills. That flame seemed uncannily bright, did it not? Yet no magecraft at all was needed for it—simply two items of knowledge. First, that a certain rare metal burns thus when very pure. Second, how to find and purify it. Simple enough—but do not scorn such trifles, for all that, when you come to master the greater craft. As you will, soon enough."

"Mastersmith . . ." Alv felt a cold tingle of excitement stir behind his belt, and an icier one of apprehension. He had to ask, and yet he was afraid—afraid he would offend the master, show himself up as stupid or unsuitable. But the Mastersmith looked at him with keen eyes, and raised an eyebrow. Alv had to risk it. "Mastersmith—why? Why me? What made you choose me? Wh-why are you so confident I'll be able to do all these things?"

The smith considered. "You feel it is a burden, that confidence? Set your mind at rest. I have reasons for it, and some I had from the moment I saw you."

"You mean—because I look like one of the old northerners?"

"Indeed. That in itself was enough to interest me. All the greatest magesmiths have come from that stock, last survivors of the Lost Lands eastward, for it was among them that smithcraft was most cultivated, and so grew strongest. True smithcraft, the art that goes beyond the mere shaping of the metal, that is a rare and strange thing indeed, and not all possess it to the same degree, or at all. If a people lose sight of it, cease to cultivate it, it will fade from them. So it has for Roc's people, who became so great and so wise in things material they felt they no longer needed it, and in time ceased to believe in it; it was some barbarian superstition they left to their less advanced cousins. In the Northlands, by contrast, it was nurtured and studied as the sothrans studied war and trade and building in stone. Yet even in the north it has dwindled now, as the old peoples have become assimilated among the greater numbers of copper-skinned folk who fled east over the Ice from the rising power of the Ekwesh realm. For though they, too, knew the art, they were a plain folk more concerned with the soil, the catch and the seasons than any deeper knowledge. So in most of them the art has declined to that level. Wise smiths, therefore, seek their apprentices among those in whom the old stock runs strongest—Ingar, for example, with his eyes and face. Very rarely they find one of almost pure northern stock, and in them the art often runs strong. Such, I would guess, are you. But I do not need to guess about what is in you. When I look closely, with the eyes of my art, I can *see* it, though you know nothing of it yourself as yet. And what

I have seen, I trust. You will make a good smith—but how good, only the future will show.''

Alv shook his head, bewildered. "Thank you, Mastersmith. I—I still don't quite . . . It's just that it's what I've always wanted—"

"Naturally. That, too, is a sign. But you will see, when we reach my new home. It will not be too long, from the lie of the land. The beasts also, for they hunt near the forest margins at this season. And indeed—" He stood in his stirrups and pointed out toward the looming bulk of the mountains, presently no more than shadows swathed in clinging mist. Alv, copying him shakily, saw a long streak of greenish-brown only a league or so distant, filling the next low hollow and spreading back over the hills to rise up among the very roots of the mountain range. The contrast of the lush carpet of treetops and the cold sterility of those slopes was amazing; it looked as if all the life had come slipping and spilling off them into the valley, leaving only their bare bones to endure the icy weather. A narrow, muddy track led the travelers in among thick underbrush surrounding cedars, ash, maples and spruce, pines far taller than the ones Alv had known on the coast—and here and there, towering above the rest, stands of red-barked metasequoias reaching for the clouds. "And this is only a sparse little outgrowth of the woods to the east," remarked the Mastersmith, "Tapiau'la-an-Aithen, the Great Forest that casts its shadow over the heart of all this land. Think of that."

Alv shook his head. "I can't, Mastersmith. But I'd love to see it one day. Have you?"

The Mastersmith's mouth twisted wryly. "I have. As I hope you will, though you will need to be well proven and prepared before you venture into the realm of Tapiau. I barely escaped, myself. But here that power is weak. You will learn more about it—one day." Alv took the hint, and stifled all his eager questions.

Ingar and the servants were looking around nervously as they rode in under the shadow of the trees, but nothing more than small green birds moved, bouncing around from bough to bough and cocking heads to eye these intruders with immense skepticism. Alv and Roc tossed crumbs to them. There were sounds deep in the forest, though; often they heard the groaning bellows of deer large and small, the snorting of wisants and, always in the far distance, the deep coughing growls of meat-eaters on the hunt. Once, looking back, Alv saw a single doe slip silently across a clearing they had just passed through. When they came to a wide river, there was a swift crashing in the undergrowth as some large creature dashed away; bright blue birds flicked up shrieking out of its path. A moment later the travelers came across its slaughtered prey on the bank, a huge beaver also as big as a man.

"A daggertooth!" muttered Ingar, twisting the tinderbox nervously. Daggertooths preyed on even the largest forest beasts.

The Mastersmith shook his head. "Look at the windpipe—pinched shut, not punctured. Therefore it was one of the biting, not stabbing, cats—smaller and less dangerous. In any case, not even a daggertooth would attack a party this size."

But the others kept casting anxious glances behind them as they went splashing through the ford, and that night they camped in a ring of thornbushes, with two fires lit, and set a watch. From there on, however, the forest began to grow thinner as the land rose sharply; the heavy undergrowth became sparse, and many kinds of tree were no longer seen. What grew around the path now were chiefly pines, firs and other hardier evergreens. Toward the end of the second day the path itself grew wider and firmer, no longer a muddy track but a well-surfaced road with shaped stones set along its edges. Here and there the resiny scent of the forest became newly sharp and strong, and looking around Alv saw the stumps of pine trees freshly hewn with the chips still lying around them, the light flooding into new clearings through the ravaged canopy. As the hours passed, he could see that a great quantity of wood had been taken from this forest, some very recently, and wondered who was cutting it. The Mastersmith, perhaps, to build his house or fire his forge—but there seemed to be almost too many stumps even for that. He could ask—but that might look stupid; better mention it casually to Roc, later. They camped that night where the trees stood tall and untouched.

All throughout the next day the trees grew thinner, the land steeper, until the forest died away to mere clumps and coverts huddled against the hillside, in one of which they camped. When they rose the next morning the travelers found they had a clear view back over the forest and out over the lands they had crossed. Alv was startled to see how high up they were; the forest lay stretched out below him, right to the moorlands beyond, silhouetted against the dim dawn sky. He turned, and blinked with surprise. He was in the mountains now, truly; they were all around him, as thickly, it seemed, as the forest had been, and the sun spilled blood down their flanks. As the travelers rode on, the last clumps of trees dwindled and finally seemed to fail altogether; the slopes on either side were covered in coarse grass, or bushes and scrub that clung to shelter as if in fear of being blown away. The only sounds of life were the drone of biting insects and the harsh screams of unseen birds of prey, echoing down the wind. By evening even the smaller plants had all but vanished, and the road was leading them across a broad slope, stony and bare, between two lowering dark peaks that looked like roots put down by the sky. The wind whistled bleakly between them, and somewhere in the distance there was the sound of falling water; it reminded him of the little falls on the hill streams, but much louder and deeper. As he watched, night fell, and the weary ponies plodded on through the pale afterglow. But the Mastersmith gave no word to halt, and with a sudden thrill Alv realized they must be near enough to reach the house tonight.

Hours went by. Stars came out, and the moon rose, and heads sagged with weariness; Ernan seemed almost asleep in his saddle, and Roc was swaying where he sat. But the Mastersmith was wide-awake, and so, to his own surprise, was Alv, drinking in the mountain air. Darkness seemed to flavor it, like cool, bitter wine. The moon was sinking by the time they neared the top of the pass, and just as they crested the slope it slid down behind the peaks. But instead of the sudden darkness Alv expected, a new radiance seemed to hang in the sky, paler and clearer even than the light of moon or star. The crest and the peaks stood out sharp against it, and their snowcaps caught it and sparkled like frozen jewels. Abruptly the Mastersmith reined in his pony and swung down. Frost crunched beneath his feet. He beckoned to Alv, who followed suit, and came trudging up to join him.

"Look, boy!" hissed the Mastersmith softly, with something as near passion as Alv had ever heard in his voice. "Do you see it? D'you see it there? Look at it, the glory of it, blazing back from the earth into the heavens!"

"I see it, Mastersmith," breathed Alv, full of wonder. "Behind the mountains . . . it stretches as far as I can see . . . shining on the clouds like a reflection from a great still lake . . . but . . . what is it, Mastersmith?"

"No lake, boy. You see in reflected glory the power that has come down to cover the Northlands, the power that ruled this world of old, that was many times dispossessed and thought defeated, and that yet holds it in its grip. And that grip is tightening! You see the Great Ice!"

The words were flung out across the mountains, their hollow echoes riding the wind like spirit voices. The glare seemed to grow more intense, and even Alv shivered in his boots; the wind sucked the warmth out of his very blood. "No," said the Mastersmith after a moment, and his voice had dropped to a deep whisper, "you do not see it yet, not truly. But you will, one day. As I did. You, when you have served as apprentice and journeyman, and become in your turn a master, you will set out alone and unattended over the Ice, walking and walking on into the emptiness, enduring its hardships and braving its terrors, and the ordeal will purify you. And if you do not fail at the test you will come at last to the heart of it and there commune with the powers behind it. In their hands you, the master, will again become an apprentice. You will learn new knowledge, new skills, new purposes—new thoughts. Thus you yourself will be made anew—hammered, tempered, forged on the Anvil of the Ice!" The Mastersmith swung round and gripped him violently by the shoulders. His eyes stared deep down into Alv's; the fierce white light blazed and rippled in their depths, and in Alv's brain a piercing point of pain awakened as if in answer. In a state halfway between terror and ecstasy Alv felt his feet leave the ground. The Mastersmith held him out at arms' length as if he weighed nothing at all, as if released he would flutter away on the wind. "Yes, boy," whispered the smith at long last, "there is power in you, true enough—great power. But that is not something you can take for granted. More than any other attribute it must be developed—and disciplined! It must be carefully nurtured, boy, in a climate of thought, pure thought, if petty humanity, the passions of the ape, are not to creep in and weaken it. Pure thought without taint or contamination—*that* is what lies out there. That is the secret behind the Ice."

He released Alv so suddenly the boy almost fell on the stony slope. "And that is why I came here," the smith went on, in his normal dry voice. "To be away from the stifling presence of massed humanity, the meaningless demands of the herd. Up here, where few things are living save ourselves, we may aspire to a communion with the Absolute. For the moment it is checked by the mountain-barrier, but not forever—no, indeed. It can afford to wait. Before ever man was, those powers set their hands upon this world and they have never lifted it; in their service we can learn much, and achieve great art and power. Here alone is true life, and here I have made my new home." He gestured down into the valley below. "There is my house—and from now on, yours also."

Alv looked down into the shadows. A little way along the valley its wall became a sheer cliff face, down which a mountain stream fell in great cascades from the snowline high above. Just beyond it, founded on an outthrust arm of the cliff wall, rose a squat square tower of stone from within an encircling wall. Its summit was open and flat behind high crenellations, but to one side rose a wide round turret roofed in metal, cold-sheened in the clear pale light. Here and there on the flanks of the tower shone squares of warm yellow and red light and plumes of smoke or steam drifted up like banners into the icy air.

Alv could only gape. He had never seen anything so large, except the Halls of Guild, and they had been low and flat, not many-storied like this. And it was all of *stone!*

He had never even dreamed it was possible to build entirely of stone, and shuddered at the difficulty and danger of it. He found his voice at last, as they remounted and went riding down the steep road into the valley. "Mastersmith—it's amazing! But how was it all built—up here?"

"It was built for me," said the smith drily, "with rather unusual help. I had to pay for that, and I am still paying, when I must. But it is strong, and houses all we need, including great stores of supplies. I think you will find it comfortable."

After the smith's words about the Ice and the meaningless demands of humanity Alv was inclined to doubt that, but when the high gate of polished granite swung silently shut behind him and the door of the tower creaked open, a welcome tide of light and warmth flowed out, and the aroma of baking bread. That almost reduced him to tears, for all his newfound dignity, because he remembered it from years of passing by homes that were not his, doors at which he might only beg, and never enter as his own. But here as the Mastersmith and Ingar went in, Ernan, Roc and the wrinkled old woman who had opened the door all stood aside, and they ushered Alv in before them. The central hall around him was simple enough, stone-walled and flagged, strewn with rough matting; the great table and benches were of plain solid wood, as were the seats around the fireplace that filled the far wall. But it seemed like a palace to him, and almost unbelievable that he was able to stand and warm himself by the fire undisturbed, then join others at the table to eat bread and meat and drink mulled ale. All this was new to him, and he thought then that for all his life long he could want nothing better. And indeed, though others might have found it a lonely or uncanny place, he was happy enough to spend all the years of his growing in that house.

In fashion it was like no other house of men in Nordeney at that time, being built of stone blocks after the manner of the great towns of the south, but far larger in size, and so dressed that not even the keenest edge of the winter wind could force a particle of snow or ice between them. They were bedded deep in foundations of living rock, not

only for strength but for heat. The fires under the Earth
burned strong and high in that place, and often the hillsides around would vent great gouts of smoke and steam,
and a fearful throbbing like the breath of some great beast;
at times the ground itself would tremble and heave, as if
that beast stirred under the intolerable weight of the Ice.
But no tremor disturbed or weakened the Mastersmith's
great house, though at its very roots there opened a deep
cleft in the rock, through which its hot lifeblood yet ran;
the stone drew up so much heat from below that often the
spray of the falls splashed into steam against the wall. But
the house was placed and built with a hand and a cunning
past that of men, and so remained warm at all seasons in
that bitter land, where living men could never otherwise
have dwelt. On the stillest of summer nights the grind and
crack of stone would resound from the far side of the
mountains, under the quarterless siege of the Ice; all
through the half year's winter the frost would grip like a
steel vise and the snowladen winds would come shrieking
down off the Ice, seeking the least crack or crevice to
begin their ancient game of splitting the stone. But crevices there were none, such was the work; frost and snow
alike steamed away to nothing.

At the base of the tower the heat was fiercest, for there
was the Mastersmith's great forge, a wider chamber like a
cave in the living rock, but with high vaultings curiously
carved. When the Mastersmith first led Alv down into it,
the day after their arrival, the boy fought not to flinch at
the thought of the great weight of stone overhead. But as
his eyes grew used to the reddened, flickering light he
forgot his fear in wonder at the look of the place. He had
grown up wondering and marveling at the village smithy;
this place so far surpassed it that he was moved with a
feeling almost of worship.

It had something in common with Hervar's lair, the firepit at one end and the scatter of anvils around it. But here,
instead of two or three, were a hundred or more of all
shapes and sizes, ranging from small shaping blocks on
workbenches to an immense slab, as high as his shoulders,
that seemed too huge for any merely human hand to work
at; some hero of old such as Glaiscav might have forged

arrows here, or Vayde his sword. As he peered more closely he saw poised over it in the gloom what almost confirmed his feelings, two immense metal hammers with wooden hafts thicker than his thigh.

"Do you wonder at them, then?" said the Mastersmith. "Yet once again they are simple things, true smithcraft's servants, rather than its creation." He strode to the wall and turned a wide wheel set there a little way, and the cavern filled with the thunder of falling water. Below the wheel were rows of levers in the floor, and he pulled first one, then another. There was a long, loud creak, a slow ticking sound, and in the shadows behind the great anvil something stirred; the firepit casting a moving, plunging shadow on the wall. Alv had barely time to see it was a bladed wheel before the Mastersmith slipped yet another lever by the high anvil. The suspended hammers jerked, rose and came crashing down in turn on the great block of metal with a mighty clanging that shook the sandy paving of the floor, echoed in the vaults of the ceiling and went reverberating through the boy, so that his body felt insubstantial and frail. The Mastersmith shut the levers off one by one. "Thus are the sternest ores crushed and the hardest metals tempered. But before you use it, guard your ears!"

He stood a moment, with the faint half-smile on his face. "You see there, a vent channels in a part of the waterfall to turn the wheel. That works the hammers, and other such devices—bellows, grindstones, heavy hammers, lifting tackle, metal-benders and wire-drawers, all with greater power than ever came from a man's arms. And that is not all . . . Ingar!"

The older apprentice, over by the firepit, took hold of another wheel, set this time on a thick shaft in the floor, and with immense care moved it a little way. There was a sudden deep coughing rumble, the flames of the pit leaped and blazed to twice their height and spat a column of dark smoke toward the ceiling, where a wide gap swallowed it.

"You see? The rock itself bleeds to aid our forging." The Mastersmith nodded, and Ingar hastily spun the wheel back, grinning at Alv.

"A forge fit for the gods!" he called. "All four elements ours to command! The stone around us, the wind in our airshafts, the water in the wheels and this—'' He locked the shaft with a bolt. ''Better than having a dragon on a leash! Here we can work wonders!''

Roc, pouring fine sand around some impossibly delicate wax thing in a mold, laughed scornfully. *''We?''*

A single glance from the Mastersmith silenced him, and Ingar's angry retort died in his throat. The man smiled. ''Ingar is a competent craftsman, but more interested in the theory of our art. He prefers—'' he gestured at a low arched doorway to the right ''—to bury himself in here.''

The door was of bronze, and heavy, and when it opened there was a sucking of air. Alv stepped through, and stood blinking in the change of light, clear, cool and coming from nowhere he could see. And when the shapes and flecks of color around the walls resolved into solidity, he was still blinded.

''You know what these are, then?''

''Yes, Mastersmith, of course! The town had some, three or four, very old—they were proud . . . But—am I stupid? I never knew there could be so many!'' From floor to ceiling, and across the center, the room was filled with books. Books of every kind, from the usual scrolls and fanfolded links to leaves of paper, parchment or even bark tied up in clumsy sheaves or, oddly, fastened together along one edge.

''No,'' said the dry voice, ''you are not stupid. It is an immense expanse of knowledge, more than you will find in any other library save that of Kerbryhaine, which is now little regarded, or those of lost Morvan itself. And yet no more than a fraction, a grain of what there is to know. Ingar prefers to be a scholar, and makes himself useful as such. But a true master of the art, as I am, as I judge you might one day be, must balance both, the learning and the craft. I assume you cannot read?''

''A few signs I picked up . . . My name, a word or two . . .''

''Well enough for you, then. Because you are late to start book learning, and this is one door you must enter soon. But be warned now! Learning is not to be gulped down as you do your food. It must come in courses, by degrees, as you are ready to receive and understand it. Otherwise it may choke you, or worse! The high mysteries of our craft are not to be taken lightly, and need to be guarded. So—you may take and read any book from this South wall, or the center cases, as you will. But on the others a guard is set, surer than any lock or key, and I advise you not to cross it. For the East and West walls, you must first ask leave of me, and it will seldom be refused. But leave the North wall alone!'' The soft voice glittered like the Iceglow; Alv shivered, and nodded. "Then go now to Ingar, he will begin teaching you your letters. He has some romances and epics which should be easy enough to begin on. Find me by my anvil in three hours if you weary. But you must be reading, and well, by next spring—no longer!''

He was reading, avidly, before winter. The spring season was in himself, all his pent-up energy and intelligence breaking the crust of his beginnings with the ruthless impatience of a seedling eager for light and air. And over the years that followed it seemed to him that no winter ever came, for he felt himself grow and blossom into new strength and confidence, both of body and mind.

Little can be said of his eight apprentice years, for little is recorded till the events which led to their uncanny ending; in manhood he was never proud of them. Only the lesser part of his early schooling, his learning of simple smithcraft, is mentioned, and that for the changes it wrought in him. Long hours of toil at anvil, vise and mandrel, wielding heavy hammers, swages, tongs and hardies, hardened his body; it was labor that might have killed a thrall, but with good food in plenty and all the force of his will, his driving need, behind it, the work redoubled the strength he was born with. He grew only to middle height, but solid and well made, especially of face. It was the fine work that bowed his shoulders and narrowed his eyes, long hours of carving out inlays in steel and tapping soft gold or silver wire into the channels, endless vigils over tiny molds in which a minute bead of electrum shivered and slid down little by little at the vibration of a stroking finger. One minute he would be hauling bar iron, heated to the point of burning, out of the firepit and under the mighty hammers, the next he would be anxiously coaxing a fire enameled sword pommel out of a miniature kiln. Then, as the snows of the outside winter melted unregarded, he would be off across the mountain land with the Mastersmith and Roc, searching for new seams and sources of metal. In all ways they went, save only to the north flanks of the mountains, against which ground the first outthrust glaciers of the Ice; Roc seemed deeply glad not to venture that way, but Alv was only the more intrigued. Sometimes, many miles to the south, the master would lead them deep into working and mineshafts evidently made by others, and equally evidently still in use. But who the makers and users were, the Mastersmith did not say, and his manner discouraged questions. There they would find many rich and precious ores for the taking, at the faces or from heaps left lying around uncollected. But though Roc was always looking nervously about, they never so much as saw the mineworkers, and only once, as from an infinite distance, did Alv hear the rattle and ring of work in the stone.

Often when they returned from these expeditions there would be horses at the gate, even a line of wagons, for the Mastersmith was no hermit; many visitors seemed to think it worth the long trek out to the house, and they were of many kinds. There were messengers, whom the Mastersmith greeted with cool courtesy but dismissed to the kitchen to await reply. There were men who came by night, hooded or masked, and stayed for no more than a word at the gate. There were pale travelers from strange lands in the south, their errands as enigmatic as their speech. Many visitors were simply merchants, come to sell supplies and perhaps treat with the Mastersmith for special work, though this he seemed to endure patiently rather than do gladly; he had no great need of more wealth. Occasionally men in splendid clothes, with haughty airs and well-armed followers, would ride up to commission weapons and armor, or fine jewelry. But often a chieftain or merchant who took away such work would return, wealthy and beholden to the Mastersmith Mylio, and then Alv saw their relations with him change; they would become confidants, partners, consulting a trusted adviser. When they next returned it would be as clients to a patron—or vassals to a lord. The Mastersmith would receive them with his usual mien—suave, reasonable, generous. But nonetheless many left him pale and shaking, or bowed as under a heavy burden.

Alv studied his master as assiduously as his craft or his books, and through such dealings came to see the iron in him beneath the gilt. Then, for the first time, the memory and the puzzlement of the Thunderbird awoke, of the close ties with the Ekwesh and the bargaining and bartering over the ashes of Asenby. But the years of training were also working changes in Alv's mind; his thoughts were no longer so simple, or his hatred so direct.

How this was is not known—whether it was a deliberate act of his master, or whether it was a thing brought about by the boy himself. There may have been many subtle enchantments interwoven among the long chants he was set to learn, and that later he was taught to amend, add to and eventually compose for himself. In these, sung into and onto their forging, lay the true magic of the smiths of old—to set a virtue in the things of their creation, to work into them powers that at their height were able to reshape the very forces of nature, or—hardest of all—to sway the minds of men. So it is possible that the will and the blame were not his own. So strong an enthrallment, though, would tend to break the spirit it was turned on, and hamper the growth of its powers. But as the years of his learning passed, Alv's skill and craft waxed ever greater, and with it his arrogant, untamed, questing spirit.

Need drove him, a desperate need to learn, to know all that there was to be known. Whenever he had a spare moment he would be delving through some volume or other, storing up masses of questions for Ingar or the master. To break the boundaries of his reading he mastered not only his native Northland speech, but also the tongue of Suderney, and many no longer spoken in south or north. Even some words of Ekwesh he acquired. But much as he learned, it never satisfied him. In his dreams he searched out all the secrets of the world, from its heart to its heights, and shouted out his questions to the silent stars. Awake, he longed to end his apprenticeship, to become his own man, free if he chose to go out and explore the world. Much as he admired the Mastersmith, Alv had had his fill of these barren mountains, the house from which he could not stir for six months of every year, the few faces he was forced to see every day. Most of all he yearned to see women again, for none had ever come there save Ernan's old wife, and she died during his third winter in the house. Knowledge was his road to escape, his path to his own fortune, and he longed for it with the fervor of love. That forbidden North wall of the library drew him like a magnet, and he deeply resented the prohibition. He would run his hands lovingly over the scrolls there, fingering the smooth dark fabric of the cylinders and their cold carved finials, as if he could somehow divine their cloth-shrouded secrets through his fingertips. It seemed to him almost that he could, that half of the hidden knowledge came through to him and that he lacked only a single clear glimpse to set it free in his mind—and that that glimpse, that essential key, should be his by right. Always he was tempted—but he never dared risk it. Even more clearly he felt the force of the Mastersmith's word. And perhaps it was this hunger, and the only source of feeding it he knew, that drew his mind toward what, in his innermost heart, he knew to be evil. He felt himself apart even from the others of the household, and quietly looked down on them all. Ingar he despised, even after the older apprentice had completed his prentice pieces and been made journeyman; his amiable lack of ambition and his decision to stay with the Mastersmith and study, rather than make a life of his own, struck Alv as cowardly and contemptible. But outwardly he showed little of this, following the Mastersmith's example as in all else.

Sure it is that he needed no urging to despise his origins and admire the man who had raised him out of them and might raise him higher yet. So perhaps it is not strange that he came to feel it right and admirable to be as hard, as detached, as his master, to feel joy in the domination of others and cloak it under studied civility and friendship. Would that not seem the very stamp of a great man, a master? But he was to learn that not all of the Mastersmith's visitors were his servants.

It fell in the last winter of Alv's apprenticeship, when he might have been some twenty or twenty-one years of age, that the Mastersmith sent for him. Alv found him by the firepit, gazing at its low flames as if reading something from them; when Alv stood respectfully by him he did not raise his head, but spoke briskly.

"Well, boy! The world moves apace, and you with it; you are molding yourself well. I will need other helpers besides Ingar in the days soon to come. Therefore, though you are young for it as yet, I judge you ripe now to try your prentice pieces."

Alv lost all his studied calm. "My . . . You're making me a journeyman?"

"If I accept your work. *If*. Strictly by rule of guild, for it would be very useful to me one day if you were to hold a mastership in it. Very useful . . . So, you must prove to me that you have some command of the higher arts of the smith—scholarship, jewelry, armory, weaponry, suchlike. You will begin three test pieces, two under my direction, but the first you must manage for yourself. We will make that jewelry, I think. A simple gold armring, the kind wealthy young pups covet to give their girls—when they can be sure there's a good virtue of binding and fidelity laid on it. They'll sell their souls for a really fine one—or better, their influence. Can you manage that on your own?"

Alv swallowed. "Y-yes, Mastersmith. With Mochain's treatise on the patterning of gold . . ."

"From the East wall. Very well, you may safely take it. Mind that the ring looks good, now! Graceful, nothing clumsy, but the pattern clear upon it. Now off about your work!" Alv fled willingly, half afraid he would blurt out the thoughts whirling around in his head. So he would become a journeyman—that he had never doubted for a moment. But the Mastersmith was assuming he'd be willing to stay on here, free or not; well, safer not even to think otherwise—for now.

"Why set you to make a daft thing like that?" asked Roc, when he found Alv shaping the fine beeswax for a casting. *"He's* got no use for it, that's for sure! And no more have we, worse luck!"

Alv sighed. He found Roc easier to tolerate than the others, but at times he could be tiresome. Still, it was true enough, what he said. The Mastersmith had no use for women, or any other desire of the body; he was cold, ascetic, saving his passions only for his work and his intrigues. His household had perforce to live as he did, which suited the younger men not a bit. Even Ingar had been heard to complain—but not when the master was around. "How would I know? Maybe he has a customer in mind—"

"Up here? Even the randiest ones won't come galloping over fifty leagues of frozen Northlands just for one of those!"

Alv snorted impatiently. "Well, maybe it's to teach me a moneymaking skill, then. Get me a stand to mount this on, will you? And a set of carving tools—fine ones, and sharp!"

He hummed to himself as he scraped at the wax, a smooth sweeping tune that seemed to fit the gentle curves; it had no words as yet. He would find those in the symbols he would engrave around the serpentine shape, symbols taken from that ancient book and elsewhere in his ardent studies. It was up to him to weld those words together in song, as it was to blend the symbols into a harmonious pattern. The right song, the right pattern, the right fine alloy of metals sunk cleanly into the mold, without crack or bubble—they would take the impress of their creator's power, and enhance it in the form he chose. When the blank wax model was complete, he laid it down gently and turned to his books, selecting and composing, scribbling on his slates, always with that smooth shape before him. A full week that labor alone took him, in which he slept little and only remembered to eat when Roc thrust food under his nose.

"Here! Stick your snout in a stewpot for a change!" Alv threw down the heavy scroll with a growl of disgust and grabbed the bowl and the slice of black bread. Roc watched him with amusement. "Don't bother to thank me, will you? The stew's not that bad, the beast's only been dead a week."

Alv remembered to stay polite and mumbled an apology. "Thinking too hard . . ."

"Not such a dawdle as you expected, eh?"

Alv gave him a withering stare. "You wouldn't understand. It'll do as it is—but I've got to be sure it's perfect, you hear, *perfect!*"

"I hear. I won't wait up, then. Don't fall asleep in your stew!"

Alv hardly heard him. That was the real problem—that half-felt memory that seemed so vital, that nagged him every time he stared down at the symbols scored on the slates before him. He had a pattern, a good pattern, and parts of it had cost him much labor. But some small characters had seemed to fall into place almost naturally, as if by instinct; the result looked good, but he couldn't work out why, or find any other remotely satisfying version. He distrusted that. He had followed a shadow, something cast in his mind, a shadow of the days when he was a child, before he'd come to this place. And that was ridiculous, because then he'd known no smithcraft. He swore, and sent the bowl spinning across the room to crack against the high anvil. Whatever the reason, this way it would have to be.

At dawn Roc found him asleep over his slates. On them the symbols were merged into a single fluid tangle of lines, and his song had found words. He sat by himself all that day, singing softly and carving the stylized pattern deep into the wax, burnishing away trimmings and rough edges, highlighting the design here and there with stippling. Late that evening he grafted on two short wax rods to act as sprue, and rousted out a yawning Roc to fetch a bronze molding flask and a pail of fine white clay; sand would be too coarse for this. By dawn the clay was dry and the flask set to heat at the firepit. Roc handed him tongs wrapped in wet rags; carefully he lifted the heavy flask, tilted it gently over an empty bowl and spilled out the steaming wax that had once shaped those delicate curves. Only their ghosts were left now, invisible in the shell of clay. He set the flask back to heat for a moment, reached deeper into the fire and seized a black crucible. The air shimmered violently about it as it rose, and he held it unmoving at arm's length above the flask, which Roc was steadying with tongs. Slowly, carefully, Alv tilted the crucible, and liquid spilled over and out, glowing like the sun. Alv had drawn the gold from the Mastersmith's deep vaults, along with tiny portions of rare metals and other substances to make it subtly stronger and easier to cast. Little by little, humming his tune, he poured the fine stream into one of the sprue holes, while Roc gently rasped a fine file over the lip of the flask, to vibrate the molten metal into all the fine detail and free any air bubbles. Steam whistled out of the other sprue hole, and every second Alv's throat tightened as he feared the mold would crack. Then a little dome of gold stood out above both sprue holes, and would sink no further, and they could breathe freely once more. Now there was only the gradual cooling, moving the flask closer and closer to the lip of the fire till it rested on the rim, and at last he could seize it and plunge it into the quenching bath. The icy water boiled up and splashed his hands, but after the stinging and scarring of forgework he hardly noticed. A tap on the loose bottom of the flask freed the mold, another cracked it. As he pulled it out it fell apart in two halves like an eggshell, and the pattern gleamed warmly up at him from the clay.

He reached out to it, but another hand forestalled him. The Mastersmith swept up the mold, and the clay crumbled to dust under his long hard fingers as he looked it over. Alv watched him breathlessly, wondering how he had known to appear just at the right moment. The dark eyes gleamed as they read the pattern, reflecting the gleams of gold and firelight with a strange added luster. He gazed at it long and silently, as if seeking to unravel some puzzle.

At last he nodded, and handed the armring to Alv, still dull and encrusted with powdery clay. "I was not mistaken in you, boy. The piece is fine, it has a true power in it—more than a virtue, a power. Do you clean and burnish it now. Bring it to me tonight, and we shall consider what may be your next piece."

But it was that night, as dusk was falling, that the riders arrived. It was Alv who saw them first, cantering down the steep valley floor from the north; he was sitting on the high outer windowsill of his small bedroom, as he often did, gazing on the last of the sunset and seeing it strike fire from the new-polished ring. At first he was mildly intrigued, no more; such cloaked and hooded visitors were not uncommon. Seldom, though, on such a beautiful white mare as the first one rode; the other was a nondescript black, but both picked their way among the uneven stones with amazing sureness and grace. Then the leader reined in sharply at sight of the tower, and Alv sat up so suddenly he almost tumbled off the ledge. The dark hood was swept back, and a swath of long hair spilled out, tinged white-gold by the failing sun. The voice that hailed the tower rang between the cold cliffs high and clear as a hammer-stroke. Then the woman spurred her horse down the last of the slope toward the gate, and Alv hurled himself back inside and onto the spiral stair, shouting for Ingar and Roc. He went leaping down the steps two at a time and out into the great bare hall. Ingar came running up the steps from the library, and Roc out of the kitchen, struggling to ask excited questions with his mouth stuffed full.

"Gate—" panted Alv. "Riders coming—she . . ."

"She?" said Ingar and whistled. He turned to the kitchen and yelled "Ernan! The gate, and be polite about it! Roc, stop your stuffing and go tell Himself, he's deep in some book down there. And then go fetch my best robe—no, wait." He looked narrowly at Alv. "This woman . . . Tall? And blond-haired, very blond—almost white?"

Alv nodded breathlessly, but Ingar's face fell. *"Louhi!"* He shook his head. "Forget the robe, Roc. Now just what on earth could be bringing *her* here now?"

"Old friend of yours, this Louhi?" inquired Alv archly, doing his best to look dignified again.

Ingar's mouth twisted, but before he could answer there was a clatter of feet on the library steps. They both stared in astonishment as the Mastersmith came running out but as Alv had never seen him, with robes and hair awry and a wild look in his dark eyes. He came striding over and grabbed Alv by the shoulders. "You're sure? You saw her?"

"Y-yes, Mastersmith! Clearly, and she called out! Riding from the north—''

As if to confirm his words came a single stroke on the great bronze bell at the gate, and the Mastersmith's fingers bit deep into Alv's arms. Then he let go, with a murmur of apology, and turned away to adjust his tunic and robe, and smooth down his hair. From outside came the soft rumble of the stone gate opening, and the clatter of hooves on the polished granite. The Mastersmith waved the others back against the wall, squared his shoulders, strode to the hall doors and flung them wide.

The great horse halted just beyond them, gleaming in the dusk. In a flurry and rustle of fabric its rider swung herself easily down, and tossed the reins to an apprehensive-looking Ernan. "Look to him well!" she called, and stepped forward into the warm light of the hall, extending a gloved hand to the Mastersmith. He bowed, took it and touched it lightly to his forehead and lips. Alv had never seen his master so deferential, but he felt no wonder in him at that. She was the loveliest woman he had ever seen. Tall and slender she stood, as tall as the Mastersmith or taller, and held her head high and proud. Her pale, fine hair was gathered tight back on her head, but fell in smooth straight cascades around her shoulders. Her high forehead and fine-chiseled features were so nearly the same shade as her hair, like milky ice, that she might have seemed a beautiful statue, but for the full lips and the flash of blue eyes under heavy lids as she glanced around the room.

"Well, Mylio," she murmured, and her voice had the tone of the bronze bell, "you seem to have made yourself comfortable here. And added to your household, too—good day, Ingar! So you are almost a man now!" At his side Alv saw Ingar bow with the practiced grace of a good upbringing. Then the blue eyes lit on him, and he wanted to imitate the bow, but dared not trust his shaky legs. "And to you also, fair young apprentice! I do not know your name?" She smiled, and Alv's throat went dry. There was something in the parting of the lips . . .

"Alv, if it please you, lady," he managed, remembering the polite formulas out of some of Ingar's romances, and made a stiff but creditable bow. To his surprise she returned it with a grave inclination of the head, before turning to the Mastersmith.

"It seems to me you have made a promising choice, Mylio," she said. "And you shall tell me what you think of mine. For Louhi also has taken an apprentice—*Kara!*"

Another rustle, a white shape moving in the dark, halting on the threshold as uncertain as Louhi was assured. The hood was not drawn back, the thin white cloak held protectively close, but Alv could see its wearer was also a woman, thinner and shorter than Louhi. The hood turned toward him for an instant, and he caught a glimpse of wide eyes and dark hair in its shadow. The Mastersmith's dark gaze seemed to penetrate it even more keenly, for he scanned her up and down and darted a glance at Louhi, running the tip of his tongue nervously over his lips.

"Your judgment places mine in shadow, Louhi, as ever. May your servant ask what it is that you require of him?"

Louhi laughed lightly, rippling like the waterfall. "Nothing more costly than an hour of your time, Mylio, and to your own great profit. Things are moving that you should know of. Then we must ride! Come, show me the prospect from your tower, and we shall talk by ourselves."

The Mastersmith bowed silently and waved her toward the stairs. She swept toward them with a confident stride that flared out her cloak like a train—and Alv gaped. Had he really glimpsed the hilt of a broadsword against the white skirts of her riding habit? Kara trailed after her, but the Mastersmith suddenly rounded on her. *"By ourselves,* you said, Louhi! Well then—*she* stays down here!"

Louhi's laugh rippled delicately. "Why, Mylio, how ungallant of you! Anyone would think you were afraid of the child! Well, girl, you may stay here and warm yourself by the fire as you will. But remember that we leave in an hour!"

The girl turned away hurriedly toward the fireplace, and the smith followed Louhi up the stairs. Ingar let out his breath with a great gusty sigh and sagged against the wall.

"What's got into you?" demanded Alv in an undertone.

"Thank the powers she's gone!"

"Why? What's wrong with her?"

Ingar shrugged. "Just her presence—and those eyes of hers—I can't stand 'em, they give me the creeps! Couldn't you feel it? No? Well, there you are, I suppose. You notice Ernan and Roc have made themselves scarce." He chuckled. "Maybe she took a shine to you. If so, you may have her, for me."

"Listen, who is this Louhi woman anyhow? Another smith?"

"Keep your voice down!" snapped Ingar, with a quick toss of the head toward the white-cloaked figure now bending toward the great fire. "I don't know! I've only seen her once before, the day she came to our old smithy at Esarka, far to the south. And that was when the Mastersmith began making plans to move out here for good! I've heard things, though—rumors, whisperings. She's no smith, that's for sure; she had the Mastersmith make her a sword, a fine one. A schemer, a troublemaker—a great lady out of the Southlands, probably. I've heard they let their women get out of hand down there."

Alv's gaze lingered on the girl. As if in answer, she raised a slender hand and very tentatively pushed back her hood to reveal a head of short dark hair. She turned her head slowly as if to steal a glance back at them, but caught Alv's glance and looked away hurriedly. "And the girl?" he asked, nonchalantly.

Ingar shrugged. "New to me—and little enough I care. If she's Louhi's she'll be nothing for you or I. And you can take that how you like."

Alv pursed his mouth. "There's no harm in just *talking* to her—"

"On your fool's head be it!" muttered Ingar, and stalked off swiftly toward the library stairs. The door banged behind him, and Alv saw the girl jump, and again when he spoke.

"Don't be frightened, lady! Make yourself at home here. May I find you a chair?"

Now she did look at him, and Alv fought to stop himself goggling. She was the opposite of Louhi, and yet in her own way she too was lovely. It was her eyes he saw first, wide and strangely slanting and as green as sea surf. High cheekbones and a firm nose made her face seem almost triangular, narrowing down to full lips and a strong chin. Her hair was roughly cropped just short enough to show her ears, neat and narrow; her skin was creamy, browner than Louhi's, rich cream against ice. With that, and those eyes, it seemed to him a face he might have glimpsed for an instant in the forest undergrowth below; she had almost an animal aspect—a hunted animal, perhaps already ensnared. For though her face was very young, suffering had graven it deep, and an unseen yoke seemed to weigh down her shoulders. The wildness in those eyes was desperation.

Alv could not speak at first, for something welled up in him, a deep wash of feelings too fiercely foreign to the image of himself he had tried to forge. He grabbed one of the rough settles against the wall and thrust it toward her almost angrily, feeling utterly ludicrous. But she slid down onto it wearily, and a smile glimmered on her lips. Overwhelmed, he slumped down beside her.

"I thank you, sir. It seems so long since I sat in peace by such a fire . . ." Her voice was startling, deeper and softer than Louhi's. She looked at him almost amusedly. "To whom do I owe my thanks?"

"I—I . . . I'm an apprentice here—candidate for journeyman, though! They call me Alv . . ." He shrugged.

"But you don't like that name much?"

Her clear sight stunned him. "I hate it! But I haven't found a better one yet—not one I could bear without, well, feeling foolish. Like flopping around in someone else's clothes, reach-me-down rags . . ."

She nodded. Her smile was grave still, but more definitely there. "You could have no pride in that. But be patient, you'll find your name, I know you will, and earn it! There's something about you, I sense it—and so did Louhi, I heard her. You're somebody special, one alone, out of the ordinary . . ."

"So are you! So are you!"

She closed her eyes a moment, and her smile tautened. "Yes. To my grief." Her head bowed, and the firelight trembled on her cheek. The white cloak fell apart; beneath it she wore a plain smock like any village girl's, but in dark soft material. Her long fine hands looked very white against it as they twisted in her lap.

The water roared, the wheel turned, the great hammers pounded, the fire came rushing through him. He seized her hands and held them tight against him. "Lady—I'll help you! Just . . . tell me how, and I'll help you!"

She stared at him, wildly again, but did not shrink away. Her grip tightened within his own, and with strength that startled him she caught his hands to her breast. "You can't! No smith welded my chains, and even if you were the greatest among men you could not unmake them! Never!" Then she subsided, and laughed a little, but there was no mockery in it. "But one day, perhaps, I can. I had ceased to believe that—or to see any gain in doing so. But knowing somebody wants to try—that itself heartens me so much, so very much . . ."

"Anything! I'd risk anything!"

Her face set, and light awoke in her eyes, light glimmering on a pool in some immense forest, far greater than any he knew. "No. I forbid you, for not only you would suffer. And you may have some great destiny ahead of you. I would not deny that to the world. In less than an hour Louhi takes me from here—let her!"

"And never see you again? Never know what—what . . ." Tears at least he could still dam, that much control he kept, but he knew his lip quivered like a child's. Twenty years old, candidate journeyman, he had briefly felt himself grown to a man. Now he felt empty, helpless.

"I promise you this!" she said, slowly, intensely. "That from now on I'll never despair, I'll watch and wait for any sane chance I have to free myself. And then I'll seek you out, wherever you are, and you'll know! Believe me, and be content!"

Flames flickered up in the hearth, a coal cracked and settled. The idea came to him in a rush. He could still face himself in his glass on the morrow. He could still risk something on a venture. He felt the fire's warmth in his smile. "I'll believe you, Kara—if you'll be held to your promise! If you'll accept a token!"

And he held out the armring.

She hesitated a moment, then took it, wondering, and turned it this way and that. The gold reddened in the light, and the flames danced along its pattern. "There is a virtue in this," she said, and her voice trembled. "I of all folk should take care, should take long counsel, before allying myself to such a thing. I should be slow to take it upon me—" Then, violently, she thrust her hand out and through it, and it rode high on her bare arm, past the elbow, and clung there.

"Be you as slow to keep your promise, then," said Alv drily, and they both doubled up with laughter, the foolish mirth that breaks the cords of fear. They swayed together, and for an instant her breath mingled with his, their lips brushed—and then they sprang apart, for they heard light footfalls on the stair, and the rustle of Louhi's robe. Her hands gripped his an instant, and they were parted.

When Louhi and the Mastersmith stepped into the hall Kara sat by the fire alone, head bowed as before. The tall woman looked around and gave a delicate disdainful sniff. "It stinks of animal in here now, after the clean air! And soot, and food, and hot metal—I long for the open road again! Come, Kara!"

Alv, at the open kitchen door, watched her rise and follow, saw the door thrust wide and heard the clatter of hooves on the flagstones as if they were stamping on his heart. But he stood respectfully, and as the Mastersmith ushered out Louhi and followed, Kara's arm darted out, gold-bedecked, from beneath her cloak, to touch his. "It will aid me!" she whispered fiercely. The cloak fell back, and he saw for the first time, as if in a dream, that it was lined with innumerable minute black feathers.

The hooves departed, the outer gate creaked softly to, and the Mastersmith returned, rubbing his hands. He looked pale and harassed, but relieved, as if some immediate burden had been lifted. He sat by the fire in silence for an hour or so, and then called Alv to him. "Well, boy! Let's be having a look at your armring!"

"*My* armring, Mastersmith? Are you giving it to me?"

The Mastersmith looked slightly askance at him. "Yes— if you wish it, since it is your own work, though the gold is mine. But not your other pieces, mind! Well for you if you do not grow to love your own work too greatly to dispose of it to advantage."

"Indeed, Mastersmith," said Alv, and bowed. "I have already given it away."

"What! To whom?"

Alv drew a breath, and told him. For one instant a blacker fury than he had ever seen crossed his master's brow, and then, surprisingly, the smith began to laugh softly. "So we have given a gift to Louhi! For what that girl has, Louhi has, be sure of that. And what precious thing did you get in return? No, save me the mawkish details, I can guess!" He laughed again, a chilly little laugh, and Alv ground his teeth at what that laugh made of his hour. The smith pursed his lips. "Well, the price was high indeed for any such . . . matter, but at least there was a price. If you must trifle with women, better you learn to keep it a matter of trade than let them assume undue importance, and distract you from serious matters!" He grew thoughtful. "Louhi herself would know the bauble for what it was, and not wear it. But who knows, if the girl happened to keep the armring . . . It might yet benefit us greatly to have a hold over one so close to Louhi's secrets. Who knows!" He clapped his hands briskly. "So, to bed now, for tomorrow you begin work on your second piece—and that is armory. You will make me a helm of fine mail, and in it a virtue of concealment, of change, of moving subtly and unseen. Dream of that!"

But Alv dreamed of nothing; he could not sleep. His head burned on his hard pillow, strange twisted images of the day unreeling in his mind. One minute he would seethe with anger at the Mastersmith for casually assuming he had been pawing at Kara—the way the old Headman used to treat his maidservants!—and then even more at himself for not having done so. It was what he wanted, wasn't it? What caused the dull swelling ache in him now? She'd probably have enjoyed it well enough, giggled and given in the way the maidservants did. With what he'd given her—for what? for the shadow of a kiss?—he might have commanded the body of a great lady like Louhi, or for its worth in gold a hundred street girls. He might at least have got better value for it. And then he turned over and groaned. If he could think like that, the Mastersmith had

made an understandable mistake, had read his character
only too well. That was just what he'd thought of trying,
might have tried—if it had been any other girl than Kara.
But then why did the image of her still torment his body
and banish his sleep?

At last he swung himself out of bed, tottered to the
window and flung the casement wide. The night air poured
in, crisp and cold enough even at the end of winter to
make his lungs blaze. He hung there, drinking in great
gulps, looking at the Iceglow and thinking how peaceful
to be out there, cool and sterile, free from the tortures of
the body—and yet, somehow, he would yearn for them
still. Then below him he heard the soft boom of the hall
door shutting, and the crunch of boots on flagstones. Startled, he looked down and saw the Mastersmith walk out
across the yard toward the main gate. It was late at night,
everybody must be asleep—except, of course, him. Alv
bit his lip; could the smith have had second thoughts and
be going after Louhi and Kara, to get back the armring?
Surely not—but . . .

A spirit of deviltry seized Alv. He had already taken
one risk and got away with it. He flung on his clothes,
grabbed cloak and boots and went padding barefoot down
the worn stone stairs, paused an instant to don his boots
on the warm hearthstone in the hall, and cautiously unlatched the front door.

The clatter and creak of latch and hinges sounded deafening against the silence of the night, but nobody stirred
in response. The front gate was securely fastened, but he
had learned the lore of locks from this one's maker, and
it was fastened from the outside only. He moved through
it like a ghost, the gate stirred, and then he was looking
down at a trail of footprints in the deep snow. He hesitated
a moment, then ran softly and lightly along their track,
carefully placing his feet in the actual prints so no second
track would show. At every rise or hummock he would
hunch down against cover to spy out his way ahead. And
that was as well, else he would not have heard the voices
in the gully beyond. He crept to the edge, peered over—
and froze.

The Mastersmith was there, but not alone. Gathered

around him on the snow was a semicircle of shadows, shapeless things—but with voices, low, dark and guttural. The
tallest of them was a head or so shorter than the smith,
and he stood stiff and dignified above the jabbering group.
Their voices rose suddenly as if in fury, but when the
Mastersmith snapped out one or two words, no more, in
a clear commanding tone they fell silent at once. Then the
Mastersmith turned as if to walk away, and Alv pulled his
head back sharply. If the Mastersmith was going back to
the house he would have to be there first. He turned and
went sprinting back to the gate, and breathed easily only
when it was locked behind him. Now his mind had something else to whirl over, as he padded carefully across the
courtyard. What were those shadow-creatures, were
they real, alive, or some kind of sinister snow-spirit? They
looked like no people he had ever heard of. He crept into
the hall and risked a moment at the low fire, imagining
himself become a master mage whose works could call
dark spirits in the night to fulfill his slightest wish, to
compel any girl he desired. And was it such a wild hope?
Soon he would be a journeyman, maybe a master while
yet young. Then he wouldn't need to lie awake at night—
not alone, anyhow. Any girl he desired—but then there
would be Kara. For surely he would find her before anything, and her he would not compel.

He sighed, turned away—and knocked over the settle
with a resounding echoing crash. Guiltily he scooped it
up, waiting for doors to be flung open and angry shouts;
should he bolt for the stairs or try to brazen it out? Either
way would look suspicious, would very soon reach the
Mastersmith's ears—and what then? He would at least sus-
pect.

But there were no doors opening, no shouts, and he was
almost aggrieved at the silence. Had everyone else vanished too? He peered into the kitchen. Ernan's thin snore
came undisturbed from his little room beyond. Alv glided
across to the storeroom, and heard Roc's loud snorts; he
even seemed to grumble in his sleep. Alv touched his
shoulder, found no response, shook and finally pinched
him. Roc snorted more loudly, but did not awaken. Greatly
daring, Alv applied the same tests to Ernan, who also did

not stir. Then, afraid of the Mastersmith's returning, he
tiptoed back upstairs—and then past his room, up to Ingar's. A light burned there, but there was no answer when
he knocked. He found the journeyman flat out on his bed,
with a book over his face and a lamp stinking and guttering beside him. Sleep had evidently struck him while he
read, and could not be shaken off him. Alv blew out the
lamp, and stole away, shaken, to his own bed. The whole
household lay under some spell of sleep, and he could
guess why—to cloak its master's nightgoings. Perhaps he
did it often, and Alv had either succumbed to it, or slept
naturally as he normally did. But tonight . . .

Tonight the turmoil in his mind had kept him awake. Or
had it unleashed something, some force in him that could
resist the Mastersmith's enchantment? Then surely he was
a mage born! In the promise of that, in images of sensual
delight, he found release and finally sleep. But the last
vision in his mind was his first sight of Kara's face.

CHAPTER THREE

The Sword

Alv awoke next morning with the first gray glimmer of dawn in his eyes, and a driving urgency in his mind. For a moment, bewildered, he could hardly remember what it was; the events of the night had turned his old world wholly upside down. Then he remembered. His second trial piece! The Mastersmith had set it. Today the work would begin.

He suddenly felt very empty and helpless, the puzzles of the night retreating before a new and immediate problem. *A helm of fine mail, and in it a virtue of concealment, of change, of moving subtly and unseen . . .* Virtues indeed! He knew something of them—how to charm a jewel setting so it tended to turn away thievish eyes, to work a sword hilt so in action its blade would blur before the eyes of an unwary opponent. But these were light powers, minor charms added to some greater work, little use if their existence was suspected. Making them strong, making them work together as the living heart of a piece—the difficulty of it loomed over him like a wall.

He panicked. He didn't have the faintest idea where to begin. And yet if he was to have any chance of ever finding Kara again, he'd have to. He slumped down despondently. It seemed monstrously unfair, a task like that—surely the Mastersmith hadn't set anything so hard to Ingar the Booklouse, Ingar of the Parchment Anvil? Then the weight lifted so suddenly he laughed aloud. Of course, the second and third pieces weren't supposed to be things an apprentice could manage on his own. They were meant to

stretch him as well as test him—well, it would, this one.
And now that he was able to think more clearly, he thought
he could see a clue in the very form of the thing—chain
mail. A whole made up of thousands of tiny, separate
pieces—

"Like the elements of a living body," said the Mastersmith, and nodded. "You see clearly, as I have always
said. Each link a distinct work in itself, with its own particular virtue, some of one kind, some another—weak in
themselves, for it is hard to make such negative virtues
strong. But joined together into a single thing with an
identity of its own—*then* they become strong."

Alv nodded, tracing the archaic words on the great scroll
spread out before them.

> *Eynhere elof hallns styrmer*
> *Stallans imars olnere elof . . .*

"There is made . . ." he translated slowly, running his
finger from word to word, " . . . one alone . . . a whole,
into a whole, I mean . . . of power . . . surpassing . . .
by many . . . being linked—why does it repeat 'one
alone'? A copyist's mistake?"

"Hardly," said the Mastersmith sardonically, "since the
copyist was I. It is a poetic form of *alofer,* an even more
archaic term for smith—literally 'shaper.' Used here in the
dative as a scholar's pun, and to heighten the assonance of
the lines. I incline to think that is important in your chant—
use these lines, and keep as much assonance as you can
in the lines around them. You see their meaning now?
'The smith makes single things strong by combining them
into a greater identity.' Remember, identity is important,
the more so the greater the virtue in an object. If a portion
of the helm is ill made, the whole thing fails, and you
must needs begin again."

"And if it was damaged, Mastersmith?"

"That would depend on the extent and type of the damage. A few broken rings would not ruin it altogether,
though they would weaken it; replace them exactly—if you
can—and it will revive. But anything that destroyed its
identity as a helm would surely destroy its virtue alto-

gether. So though you would not wear it as armor to ward off blows it must be made strong in metal and frame, as the pattern shows. Go as far as you can with it, ask my help at need, and when I judge you have done enough I shall complete it. But you will need to study first. There is a text on ringmail in the sothran tongue which you may find useful, somewhere on the East wall, and various odd passages in other books. And you must read some works on the powers of concealment and the guise of forms. You will find some references on the slate below the pattern. You may study to your heart's content the first scroll of the *Alhvarthen*. And my own notes on the *fjoth* characters, added to the third chapter of the *Book of Tarn*. I may find you others as you plan your work. Begin now!''

The first thing Alv did was seize the large slate with its precious pattern, and scan eagerly through the references. There were many texts from East and West walls he had not so far been allowed to read, but still none from the North. He sternly repressed the cloud of disappointment that settled about him; why should he expect his master to scatter his hard-earned lore before mere apprentices? Surely the quickest way to it was to get on with the task in hand, to the utter limit of his abilities. And this he did.

This time his preparation took not one week but four. He soaked himself in every authority he could find, till at times he had to force himself away from the books, head buzzing, and find relief in simpler tasks. Roc watched all this with cynical amusement, brought Alv the occasional meal and loudly blessed the powers that had never made him a magesmith. But for all his concentration, there were other thoughts nagging away at Alv. Some were of Kara, though those he could escape by reminding himself that this work was also his quickest way to her. But there were some, however trifling, that he could not escape, for he was reminded of them on almost every page or column of scroll he came to. Somewhere on them, often across the bottom left, he would almost always find slight chalky smudges. He wiped them off carefully, in case he was blamed for them—the Mastersmith cared for his library—and remained mildly puzzled as to their cause. He had not yet found it, however, by the time he felt ready to begin.

With the Mastersmith's wire-drawing devices he had made great coils of heavy wire in many metals, copper and gold and delicately alloyed steel. He had patterns ready to be minutely engraved round the edge of every single ring; he had characters into which the rings would be woven, in carefully balanced combinations, and patterns to be inlaid, embossed or enameled around the main frame of the helm. And for each of these he had its own chant, distinct but linked as closely as the finished rings.

First, though, he made the frame, and that was a simple enough business; it resembled the ordinary light helm worn by warriors for skirmishing or scouting, where swiftness was their best protection. One band of fine bronze circled the brow, two hoops crossed the head from front to back and sideways; between them went a stiff leather lining and over that a layer of mail rings. The rings hung down in a curtain to shield the back of the neck, and could be fastened across the throat or the lower part of the face. Then he began on the long labor of crafting the rings, engraving the lengths of steel wire and shaping them, not into plain circles but into peculiar distortions which would let them mesh easier and lie closer, to the good of both armor and virtue. These he would blend piece by minute piece into the pattern, sometimes overlaying them with smaller rings of gold and copper to highlight its lines. It was a long labor, almost another month, and when the mail was complete he held it up in the light of the forge. It was as if the waterfall had overwhelmed the chamber, for the mail reflected a great shimmering wave of light across the dark walls, and the rings rang and chuckled like water among stones. For a moment Alv thought of the hillside streams of his childhood, and felt suffocated in this shadowy, seasonless place. Then, shrugging, he turned to the frame, secured the mail to the leather interior, fitted these together to the frame and hammered the last bronze rivet flat with a die that stamped a binding symbol. "Well?" demanded Roc, who had been holding the die for him. "That's as much as was on the Master's pattern. What're you waiting for?"

Alv stared a doubtful moment at his creation. There

seemed to be nothing inconspicuous about that glistening thing. Still . . . He raised it as if to put it on his head—

And the Mastersmith reached out and received it graciously. He too looked at it a moment, as if puzzled, and then quickly placed it on his head, smoothing the mail out around his neck. The rings rang more quietly; nothing else seemed to change—but then the Mastersmith reached up and fastened the mail across his face. The rings shone as brightly in the forelight, but somehow the tiny gaps between them grew harder, deeper, more black, until night seemed to seep out of the helm like thick lampblack ink. The highlights still shone, but behind them it was as if the mask itself and its wearer drew further and further back into the shadow, blurring, quietening, becoming indistinct. It was like a pond draining and drying in the darkness, leaving nothing but a few gleaming puddles. Knowing someone stood there, Alv and Roc strained their eyes and could just make him out. Otherwise he would have seemed nothing but one of the insubstantial shadows that darkness creates. In a forest, anywhere with cover, he could have walked unheard, unnoticed, as good as invisible.

Behind the young men the library door swung open. Ingar walked in, and stopped short at the sight of Alv and Roc. "Seen the master anywhere—what're you two gaping at?"

There was a sudden trill of metal, and the Mastersmith stood bareheaded before them with the helm swinging from one hand. It was Ingar's turn to stare; the younger men whooped with laughter, but Alv's faded in him as he caught a flicker of some deeper disquiet on the journeyman's heavy face.

"A pretty enough prentice piece, Ingar, do you not think so?" inquired the Mastersmith with quiet satisfaction.

"A fine work," said Ingar, equally quietly. "May I see it?" The Mastersmith looked at him a moment before handing it over. He rolled it around in his thick fingers, held the mailwork up to the light, and let out a long slow whistle. "There's more powers than one in this, if they can be tapped! Complete it, and—"

"That is what I intend to do," said the Mastersmith

calmly, taking it from him. A look passed between them, one Alv caught but could not understand. "But that is beyond Alv's concerns, for the moment. Your second piece is accepted, boy, with honor. But now to your third! Rest now, and what it is you shall learn—in the morning. You also, Ingar and Roc, it is late enough. Sleep you well."

But again Alv found himself unable to sleep. His mind had grown used to racing, and without the effort of the work in hand to distract and exhaust him it kept him awake long hours into the night, worrying over everything, great or small. What would he be given to create next? Why had Ingar reacted so strangely today? Could it be jealousy, perhaps? What more could the helm do? And, as every night, he thought of Kara. Where was she now? He laughed to himself, bitterly. How wide was the world? He had lost her, failed her—

A sound of thunder shook him, and he sat bolt upright in bed. A storm? But there'd been no flash at the window. It came again, and this time he knew beyond all doubt. It was coming from below. The great hammers were at work. He sat and listened for a moment. He slipped into his tunic and went to the door. Why wasn't the house in an uproar, with that din? And yet in the intervals he could hear Ingar's snores drifting down the stairwell. So it had to be the Mastersmith again, about some secret work . . .

He closed his door and stood there indecisive, torn between his desire to slip down and see what was happening and his fear of having his immunity found out. There was no telling what the Mastersmith might do, then. Why risk anything now, when he was so near his goal? But the need awoke again in him that was to rule his whole life, the need to know, and step by hesitant step it forced him down the cold stairs, through the hall and down to the echoing forge below.

The door was shut, and he did not dare lift the latch; sound and movement might be noticed. He stooped to the keyhole; it was wide, and he could see right across the forge. There were the plunging shadows of the hammers—but even as he watched they fell silent, and he shrank back, afraid the Mastersmith was somehow aware of him. But then he heard the explosive hiss of something being plunged into the quenching trough, and a moment later the rasp of a heavy file. He dared to look again, and saw the Mastersmith clearly, at his bench now, working away at something clamped into a large vice. After a few moments he freed it, picked up something else, tried the two together and nodded calmly to himself. Then he took a hammer and what looked like a die, and began to tap in rivets. Something rang and rippled as he worked, and Alv felt a sliver of the Ice against his spine—it was the helm, the Mastersmith was completing it! And sure enough, when he had finished he held it up, just as Alv had, turning it round and round to look for any slight damage. Alv gaped. The helm now had a front to it, an eyemask that looked to be of silver steel, cast in the form of hawklike glaring eyes. These were outlined by a thick rope of twisted wires, flattened onto the metal; the hammers must have been for making that and welding it onto the mask. The Mastersmith stared at this for a moment, then lifted the helm and placed it on his head with careful ceremony, like a crown. He made no move to fasten the concealing mail. For a minute he strode back and forth, crossing and recrossing the narrow viewpoint of the keyhole; Alv could see his lips moving, but heard no sound. Then a hand swept up the mail to hide his face, the shadows seemed to deepen and he strode out of view. Alv waited for him to reappear, but he did not. The moment grew longer and longer, and Alv felt less and less safe where he was; the Mastersmith, visible or invisible, might come out of that door at any moment. At last he straightened cramped legs and tiptoed slowly and carefully back up the stairs. But when he reached the hall he froze in horror. There were footsteps on the stairs! He scuttled back into the shadows by the front door and crouched there, quivering with fright, as he saw the Mastersmith himself, still wearing the helm, but with its mask now open, come down the last few steps, walk casually across the flagstones and down the stairs Alv had just come up. The stairs which were the only way down to the forge . . .

Back in his bed, Alv lay awake and brooded. The smith might easily have gone through into the library and up those stairs to the far end of the hall—but then Alv would have heard him, his footsteps, or the creak of the library's heavy outer door. Could the completed helm now mask all these sounds, as well? What other, stranger, powers did it now confer? *Of moving subtly* . . . He drifted off to sleep, trying to draw comfort from a vision of Kara—but why were her eyes so cruel—predatory—hawklike?

"This technique is called pattern-welding," said the Mastersmith. "Do you remember reading about it?"

Alv screwed up his eyes. "Yes, Mastersmith, I do. An ancient method of forging a strong blade, when they had little good steel and no easy way of making it."

"Indeed," said the Mastersmith, running his fingers over the short rope of twisted wires. So far there had been no mention of what the rest had been used for, and Alv was not going to admit he knew. "But its very antiquity makes it more than that, for in the course of time it has gathered about it much, much lore. The first great smiths of our kind were taught it by those of the Elder kind, and they in turn by the powers they had revered and abandoned. Like the craft of mail, it takes complexity and makes unity of it, but greater complexity and a more solid unity. Great virtue can be bound up in it by those who have the skill. So—for your trial piece of weaponry, you will make me a sword! But a sword such as you might one day craft for kings, a sword with a virtue of command and obedience, of order and submission. You will prepare everything and shape the blade, but the completion is delicate work, and that may be left to me. It will be long in the forging, many months, I am sure—but when they are over, so will end your apprenticeship. And great things will await us all then, for the world is moving, moving . . ." He paused and sat back, staring into an infinite distance. At length he reached out and tapped the roll of parchment on the table. "Some references to start your studies, boy. More than one or two slates will hold, as you see. Open it and read!"

Fascinated, forgetting the mysteries that gathered around him, Alv unrolled the stiff crackling stuff and read the crabbed script. A page here, a page there, notes—a chapter—the reading alone would take weeks. "And that is not all," said the Mastersmith somberly. "You will require the ancient text *Ysthihain,* its first section on the symbols associated with command and dominion. I have made some notes in it of forms I found used by Ekwesh shamans, which appear to resemble many of ours, but in more archaic, purer forms. Also the *Skolnhere-Book,* left by a great smith from the east many centuries ago; it has pages on pattern-welding, and others on the powers of command."

Alv looked at him. "I do not remember even seeing those on the shelves, Mastersmith, let alone reading them."

"No indeed," said the Mastersmith drily, "and little it would have profited you if you had read them. They are on the North wall."

Alv's eyes widened, and he started to say something, but the smith held up a hand. "Wait! I am not making you free of it—not yet. Come with me now." They threaded their way between anvils and machines toward the library, where Ingar, scribbling furiously on a slate, paid no attention as they went past. The Mastersmith stopped before the racks of scrolls on the North wall, drew out one, and lifted a heavy fanfold book from a high shelf. Alv could see long tongues of parchment protruding from them both. The smith carried them to a table and opened them carefully. He touched the parchment strips. "I marked these for you, last night. See, from here to here in the *Ysthihain* scroll—and in the *Skolnhere-Book,* between this marker and this, to the end of this page." He pointed to the end of the leaf, crammed with crabbed black lettering in an archaic cursive script, interspersed with tight little drawings of symbols or elaborately ornamented characters in red and black. One, the distorted face of some crouching beast, grimaced out from beside the Mastersmith's finger. The wide margins were filled with his flowing script. "Thus far, and no further! Do not let your eyes stray to an earlier or a later page, to another book—not even by chance! You would find little profit in anything you chanced to learn!" Alv nodded, a little rebelliously. "Very well. And do not take them into the forge, they are too valuable."

That was reasonable enough, but Alv, watching the

Master's retreating back, felt like disobeying it, simply out of spite. It was like having a drink snatched away from your lips after the first sip. What he had done so far might please his master, but not him. He felt he had learned almost nothing from any of it—not enough to let him strike out confidently on his own, as he planned to do. He might, with luck, be able to reproduce such a bracelet, if he could get the gold. But the helm was another matter. Information had been carefully measured out for him, so that he knew well enough what he was doing, but had only the barest grasp of why; there was nothing he could apply to any other work. And he had not even been allowed to bring it to its full strength, to appreciate all those powers his own skill had invested in it! And now it was happening again. Why? To make sure he'd stay? To tether him firmly to his master's apron strings?

He didn't want to believe that. He reined in his temper, remembering the gratitude and admiration he still felt, afraid of hasty judgments. But the doubt still hovered blackly around him. He looked across at Ingar, blissfully engrossed in transferring his notes onto parchment. *Does he ever feel like this—fenced in—cozened with false hopes—cheated?* Probably not. He had no driving ambition, no great reason for it; apron strings suited him very well. Ingar tossed down his pen on the slab, scattered fine powder onto the wet page and threw it aside with a satisfied grunt. Then he snatched up his slates and scrubbed them clean with a fold of his left shirtsleeve. He tossed them down, and caught Alv's eye. "Filthy habit," he said unapologetically. "I can never be bothered hunting for the cloth when I'm busy!"

"It's sticking out of your pocket," said Alv, striving to keep his voice level. "Ingar, I never did ask you just what your prentice pieces were."

"Can't tell you—not till you're a journeyman yourself. Guild rules, remember—and the master's a stickler for them—*he shall not seek nor have help or advice save from his own master . . .*"

"Not like that, ass. All I meant was, I don't remember seeing you bent over an anvil for as long as I look to be."

"Should hope not!" grunted Ingar. "Guild rules don't

undervalue scholarship the way tykes like you do. You can substitute dissertations for the two higher pieces, if your master thinks fit. So I did.'' He pointedly unrolled the next page of the work he was studying and leaned forward over it in his customary reading position.

Alv nodded slowly, and looked down at the page below him. There was the slight chalk smudge, much the same as the others, including, no doubt, one on the column Ingar now read. The fastidious Mastersmith would never treat clothes or books thus. So—Ingar had trodden this ground before him. And read almost every other page Alv had had doled out to him.

Alv drew a deep breath. He could guess just what those dissertations had been about.

Deep in his mind, almost sooner than he could admit it to himself, his doubt was becoming a certainty. The Mastersmith was seeking to tether them both, not only rationing the knowledge he was giving them but carefully separating it, encouraging them to stay within their specialties. Ingar the scholar, seeking knowledge without the craft to put it into effect, Alv the man of skills denied the learning to use them—both of them less than a whole craftsman, both of them dependent on their master, doomed to use their gifts for him, as he chose to direct.

Black anger rose in Alv's throat, the worse for being wholly helpless. What could he do? There was nobody he could even talk to about it. Ingar had seen it already, last night if not sooner; Alv remembered his strange look, when he was confronted with the powerful reality of the helm his studies had given shape. He had seen it, and accepted it—perhaps even liked the idea, because it gave him an easy, congenial living without sweating over an anvil. *Which is all very fine for him—but me? Where does it leave me?*

"Right up your own chimney!" said Roc, and laughed raucously. Alv glared at him. He had had to talk to someone, and while he had tried to avoid becoming close or familiar with the forgeboy, Roc had somehow remained the nearest thing to a friend he had. So in the end he had swallowed his pride and told him something of what he feared—putting the best possible complexion on it and with

no question of seeking advice. But of course the first thing
Roc said was, "If you want my advice—" He seemed to
be waiting for Alv to deny it. "If you want my advice,"
he repeated inexorably, "stick it out, then get out! Getting
to be a journeyman, that's the thing, getting the badge and
script. Then push off and find some other bolthole!"

"Maybe I don't know enough yet—"

Roc shrugged. "Pick it up as you go along! The rank's
what folk'll pay heed to. Take what you're given and use
it, that's what I say."

"Maybe you're right," Alv admitted. After all, it was
no more than he'd planned, wasn't it? But he hated the
idea of leaving without at least some of the unique learning
that was here, and was denied him. His anger turned round
then, and became a cooler, more calculating thing.
"Maybe you're right," he repeated, and Roc looked at
him shrewdly. But Alv kept his own counsel then, though
he did not cease to think. Go he would, but not without
at least some of that special knowledge, knowledge he
could rely on to make his living and let him search for
Kara. And he would gain it by turning the Mastersmith's
own methods against him; since Ingar was so content to
be used by his master, why should Alv not make equal
use of him?

And so he threw himself into what was to be the hardest
labor of his life till then. Throughout the long weeks of
study he kept returning, again and again, to those texts
from the North wall. In them he at least found a foretaste
of the knowledge that he wanted so much, that in truth
was as necessary to him as meat to the starving, so strongly
did the craft within him burn to find its fullest expression.
But what little he learned served only to awaken further
that appetite, never satisfying it. Often he felt tempted,
driven, to disobey the Mastersmith's injunctions, but
though he was no longer sure he believed the books were
guarded, still he never once dared to let even a page too
many fall open. What he was allowed, however, he read
and reread, draining the last fine drops of learning from
it, and most of all the Mastersmith's own notes in the
margins. These came from many sources, but the ones he

found most illuminating seemed to stem from comparisons with the lore of the Ekwesh.

"Indeed," said the Mastersmith gravely, when Alv sought counsel from him one day. "Their smithcraft is often rough and savage, for it is the preserve of their tribal shamans, who must also be priests, chroniclers, bards, healers and counselors to the chieftains in peace and war. Their metalworking is elementary and knows little of fine alloys and precious metals. But they have some special skills, little practiced in more civilized lands; one of these is the use of masks, in which the wearer, as it were, becomes his own living symbol. But these they make chiefly from wood, as yet. I have experimented at combining their skills with ours, and have often found the results very potent." Alv thought of the Thunderbird, the beautifully crafted metal death's head within, and the keen cold mask that now fronted that strange helm. He nodded with polite interest, but said nothing. "They are also concerned," continued the Mastersmith, "with the swaying of wills, and that is what makes their work relevant here. In their tribes, where the chieftains enjoy all power of life and death over their people, such things are more easily and openly studied than among our own, and more greatly valued. So I feel that by considering their equivalents, these characters of ours, here and here, could well be modified thus . . ."

It was not the first or the last advice he gave. He never hovered over Alv, but he seemed to be constantly on hand when he was needed. His counsel was always good, always helpful when Alv had a choice to make. But about the reasons for that choice he was given only the most general ideas, little or nothing he could apply to other works. Alv was careful never to appear less than satisfied and delighted with what he was given, choking down the frustration he felt. And in truth he often forgot it, as the sword seemed to take shape among the piles of slate and parchment before him. More than once he dreamed of this, of sliding his fingers down among the litter of papers and touching cold metal there—but metal that quivered at his touch, and went slithering away through the rustling layers like a snake among fallen leaves.

But day by day the image of the sword grew less elusive, more real, till it came to occupy his mind almost to the exclusion of all else. He had not forgotten his other concerns, his fears and hopes and desperate love, but it was as if he poured them into a single mold, and sought to hammer them all out at the same anvil where he would forge the sword. It seemed so clear before him now that his arms grew taut and tense as he sat, impatient to be striking the first hard blows. But he knew where impatience led, and what flamed in his mind he quenched with the cool precision that he would first of all need. For no work he had yet attempted, not even the helm, had been so minute and so complex. And as at last he drew all his patterns together, and scribed the final design onto stiff yellow parchment with a fine silver-tipped quill, he almost quailed at the weight of the work that lay upon him.

Five rods of metal would make up the sword, one for a spine, two for the body of the blade and two, longer and thinner and of harder stuff, set round the outside to take the fine edge essential to a good weapon. Each of these rods he would make from many strands of metal, twisted together like ropes, and these strands themselves he would in turn twine out of many finer ones, cords and bowstrings and threads of many metals and alloys, starting with strands thinner than his own fine hair. And each of these would have its own symbols, its own virtues, to be sung into it with its own proper song.

He stopped suddenly, pen hovering over the paper like the great condor that had borne it. He had planned them all. He had command of the songs, the symbols, the metals, and surely above all he had the skills. Then what could he not do? What was lacking in him now for the Mastersmith to fulfill?

"The five rods you will make as you have planned," said the Mastersmith approvingly. His dark eyes flashed as he scanned the crammed parchment. "And though I would not entrust it to every apprentice, I see no reason why you should not also make up the spine and body of the blade."

"And the edge, Mastersmith?" Alv strained to sound no more than normally eager.

The Mastersmith smiled, faintly. "In the edge of a sword is power. In the edge of a sword is what gives meaning to its presence—force fined down to a cutting thinness, to strike where it will profit most, the final sanction that enforces the command given. The body is the command, the threat—the edge is the enforcement. The execution. Without its edge the sword would be only a dull threat, a club at best, its violence dissipated, ineffective. So, this edge is crucial, and must be invested with extra strength. It needs not only the symbols sung into it, it must bear others." He shook his head sadly, and his long dark hair rustled against the rich collar of his robe. "These I cannot trust you with, not yet. They are of my own devising, and difficult to use—perhaps even dangerous. So I will take that work upon myself—" He smiled more widely. "But I am sure that you would find the stamp of a journeyman some balm for your pride, at least. We will see. But for now—to your forging!"

The first days of it were long and wearisome, and they grew to weeks as Alv struggled with the metal that seemed to grow willful under his hands. For him the passing of time became measured by the chime of hammer on anvil, the slow deep gasping of the bellows, the verses of the chants that hung leaden on his dry tongue. The Mastersmith had predicted he would often fail, and often he did—most often of all within reach of success. It was then that an overstrained filament would weaken and snap, or welded cords would part at a blow. Alv would simply stare at the remains and hurl them aside. If it was time then to eat or sleep he would; otherwise, with unfailing patience, he would simply start again. He lived to a strict order, never working long hours or missing meals, because he could see that haste would not help him here. Later it would be forced on him, and he must save his endurance for then. So it was long months before he had even completed enough of the long cords of iron and steel, as thick around as his thumb, that would become the five rods. Some were entwined with threads of bronze and gold, others with thinnest webs of rarer metals and fine alloys. But those for the edges were made all of steel, hardened with traces of strange metals and other substances.

"So far you have done well," said the Mastersmith, "and quicker than I feared." Alv looked up sharply, and caught Roc's eye; the forgeboy shrugged eloquently. Feared? Did it matter how long he took? The Mastersmith had never even suggested that. But he did not press the question; the smith was looking odd now, troubled—almost afraid, if you could imagine that in such a man. It seemed to have been growing on him for some time, since that night in the snow, perhaps. He spoke often of the Southlands, though he seemed never to go away now. Alv remembered what Ingar had said, that Louhi's last visit had begun the Mastersmith's plans to move here. What had she set in motion now? The Mastersmith laid down the length of metal he had been examining. "You cannot linger over the rods. Now comes the race!"

Then the bellows must needs blow faster, and Roc was kept busy topping up the firepit with coal and charcoal, and silver sand to keep it and the metal clean, till the airshafts could barely cope and the stink of soot and sulphur hung in the air. Alv bound together seven of the stiff cords, carefully chosen and matched, with thin wire and thrust their tips into the glowing heart of the pit, plucked them out an instant later and beat them together on the anvil. Then they went back to the fire till they glowed red-white, had a cloth wrapped round them and were jammed into a ring swage set in the anvil's side; Alv set a lever under them, tensed his foot on it and by the sheer force of his arms and shoulders, twisted the thick metal strands about each other a handspan or so, with the words of his song hissing through his teeth. Then the glow died and the cords went back to the fire, the bellows wheezed, and again Alv strained till the sweat rolled in rivulets down his forehead. For another handspan or so the separate strands became a thick coiled rod, threaded like a screw, coated with gray dust from the fire. But as Alv's fire and strength and song bore down on it, the coating cracked and fell away to uncover the clean glowing metal, the threads twisted closer and closer until they met and became a single surface with only a faint coiled tracery to show where they had been. And so, in twenty hours of unstinting, unceasing work, the first rod was made. Each of the others took as long, but on the tenth day after that they were complete. That night he slept the long sleep of exhaustion.

The next day, at first light, Alv went upstairs instead of down, up past Ingar's room and the Mastersmith's many chambers, right to the towertop. Now was the time that the sword must be made whole, and he wished to clear his mind before beginning anew. And when the great slab had slid back at the stairhead and he mounted out on the high pavement, he was startled to see only a light frost on the tesselated stone, and mere remnants of snow on the Mastersmith's turret and the rocks around. He flexed his muscles, and felt new strength arise in his arms. The wind blew from the south, and the smell of woodland and plain and shore hung on it, all fresh, all new. He breathed deeply, blinking in the daylight, for since he last saw it he had worked away the winter, and spring would be coming soon.

He jumped at the hollow creak from behind him. The turret door was swinging open, and the Mastersmith stepped out. He, too, blinked at the light, and his face was drawn and anxious; his rich blue robe was creased, and he looked as if he had not slept. But when he saw Alv the weariness fell away before his usual suave good will. "So you also seek wisdom on the heights, boy? No doubt about what you undertake today? No need of my counsel? Good, I am glad, for I fear I must leave you for a day or so. I hate to do so, at such a time, but it must be. The world presses on me, as I had hoped it would cease to in this place."

Alv smiled ruefully. "I am sorry, Mastersmith. It will be difficult, but I am rested and ready."

"Good. Then try to have your work completed by tomorrow, when I return."

Alv bowed his head to hide the grin he couldn't suppress. He could have asked for nothing better! "Indeed, Mastersmith. I will."

The gloom of the forge seemed to hang more heavily around him after that, and with it the note of tension in the air. For a while he prowled around the anvil, nervously selecting hammers and shaping tools and laying them out within easy reach, pinning endless sheets of notes to every surface he could easily see. But at last he took up the rod that was the sword's spine, and the others that were its body, and sang long slow words over them as he bound them tight in metal bands and thrust them into the fire. Now the note of the bellows changed, for moments of great heat were needed. Alv set Roc to work the piston of the hand-bellows, and its quick panting breath echoed his own as he grasped the rods with pincers and maneuvered them in the small circle of blue-white flame. Then he pulled them out in a flurry of cinders, struck three quick blows with the heavy hammer, and thrust them back into the fire. After a minute or two more he repeated this, and motioned Roc to stop, letting the wheel-driven bellows take over. He sang when he could, in eerie harmony with the soft song of the charcoal, squinting at his notes and listening for the moment when the sword itself would begin to sing, and spit out a few light sparks—the first sign that the steel itself was beginning to burn, which it must not do. He sang of the tree that had once grown, drinking in the wind and the light of the sun, and of how he had mastered it, cut it down and burnt it to charcoal, because the time had come for it to give back the air and the fire. He sang of the metal that had lain deep in the veins of the earth, unshaped, unseen, till he had mastered it, dug it out and purified it, commanded it to take other shapes and forms. As they had been mastered, let wood and metal combine to teach mastery; as they had obeyed a mightier command, let them in turn enforce obedience. His words fell into time with the vast strong breath of the bellows.

> That mighty ash tree,
> How boldly it burns,
> How noble the blaze it's made!
> To leaping sparks of light
> It returns
> But its strength it leaves to my blade!
> Bellows, blow!
> Brighten its glow!

And when the thin voice came from the steel, the note harmonized with the tones of his chant. That was it! He hauled the body of the sword out, the top of it an erupting fountain of yellow sparks, and struck, and struck, and struck and struck till the mighty anvil rang and rocked on its huge hardwood base, twisting the spitting steel this way and that across the anvil, narrowing his eyes against the exploding haloes of sunbright metal. As it darkened he brandished it at Roc, who sprang to the bellows, and he thrust it deep into the charcoal, twisting it about to clean it. Then, verse after gasped verse, he was wrenching it out again and striking with all shapes and sizes of hammer. From time to time he would seize a page of his notes and rush into the library, wiping his hands on any rag he could find. Once or twice, unable to leave what he was doing, he would yell through the open door to Ingar, who fussed and grumbled somewhat, but was willing enough to read out or copy a particular passage or symbol for him. Most often it was to the North wall he was dispatched, to those pages of the *Skolnhere-Book* the Mastersmith had annotated.

Alv's labor was backbreaking, but as he worked through long hours of the day, his intense frown began to lighten; for all his weariness, he was grinning with delight as at last he plucked the steel from the fire, braced it against the anvil, seized one of his chosen fullering tools and with minute precision tapped it home to narrow and shape the tip. Roc expected a war whoop of delight as Alv finally plunged the steel into the quenching trough, but when the steam cleared he was gazing at the narrow dark blade he held with only the faintest and tightest of smiles. He stroked a finger along the raised spine, feeling how smoothly it merged into the sloping surface of the blade.

"Is it all right?" demanded Roc. He exchanged anxious glances with Ingar, who had heard the hiss and was peering round the library door. "You haven't gone and—"

"Oh no," said Alv quietly. "It's fine. It's perfect, in fact. All it needs is . . ." He picked up the two remaining rods, and clanked them against the thick dull edges. "These. D'you feel up to another few hours of this?"

Roc stared. "If you do, yes—once I've had a drink

and a bite, that is. But . . . you mean you're going to finish . . ."

"Yes, of course. But off with you quickly, if you want some food—and bring me something I can eat here—"

Roc scuttled off, but Ingar stayed, frowning. "Wasn't the Mastersmith going to—"

"He's in a hurry for it, it seems," said Alv. "Remember I met him on the tower this morning, before he left? He told me he wanted it finished when he gets back tomorrow. So finished it will be." He held the cooling blade out at arm's length, squinting own it for tiny irregularities, and his bright eyes met Ingar's. After a moment the journeyman turned away, shaking his head in confusion.

"Whatever you say yourself! Well, I'm going back to my work."

"Oh, before you do," called Alv, "could you just check these characters for me—my hands are covered in soot—" He reached out and plucked off two leaves of thin parchment he had tacked to a shelf. But hampered by the blade, he missed his grip; they went fluttering into the draft of the firepit, twisted upward and were consumed in an instant. Alv, goggle-eyed, burst out in a stream of curses that raised Ingar's dark eyebrows.

"My," he said mildly, in his best-bred voice, "really, you must have quite shocked those cattle of yours. Well, don't take on so, if you remember the reference you can copy them again—"

"Before this cools? I've got to match the edges!"

Ingar sighed deeply. "Oh very well, if that's important I suppose I can copy them for you—that's not really helping you. The North wall again? The *Skolnhere-Book?* What page?"

Alv remembered the page that set the limits of his knowledge, saw in his mind the ugly, mocking little countenance, and beside it the Mastersmith's forbidding finger, resting on the long parchment marker—the marker he had that morning detached and, without opening the book enough to read, slipped in several pages further ahead. "Everything beyond the *nakina* character!" he called, and held his breath.

From the library silence drifted like a freezing cloud.

Then there was a sudden rustle of paper, exactly as in Alv's dream. He jumped violently—but then Ingar's voice called out cheerfully, "Well, that's only four or five figures, before the chapter ends—and they're simple enough. D'you want the notes as well?"

"If you would!" Alv called back, trying to keep the unsteadiness out of his voice. Four or five, only? Surely, then, his suspicions had borne rich fruit. All the other symbols from that chapter had ended up in the sword, in one form or other, buried deep now in its twisted heart. So there was a good chance it was the remaining ones the Mastersmith planned to incorporate in the edges—how logical, and how typical of him, that there should only be four or five! And on that chance Alv had taken a greater gamble—either that there was really no mysterious power shielding the books, or that Ingar would be immune because he'd been through them before in his researches, as the chalk marks proved. The Mastersmith wouldn't have bothered stopping *him* before the crucial page, because he hadn't a quarter the skill to make use of his knowledge. A logical gamble, but a good one—*if* he'd won!

Alv seized an oily rag and wiped down the sooty blade, staring along the thick edges for irregularities that might hamper the welding—anything to keep busy, to think about something else. He set the thin edge rods to heat near the rim of the firepit, fixed the blade in the leg vise on the far side of the anvil and set to work tapping the edges into a gentle curve to match the blade. The purer steel was much harder to work, and he had only just finished the first one when Ingar tapped him on the shoulder. He laughed at Alv's convulsive start. "Don't get so wrapped up in your work! You might wreck everything, jumping like that! This is what you needed, isn't it?"

Alv swallowed, and forced himself to look down at the slates clutched in Ingar's plump hand. "Y-yes, it's everything I need—I'll have to work out a couple of my verses again, though . . ."

"Well, that you can do for yourself. I'm only a channel, remember? A conduit. I contribute nothing."

And may that save your soft hide for you, thought Alv, *when the Mastersmith finds his bluff's been called!*

But aloud he said, "I thank you, sir journeyman! If I get through this—"

"Oh, you will, you will," said Ingar patronizingly. "Well you may labor all the watches of the night, but I don't have to. I'm a tired conduit—and dry, too, with all this smoke in here. Me for a stoup of sothran wine, and then bed."

"Sleep well!" said Alv, and was surprised to find the gratitude in his voice genuine enough. Ingar might infuriate him in any number of ways, but he was not a bad man at heart. Not his fault, perhaps, if he preferred the security of serving the Mastersmith to striking out on his own; he'd just never had to struggle for anything. And because he'd never disobey the Mastersmith, it hadn't occurred to him that Alv would. *Well, let one person use you, and others may also. So turns the world!*

He perched the slates on his workbench and read through them carefully, struggling to make out Ingar's script, which disintegrated when he was hurried. And as Alv did so the cold certainty grew in him that these strange bastard things were the final symbols, the only ones that would have to show on the surface of the sword—inscribed around the edges, perhaps even inlaid for clearer effect, but that could wait. As long as they were there . . . But *why* was he so sure? And what on earth was the right way to arrange them? *Difficult . . . perhaps even dangerous . . .*

Roc brought him a bowl of something hot and meaty, and he supped away at it absently while he read. The notes were tantalizing, all about the shape of the characters, hardly anything about their symbolic associations or effects. And yet as he gazed at the forbidden characters he seemed to see them in an order, a definite grouping. He clawed at his hair. There *was* something he recognized, a memory he couldn't quite grasp, but felt was terribly important. A pattern, a web of symbols set in metal . . . In his mind he traced and retraced all the studies he could remember, and found nothing like it. Such a faint memory— it seemed to date from a time before . . . Before he'd come here? His childhood? Impossible. Where would he have seen smithcraft then?

And then memory washed over him with the clear cold thrill of the waves he'd once played in. That ancient thing, that cattle goad! The markings on it! He could see them clearly, glinting in the sunlight—small wonder, when he'd studied them so long. Symbols, of the kind he was using now—one or two among the commoner ones he had already chosen. They were, now he saw them, very like the ones he had set upon the armring; a memory of them, perhaps, had inspired his design. But there above them, enclosed in a cartouche of tracery, were counterparts of the characters he was looking at now—simpler, but unmistakable. A simpler power, possibly—but the way they were arranged, the pattern . . .

His mind seemed literally to spin, the symbols scrawled across the slates tumbling together in a whirlpool, slotting almost of themselves into an arrangement that was intricate but logical, fluent—*perfect!*

For half an hour or so he scrawled feverishly on his own slates, terrified that in writing down one thing he might forget another. But the pattern held with its own inner strength, and he had it all, and the song to go with it. Then he was up and running for his anvil. The bowl went clattering unnoticed across the floor.

In minutes he had the second edge worked fine and tight, and he bound both to the body of the blade with wire and metal bands. Ignoring the scorching heat, he leaned out over the firepit to choose a clear spot, and slowly and gently slid the bound pieces into it. This was the most difficult part. Ordinary pattern-welded swords were made with the edges welded to the body pieces before they were attached to the spine, but the unity that gave this sword its power had to grow from the center outward, like a leaf. And if, once welded, it broke, then like a leaf it would wither and die, and all his effort go to waste. With long pincers he lifted the pieces, but swore and pushed them back down.

"It's got to be hotter, far hotter!"

"Push 'em further in, then!" gasped Roc, panting like the hand-bellows he worked.

"Can't risk that—too hard to control!" Alv bit his lip a moment, then ran to the wheel set in the floor and forced

it open a full half-turn. Great gusts of heat came roaring
up from below, through the layers of coal and charcoal,
sending a high flame up from the heart of the pit to lick
at the vaulting. Alv turned to the wheel that controlled the
waterflow, but it would open no wider. In a burst of sheer
fury he canted the great bellows lever loose and worked it
himself. Sweat poured off him, he could hear his shoulders
cracking with the effort, but the airblast roared through
the pit faster even than the wheel could drive it. A white
glow crept outward toward the rim, sizzling and crackling,
spreading around the half-buried blade.

"It's going, Roc, it's going! Just once more—pump,
man, pump, and sweat some of that lard off yourself! Here
am I breaking my back and you just sit around twiddling
your fingers—"

Roc, purple-faced and gasping, threw all his bulk onto
the piston of the hand-bellows, the fire blew white at its
heart and the steel sang again. Alv caught it out, swung
round to the anvil and caught up his great hammer. To
Roc's dazzled eyes he seemed to vanish in an aura of sparks
each time he struck, and every blow rang as hard as the
machine hammers. But louder and clearer rang his voice,
though few of his words could be heard.

> As sundered I found you
> In flickering flame,
> As once then I bound you
> I bind you again—
> Shape, sword, in the firelight!
> Encircle your blade with sharp steel!

Almost before Roc could see again, the blade was back
in the heat and he was thrusting and heaving at the bellows
once more till his mind grew cloudy. Then again a hammer rang, and the voice echoed it, but more lightly now,
and from time to time there came the clang of a tool discarded, another seized. The blade lay wedged on the anvil, its heat turning the smoky air to a rippling velvet
curtain. Alv, bending over it, tapping around its rim, became a strange hunched shadow, his voice no more than

a whisper as he worked the chain of characters round the blade.

> *Master, my hammer,*
> *This stubborn steel,*
> *Teach it to know*
> *My skill's command—*
> *That in its turn*
> *Shall hammer home*
> *The will behind*
> *Its wielder's hand . . .*

Then it was back to the firepit for a moment, a few strokes to flatten the tang and punch it for rivets, the glowing shape poised over the quenching trough—and then there was a loud searing hiss, like a voice that screamed. A blast of steam leaped upward and burst across the roof; boiling droplets rained down over anvil and firepit with a sizzle and a roar, spattering agony across sweat-ridden skin. Great gusts of steam washed through the reeking air and, murk-heavy, condensed like black rain on every metal surface. As the steam blew aside Alv stood there with the blade in his hand, and he slapped it down on the flat of the great anvil, which tolled like an awesome bell. *"It is done!"*

But it was not long before dawn when the weary young men at last climbed up the stairs from the forge. The blade had had to be trimmed down with light hammer and file, and soaked for some hours in a bath of weak corrosive to remove surface impurities. Meanwhile Roc and Alv labored to clean up the forge, which the Mastersmith always insisted upon, and make it ready for his return. Alv was acutely aware of his bold disobedience, and in chilly dawn afterthought it no longer seemed such a marvelous idea. But he had done it, and there it was, and nobody the worse for it—not even him, for the Mastersmith might rage, but he could not deny the power of the work. When Alv took the blade out and washed it he seemed to see a peculiar sheen, in rather than on the metal, and wondered if he saw with the eyes of a true smith; Roc could see nothing. Alv gave the blade its first edge with the grindstone and finer whetstones, then very carefully wiped the blade with a stronger corrosive, and polished it away at once. The rippling weld patterns, relic of the many strands that made it, ran in strange twists and coils across the blade; he turned it one way in the lamplight, and they seemed to hold depth and perspective, like one of the strange drawings in the Mastersmith's sothran books, but a very peculiar perspective that suggested immense distance to the eye, and sought to draw it down. It was almost like looking over a cliff. Another way, the light rippled across the patterns, and they suddenly reminded him of the folds and convolutions he had seen on a drawing of the human brain in the Mastersmith's great anatomy text. Another way, and they were like some ancient, esoteric writing—*very* like writing, he could almost read it now, surely he could catch a word or two—then he tilted it slightly, and the patterns became that weird suggestion of the abyss once more. At last he wrapped it in soft leather, and tucked it under his arm, and beckoned Roc to follow.

"Breakfast?" inquired the forgeboy hopefully as they came out into the hall.

"Yes, I'm ravenous! But let's go roust Ingar out of his nice soft bed first, I want to see what he makes of this."

"He'll probably thump us with it! Oh well, I'll hang on . . ."

Alv drummed merrily on the door of Ingar's room. They were not very surprised to get no answer, and kicked the door wide. "On your feet, journeyman, and meet your new master!" But then they stopped, slightly surprised. Ingar lay peacefully in his bed, sleeping on his side much as usual. But though he was facing the door, he had not stirred at all. Alv stepped forward, grabbed him by one heavy shoulder and shook him—and then fell backward with a yell of sheer horror.

With a crisp dry rustle, exactly like the sound in Alv's dream, like the sound in the library, Ingar's body had caved inward where he lay, collapsed and crumbled to a heap of dark fragments, like a pile of dry leaves before an autumn wind.

Roc, eyes wide, backed slowly out of the room and onto the landing, till he could back no further. Alv scrambled up, half-fell against the doorframe and out, and stood there staring back into the room—staring, he knew now, at what he himself had done. The back of his hand was against his mouth, and he bit into it to stifle a scream. The blade dropped, dully ringing, to the floor—

And the Mastersmith stooped to pick it up. Whether he had come up or down the stairs they could not say. He was there now, unwrapping the folds of leather, and his dark eyes flared wide in his haggard face as he saw the completed blade inside. Then he looked up at them, and quickly past them to what they had seen. For a minute he stood there expressionless, then he looked down at the blade in his hand, and complete understanding dawned in his face. He threw back his head and laughed—a rich, carefree laugh, the laughter of sudden release. Then, abruptly, he rounded on them.

"Well," he smiled, eyes still ice-bright with mirth, "so you were that determined to prove yourself! And you have cost me a fine journeyman in the process—though perhaps you didn't quite believe in my sentinel. Now you do! Still, it would seem that I have another journeyman to replace him . . ." The Mastersmith's voice had gone vague, almost dreamy, as if he was voicing his thoughts. He raised the hiltless blade high, and Alv could not but flinch, though in truth he would have welcomed being struck down in that hour. But the Mastersmith was only examining it. "Yes—yes . . . And there, yes, perfect . . . another journeyman, yes, and one who might well be capable enough to fill Ingar's shoes as well as his own . . . For boy, boy, this is craft of great power . . . Master's work . . ."

And then suddenly he was himself again, and gazing at Alv with the same intent look as he had when they first met. "Who are you, boy?" he whispered, and his hand fell heavy on Alv's shoulder. "Where have you sprung from? Who was your father? Your mother? What strange hour, what remote place gave you birth?" The hand sprang to Alv's chin, tilted it back fiercely, so he staggered on weak legs.

In that instant came a sound Alv had never heard before, echoing through the high windows of the tower, distant but deep and clear, like the ghost of a great bell tolling.

The Mastersmith's hand fell away; Alv staggered and almost toppled down the stairs, but the smith hardly noticed.

"Boy, this comes timely!" he said softly. "You have pleased me well—forget the fool, he pays the price of his own stupidity! Later today I shall set the stamp of journeyman upon you! But for now, get you to bed and rest, and you too, Roc! Until later!"

He gestured with the blade, and Alv stumbled away down the stairs, hardly knowing what he was doing but wanting to be away, to escape, to run till he could run no further. But as they came to his room Roc thrust him firmly inside and thumped the door shut behind him.

"*You* . . ." Words failed the forgeboy, and he almost threw Alv flat on the bed. Alv thrust his head in his hands, unable to think, unable even to weep. The forgeboy slumped into the single chair. "What'd he ever do to you, that was worth *that?* I suppose if he hadn't fallen for it you'd've tried to cozen me into it . . ." And then Roc's voice suddenly ran down like a spinning wheel, slowing, slurring, weakening. Alv looked up, startled, and saw the forgeboy swaying where he sat, eyes glazed, about to topple onto the floor. The surprise triggered something in him; he sprang forward and hissed in Roc's ear. "It's a spell! An enchantment! Something of his! Fight it—"

Roc stared up at him and mumbled something. Alv shook him, slapping him—and abruptly the forgeboy was awake, eyes wide with horror. "I was just falling asleep— I couldn't help myself, I was just . . . Like something dragging me down!"

"A spell," growled Alv. "He's going out . . ."

"Ah," breathed Roc. "To answer whatever that bell-thing was." He shook his head. "He was going to kill you then, you know that? For finishing that sword, not . . ."

Alv shuddered. "Yes. I wish he had . . ."

"Could be you'll get your wish soon enough. Meanwhile we'd better be hopping!"

"We . . ."

"Yes! Come on! He'll stick us both, sure as sunrise— me just in case. And if he doesn't I reckon something else might, if we stay here—you saw how worried he's been these last weeks. What might that bell be about, then? So I'm off, and I don't give much for my chances alone in these mountains, so you'd better come along, you hear?''

"I hear," mumbled Alv. "If you think I'd be of any help, I'll come."

In truth, as he realized afterward, Alv was no help at all, for it was Roc who had to take the lead in everything. It was Roc who listened till he heard the great door thud softly closed, Roc who led their hesitant way downstairs with Alv trailing behind, in every sense a shadow, Roc who collected clothes and cloaks and boots and swords, and filled wallets with food from the kitchen, with Ernan snoring peacefully in the next room. Alv went and did as he was told without apparent sense or feeling, save once only. That was when Roc vanished down into the forge and reappeared with a bundle that rang of metal, which he thrust at Alv. Alv fell back as if it contained a poisonous serpent. It was Alv's own set of tools, which all smiths crafted for themselves early in their apprenticeship, and which held an affinity for their hands.

"Grown too dainty to carry our own, are we?" sneered Roc as he gathered up the spilled tools.

"I'll touch them no more!" Alv spat out. "They're tainted—"

"Aye, well they may be, but tainted or not, they've got to earn us a living once we're out of here! We can't afford to be particular—speaking of which," he added hopefully, "you couldn't manage to open his strongroom, could you? All that gold?"

"You saw how he guards his knowledge," Alv grated. "Do you imagine he would set any lesser guardian over his wealth?"

"Pity," grunted Roc. He shouldered the tools himself, but tossed both food wallets at Alv. "Ah well, he'd surely hunt us down then. You can manage the gate? So be it. Off we go." He swung the door wide, but paused, and looked around. "Not a bad berth, if you didn't mind the swink. *And* Ernan. Let's hope you can earn us a better." Alv drifted out after him, unheeding.

At the gate they delayed long while Alv fumbled with the lock. His fingers seemed as numb as his heart and grown clumsy, as if unwilling to leave the place. And in that they reflected some part of him, for here he had found his first true home, and had first been treated with any humanity, any dignity. But at the last it slipped open, and the bare valley lay ahead of them in the last light of the vanishing moon. "Uphill!" said Roc decisively. "He'll think we've taken the forest road, if he cares to go after us." He looked up at the cascades of the waterfall, and the stair of rocks alongside, no longer icy in the growing thaw. From the summit of the first fall a long ledge led back to the crest of the pass. "Might save ourselves a step that way. Allowing we don't miss a longer one, if you take my meaning. Well, are you game?"

It made little enough difference to Alv, and he clambered up obediently after Roc. They were both climbers of experience from their excursions with the Mastersmith, and much stronger than the run of young men their age. Roc's weight told against him, and he was puffing and blowing before they reached the top, but Alv hardly seemed to notice the effort. He sat patiently and waited while Roc bathed his scarlet face in the fall, yelping with the chill, and when they set off again trailed after him as before, saying no word. They came upon thick snow as they neared the summit of the pass, for it was above the margin of the mountain's snowcrest at that season; Alv trudged through it unnoticing. But as they breasted the summit, he seemed suddenly stricken; he leaped at Roc, seized his arm and threw him violently down in the snow. Gray-faced and panting, he pointed down into the pass beneath.

Roc's angry outburst died on his lips. A hundred feet or so below him stood a tall boulder, just where the road across the pass flanked a steep drop. The moon had fallen below the mountains now, but snowglimmer and the lightening sky were enough to show him the shape that lurked in its shadow. A human shape, its face hidden from him— but not its dark robes, and he knew them at once. "Our late beloved master!" he whispered. "May he wait there for us till he freezes!"

He made to get up, but Alv pulled him down. "Not for

us! Or he would be waiting on the other side of the boulder—
hsst!''

Roc's eyes widened, and he flattened himself down in the
snow. Further along the slope, just below the level of the
ledge, a shadowy group of figures had appeared round
the side of the mountain, marching surefootedly down the
steep snowbank toward the road. Alv caught his breath.
They were unmistakably the same strange shapes the Mastersmith had dealt with before, whom he had taken for
mountain spirits or something of the kind. But as they
passed below him they sounded all too solid, with a crisp
crunch of boots in the snow. He heard their voices, too,
speaking a tongue he did not recognize, gruff and peculiar
but not in any way sinister. There was even a brief burst
of laughter, silenced by a sharp word from the head of the
column. There might have been thirty or forty of them,
and from the tall shafts many of them shouldered, and the
subdued metal jangle of their gear, Alv judged them to be
a party of warriors. They came to the road, and their boots
rattled and clattered on the ancient stones as they headed
up the pass, and the first dawn glimmer filled the sky.

Then Alv and Roc realized who it must be that the Mastersmith awaited. A kind of sick apprehension grew on
Alv as he saw the Mastersmith step out from behind the
rock into their path, though they were still some hundred
paces away. He spoke, and then the leader of the column—
quiet voices, but angry words, that was clear. Then Alv
saw the Mastersmith snatch something from his shoulder
and cast aside its wrapping, and the Iceglow gleamed on
the strange blade he himself had completed only five or
six hours since.

For an instant Alv's mind writhed in torments as twisted
as the substance of the sword. His skills, his learning, his
very life he owed to the man who waited below, though
he had long since lost any illusions about why they were
given. He had seemed useful, that was all. But whatever
his motives, it was the Mastersmith who had first treated
him with any human decency. A metal once alloyed is not
so easily made pure; a great debt there remained. And
these nightshapes, what did he owe them? They were many
against one, and well armed, against an untried weapon

of a different kind. But something deeper in him, some clearer sight, saw differently. Everything about the smith seemed colored with a treachery blacker than the shadow he lurked in, a menace darker by far than the bluff and open manner of the warriors. Rightly or wrongly, Alv could bear it no longer. Before Roc could catch him, he sprang up, cupped his hands and yelled. His voice rang between the mountainsides. *"NO! Get you back, get away! The blade has a power—"*

The little knot of figures scattered in the instant the blade was leveled at them, bounding up the mountainside with the speed of squirrels. Only the leader and three or four others failed to run in time, or perhaps stood their ground regardless. Nothing visible happened, but something seemed to pass across them with the force of a blow; they crumpled before it, staggered and howled as if in agony or madness. The leader tottered to one side, clutching at his head, and stepped straight out over the side of the road. Another ran wildly in a circle, slipped and went skidding out after him. The others tumbled threshing into the snow, heaved and lay still. And in the next second the blade swung up toward Alv and Roc.

Panic descended on them both like a cloud, and they turned and fled wildly up the mountainside. They ran and ran, slithering and tumbling in the snow, barging blindly into rocks and into each other, hardly seeing. It was accident only, perhaps, that they ran in the same direction and passed behind a tall outcrop of the cliff, into deep shadow.

Without warning hard hands grabbed them and forced them struggling to the ground. With all their strength they could not break free, nor could they reach their swords. A lantern flickered, and a burst of yellow light shone in their eyes. Alv stared at the ring of faces that bent over his—strange faces, all with the same cast, broad and coarse-featured with heavy brows; some were grim and gnarly, some round and wrinkled like a winter apple, and one alone was smooth-skinned, snub-nosed—a girl's face, grinning. Then the light vanished, and the strong hands scooped them up in the air, bouncing them along to the crash and crunch of boots in snow. Alv, too confused to struggle, felt the icy air flow past him at an incredible rate, and realized he was being carried up the slope toward the mountain crest. But all of a sudden the air became warmer and the echo louder, and the shadow around him as deep as midnight. For what seemed like hours he was bumped and bounced along, and the only recognizable thing he heard over the grind of boots was an occasional strangled protest from Roc. Then, equally abruptly, he was pitched forward on his face. Something hard struck him in the small of his back as he tried to get up, and then the mountain seemed to collapse onto his legs. But as it struggled away he realized it was Roc. He sat up, and the light flicked on again in front of him. There was the girl's face, grinning impishly, and a hand waving. With a final roguish waggle of her eyebrows she receded into shadow, and the light went out. From some distance away they heard, or more truly felt, a soft heavy impact, and then nothing.

Alv could do nothing but sit there and stare stupidly into the darkness. It had all happened too quickly. After a moment he felt the wind on his face, and realized he was out of doors—still, or again? But it had been on the edge of dawn when they seized him, and here it was dark. He turned and looked around, and saw the peak of a mountain silhouetted against grayish clouds, and others to left and right. But in front of him there were none.

"We're on the other side of the peaks," he said wonderingly. "And further down. The sun's not reached here yet."

"Don't be daft!" gurgled Roc, sitting up next to him. "You know that'd be a long day's climb from the house—a week by the forest roads!"

"Be still, then," said Alv softly, "and see. For dawn is upon us."

And before long the clouds above were turning to white, the sky to gray and then blue, bright blue, and in the clear air the land spread out before them. They sat at the high head of a mountain valley, on barren rock among the last thin shreds of snow. But not far below them green growth circled a little lake, and below it another, and another, all the way down the valley like a giant's stair, until at last all they saw was a glimmer of blue water between the burgeoning trees.

"We're away," whispered Rock, in utter awe. "We're only a morning's march from the lowlands, we've a head start. *We're safe!*"

"Yes," said Alv. "We're safe." And he bowed his head upon his knee.

CHAPTER FOUR

The Smith of the Saltmarshes

So began his first great wanderings, in a lifetime filled with them. Terrible enough he was to find them, for he had lived all his life enclosed in small spaces, first in little Asenby, where he found no happiness, and then in the Mastersmith's house, where he believed that he had. His flight had been all in panic, driven by starkest need, thinking only of what he was escaping, the memory of what he had seen that moment in his master's eyes; he had not stopped to consider all that he was leaving behind. Only later, that night and through the harsh days that followed, did the true sense of what he had lost settle upon him—his past security, his promised future. At the first he was glad enough of his freedom, and went with a light heart for all the grief and guilt that haunted him, and the fear of pursuit.

To avoid it, that first day, they walked down the valley to the south and out into the woodlands beyond, stopping seldom, eating as they walked, saying little. They halted at last only when darkness forced it; the moon had long since risen, but shed little light through the trees. They made camp among thorny bushes under a high cedar tree; Roc thought to build a fire, but Alv would not let him. "Have it your own way," grunted Roc, cramming his mouth with dried meat. "Our cloaks'll keep us warm enough, but there'd better be no hungry beasts about. Beardogs, bears, the odd daggertooth—"

"Better a beast than a searching eye. And we have our swords, and the bushes are some shield. Anyway, I will sit watch for what remains of the dark. I have no taste for sleep."

"Better find one, then. We've a long way to go before we come among men again." Roc laughed. "Makes you a real journeyman now, and all!"

"Don't mock me!"

"Ach, I only meant you'd let yourself in for a bitch of a journey—"

"I know what you meant. It was still a mockery. I wanted it so much—but I had to have the journeyman's stamp, and now I have not, and that, that loses me . . . more than you know."

"Can't you just fake the stamp? Damn, I wish I'd thought, I'd have taken Ingar's. He won't be needing it now!"

"Do you imagine I could ever have worn *that?* And no, I could not counterfeit a convincing stamp, for I do not know the mysteries that go with it. Any real journeyman could unmask me."

"Aye, I see. And the penalty for impersonating a guildsman—it varies, I hear. They don't always chop your hands off."

"No. It makes you worthless as a thrall."

"Well, well, we'll try something else. I'll settle for some sleep for now. Do you the same."

"I'll try, in a while. And Roc . . ."

"Mmnh?"

"Thank you."

"Hmmph. You'll have plenty of chances. Won't let it slip your mind. G'night!"

Alv sat awake, listening to the night sounds of the wood, the scuttle and slither of small creatures among the damp leaves, the thump and rustle of larger bodies, the eerie cries of the hunters on the ground and in the air that silenced all else and made his own breath sound deafening. In truth, sleep weighed down on him, but he was afraid of surrendering to it, of releasing the tight rein on his thoughts. Always a vengeful shadow hovered beside them, awaiting its chance, and he shrank away from confronting it. But very soon weariness overtook him, his head dropped on his chest, and he was sinking down, down into dark dreams of noise and fire and squalor, hatching a snake that turned to strike at his heart. Then he was digging frantically into a vast mound of papers, trying to find someone lost beneath, coming upon a slender arm ringed with gold, but when he clutched at the shoulder it sank inward under his fingers like rotten wood, with a soft popping rustle—

He sat up, hearing his own whimper, and found himself staring at a wide shadow with glimmering eyes and pointed quivering ears. It tensed rigid as he snatched up his sword, whirled and bounded away back through the bushes with the selfsame rustle. He stared around, shaken and shivering—some beast, more curious than hungry. He had slept most of the dark away, and dawn was graying the sky. What would the new light bring him? Release? Hope? He grimaced. Could he face her now, even if he found her? He turned stiffly onto his side, pillowed his head on his arm and slept on uneasily.

For most of a week they walked through the woodlands, down trails made by animals, not men. Early one cold morning they came upon the makers, a great herd of wisants feeding among the trees. Their breath steamed around their shaggy heads as they chewed cud and belched thunderously, and their deep rumbling lows echoed as they tossed their horns at the newcomers. Alv, used to the even larger white cattle, simply skirted the herd, avoiding bulls and young calves; Roc sidled nervously from tree to tree. "They're not so dangerous," Alv told him. "They say there are far bigger beasts than those in the Great Forest across the mountains—"

"Then spare me the trip!" Roc hissed, looking nervously back up the trail.

"You never know," Alv said drily. "If we don't find ourselves somewhere to work soon—"

"There'll be plenty of towns needing a good smithying team like us. Stands to reason!"

"Does it?" said Alv, and strode on without waiting for an answer.

His misgivings were to prove true. The trees grew thin

and sparse, and they left the woodlands at long last, coming to many places of men under the roots of the mountains. They had little real idea of where they were, or where they were going, for the Mastersmith had taught Alv much about what lay under the land, but little of what lay above it, and there were few maps in his library. From the sun and the look of the land, Roc reckoned that they were now almost level with Harthaby, but they avoided it for fear of the Mastersmith's connections, and stayed among the inland villages. The first of these lay among open, wind-scoured moorland, one step from the tundra that lay ahead of the Ice in the heart of the land, where there was no mountain barrier. Sheep grazed among the flinty rocks, with shepherds to watch them; they were polite to the well-dressed travelers, but quick to point out that their own villages had each its proper smith, seldom a full guildsman but adept enough for them. They could often find a bed for the night at such a smithy, but no proper berth, and they had to suffer many embarrassing questions about where they came from and what they were doing. Roc represented them as followers of a master who had died suddenly before he could set Alv his prentice pieces; that won them much sympathy, but no more help, and they were obliged to move on. Journeying ever southward along the smaller roads, often no better than hill tracks, they came to towns, farming centers of a size with the one Alv had grown up in, and found all of them, too, had smiths enough. These were usually older journeymen with no chance or ambition to become masters, content to work out their days with thrall assistants or locally born apprentices whom they would send to masters elsewhere to finish their training; they sought no stranger apprentices, however skilled. Masters there were in some of the towns nearest to the High roads, but chiefly less able ones such as Hervar had been. Almost every man, though, looked askance at Alv the moment he entered their door, and when in the town of Rasby one at last consented to give him a trial, a terrible thing was revealed.

The master's name was Hjoran, a huge jolly fellow grown almost too fat to reach his anvil. He had a name for tolerance in the town, to the point that he had once taken a girl as apprentice, which was reckoned strange enough though not unheard-of; she had become a jeweler in a nearby market town. But he seemed wary of Alv, watched him closely throughout the work, and squinted dubiously at the knife and axehead he had commanded.

"Fine craft enough, laddie, fine enough," he wheezed, turning them over in his fingers. "A trifle fancy, maybe. Truth be told, best I've seen from a younker so long's I can recall. But—" He shook his head. "Where's the feeling in 'em? Where's the virtue? These're just lumps o'metal, there's never a bit of life between 'em."

Roc gaped, and Alv sprang up from the hearthstone where he had slumped. "But . . . I did everything aright! You saw, you heard—"

"Aye!" protested Roc, "and he's made many a strong work before now—"

"I don't doubt it!" shrugged Hjoran uncomfortably. "There's something about those tools of yours, though it's a strange thing to me. And no master in his right mind would've taught you the things you know 'less you showed more'n a trace of craft in you. But look, lad, can't you see for yourself?" He wheezed and rumbled over to his shelves, and pulled down a neat but unimpressive axe. "Piece Marja made. I save it to show women can do well's most men at this game. Truth is, it's not that good beside yours, you've got an uncommon hand—but there! What's the virtue in that?"

Alv rubbed his fingers over the fine markings in the steel, traced a flicker of light that seemed to be not all reflection. "To go where it's aimed, as mine was—"

Hjoran drew a line on his untidy workbench and let the axe fall lightly. It struck a hair's breath from the line. He thrust a handle into Alv's piece, and repeated the test. It fell three fingers' breadth away, and skidded sideways. "There you are, laddie," he muttered. "And don't think I'm not sorry."

"Listen here, Master Hjoran," Roc spluttered indignantly, "almost the last thing our master said to him was that he'd made master's work!"

Hjoran weighed the axehead sadly. "Don't doubt that either, boy. And I don't understand it anymore'n you.

Smith don't lose the power he's born with! Can use it
badly, maybe not at all—specially's he gets older—but lose
it? Like a fire going out? No, never. But it makes no difference. Not a rich man, me, not like your big-town
smiths. Can't afford an apprentice who's only half a smith.
Can't even set you your prentice pieces.''

Alv had sunk back onto the hearthstone, his face the
color of the ashes that coated the earth floor. ''So what
then must we do? Approach one of the wealthier smiths?''

''Aye, and get a boot up the arse for your pains! They
get *paid* to take apprentices, boy, big sums too, and run
'em like a manufactory. They'll take a talentless nothing
if his folks pay well enough, there's always odd jobs for
them, but not a couple of wandering tinkersmiths—sorry,
but that's how they'll see it!'' Hjoran looked at the young
men, Alv with shoulders bowed by shock and despair,
Roc huffing and fidgeting. ''If you want my advice,
though . . .'' he began, after a moment.

''Yes, Mastersmith?'' they chorused.

''Well, you lads with your fair skins, you've got a sothran look to you. You could do worse than head for the
Southlands—not just south of here, the real rich Southlands, Great Suderney across the Marshlands, Kerbryhaine
as they name it themselves. Not that I've ever been there,
but I have met a few traders who have, and they do say
that they don't believe in true smithcraft there! Mostly
never heard of it, and those who have pay it no heed.
Think we're a load of savages to go singing to our work.
Well, I've never seen any sothran smithcraft, to my ken,
but I'd be damned surprised if you with your touch couldn't
do a damn sight better. Teach 'em a thing or two, maybe
make your fortune.''

''That's it!'' whooped Roc, springing into the air.
''That's it! Thanks, good master, thanks a thousand times!
Alv, Alv, what say you? Shall we go south, and see my
people's land? You know I've always wanted to!''

Alv looked up. He was pale of face, and there was a
distant, remote look in his eyes, but he nodded willingly
enough. ''If that's what you wish, Roc, I'll go southward
with you.''

''Good! Good!'' wheezed Hjoran, obviously glad to be

quit of an embarrassing situation. "That's the spirit, eh? Break new ground, yes, yes . . . Well, getting late in the day, eh? You can give me a hand here in the forge today, sleep in my loft tonight—now Marja's not there, hahaha!—and be on your way the morrow. Give you some grub to tide you over, hah? And don't hang your head so, laddie. Sure you'll get it all back one day—and when you do, you just come back posthaste and see old Hjoran, hey? And he'll have you a master yourself before you can say solder, you'll see! Now—to work! Let's get this place cleaned up a bit!"

They took leave of Hjoran the next morning. He set them on the track south with directions to where it joined the High roads, and their wallets well stuffed with provisions for a week or more. Not slow to take advantage of his opportunities, he had worked them almost until they dropped, but the food was fair pay for it, when he had owed them nothing. Alv had been glad of the distraction, for the pains of hard labor had helped numb him to the blunter agony of emptiness, of loss. One after another all the things he had gained or hoped to gain had slipped from his grasp, and latest of all, it seemed, that single thing on which all his arrogance had been based, pedestal of the pillar that raised him above other men. And yet now, past the first sharp pain of discovery, free at last to brood, he found he could in some wise accept what had happened. He had misused his gift, he could use it no longer; that seemed like a natural consequence. In betraying, in wounding, was it not also his own flesh he had wasted?

Roc, munching on a sausage, was full of ideas and speculations about the south, which he hardly remembered. His parents had been small traders to the Northlands; he had been orphaned when plague swept the caravan they were traveling with, and sold off as a servant by the caravan's survivors. But half of what he said seemed to pass Alv by, and finally Roc burst out, "Aren't you excited, damn you? It was you who wanted to see the world! It was you who wanted a chance to make your fortune—"

Alv kicked at the weeds covering the gravelly face of the road. "Once, yes. But that's not what I need now."

"What then? The moon?"

"If I could find there what I need, maybe."

"What's that, then? And where will you find it?"

Alv shrugged, and Roc raised his eyes to the sky.

On the second day they came to the High roads, and Alv, coming out of his daze, marveled at the wide expanse of metalled trackway that lay across the hills like some pale gray ribbon, until it seemed to lead right up into the clouds on the horizon. But as they clambered up the bank he saw that the road was sadly ragged and cracked, and the wheelruts had long ago grown deep enough to churn up the bed, with no attempt made to fill them in. Here and there were potholes, where the ground under the bed had subsided; some were full of earth, and grass, fireweed and pale lilies grew in them undisturbed. Still, it was a good track for travelers on foot, and from thence their way south was swifter. But it was no easier, for though many great towns such as Saldenborg, Arlaby and Thuneborg lay alongside the roads, and there was much demand for good smithcraft in them, in these towns the guild's hand was heaviest, and Alv and Roc found themselves treated as little better than tinkersmiths. They looked like them too, for their once-respectable garb had grown ragged and rough, and only Alv's fair speech won them some consideration. Once in a while they would find some master or journeyman, less scrupulous or more needy, who would let them do petty work for a night's lodging, but more often they were driven out with a curse, or the dogs set on them. Once when this happened, Roc turned on a mocking apprentice and felled him with a blow of his ham fist, and they were hard put to escape the town watch. That night, as many others, they spent like outlaws, sleeping rough among the scrub, and stealing a fox's kill for their meal. And on the next day, as ever, they turned their steps onward to the south.

In truth, they had no clearer idea than that where they were going, for if they knew little of the Northlands they knew nothing at all of the south, and there were few who could tell them what lay ahead. Not many northerners now bothered to go south, and it was still too early in the year for traders coming up from there. But they saw one thing, that the people themselves were changing; their skins were lighter, their faces longer, and here and there were eyes of blue or green, all reminding them both uncomfortably of Ingar. Alv spoke less and less, and there were nights when Roc suspected he had not slept at all. The towns were growing smaller and sparser again, and the land wilder. At last, after some days' walking through wholly empty country they came to a small, poor town with a strange name, Dunmarhas, in which many seemed to have pale skins like theirs—not that it made their welcome any warmer, for folk seemed deadly afraid of what came from beyond their walls, fair-spoken or no. But here at last simple smithcraft was valued, for the town smiths were poor craftsmen indeed and kept no rules of guild. In return for teaching them some simple skills the travelers could at least get food and a pallet by the hearth, and by then that seemed much to them. When they left Dunmarhas they found that they were leaving the mountains behind, the range curving away inland. As the land fell and flattened out before them, the weather grew wetter and the woodlands lower and very thick, with a few tall firs standing out proudly over a mass of aspens, junipers and other lesser trees. Dogwood, ferns and sedge bloomed by the road, daisies, lilies and columbines in its wide crevices, and willows hung over the many little brooks and rivers it crossed. Mists rose swiftly and hung dank about them, and clouds of insects made the noon hours a torment. The road ahead became a long, dead straight ribbon leading toward a horizon on which there was nothing—no rise, no fall, no wall or building, no feature taller than clumps of misshapen trees. The land became covered with tall grasses that hissed in the clammy breeze, and every so often gave way to expanses of soft green rushes. Mists and haze became more frequent, and the wind often brought them a tang of the sea Alv knew so well from his childhood. The rivers were fresh, though stained brown and sharp-tasting, but many of the stagnant pools were brackish, and the water that oozed into every footprint beyond the raised roadbed grew saltier day by day. They took to sleeping on the hard road by night, for nowhere else was dry enough, and there was seldom clear moonlight to walk by.

They had walked through this fenland for days, and their last food was all but gone, when, as dusk was falling and the mists were rolling across the roadbed, they saw the flicker of fires ahead. Alv seemed reluctant for company, but did not refuse Roc, who went stumping ahead at a great pace. As they came nearer they saw that the fires were dotted around a long train of wagons, forty or fifty at least, which had stopped beside an old ruined shell of a building, the first they had seen for some time. Some of the wagons were small two-wheeled tiltcarts drawn by a single horse, others heavy four-wheelers drawn by teams of horses or oxen; a few even had trailers. Many men moved around the fires, a strong party indeed, and yet as the two travelers appeared out of the mist, shouts of alarm spread across the whole encampment, and men came charging up with swords and bows. Nor did they lower their weapons when they saw they faced but two men, young and ragged at that, and as pale-skinned as themselves. Tense questions rained at them from all sides in a tongue that they recognized but could not summon up in the stress of the moment. It seemed that any minute one of those taut bowstrings would loose. Then a tall bearded man in a fur-trimmed robe and hat shouldered his way through the crowd, waving the people aside, shouting something. Four bowmen remained with him, and one or two other men in robes with drawn swords, but the rest dispersed warily. He himself drew no weapon, but stared doubtfully at these two strangers for many slow breaths before he spoke, in the northern tongue.

"You wear our skins, but you don't seem to know our speech. Would this then be yours?"

"It is that I grew up with," Alv replied, "and my companion here from his youth, though he is one of your folk, by name Roc."

"And you are not?"

Alv shrugged. "I have not that honor, that I know of. A foundling I, raised a northerner and named Alv, that is all. Roc has forgotten most of your noble tongue in his long exile, and I know it only from books."

The bearded man smiled a smile as impenetrable as a stone battlement. "Well then, my fair-tongued foundling, my name is Kathel Kataihan, called the Honest, a dealer in things of small account and the elected leader of this paltry troop of peddlers you see before you. Are you come to sell, or buy, or how else may we oblige you?"

"A seat by your fire on this dank night, honest sir," chimed in Roc, "and perhaps a trifle of supper, as it's some hours since we dined. Nothing elaborate, you understand, for it would not agree with the digestion this late of an evening."

"Oh alas," intoned Kathel, "we are only poor traders with the least of victuals, sufficient only to get us across this godforsaken land without actually starving. If you were calling on us at our simple homes, why then we'd share our last crusts with you gladly, but as it is we dare spare no morsel or crumb for the sake of the loved ones we have with us."

"Ah, but how remiss of us not to explain!" said Roc smoothly. "We are not the common beggars or riff-raff as you would find in such places, but honest men of craft and lore traveling to the Southlands in search of other honest men who will appreciate our hard-earned skills, namely the working of metals . . ."

Kathel's eyes widened, and one of the other men, short and baldheaded, lowered his sword. "You're smiths? Northern smiths? Out of the far north?"

Roc repeated his tale about the unfortunate death of their master, and the short man rounded on Kathel and spoke a few crisp words.

"Yes, I have the skill of repairing wheel and axle," said Alv, in halting sothran phrases.

"And of understanding our tongue, indeed," said Kathel. "Can you make our carts whole?"

"I will not say till I see them," said Alv drily. "I have my tools, but not the whole equipment of a forge. With no smithy to hand—"

Kathel inclined his head at the ruin beyond. *"This* is a smithy," he said, with an air of having arranged it on the spot. "Or it was. That's why we stopped here. We've been trying to get it back into order, but we know no more of the craft than any traveler picks up over the years. We have four carts crippled by this worthless road, barely dragged here in one piece, and another ten that might fail us before we even reach Dunmarhas—not that the best of their blasted smiths will avail us much.''

Alv smiled. ''You may find them a touch more adept since we passed. Let us see the damage, then, and the forge, and I will do what I can.''

''Wait a minute!'' protested Kathel. ''We've not fixed a price yet!''

''Fire, food, bed,'' said Alv. ''The rest we'll settle later, depending on how much is to be done. We won't haggle.''

''You trust us?'' cried Kathel, as if the idea offended him.

''Of course,'' chuckled Roc, ''since you're called the Honest.''

''Oh dear, oh dear,'' breathed the trader, ''what is the world coming to, to be sure? Well, come and have a squint at what's to do, and then you may share what poor scraps we have.''

The poor scraps turned out to be as sumptuous as anything they had tasted, and in quantities enough even for Roc. Alv ate little, but the prospect of work seemed to hearten him.

''So,'' said Kathel when they had finished, ''you reckon you can do it, then?''

''The most of it,'' said Alv, ''if your men can get the smithy clear and working. Those ten damaged wheels only need a fastening and a new iron tire; Roc can do them for you on his own, he's a fine craftsman.'' Roc sat up and stared at him, startled. ''And those with the bent axles and spokes I can straighten and weld so they'll bear you all the leagues you'll travel this season—if you keep to the roads. But the two with broken hubs—well, I can patch them up to last thirty leagues, maybe, but no more.''

The trader sighed gustily. ''Two? Ah well, that's nothing, nothing at all. We always start with a few extra wagons for just this kind of chance, they carry the victuals we eat on the way, see? So we can just shift the loads and send the patched ones home. But we couldn't afford to lose fourteen, no! Take the cream of the profit off the trip.

So it seems to me you lads're a godsend, that's it, a godsend. Finding you just where one always needs a smith, after the worst of the road. But devil a man can you bring with you, these days!" He swigged at his ale, and gazed up at the shell of the building above. "Used to be a smith there always, a century or two back. A good place, y'see, for all it was a bit lonely, because there was so much traffic up and down the roads at all seasons, and things always coming adrift in the wilds as is their cursed way. So there was a whole huge hostelry here on the end of the Great Causeway, with a forge to serve it. Times changed, fewer came, the hostelry fell out of use, but the smithy remained. It lay unused from time to time, but smiths'd come and keep it up for a few years. The last one, he was still alive when my father passed this way on his first trip, so he told me. Would've been, let me see, fifty, sixty years back. But he died, and nobody came to take his place." He looked keenly at his guests. "Now *there* might be an opening for two young lads not afraid of a bit of hard work. Very glad to have a smith here again, all us honest trading men'd be! Plenty of work for you there, caravans passing back and forth all the summer—"

"And the rest of the year nothing and nobody but the marshspooks!" grunted Roc. "No thanks, worthy sir! Too empty and too lonely for us, eh, Alv?"

But Alv was looking up at the bare old walls and rooftrees, still thick, still strong. A flicker of flame kindled within, where the old hearth must be, and one of the workers began to sing. Others took it up, a soft, melancholy air, and even Kathel hummed along.

> *They're worn, my sturdy feet*
> *From the wandering day,*
> *From the wandering day!*
> *They're sore, my willing hands,*
> *From the hours of toil,*
> *From the hours of toil!*
> *Yet I cannot rest*
> *Now the day is done!*

"I don't know," Alv said quietly. "I don't know . . ."

It aches, does my ardent heart,
Till I know no more,
Till I know no more
What I must do, how far to go
To forget my love,
To forget my love!

But he said no more about it. Kathel grew sentimental
with the song, snuffled into his ale, and then abruptly
turned businesslike and led them all off to supervise the
fitting-up of the forge. Roc bustled about, showing the
workers how to fit a new leather to the corroded old bellows, but Kathel and Alv stood and looked around the
ancient building. "Good strong walls!" said the trader,
slapping the stonework. "Could make this a place to live
in in a day, my boys could! Take some timber off the spare
wagons, that and a few good solid strips of turf'd make
you a grand roof. You want food, you've got rivers full of
fish, birds all over the place, and all the dainties you like
from your customers. And you needn't stint yourself! With
never a rival within thirty leagues, south or north, you
could charge what you liked—'cept to your worthy old
friend Kathel, to be sure. You could make your fortune!"

Alv smiled, but said nothing, and that night once more
he lay awake. But next day he betrayed no fatigue, nor
gave away anything of what was in his heart, but labored
with a will. From dawn till dusk of a dank, drizzly day he
sweated over the rebuilt forge, straightening wheels and
axles, banishing the deadly hair-thin cracks and distortions
that could overturn a whole valuable load in the middle of
a ford or a steep ascent. It was crude cartwright's work,
but all marveled at his strength and perseverance, Kathel
most loudly of all. Only Roc, engaged in welding minutely
measured hoops of iron and setting them over the wooden
wheels, would occasionally stop and look at him with a
blend of anger, confusion and concern. But it was only
late that night, when the labor was done at last, and they
all retreated silently to their pallets and rugs, that Alv at
last spoke.

"Roc, my friend," he said, staring into his mug of
mulled wine, "I believe Kathel has the right of it." Roc

spluttered, but Alv held up a commanding hand. "There is a place for a smith here, a useful, a—a vital place, and here I mean to remain, for a few years at least."

"You've not been taken in listening to that silver-tongued bastard, have you?" burst out Roc. "You're sick in your head, d'you know that?"

"In truth, I am sick in my head," agreed Alv bleakly. "And in my heart, my hand and all of me that can feel. I have grown crooked, and I must be set straight. And if I mistake it not, this is the place set aside for my cure, and no other."

"Ach, Amicac have your sickly fancies! This place'll only feed them—or cure you of them and all else beside! You should hear some of the tales I've been hearing from the lads about these thrice-damned boglands—a brimful breeding ground for sicknesses, and worse! Every marsh-fever and bog-ague known to man, here for the finding, to rot your innards and pain your bones and set your blood to boiling. And if that's not enough, they're awash with spooks and specters and nightwalkers and fearful things wandered downriver off the Ice, they are!"

"Men have lived here before, nonetheless," said Alv calmly. "It is driest by the road, and we have seen no terrors as yet."

"Time enough!" growled Roc. "Ah, see sense, Alv! Or if not, leave the maggots in your mind and try thinking of me—for a change! That you said about me last night, me being a fine craftsman, you've never thought to say a single word of that before now—"

"Because I never realized it mattered to you; your feelings are not so easy to read. Don't ever think I don't know how much I owe you, Roc—and I *am* thinking of you now. If it's true what Hjoran said, and from these folk it seems to be, that in the south the power of true smithcraft is unknown, then to them you will be as good a smith as I—"

"You know that's not true," Roc growled, lowering his round head, "power or no power, you've ten times my craft—"

"You had to learn it to serve us, though we gave you little chance to use it. But in the south you can, on your

own account, and need be forgehand and servant no
longer—''

''Ach, the bog's rotting your brain already! If that's so,
it's true ten times over for you. Do you come too, and be
a master, an apprentice no longer! Sink these shadows of
yours in the mud like the dung they are. What's done's
done. If I blamed you I'd never have helped you out then—
left you to our dear master's mercy, I would, and cheerfully! He was striving all he could to turn you down his
path, because he needed your power—even I could see
that, and who were you to resist, the age you were? It's
him I blame—what you did, you did in his shadow, that's
all.''

Alv nodded grimly. ''Yes. And his shadow is with me
yet. Roc, my friend, when Kathel sends his carts back
south tomorrow you should go with them. But I will not
be coming with you. Not yet.''

''Then to the River with you!'' spat Roc, and turned his
back, and spoke no word more that night.

He said nothing, too, when the next day dawned, bright
and blustery, and made his preparations in silence. Kathel
was volubly surprised at the two friends' parting, and all
the more that Roc should blame him for it; as a kind of
expiation he presented him with a fair sum of money and
a wealth of good advice and useful names, to get himself
started in his trade. Roc, no fool, took both, but reluctantly. At last he swung himself up on one of the carts,
whose driver he had already made a friend, and did not
look back as the carts clopped and creaked away. A few
hundred paces beyond the ruined smithy the High road
left the dry land and set out across the marsh on the low
wide arches of the Great Causeway. In this fashion, only
occasionally lighting on small islets of solid ground, the
road stretched far into the misty distance. Two broad pillars, weathered into shapelessness, marked the place, and
beside one of those pillars Alv was waiting.

''Well?'' said Roc coldly.

''No,'' Alv answered. ''But fare you well, my friend. I
can never repay you for all the trouble I have given you,
all the good you've done me—but I hope I may at least
try, some day.''

He held out his hand, and Roc reached down and shook it, once. But all he said was, "We won't be traveling fast. If you change your mind today, you'll catch us up easily enough. Run'll do you good."

Alv chuckled, and raised his hand. He made no move to follow as the cart creaked and ground out onto the road, but he stood and watched until it vanished into the sunlit haze.

Behind him came the sound of laboring, as the traders' men toiled to make the shell of the old smithy habitable. The other merchants had joined with Kathel in making him all kinds of extravagant promises, not realizing that it was not profit that tempted him to remain here. Far from it. Before—if ever—his life became his own again, he had a heavy debt to repay.

That day he labored on the smithy with Kathel's men, and sat late into the night under its new-made roof, talking with the merchants about the state of the world and drinking their mulled wine. It seemed that the world grew ever darker, roads longer and weather worse, customers stingier and tolls more rapacious. But under the light habitual complaints Alv found a note of real disquiet. The North-lands were sorely changed from Kathel's youth, and he was only middle-aged now. Then the Ekwesh were only a minor menace, harrying the far north from time to time; native corsairs and outlaws were far more to be feared, and the independent towns stood in powerful federation to protect their citizens and the trade on which they depended. Now the outer fringes of the federation were in frightened disarray, the towns retreating behind their own walls and failing to answer the general call, and in this disarray the Ekwesh grew bolder than ever, and fared further south.

"A dark time for honest traders, indeed," sighed Kathel. "True that we prosper, and yet that is in part because so many rivals have failed or no longer care to risk the long journey north. So though business is much lessened, it does not have to stretch so far, and often buyers must take what we have at our prices, or go without. But that is an advantage I would gladly forgo, seeing the cause; it will work ill in time. Still, there will be many caravans yet this summer, lad, and work aplenty to feed your forge—even if it must burn peats and not fine coal. You will do well enough here. And now to bed, for we must set off early to catch the best of the light.''

That dawn Alv stood at his door, watching the long line of carts and wagons go trundling off up the road, the oxen stolid as ever but the horses whinnying and frisky, as if glad to be escaping the marsh. It was a long time before they faded into the distance, and longer yet before the noise of wheels and creaking wood and the voices of men and beasts was wholly lost to the ear. But when it was, a great silence seemed to descend, as cool and gray as the sky. Alv closed his eyes, and leaned against the huge heap of peat they had cut him, smelling its rich earthy scent. Around him the voices of the fens seemed to grow louder, the chatter of running water, the bubbling and gurgling from the stagnant pools and the hoarse croaking of the things that lived in them, the thin whine of insects and distant, mournful bird cries. There was little of warmth or comfort for human ears in those cold voices, but for the first time since he had fled the Mastersmith, Alv found in them a promise, at least, of peace. He felt utterly alone.

After a while he turned and went into the house—if house it was, for there was only one room roofed, the forge itself. It was little better than a shack, but the roof was solid and the old front door of ironbound oak still strong; he would set more iron around its rotten edges, and remake the rusted hinges, till it could have defended a fort. Walls, roof, door and a warm bed on the brick ledge by the forge—he needed no better. He busied himself arranging the great heap of provisions they had left him, enough by themselves for a month or more. He had hooks and line here, too; later he would go fishing, and find dead wood to dry as kindling for the peat. He need look no further ahead than that; let the future dispose itself as it would. But even as he thought that, the face of Kara arose before him, and for a time he felt utterly and completely bereft.

So began his life in the tumbledown smithy on the salt-marshes, and a lonely life it was to be. Over the remaining months of that first summer he lived by tending to the travelers who passed that way, usually in caravans—shoeing their horses, making new knives and weapons to replace those lost or broken, repairing their harness and their trade goods, their wagons and carts and occasionally the carriage of a more important traveler. He did his work well, for it had no call for any power in it, and he could have been very well paid. But most often he took his fee in metal, the stuff of his trade, or food, of which all who journeyed through the Marshlands carried a good surplus against emergencies; he supplemented what he had with catching fish and trapping birds—or shooting them, when he found enough sound wood to make himself a bow and arrows. For the most part it was a meager living, for travelers were rarer even than usual on the road that first year, and he feared the coming of winter, when none at all would pass; he knew he had to hoard his small store against it, and smoked his catches over the forge, or preserved them in salt he made from the pools. He might have fared better by taking advantage of those who needed his help most, as Kathel had suggested, but that went against his nature.

So his existence was harsh, harsher even than his childhood, and he had had many years of good living since then. And the marshes themselves made it harsher still, for they were a dank and sinister place indeed. In the heat of high summer they seemed hotter than his forgefire, hazy, fly-ridden and fetid; strange fish stirred sluggishly in the lukewarm pools, and foul gases rose from the quaking mud. The tall grasses yellowed and wilted, and dangerous bogs took on a thin deceptive crust to tempt the unwary foot too far. The road shone mirrorlike under a rippling curtain of air, and in it travelers approaching or departing seemed to appear and dissolve like visions, from and into nothing. But for all this, as summer drew into autumn and travelers became rarer still, Alv began to range further and further afield among the marshes. He seldom worried about missing a traveler, for in that flat country his sharp sight could make out anyone approaching along the hummocked crest of the road a long way off. At first he went in search of better places to fish and hunt, and these he found. But also he had not forgotten the lore of metals he had learned, and knew that strange stones of good iron could be found in such huge marshes, though none knew why or how they came there. It was in searching for these, with a crude rake he had made, that he found the place he named the Battle Lands.

It was a wide space of the marshes which began some two leagues away near the first island on the Causeway; he never found where it ended, for it seemed to span the whole heart of the marsh. And surely the place was as black and hazardous a heart as that fell place would have, all overgrown with thick clusters of black rushes whose stiff spear-tipped leaves could leave deep stab wounds in leg or questing hand. Worse, the whole area was spotted with broad shallow depressions, up to a hundred paces or so wide. These seemed to mark the path of some watercourse far below ground, for they were brimful of mud that was always liquid and sucked down what fell into it like the maw of a giant. And they were not constant, but would change from week to week, as if the water were seeking new courses under what had once been solid ground. Alv found them first by falling through a thin skin of rotting vegetation, and only pulled himself free with his rake. But when he had rested a little he thought the pit a likely place for iron, and raked as far as he could reach. He was surprised when at the first pass the tines hooked something that could not possibly be an ironstone. But it felt hard, so he drew it in, expecting some half-decayed root or branch. So he was even more startled to see before him the blackened remains of a breastplate with corroded rags and tags of chain mail still attached to it, and of no type or style he knew. There was enough metal left to be valuable, so he took it and thought little more of it, until some hundreds of paces further on, in more solid mud, he pulled up a clump of colorful marsh samphire to pickle and found an arrowhead tangled among its roots, and after that the peak of an iron helmet, again of no kind he knew. He raked another pit, and came up with yet more armor, but to his horror there was part of a body yet inside it, a headless trunk, withered but tanned brown and preserved by the marsh.

He let it fall then, and left that place, but he soon conquered his loathing of it enough to return, for the whole land was a treasure trove of metal. Some immense battle had taken place there once, or perhaps many, and other tragedies besides, and the ceaseless ferment of the bog brought many sad remnants back to the daylight. Once he came upon a whole wagon standing proud of the mud, with rags of its hide cover clinging to the metal hoops, and tackle dangling stiffly from its front. And when he waded cautiously out to it over the half-hardened ground, he found in the mud inside those it had carried, the bodies, still recognizable, of a man, a woman, two children; their hair gleamed golden in the slime, though their clothes had rotted to shreds. One of the man's hands yet grasped at a length of hide cord, which had surely been reins, but the other clasped at the fragments of an arrow in his chest.

"You were fleeing," said Alv aloud to the dark dead faces. "Who knows what from, or why? But they shot you, man, and your cart ran off into the marsh. And they cut your team free, and left your wagon, and your folk, to sink . . ." He felt his eyes prickle, and with a sudden surge of revulsion he ducked down, put his back to the rotting wood and with a single fearful heave tipped it out and over into the still liquid heart of the pit. The upturned wagon sank slowly from sight, its burden hidden beneath. "Sleep again," he said harshly, as the blood-red grass flowers hissed in the wind. "Sleep, and forget. There is injustice enough walks free and alive in the light of day."

As autumn drew on, and darkness closed around the day, the marsh became yet more terrible for him. Rains pounded the land, washing what had been firm paths into treacherous slideways to the dark pools. The song sparrows and mockingbirds fell silent, and the sad notes of plover and sandpiper, the harsh croaks of rails and faraway screams of seabirds echoed across the flat land. The mists came rolling in off the distant sea till only the scant tree-tops could be seen, like stark fingers clawing up, and in that mist the shadows grew weird and treacherous. Some seemed to walk by themselves, strange thin forms stalking beside him or behind him, whichever way he turned. At night eerie cries echoed under the black obscuring clouds, pallid lights danced in the shadows beside the Causeway, and sleet and moaning wind battered at his door like great hands knocking. He kept it well barred, and seldom stirred outside. When once he did, on a night that was crisp and clear, he saw an immensely tall figure, glimmering gray in the starlight, go gliding across the frosty grasses like smoke in a breeze. He stood rock-still till it had passed, then backed slowly inside, softly shut and barred the door and sank down behind it, shaking.

Not long after that, as autumn merged into a black, biting winter, he was just settling down for the night when he heard the unmistakable clop and rumble of a caravan approaching from the north. Wearily he went to the door and watched its lanterns advancing through the mist—a small party, eight or nine wagons and a carriage. He was glad when its troubles turned out to be even smaller—a single sheared axle-pin on the lead wagon, which he was able to replace from his prepared stock, filing and beating it to a solid fit with a few minutes' labor. He turned to store away the fine slab of bacon and pitcher of wine that were his fee, ignoring the caravan as it rumbled off. But he glanced up at the carriage as it came toward him. At the half-open window a slender arm rested; its long sleeve fluttered aside, and in its shadow he glimpsed the serpentine shape of his armring.

What that girl has, Louhi has . . .

He stood in desperate confusion. If that was Kara—but if it was Louhi . . . And Louhi might well be there also—heading south—*why?* He remembered what Ingar had called her—*a schemer, a troublemaker—a great lady out of the Southlands, probably* . . . Was she returning there? As the carriage drew level with him he craned his neck to see, and made out another indistinct shape inside. He could dimly distinguish the face of the woman at the window, wreathed in something light-hued—but whether that was blond hair or a white hood, he could not tell. The woman did not see him; she seemed to be looking straight ahead, toward the Causeway. He had only to call out . . . And risk an encounter with Louhi. That might be almost as perilous as meeting the Mastersmith. Doubt held him a crucial moment, and the carriage rumbled by. And as it passed he saw the dim face turn; whoever she was, she was glancing down at him but without any sign of recognition. He stood, frozen, realizing only then how great were the changes that wanderings and labor and hardship had wrought in him, and the shame of them rose like bile in his throat. He felt then that even if it was Kara, he dared not move or speak to acknowledge himself, in the state he was. He let the carriage pull away. But as it passed her gaze seemed to linger on him, and as the carriage reached the Causeway he heard the window slam down, saw the white-wreathed head half lean out and look back. In a spasm of anguish he turned away as if uninterested, cursing himself for every kind of coward. He did not look again till the grind of the wheels had dwindled into the distance, and the caravan was fading like a dream beneath the livid face of the rising moon. Then he walked stiff-legged back into the mean forge, and collapsed onto his bed.

That midnight Alv awoke bathed in sweat, though the fire was low, and racked with sudden shivers. When he tried to stand, it was as if the marsh had run under the floor, and quaked. His bones ached, his teeth chattered, and before long his lungs seemed on fire. When he looked down at his hand the firelight seemed to shine right through it, as if he was fading away. With the last of his strength he fetched in more peat; he laid food to hand, and an infusion he had made from the bark of a certain tree which he had learned was a specific against some fevers. It was this, perhaps, that brought him over the worst of his illness, but it lasted many weeks and all but killed him. At times he lay raving beside the dying fire, seeing faces arise to haunt him in its lambent flames. The dead of Asenby came shimmering around him with the Headman and Hervar, all blackened, leading them, showing off their wounds with malign pride; the family from the wagon gathered around his bed, staring at him with wide shriveled eyes, and Kara moved among them, let fall her cloak to show herself as naked and withered as they. And in the corners of the forge, now here, now there, calmly surveying it all, stood the bulky frame of Ingar; as Kara appeared he threw back his head in a hearty laugh, and as he laughed he slowly, very slowly, cracked and crumbled away. Alv felt streams of whitehot silver run down his cheeks, but they were only tears.

Mercifully he grew lucid long enough to feed the fire before it died, and once to rekindle it when it had, though he was very weak and had to crawl. At times he choked down a draft of the bitter drug, and sometimes even a morsel of food when his stomach did not revolt. So he lived, and one night before the turn of the year the fever broke, though the morning found him almost too weak to move. The worst of winter was not yet upon him, and though it sorely taxed him and he had barely enough food, by degrees his health returned. Cocooned in his blankets, he huddled in the smoky darkness while the winds howled outside and the silent snow fell, and grew used to his misery, and patient under it, and awaited its ending in peace.

And one morning, though the marshes still gleamed with ice, and snow clung to the flanks of the Causeway, he was able to come out into the fresh dawn air, and find in it a taste and promise of spring. He breathed deeply, and spread his arms wide, and found room in his mind and heart for nothing but sheer delight at being alive. It was as if in those hours of illness he had at last faced what tormented him and met its agonizing price; the fever-flame had burnt it out of him. He could still suffer for what he had done, feel a chill shiver of horror and regret, but it had faded now into a memory, no more. He was cured of more than his sickness.

The sun arose in glory, reborn from the old year that was gone. "And I also am reborn," he thought, "here all alone. Am I still the boy they called Alv? Surely not. That was never his name. Better to be a nameless, lonely smith of the saltmarshes—one alone, but one made whole . . ."

And then he remembered the lines from the ancient book, the words in the old tongue he had found when he made the helm, and among them the one that had two meanings. *Elof*, one alone; *Elof*, the smith.

So that is my name! he thought, as if he had known it all along.

Elof, who had been Alv, sat there in the sunlight for as long as it lasted, and moved little, for he was in truth like a newborn infant; all his great strength had deserted him, and it was slow to return. But he was patient, and ate as much as he wished of his provisions, knowing that he would soon be fit to hunt and forage again, and that before long the caravans would be rolling along the roads once more. The first of them came southward only a week or two later, and he greeted it with joy, for it was Kathel's returning, having overwintered in the north. The trader was equally pleased to find him.

"Look at this! Thirty wagons dragging, out of forty-five! Wheels, hubs, axles, sometimes it's only the dirt holding them together, and that's what your misbegotten bitches of northern roads are doing to an honest man's profits! Well, Alv, how fare you? Thinner but happier, by the face on you—"

"I've been ill, but I'm better. And by the by, my name's Elof—"

"Ahah!" thundered Kathel exultantly, leering and tapping a finger to the side of his red-veined nose. "So you *were* being close, then, and not giving me your right one, and didn't I always say it, Master Ourhens?" He nudged the small bald man violently in the ribs. *"Didn't I? Alv, no name for a man, that, I said. Changeling indeed! Well, far be it from me to blame a lad for being careful at first, far be it. Let's have a drink on it!"*

Elof let him assume that was how it was, because changing Kathel's mind over anything was hard work, and he had enough of that with his carts. It took nearly four days to work all the repairs, and Kathel in gratitude left him so much food it almost filled the little space in the forge. And as his caravan filed away southward, with many shouted promises to return northward next spring, if they could, Elof suddenly felt he would welcome that, even with the prospect of another winter in between. For all their strangeness, for all the frost that still lingered late into the mornings and the storms of driving sleet and rain that came rolling in from the distant sea, the marshes were becoming a home to him, almost a shelter from the bitter demands of the world. Here he need worry only about himself, and that not so much now. They were a peaceful place as spring drew nearer, and even the echoes of an-

cient strife seemed to ring less loudly among the unheeding chatter of the birds.

But later that day they rang out once again, for as he
went searching the margins of the Battle Lands for more
iron to replenish his dwindled stock of hoop tires and
horseshoes, he came upon a whole heap of corpses thrown
up by the flooding after the thaw. Most of them were frag-
mented past recognition, but one huge form lay whole,
face down and a little apart from the rest, half out of the
mud as if he were even now trying to escape. He seemed
to be wearing black ringmail, which Elof had always found
too corroded to reforge. This looked better than usual, but
as Elof waded out unsteadily to examine it he saw something gleaming in the mailed hand still clutched by the
mud. Gently he reached down and parted the stiff fingers—
and saw the sword hilt they grasped crumble to fragments
in that instant. Below it something black went slithering
back down into the mud; he grabbed it—then yelped with
surprise and pain. But he held his grip, and with great
difficulty managed to pull it free, and wiped it clean on
the grass. It was the blade the hilt had held, black like the
mail, and it had cut deeply into his palms. Forgetting his
pain, he whistled with admiration, holding the dark metal
up to the sun and seeing drops of his blood run gleaming
down the rim. "And what smith of old made *you*, my
beauty, that you've still such a cutting temper, eh? I'd have
liked to meet him, and tell him you're every bit as sound
and as sharp as the day he made you. And find out how!"
he added, with a deep sigh of envy. He held it by the tang,
weighed it, balanced it, flexed it and finally swept it up in
a great arc, lopping the heads from the nodding grasses.
And that put a thought in his mind, and he looked over to
the pile of cloven corpses, and nodded thoughtfully. It was
hard to number them, but there might have been thirty or
more. He whistled again, looked down at the dark shape,
and made to turn it over and look upon the face of one
who had wielded such a weapon and to such effect. But
the very movement and the touch of his hand disturbed a
delicate balance. With a soft whispering sound the mail-
clad figure slid back down into the mud, and was instantly
sucked down. Only the mailed hand stood upraised an

instant, then it was gone in a swirl of bubbles. For two
breaths Elof stood there astonished, and then he raised the
dark blade to his forehead in silent salute.

He took the blade home with him, and he worked long
into the stormy night, crafting the best hilt he could for it.
He longed to make one worthy of such a weapon, if only
to be about something more demanding than cartwright's
or farrier's work. But how could he, maimed in spirit as
he was? He sighed, like the wind in the old stone chimney.
It was not only fine materials he lacked, but the power to
make anything worthwhile of them. So he toiled at reducing and reforging scraps of the finest steel he could scrape
together, and sighed often, and not only with the weariness of the labor. But as he worked, watching the flames
dance to the singing wind, he found a rhythm and a harmony that gradually became a tune he could hum, a theme
as sweeping and spacious as the fens that gave it birth,
noble in tone but with a darker, sadder undertone. It
seemed to reflect the origins of the sword only too well,
and in the end the hilt he made pleased him. Its bold shape
suited the straight sweep of the blade to perfection, and
for the grip he had found a coil of silvered wire he could
weave into a fine pattern. Most important of all, though,
he had calculated the weight exactly against the blade's;
the new-made sword balanced beautifully in the hand. It
was the first fair thing his hands had shaped for many a
day. When he had flattened and fined the last rivets holding it to the tang he set it on the anvil and sat for a long
time gazing at it, watching the strange cloudlike patterns
the firelight sent chasing across the tight coils of the grip,
as if he had somehow put the wide fenland skies into his
work. Or was it only the firelight? He turned it this way
and that, hunting the faintest glimmers like minnows in
the pools, refusing to admit even the faintest cool chill of
hope. He paid little heed to the new song of the wind,
rising in a gusty urgent howl across the marsh, pressing
the fire down like an unseen hand and setting the door
rattling.

At last, when the best of the night was past, he thought
reluctantly of his bed. But even as he rose and left his

anvil, the door shook violently with a sound that was not the wind, a thunderous knocking and a gruff voice shouting.

"Come out! Come out, you smith of the saltmarsh, and shoe me my horse! Day is near, and I must be on my way!"*

For an instant Elof stood shocked and indecisive, and all the eeriness he had seen and sensed in that place seemed to gather around him. But then he took hold of his courage. He had no choice. Why was he here at all, after all, if not to help somebody in trouble on such a night? But he snatched the sword up from the anvil before he strode to the door. He slid back the bar, opened it a little—and an instant later, in a sudden gust of terror, he all but slammed it shut.

On the road outside, its breath steaming in the wind, stood a horse of immense size, a very warhorse, and the stately rider in its saddle matched it well, for he seemed taller than mortal man could be. He was muffled up in a dark cloak, but at his back he bore a long, pointed black shield, and he was sliding a long spear back into its saddlerest; its butt had left its mark on the door. Then he swung himself down, and as he did so the cloak parted, metal rang softly, and the firelight glimmered on the black armor beneath.

But even as Elof's hand tensed on the door, a hot onrush of contemptuous anger drowned his fright. What good would skulking behind a door do? Let this be the warrior from the pit himself arisen, he wasn't going to show he was even remotely afraid. He hefted his new sword, and swung the door wide. And as the newcomer stepped forward, Elof saw that he wore a breastplate as brightly black as a moonlight lake, wholly unlike that strange dark ring mail. At his side swung a great broadsword in a scabbard of the same hue, and he threw back his hood to reveal a high black helm. The visor made shadowy pits of the eyes, but beneath it the pale-skinned face was imperious, a great eagle nose and a bushy gray-black beard revealing thin hard lips set in a strange ironic smile. Behind him the great horse whinnied impatiently and pounded the road, and slowly Elof lowered his sword. "Where to, at such an hour? And in such haste?"

Without lifting his visor, the tall man looked Elof up and down before he spoke, and his voice was deep and stern. "This last night I was in Nordeney, and before the day breaks I must be in the Southlands."

A distance, all in all, of some thirty or forty leagues, at the very least. Elof stared, and barely repressed a chuckle. "Well, I'd gladly believe that, if you had wings—"

The tall man's gaze did not falter, nor the twist of his lips, but it looked less like a smile. "If the wind may, so also this horse of mine." He lifted his head and gazed around the sky. "But even now the stars grow paler! So out with your shoe, smith, and be quick about it!"

Elof stiffened in anger, but the madman was right, he was wasting time. The sooner he was shot of him, the better. He shrugged contemptuously, hooked the sword into his belt and turned to the rack of horseshoes he had made, looked dubiously at the great brute outside, and set the largest to heat, working the bellows till it glowed. The tall man turned without another word, and backed the horse up before the smithy door.

Putting his shoulder to the great beast's rump, Elof seized its leg and bent it up against his knee. Its weight seemed immense, the play of the muscles hard and taut— a real warhorse, worthy to bear this armored giant of a man. But it submitted calmly as he checked that the old shoe had been cast cleanly, leaving no nails behind in the massive hoof, and that no dirt had fouled the site. Then he reached out for the pincers and seized the shoe out of the fire with the air rippling about it. But as he brought it to the hoof to try it, he saw with dismay that it was narrower by a third at least than the huge hoof must have. And he had no suitable metal to make more, short of melting down smaller ones. Sullenly he held it up to show the rider, who gazed down at it impassively.

"It's too small—" began Elof, but he stopped, choking with disbelief. The heated air rippling about the red-hot shoe distorted it like a deforming mirror, thicker and thinner by turns, until it almost seemed to be flexing—swelling—stretching itself out . . .

Unable to credit what he saw, Elof brought the shoe down against the hoof. A cloud of smoke hissed upward, though the huge horse did not stir. And when the smoke cleared, Elof found himself looking at a perfectly fitted shoe.

The wind howled through the open door, the forgefire juddered and shrank away, and Elof felt the hairs on his neck bristle. Without looking up, he snatched up the hammer and nails laid ready and, doing his best to ignore the icy shivers in his back and his guts, he quickly and expertly nailed the shoe firm.

Letting the leg fall, avoiding the stranger's eyes, he reached around for the rasp to make any trim needed, but a plate and mail gauntlet closed ice-cold upon his bared arm. He had to look up, and saw the stranger shake his head. The warhorse neighed and stamped like thunder, and the huge man sprang to the saddle, his sword ringing at his side.

"Fit for the steed of a god. And now good night to you—Master Elof!"

"I'm no master!" said Elof between his teeth, and then, because the smile grew positively malicious, and he felt he was being toyed with, he shouted above the rising wind, "What did you do, damn you?"

The tall man laughed, like high surf breaking on gravel-stone. "I? Nothing. All that was done, you did. But there's light in the east, and battle bids me haste—here's your fee, Master Smith!"

The gauntleted hand swept out from behind the cloak, and a thick disk of silver was tossed to him. It rose and fell slowly, as if through water or oil—very slowly, but with a dizzying spin that held his gaze fixed. He reached out for it, leaped up, his fingers closed around it—and something black rushed between and snatched it. He tumbled in the mud with a jarring, derisive croak ringing in his ear. Two huge ravens stooped over him, squabbling over the coin one held in its beak, then they wheeled up and after the horse as it sprang away and went thundering down the road toward the Causeway. Elof, dizzy and light-headed, sprang up and stormed after it, shouting he knew not what crazy insults into the teeth of the wind. But the

great charger did not gallop out onto the Causeway, but
sprang lightly down the slope beside it and out into the
marsh. And Elof, mad as he was with the ravens mocking
overhead, leaped after it. The strange steed sprang away,
over land, over marsh, over sheets of open water, seeming
to gallop effortlessly on, and Elof ran behind it. The great
wind arose again behind him, and seemed to bear him
along in great bounds, till he hardly knew whether his feet
touched ground or ran in the empty air. Ahead of him now
the ravens rode it and flew faster still, but they could not
catch up with the rider. A great light shone around the
black helm, and the dark gray cloak streamed out behind
him, flapping and spreading in the wind of his passage
until it seemed to fill the whole sky around him, and blot
out all the light, until suddenly he was running in blackness, and came to a hesitant halt, swaying and panting.
How long he had been running, or where to, he had no
idea, though he felt only a little out of breath. Surely dawn
couldn't be far off . . . He took a hesitant step forward,
heard a slight splash, and swore as he felt chilling water
running around his ankles. Then he looked up, and the
blackness had turned to gray, but it was the gray of evening, not dawn. He stared wildly around him. It was the
familiar fenland he saw, with wisps of mist drifting over
the grasses, and small birds swooping low across them,
calling the rain. But it was no part of it he had ever seen
before. He was alone in the midst of the marsh and the
mist, with the night falling and no idea where in all the
wide leagues the smithy or the Causeway might be, and
no way to get back.

CHAPTER FIVE

The Corsairs

For a moment he believed he was back in the throes of his fever, and that this was just another trick it played on his senses. Then his numbed feet protested; it was no dream, though he might as well have wakened out of one. He stepped gratefully out of the icy rivulet he had landed in and sat down on the bank to wring out his boots and stuff them with what dry grass he could find. They were stout ones a trader had given him, and he was glad he had been wearing them, and his cloak, when he went to the door. He was tired and cold, and hunger grew on him as he sat, a ravening hunger. He had hardly anything with him, less even than he had had when he came to the salt-marshes; he was without even his valued bird-bow and fishing lines. A thought struck him, and he fumbled at his belt. The sword was not there, and he panicked for a moment before he noticed it lying on the bank a little further upstream, presumably where he had first halted. That was something, anyway, the minimum to keep him warm, and protect him. As he stooped to pick it up he saw beside it a single wide hoofprint in the mud, with water still oozing into it. He sprang up and stared around, but nowhere on earth or sky was there a rider to be seen. The blood roared and rumbled in his ears. "You bastard bitch's son!" he muttered, gripping the hilt tightly. "What've you done to me? Where've you taken me? How . . ." But he left it at that. He did not dare voice the question of how he was going to get back; it might have no answer.

First things first. He had to look around, find at least

some indication of where he was. By the stars—but there would be none visible tonight, nor moon either. Somewhere behind those clouds the sun was setting; he could make a rough guess where, and marked the direction as he tramped back to his boots. They were nothing like dry, but he could not afford to be fussy. He hauled the grass out, and cursed when it came out covered in fine sand—*sand?*

He peered at the rivulet, dug his fingers into the bed. The soft heavy stuff poured through his fingers, and a salty, seaweedy smell rose to his nostrils. He looked up and down the winding bank. The grass here was much taller, head-high in many places, and with broader leaves. In between the tall stems grew spearscales, saltworts, beachbur, bright sand verbena, all plants he remembered from his childhood but had never seen by the Causeway. He swallowed, stood up, sniffed the air again, and listened. The smell was strong in the air, far stronger than the slight tang he was used to. That rumbling sound—it had not been his blood, not entirely. Somewhere not far from here, more or less in the direction the sun had gone, surf was beating upon a beach. He swallowed again, with difficulty, for his throat was very dry. Once, when they had been talking about the Ekwesh beginning to raid inland, he had asked Kathel and his partners if the Causeway was safe at such a lonely point. And Kathel had replied with a laugh, "Surely enough! The marshes are really a river delta, they spread wider as they near the sea. So naturally they built the Causeway high up the delta, inland, to keep it short. So you know how far your smithy is from the sea? Nigh on seventy leagues! That make you feel fine and safe?"

Once it had. Once. Now it crushed him. He knew now where the smithy was; he could walk there simply by keeping the sunrise ahead of him, sunset behind. But seventy leagues! When two or three was a good day's walking over marshy ground? He sat in silence, and listened to the surf, and despaired.

But as his hearing became more used to the rumbling sound he began to hear other noises through it, some high-pitched sounds that might be the voices of birds, or seals

. . . or men. He delayed only a moment before getting up
and cautiously wading out through the mist that was rising
and flowing like the ghost of a flood. Men meant fire, and
food, and company, a chance to survive in this dreadful
place. They might be hostile, of course—but he had his
sword. It was a shorter walk than he expected before he
found the flatness of the ground changing to grassy dunes
through which the rivulets cut as their greater selves cut
mountains. Through one of these deep clefts he heard the
voices more clearly. The mist hung thickly now, but as he
peered cautiously round the end of the dune onto the open
beach, the red glow of a fire shone out through the mist
like a welcoming beacon. A looming silhouette hid the
actual flames, a slender neck curling upward from a dark
bulk on the sand—by the look of it the high prow of a
ship. It did not seem to be of Ekwesh kind; that did not
necessarily mean it was safe to approach, and he hefted
the sword thoughtfully. The Mastersmith had taught him
enough swordplay and other warrior arts to judge what
made a good or bad weapon, but he had never used them
in anger, and was not eager to. There was no cover at all
here; the sand was so flat he would gain nothing even by
crawling up on his belly. He would just have to walk in
openly, and trust to his luck.

He hooked his sword onto his belt again, but as he strode
briskly across the crisp damp sand his hand hovered near
the hilt. From time to time great beams of light and shadow
played up across the mist-curtain as unseen figures crossed
and recrossed in front of the flame. But he reached the
dark side of the hull without challenge and stood there a
moment, resting a hand on the barnacled timbers. It came
away slimy, flecked with weed fragments. As he slipped
along the length of the vessel he saw tangles of half-dry
weed hung from a mass of twisted metal at the outthrust
curve of the bows; evidently it was not long beached. He
could hear voices on the far side, but no clear words; he
must needs take his chance.

Cautiously he stepped round the bows—and found himself suddenly in a circle of firelight, with a host of astonished faces staring up at him.

They were pale faces, mostly, but as wild and wolfish

as any Ekwesh. Their eyes widened, and in an instant the
whole crowd of them, twenty or more, were on their feet,
with a hiss of weapons drawn. Elof held up his hands,
then ducked violently as an axe flew past his head and
boomed against the hull. Quickly he put his back to the
wood and swept out his own sword as the menacing semicircle of men closed in. "Stand back!" he shouted. "I
don't mean you any—"

A heavy blade cut out at his head, and he met it with a
two-handed parry which tore it from its wielder's hand.
His attackers fell back a pace, but a fat fair-haired man in
the middle bellowed and sprang forward, lunging at him
with a halberd. As Elof jumped aside the lunge became a
sideways cut and he had to swing round to fend it off; the
halberd dug into the hull, was hauled out and jabbed at
him again. Elof flailed his sword out against it, and sent
the fat man stumbling back. Furious at being harried, Elof
shouted and leaped forward, whipping the black blade
whistling around him, and his adversaries stumbled over
each other in their haste to give ground. He heard somebody shouting in the sothran tongue for spears and bows.
But the fat man stood his ground; Elof had to meet him,
and aimed a chopping downward cut that should have made
him jump. Instead he brought up the butt of the halberd,
and Elof's blade skidded ringing down the iron rods that
bound it. Immediately the halberd seemed to spin round,
and the blade scythed at his throat. Elof cut at it with
desperate strength; this time the sword struck the haft
squarely and sheared right through it, iron, wood and
all, leaving the fat man staring stupidly at a useless trun-
cheon. Elof kicked the fallen blade behind him and stepped
back. Maybe now they'd listen—

He heard the pad of feet an instant too late, saw his
other attackers jump back, and whirled to meet the man
who came running round the prow. He saw only a blurred,
crouching outline, taut and compact, and a flash of red
hair. Then a long sword licked out to meet his. Elof hewed
at it as he would a tree, and with all his strength, and the
sheer force behind the ringing collision sent the newcomer
staggering back. But he recovered at once by spinning on
his heel, and his sword leaped at Elof from an unexpected

side. Elof just managed to parry, but the other's blade seemed to turn supple as a serpent and flow around his, till, with a sudden violent twist, it wrenched it right out of his grasp. Every muscle and joint in Elof's hand shrieked with the pain of near-dislocation, and he stumbled back clasping it under his other arm. His sword thudded into the sand. A heavy boot rested on it.

The other men raised their weapons and rushed forward with a yell, then stopped abruptly as they came up against the flat of a blade. The newcomer was holding them back as he looked Elof up and down. "Spears and bows just to deal with this?" he demanded coldly, in very clear sothran speech. "One man?"

The fat man glowered. "If 'e is a man! Don't look canny t'me. Came at us off the marsh, 'e did! Can't take chances—"

"I think we may delay butchering him long enough to ask a question or two. Well?" the newcomer asked, turning to Elof again. "Do you understand me?"

"Yes, I do," said Elof. He took a second to study his opponent before saying anything more. The man had attacked in a stance which made him seem small, a hard target—the ploy of a master swordsman. Now that he was standing straight, he was a full head taller than Elof, but much leaner and narrower, hard and ageless. His garb of dark green tunic and breeches, though worn and stained, seemed plainer but sounder than the others' crazy blend of rags and soiled finery; it enhanced a certain dignity in his face. He had the same cast of features as Roc or Kathel, but less rounded, longer and harder, with a stern straight nose and firm cheekbones and chin, the pale skin gold-tinged by the sun; his hair was a darker, somber bronze-red, his eyes blue-gray as the sea mist and as hard to penetrate. They had a calm assessing quality which reminded Elof disturbingly of the Mastersmith, but seemed somehow less alarming. "I meant no harm," Elof said. "I was lost on the marsh, wandering. I could not survive long out there without fire and shelter. I came to ask for help."

"With a drawn sword?"

Elof bridled. "Not till your friends set on me! Without giving me a chance to speak! I tried to be civil, but—"

"—never had the chance. I see!" He raised his eyebrows at the fat man, who was aggrievedly picking up the pieces of his halberd. "Well, it may be as you say, but do not blame these lads too much. You obviously know what manner of a place the Marshlands are; travelers are always very nervous of what might appear off them. Rightly so! How did you come to be lost in them?"

"I dwell in them," said Elof, and there was a murmuring among the men. Some drew back, others hefted their weapons. "I'm no spook!" he said irritably. "Over by the Causeway—"

"Then what're you messin' about 'ere for?" growled the fat man.

There was nothing to be gained by telling these superstitious creatures the full story. "I was exploring far afield for metal, and lost my way."

"Metal?" barked the swordsman, with a look like a bird of prey stooping.

"Yes," said Elof calmly. "Iron, and old armor, for my trade. I'm a smith—"

Among the onlookers there was a sudden stir of interest, even of relief. The fat man rounded on them, but the swordsman snapped his fingers. "The Causeway? That's right, I'd heard that there was a Causeway smith again, this last year or so . . . And you have a smith's sinew, that's for certain." He turned to the fat man. "What say you? A stroke of good fortune at last?"

"It'd make a change. If 'e's what 'e says. If we can trust 'im. If 'e's any good. Almi drank, but at least you knew where you were with 'im. I mean, what smith worth a damn'd set up *there*, of all places?"

"Why don't you try me, and find out?" growled Elof, cold and hungry and irritated beyond measure.

"An admirable suggestion, smith," said the swordsman. "By your speech you're a northerner. Do you know anything of ships?"

Elof shook his head. "I've only ever been on one, and that by no will of mine. I know nothing of their making."

The swordsman sighed. "Well, neither did our last

smith, and you cannot be any worse than he. See, smith, we were damaged in a seafight, barely limped back to this beach of ours, and the only smith among us dead—not in the fight, but of his drinking. Come and see—by your leave, skipper?'' The fat man grunted, but let them pass, and trailed along behind with the other men. "The wood-work we've managed," said the swordsman, "though there are precious few good trees in these parts. But there's the worst of it, there at the keelscarf.'' He gestured at a point just under the outward curve of the prow, where a scarf joint secured by heavy trenails joined the long single tim-ber of the keel to the rising forestem timber. Here were the roots of that tangle of metal, braced against both tim-bers. Elof, peering past the weeds, could see that the metal had once been a great harpoon-head of steel, with a comb of barbs along its heavy shaft. Outthrust beyond the bows, it must turn the whole ship into a gigantic spear, but now it hung sadly askew, the barbs twisted and cracked. "Our ramming skeg," said the swordsman. "What you north-erners would call *iarnskekke,* I believe—the iron beard. Without it we've no chance against bigger ships. If you can make that whole for us again, you're welcome to fire and a blanket and such food as we have. Well?''

Elof stepped forward to peer at the wreck, wondering furiously just who these men were. The fat man and the others could easily be corsairs, but this big swordsman spoke like something better than a brigand, or at least more intelligently. Elof had more sense, though, than to ask outright, at least for now; he bent all his attention to the broken skeg, running his fingers over the twisted metal. It had been solid and sound once, but there must have been one impact too many . . . Suddenly he straightened up and swore. "This was damaged before—wasn't it?''

The swordsman looked tellingly at the fat skipper, who ducked his head unwillingly. "Aye, t'were so, a few months gone. Almi fixed it good enough—''

"He did not! Look here and here at the barb, these are cracks, but there's rust inside them, and some other filth! He must just have covered them over, so no wonder they've failed you now. And here he's just soldered the break, where it should have been forged fast again—''

"Typical," murmured the swordsman. "Well, smith, it speaks well for you that you're so keen of eye. But can it be remade now?"

"Oh, easily enough . . ." began Elof casually, and then faltered. An awful ache of loss and helplessness settled on him, so strongly it must have showed. The captain's face hardened, and he looked significantly at his men, but Elof caught his breath. "If I had my tools here, that is. Naturally enough I wasn't carrying them when I—got lost."

"Naturally enough," said the swordsman unconcernedly. "Down by the fire there you'll find Almi's. I was about to try to use them in default of all else. But I know of this art only from books, I would not set myself against any smith and least of all a northerner. Will they do?"

Elof handled them distastefully. "They're poor things for the most part, the only good ones among them old and worn beyond belief. And little or no feeling of power or even personality on any of them." Only now, encountering a lack of it, did he realize how strong it had been in his own and the Mastersmith's gear. "I can't imagine how your southern smiths manage without it—"

But the faces around him, even the dark-skinned ones, ranged from baffled to contemptuous; even the swordsman's bore a look of tolerant amusement, as at a popular superstition. So even a sothran with some reading—wide reading, if he'd studied smithcraft—made nothing of the true craft. If only he could show them—

It might be that he could.

"They'll do," he said. "Yes, I can repair it. But I'll need a proper anvil—"

"Almi'd a little block of metal he used," grunted the captain. "Popped it on a stump or anything 'andy. That do?"

"Very well, I expect. And a better forge—you can build one here on the beach, with stones, like this . . ." He drew a square box fireplace on the sand. "We can improvise bellows, of a sort. But if the wind gets up we can pull out a few stones on the right side and channel that instead."

"Clever!" murmured the swordsman. "And how long—"

Elof shrugged. "A day, a day and a night—"

"Too long!" barked the swordsman, with a sudden lash of anger that triggered Elof's own.

"That's no damned fault of mine!" he snapped, standing up and glaring furiously into the lean hard face, fists clenching. Oddly enough, it was the captain who intervened.

"Let 'im alone, Almi'd take a week, and you or I longer if we did it at all. You want t'give 'im a whack, make it a fair whack. There's a good chance we can still catch 'em in that time."

Slowly the lean man relaxed, and Elof realized that he had been tense and worried all this time. Many lines smoothed out of his brow, and suddenly he looked only a few years older than Elof, in his mid-twenties at most. "So," he said. "I agree, we should be grateful for what we have. To work, then, my lad—"

"After I've eaten, by your kindness," said Elof calmly, "and slept a bit; I'll need that, to give you of my best. Oh, and had my sword back, *if* you please. I can't do much till the forge is built, anyway."

The captain growled his wrath, but the swordsman laughed suddenly. "Very well! I will go bail for your good faith. You shall eat and rest while we labor on it, that is fair exchange for our rough handling. The sword, though—" He turned and scooped it up from the sand, and hefted it admiringly. "A fair blade, I confess I covet it. And I did best you of it . . ." Elof frowned. "But that only makes me understand your concern all the better. I was going to say you would have it when you were done, but you might rest ill without it. Here!"

He passed it over formally, hilt forward across an arm. Elof took it, and bowed equally formally. "You are generous, and I will honor your trust. I will do the very best I can, in the least time."

The swordsman nodded. "A fair-spoken smith for your boldness. My name is Kermorvan, second-in-command of this desperate crew under Captain Ermahal here. May I know yours?"

"Elof, smith of the Causeway, now of no guild or master."

"And all of the better for that, I am sure," said Kermorvan lightly. "Well, Elof, you'll be wanting your food and rest—Maile, do you go and find him some. The rest of you, up, about and find big stones, flat if you can, and bring them up the beach there—"

Later, when his stomach was full, and he was winding himself in a coarse blanket by the fire, Elof thought over all that had happened. It had been a dangerous spot, that, at first. But he had been right to be bold with this Kermorvan fellow, who seemed to be the real power in the crew; it had got him what he wanted. Or had it? With a slight shock he realized that the swordsman's generosity and courtesy had effectively turned the whole scene on its head, had been calculated to do so. He was now under obligation to these people, instead of the other way round. For a moment he bridled at that, but sighed. It would only bind a man of honor—which meant that Kermorvan considered him one. It was a compliment, of a sort, but a mightily awkward one, when he had no idea who these cutthroats were, or what use they would make of that fearsome skeg. But he simply could not worry about all that now, his whole frame was one leaden ache of exhaustion. The soft sand drifted away from under him.

To his surprise Kermorvan was waiting by the new-built forge, tapping experimentally on the little anvil erected next to it. The clear ringing knifed through Elof's head; he had slept no more than an hour or two, after missing what might be one night or many. But the swordsman was eager to be about the work, for which they first had to detach the tangled mess from the prow. That meant hammering parts of it away above and below to get at the big rusty bolts, and while Elof was perched on a stack of seachests, straining at one of these, his hand barked painfully against a rod that felt like wood, not metal. Reaching down into the tangle, he found it was a heavy catapult arrow, stuck into the hull timbers, and he worked it loose with his pincers. But as he pulled it out he let out a gasp of surprise, for he remembered those black and white fletches only too well. Kermorvan looked up from the bolt he was working on, and nodded. "Yes, smith, those are our enemies. And if I guess right, yours also. It is the Ekwesh we fight. And in that lies our need for haste!''

Between them they manhandled the unwieldly ram up the sand to the forge. ''From what we hear,'' Kermorvan panted, ''a strong flotilla will be sailing northward along this stretch of coast before night tomorrow, and it would burn my heart to let them pass unchallenged!''

Elof nodded fiercely, and turned to stoke up the forge-fire. ''Then haste you shall have. And . . . anything else I can bring to the work.'' There were words he remembered, fragments of chants, snatches of verse, that had to do with the striking power of spearheads. If some of those could be adapted to the ram, if he had truly seen more than the firelight in that swordhilt— Then a thought struck him, and he turned again, in sharp and sudden puzzlement. ''You say *northward?* When the Ekwesh are on their way home? But why not attack when they're headed south in the first place, before they've done their pillaging—'' Then he saw the look on Kermorvan's face. ''Oh,'' he said, ''I see.''

''It is the only way they will give battle,'' said Kermorvan, his face sullen and defensive. ''When there is loot to be gained, profit to be made. They are corsairs, after all, these lads; I cannot change their nature all at once. And they are few, and must lurk here in the cover of these mists, picking off a boat at a time here and there. But at least they *will* fight! And that's more than anyone else I could find!''

Elof stood there horrified, the true import of what he had heard only just coming home to him. ''You mean— the Ekwesh have come this far, and beyond, into the rich south itself? And nobody will resist them, not even there?''

''Not after what happened to the first who tried. Every year they have grown bolder, working their way down the coasts of your lands and nearer to Kerbryhaine, that you call Suderney, till at last a sizable fleet came to harry our northern ports. The Marchwarden of these parts, a power-ful lord and a kinglet in his own domain, he grew impatient waiting for the syndics to act. He raised his own levies against the raiders without waiting for help from the city. By weight of numbers it should have been enough to obliterate them, ten times over. But the levies were cut down to a man, an utter rout and massacre. So now nobody will march against the raiders.''

''But—but we always thought of you sothrans as so rich, so powerful, with high walls to dwell behind and armies no lord would dare challenge . . . I don't understand it.''

Kermorvan shrugged. ''We have armies but no fighters, captains but no leaders. We have been at peace too long, no bad thing save that we cannot now preserve it. The Syndicacy is all the government we have now, a gaggle of fat men who cannot agree the time of day without a full session in council. The Marchwarden, being charged with the peace of our northern borders, he had more knowledge of war than most, but that only in skirmishes with reivers in the Debatable Lands, and corsairs such as th—as we. And the syndics squat behind the city walls and find reasons in their purses not to fight, hoping the blow will not fall in their time.'' He drew a deep breath. ''And since they cannot vent their fears on the cause of them, instead they do so upon any who—never mind! Something must be done, however little, to convince the barbarians that they will not have the Southlands to themselves as they have had Nordeney—''

''*My* folk didn't just lie down before them!'' said Elof sharply, levering at a cracked joint with heavy pincers, surprised at how easily he could forgive the poor folk of Asenby now. ''They fought!''

''Aye,'' said Kermorvan, ''when they had no other choice, I would wager. So no doubt will mine, when the enemy is at their gates. But by then it will be too late, because he will have dealt with the country piecemeal, as he did with yours, instead of finding it a solid bulwark against him. If they could wipe out the Marchwarden's troops without crippling loss to themselves, then no one region or town, not even the city itself, can stand against them alone.''

Elof nodded, remembering the well-fed complacency of Harthaby, while the ruins of Asenby, only a few days' sail away, were still smoking. Was Harthaby yet standing? ''You have the right of it. So it has been with us, indeed.''

To his surprise Kermorvan shook his head. "I blame
your land much the less. It has never been united, nor had
much chance to be. Its first settlers deliberately chose independence over dominion, and I shall not say they were
wholly wrong."

Elof looked at him, surprised. This was a man of lore,
in his way, and no mere swordswinger. "You seem to
know more of the histories of the north than I do. I used
to think my master had led me deep into knowledge, and
so he did—but along a very narrow path, I now see. Tell
me something of this lore as I work!"

"As *we* work!" said Kermorvan, more cheerfully. And
at first he did his best to make his boast true. In the taking
apart of the damaged ram his wiry, unflagging strength
was a great help, but he had scant breath left for talking.
When that was achieved, though, there was little he could
do save stand and watch Elof at his filing and hammering
and grinding, and take a turn at the crude bellows when
needed. Then he did indeed tell many tales, as the night
wore on, in the tongues of both south and north, in which
he seemed almost equally fluent. Elof could only marvel
at how little he had known before of either Nordeney or
Suderney, and the wider world around them.

Of the land of Kerys the swordsman told, now a name
of legend, no more, and of how the first coming of the Ice
was there foreseen, and of the many of its two kindred
peoples who then ventured across the wide oceans to settle
in the eastern lands of this vast country they called Brasayhal, hoping that their children would live free of its
malice forever.

"But that was not to be," said Kermorvan, the dark
burr of the north as deep in his voice as any native's, "and
when after many generations the Ice made its dread way
down toward them, there was division in their state. As
our Southlands are today, it was centered around the great
city known as Strangenburg in your tongue—the City by
the Waters, heart and mind of its realm, and to which the
other towns, even their first strong settlement on the eastern shore, were as mere outposts. They dearly loved that
place, high and fair, mirroring the lost splendors of Kerys.
But many in terror of the Ice now wished to abandon their

lands altogether and to flee southward and westward, despite the dangers of the forests and the mountains in the heart of this land which they must either brave or skirt round. But they did not know how long that would take, or even if it was possible, or whether it would lead them to habitable lands at all. In the end, it came to a sundering of the kindred; most of one chose to go, most of the other chose to stay. Those who stayed had come originally from the more northerly ranges of Kerys, and perhaps yet endured the worsening cold more gladly. Their kings, though, came of both peoples blended many times over; *they* stayed, and tried to persuade or compel as many as possible to do the same. But the others fled.'' He fell silent for a moment as Elof chanted a scrap of harsh verse over one of the tines of the comb, and he stood staring into the forgeflames.

> *Shining steel! Spirit of falcon!*
> *Spearpoint, mark you my word!*
> *As a shaft of sunlight*
> *Cleaves the cloud-roof*
> *Strike asunder where you are sent!*

''Some called them brave,'' said Kermorvan at last, ''to undertake so perilous a journey. Others said that by fleeing they were only serving the will of the Ice, and called them cowards and fools for choosing to risk terrors unknown rather than helping preserve what they could of their own hard-won domain. Myself, I do not know; but I think I would have stayed. As it befell, in the end there was much bravery on both sides. For the ones who fled came across the mountains to these warm Southlands only after many trials, and a good half of their number perished along the way. There are tales of high heroism and great sacrifice in the journey, and the forging of the new realm.

''But in the east also there were heroes. Then, if ever, lived Vayde and many other mighty names. They held the realm together for two generations more, as the cold grew worse around them and the Ice and all it brought with it came sweeping across their northern borders. But in the end it made a great spearhead southward, and the glaciers

came right up against the whole proud City by the Waters
and ground it to powder beneath them. And there it lies
to this day. Then those who were left abandoned their
kings in bitterness, who had persuaded them to stay, and
they too fled. Some went to the lesser towns in the east,
but a good number went in the wake of their brethren,
west and south. Many perished; some won through, at a
cost even more appalling than their forerunners, for they
were fewer, and ill prepared. That too was a time for heroes. But they found scant welcome in the birthpangs of
the new realm of Kerbryhaine, for the bitter words and
names once given had not lost their force, and some, it is
said, yet lived who had endured them. So against heroism
must be set great cruelties, and treachery and villainy on
both sides. In the end the newcomers left their brethren
and escaped to the more northerly parts of the lands between mountains and sea, which the first-come, preferring
warmer climes, had not cared to settle. There, as time
passed, they met and mingled with fellow refugees, brown-
skinned folk from far westward across ocean and Ice. And
that was the origin of your Northlands.

"The new settlers made widely scattered settlements,
for the northerners had always been the outlivers of Kerys
and the Eastlands. But without a central city to serve, this
left them poor and weak, and though the enmity between
north and south long ago grew cool, and there has been
trade and a measure of friendship between us for many
centuries, still the cities of the north cannot combine with
each other to defend themselves, let alone with us. The
habit of independence is grown too strong."

Elof nodded somberly, watching the two ends of a weld
begin to glow in the fire. "I remember my own little town.
The only link with the world beyond the walls was the
guilds and the traders, and the word of Headman and elders the only law. They would never dream of submitting
to a greater."

"Yes. It was only reinforced by the brown-skinned folk,
for they were fleeing the bloody rise of the Ekwesh empire, and feared nothing more than creating another. They
were peaceful farmers and fishers, not used to looking
much beyond soil, sea and season, and they had paid their

own toll in blood to find that peace. The settlers then were
realizing how few they were against the south, which they
feared, and how slow to increase; small wonder they made
these sturdy newcomers welcome. So today's northerners
are a good folk, but ever an inward-looking one. And that
is a perilous thing to be, when the Ice is shaping its malice
against you!''

Elof put down his hammer a moment, and looked at
him. ''My master talked as you do about the Ice, as if it
was a live thing—''

Kermorvan's eyes widened. *''But it is!* He told you no
more than that?'' He shook his head in wonder. ''Then it
was no narrow road your master led you down, but a
crooked one. Know what every child of our land learns!
There is indeed a living will behind the Ice, and a malign
one. It—or they, for it is said there may be more than
one—hates all living things; I do not know why, but it
does. Most of all it hates us, we humans, and what little
order and civilization we have won for ourselves. It may
make use of men for a time, but it seeks to drive us back
to the level of the beasts, so that it may destroy us as freely
as they. Thus it especially hates we of Kerbryhaine, furthest from its grasp, strongest against its purpose. The Ice
is its weapon, slow but inexorable in its advance. Did I
not tell you how it spearheaded south to cover the great
city? Nowhere else has it yet dared come so far, though it
chafes ever at the mountains north of your land—''

''That I know,'' said Elof quietly, as he drew the pieces
from the fire and set them together with a rain of light
taps. ''I have heard it.''

''You have heard . . .'' Kermorvan shook his head, momentarily lost for words. Then he burst out, ''But how did
you dare go so close? The Ice is not empty, but peopled
with fearful creatures, fell beasts and other terrible things
that I can give no names to; that will draws them as it
draws all unhallowed things, they ride the Ice as they might
a ship and fare ahead as its vanguard, spreading death and
terror. They come whenever its power is strong, at times
even down to the marshes here with its meltwaters. How
did you *dare?*''

Elof was silent a moment. The hammer stood poised

in his hand, but did not fall. For he was thinking, remembering, as he had not for a long time, his first sight
of the gleam in the sky, and the Mastersmith telling of
his pilgrimage, his new apprenticeship, his reshaping,
reforging—

Upon the Anvil of Ice.

Savagely Elof smote down upon the weld, with blows
so fast and heavy that the sparks went dancing and skit-
tering across the little anvil, and the pieces of hot steel
seemed to flow together as one. He looked up, to see
Kermorvan gazing at him with keen eyes. "I was astray,"
he said, but nothing more.

Kermorvan shrugged. "Who in this world is truly astray,
I wonder? There are other powers than those of the Ice,
they say. Certainly it was a timely straying that led you to
us." He looked questioningly at Elof, seemed about to
ask something outright. Elof hastily turned away and
plunged the fastened metal into the improvised quenching
trough, and was grateful for the concealing cloud of steam
that arose about him. There were too many questions he
did not yet wish to answer, even to himself—least of all
to this strange man, who had been careful to say so little
of himself.

And it was as if Kermorvan himself sensed that, and
approved, for he added, "At least, timely if I do not keep
us from our work." He looked around him, at the first
faint tinge of gray in the mist. "Dawn approaches. How
long . . . ?"

"Seven hours, perhaps eight. And another hour to refit
it, I think. The mount should be reinforced."

Kermorvan growled. "Let us hope we have that long,
then. These chants of yours, these symbols you're scratching . . . Will they really achieve anything?"

Elof smiled as he selected two more strips of metal and
jabbed them into the fire. "That's to be seen. They are
not slowing my work. Not by more than minutes."

"No? Those minutes may count!" He spoke harshly, in
the effort to rein his eagerness. "But go ahead! You must
work as you know best how."

"I thank you!" said Elof, and meant it. Once again, a
compliment, once again a burden of responsibility; this

Kermorvan did know how to sway people to his purposes. "I think . . . I think they are worth trying, though they will be less effective on something not new-made. You understand, it is not the power of the art that I doubt. It is myself."

Kermorvan, suddenly nonchalant again, rubbed a thumb over his stubbled chin. "Then I think you need have no fears."

Elof shrugged, turning the metal in the forge. "We will see, in a few hours."

"Perhaps. And what then, Elof?"

"You set out to fight the Ekwesh."

"And you?"

"I? I turn for home," Elof plucked out the longer piece, and began to straighten it. "Though if you could set me ashore above or below the heart of the Marshlands it would make my path shorter and safer . . ." He hesitated, and did not know why.

Kermorvan appeared not to notice. "We cannot leave this area before we fight, here where there is always mist to cloak us. And we cannot return to it afterward, not for weeks; the fleet may stay and search, or leave a force to trap us. So we can only land you if you take ship with us, now." He leaned forward fiercely, and red forgelight shone against his keen gray eyes. "Why not, Elof? It'll be uneven enough as it is—fifty of us to maybe a hundred of them. Someone like you might well turn the scale."

Elof snorted. "I'm no warrior—"

"No? If you're not, who is? You're strong even for a smith, and fast. You've some swordplay, at least. And you hate the Ekwesh, that's clear. So come with us!"

"Aye, come!" grunted the captain, stumping up through the mist. "Got the better of me, and there's not so many 'as done that, eh, Kermorvan? And speaking of that, if you've a moment, perhaps you wouldn't mind fixing some bands on a new 'alberd-shaft . . ."

Elof gave a splutter of laughter. "That, at least, and ones that won't cleave so cleanly. For the rest—we'll see! Now, somebody put their back to those bellows, or we'll never have this thing straight—"

The sun stood past noon before he had done, and the

mists had thinned to a heavy haze. A new strong mounting
was prepared, and the reforged ram swiftly bolted into
place. At once the captain had the corsairs scurrying about
to raise the mast and reload their gear, but Kermorvan
seemed unable to tear himself away from the weapon, running fascinated fingers over the dark menacing gleam of
the metal. "I take back my words!" he said with soft
exultation. "You have made this a finer thing than ever it
was—stronger, sharper. There is a faint strange shimmer
on it . . ."

Sprawled exhausted on the warm sand, Elof took a moment to understand what he was hearing. Then abruptly
he rolled over and scrambled up, eager to look but hardly
daring. What was the swordsman seeing? Could it be that
he also had a touch of the art in his blood?

"Like fish darting in a pool!" added Kermorvan, en-
tranced. "As if sunlight truly were forged into it, as they
tell of the duergar smiths of old—ach, I waste time! But
now we've a real chance!" He turned away to call for
ropes and rollers to be readied. Gingerly Elof reached out
and touched the warm metal, peered at it, into it. Under
the greenish sheen of the steel a light coursed indeed, now
strong, now pale, pulsing like blood in veins. The work,
crude as it was, had come alive under his hands.

On impulse he plucked his sword up from where it lay
by his cloak and jerkin on the sand, and gazed hard at the
hilt he had made. Clouds gleamed back at him though the
sky above was clear, glancing and shifting in the mesh,
vagrant as thoughts. The realization, the honing of hopes
he had deliberately dulled, was almost painful, like stirring a limb long unused. But there was no escaping it, and
pleasure in the very pain. He should have suspected as
much the moment he touched the clumsy old hammers and
pincers, felt the emptiness in them; he had not even noticed it in his work for Hjoran. It took power to perceive
power—and the lack of it. With a surging yell of sheer joy,
he hurled the sword wheeling into the air and caught it,
closing his fingers round the cool glitter of the hilt, clutching it to him. What it might be he could not guess, but a
virtue dwelt in that hilt. His art was his again, and his
long healing complete.

"A martial sight you are, of a sudden!" laughed Kermorvan, striding up the beach. "Well, sir smith? Are you then thinking of coming to fight alongside us, or of slinking away to rot in your smithy—assuming you ever find it again?"

Elof thrust the black blade vertically down into the sand, to stand like some sinister outgrowth. How strange, that he should have worked some quality into the hilt, and not know its purpose. But then, what did he know of his own, now? Go back to the marshes and live as before? The fenland had seemed so right for him once, a place of hiding, not so much from the Mastersmith as from his own self-loathing, a bitter purge needed for a mind made sick. He had found punishment in suffering, and made some restitution, perhaps; there were many travelers now safe who would not have been but for him. And in that, it seemed, he had also found healing. Now, for all their bleak loneliness, the fenlands had almost become a safe haven, a retreat where he could go on living a simple, useful life with few demands beyond staying alive, forgetting his cares and fears. But was he right to forget them, now his health and his craft had come back to him? Was it right to go on riding? The world marched on and would not wait for him, squatting in the rushbeds. What of his vengeance on the Ekwesh? What of his debt to Roc? What of his pledge to Kara? And what of the grim power he had unwittingly set in the hands of a ruthless man?

For a moment he felt bewildered, but a moment only. Then he nodded, at once angered and amused. Whatever strange power had brought him here, it had chosen its time with care. The Ekwesh were growing bolder, and he aided them who failed to resist them. Whatever good he could do in the smithy, he could do more in the world beyond. And there was so much of that to see, so much to learn, and he was yet young.

He turned to Kermorvan, and plucked the sunwarmed blade from the sand. His path was set clear before him. "All right, you sothran pirate! I'll come! But on one condition only! That when this fight's done, if I choose I'll count myself quit. And you'll set me ashore then within easy reach of a town, and food and gear to get there. Agreed?"

"So be it!" barked Kermorvan, with gusto. "We could clasp hands on it, but I've another idea. It's still too clear to launch, the Ekwesh would spot us leagues off. We must needs wait. That maddens me, so as well pass the time making you some semblance of a swordsman. Shall we cross blades on it?" Kermorvan's long sword hissed out, gray steel glittering before eyes that matched it.

Elof grinned, and the black blade gleamed in sullen magnificence. He copied the stance Kermorvan had used. "Fair trade, for the smithcraft I've taught you . . ."

So they swung and sparred through an hour or more of the afternoon, edge on edge chiming through the thickening haze. The loafing corsairs gathered round to watch and laugh as Elof was stung by the flat of the gray blade, or sent sprawling on his face with the surf lapping round him like an anxious dog; they had all suffered under Kermorvan's instruction. But soon enough as the mist came rolling in across the little bay, they ceased to laugh, and nodded thoughtfully, and laid small wagers against the coming plunder. For Elof's sheer strength told against the subtlety he lacked, and the same eye and hand that placed blows so accurately on the anvil he could turn against his opponent. At length, hilts locked, they swayed eye to eye, breath hissing through dry lips. "Better!" Kermorvan gasped. "One day—a great manslayer—had you only the will!"

"Sooner—beat metal—than men!" wheezed Elof. The tall man laughed, and was about to answer when there came a shout from the high dunes behind the beach. "Sail ho! South away! A black sail!"

"Hands to launch!" bellowed the captain, bounding to his feet. "Shift yer scuts, to the ropes!" Kermorvan dropped his guard and sheathed his sword in one fluid movement, and went pounding off to join the other corsairs, dragging Elof with him. A spring cable, rigged between the sternpost, a solid old tree stump and the bow capstan, pulled the vessel forward on its rollers, while those crewmen not straining at the capstan bars rushed back and forth taking rollers out from under the stern and thrusting them under the advancing bows. Elof, scrambling over the stern, was amazed nobody was crushed, but it was a practiced operation, and the long sleek hull slipped into the oily-calm waters of the bay with hardly a splash. The mist curled around her low gunwales, and wreathed itself around the legs of the roller crewmen being hauled aboard, as if it wanted to hold them back. Many of the men clutched amulets, or made superstitious signs; even Kermorvan rested his forehead against the mast a second, uttering low words. Elof, for his part, simply looked back at the shore, but it was already no more than a shadow in the mist, and even the marshy odor was lost in the myriad smells and stenches of the ship, from tar and damp seal-skin sleeping bags to unnamed foulness in the bilges. The captain brought a heavy oilcloth bundle forward, and as he unwrapped it carefully the bow lanterns glinted on a great beast-head, carved and gilded, with staring eyes of red glass and long jaws filled with brass fangs. He reached up and fixed it into a socket atop the forestern, so it rode high over the bows as if on an arching swan-neck.

"Amicac!" cried the crew, and cheered wildly. Elof shuddered.

"Why do they bear the Sea Devourer so gladly as an emblem?" he whispered to Kermorvan.

"What better sign for a corsair?" said the swordsman darkly. "A terror, a scourge and a curse, that may very well be our ensign. We are outlaws or exiles, who might as easily be slain by our own folk as our enemies." He laughed bitterly. "Perhaps we have made our own compact with the Devourer. We send him food, or are ourselves sent down to feed him. Why should we not claim his protection? *Out with your sweeps there! Fix locks!*"

The oarsmen took their benches, and the long heavy sweeps were passed out over the gunwales and mounted on the heavy pivot pins that served as rowlocks. They were held poised a moment, as if about to row through mist rather than water, but as the captain gave the word and struck his halberd upon the deck they dipped and strained in perfect unison, and the lean craft lifted its bows and flew forward, the dark glassy water chuckling and gurgling delightedly around the new ram.

Someone began to sing softly, and after a moment the

others took it up, a slow, rather sad chantey, in time with
the stroke.

> *Riding the waters,*
> *Fair is she,*
> *Fair the body of Saithana Sea-Maiden!*
> *Streaming her tresses,*
> *Bright as sun,*
> *White her breasts the gulf's-road cresting!*
> *Body so slender,*
> *Pale as foam,*
> *Silken her flanks through seaswell gliding!*

Kermorvan's clear voice rang out over the chorus.

> *Saithana, come to me,*
> *Leave me not drifting*
> *Sleeping so lonely*
> *Where tideway takes me*
> *And the cold claws tear!*

"Aye, let 'em call on Saithana while they may," grumbled the skipper to Elof, "for d'you know, sir smith, that
she's the promise of drowned men! Now we'll needs thrash
about till we find the bleeders, and that's chancy business
in night and murk."

"But that's when it must be," added Kermorvan calmly,
"for we cannot match the Ekwesh in daylight and under
sail. But they are poor navigators, and sail always by following the coasts, and in that is our hope. They must pass
the delta, where there is always mist somewhere, and in
that we may have them!" He stared out into the thickening
fog, where Elof could see nothing. An instant later Kermorvan rapped out an order, and the chantey died away.
He rested an ear against the gunwale, as if listening.
"Passing the headland rocks, by that swell—eh, skipper?"
The captain listened a moment, and nodded. Elof felt the
gentle rise and fall beneath his feet grow slower and
stronger as they moved out into open sea, though there
was still only the faintest breath of a breeze. "Right then!"
added Kermorvan. "Douse lanterns, muffle your row-

locks, batten down anything loose and most of all your mouths, for there'll be no more shouted orders! We want to hear those reiving bastards before they hear us, remember? Stick to it, then, and this voyage'll see us all rich men!'' One subdued cheer answered him, and then a silence thicker than the fog fell about the ship. He turned to Elof. "Do not think the worse of me for holding out the promise of riches. I need them myself."

"How so?"

His hard fist thumped the tiller of the steering oar. "To buy and equip ships of my own! To strike before the raiding, and not have to hover like vultures over the kill! We have engaged four Ekwesh ships so far, and taken three, and I, poor exile as I am, I have saved all my shares—little enough so far, but I was not then second-in-command. Tonight we may see!''

Hours passed, and the corsair beat about, back and forth, searching for some trace of its foe, Kermorvan and the captain plotting their position only by the changing sounds of tide and current. A rare puff of wind would thin the fog, but for the most part the sail hung empty and lifeless, bedewed with the damp, while the corsairs strained at the oars and grew ever more tired and disheartened. Many said the Ekwesh must already have gone by them. Elof took turns rowing, then on watch, standing in the high bows behind the hideous head, one hand tight on the forestay. He glanced down at the ram, cleaving the low swell beneath him, no longer sure he had done right to come, or whether he trusted the swordsman's words. This clammy chill fogged his feelings, forever blank, pallid, silent . . .

Or was it?

He leaned forward suddenly, holding his breath so it would not drown the faintness of the sounds he heard—creaks, splashes, rumbling of water under a hull, like an echo of the sounds from the ship beneath him, but far, far away in the paleness of the dawn. Could this somehow be a trick of the mist, mirroring and dispersing sound as it did light? But he listened again, held his breath longer till he almost choked, thought he heard the laughter of harsh voices, as if the echo came now out of dark dreams of his

youth. He slipped back down onto the deck and passed
word aft to the captain and Kermorvan. The oars were
stilled, the crew rose and lined the gunwales, listening,
and now the sounds grew clearer, drew even closer, till
there was no mistaking them.

"But whither away?" puzzled the captain, " 'Ere one
minute, there the next—can't get 'old of them at all—"

"From ahead there!" said Elof.

"Off the port bow—"

"No, starboard and moving up—"

"But that drum's astern!"

"*Quiet!*" hissed Kermorvan suddenly, and rounded on
the rowers in fury. "Back to your sweeps, damn you! And
row! Row for your lives! Helm, due north and be ready
for anything! Archers, to your posts! *They're all around
us—*"

The corsair boat surged forward, a momentary breath
of wind arose around it and the mist rippled like a sail
and grew briefly thin. Every man on board ducked down
in that moment save Kermorvan, and he stood rooted to
the spot. In the faint light, long dark shadows, half again
their own length and higher in the water, went knifing
through the swell on every side—not just one or two, but
twenty at the least.

Then the breeze slackened, and they blessed the mist as
it fell again. There was no alarm, no hail of challenge, no
creak of catapult winders; the watch had not noticed them.
Kermorvan grabbed Elof by the shoulder. "Into the bows,
you and Maile, and listen out well! There was one running
in toward the shore, we can take him right now if we're
quick! Boarding party, arm! Helm—"

Elof scrambled back to his perch with Maile the bosun
on his heels, and they hung there listening, relaying whispered commands back to the helm as dark outlines loomed
out of the mist around them. A faint thudding rhythm
drummed through the hull under them, and the rise and
fall of the oars quickened in time with it, the bows leaped
and plunged hissing through the dark smooth ocean. The
corsair craft weaved on an insane race through the fleet,
slipping under bows and bouncing over wash. "Aft,
Maile," said Kermorvan's voice from behind them, "and

to your post! We're through the thick of them now, and on
his heels. Hear?''

Ahead of them now was a deeper, slower sweep of oars,
the slow rumble of a drum and harsh voices chanting.
Something or somebody was not chanting but wailing, on
a high rising note of utter misery. Old memories rose bitter in Elof's throat. He turned to Kermorvan. ''Well?
Where shall I—'' He stopped in astonishment.

In the figure that stood there he saw nothing of Kermorvan. A high helm of dully gleaming metal, richly
worked, reared on his head, and below it a mask visor in
the form of a face, regal and proud but with a dire rage
and cruelty in its slanted eyes and flared nostrils. A shining steel collar circled the throat, and below that a casing
of dark mail from head to toe, set with plates at shoulder,
arm and knee, and bound about with a great belt of leather
bearing axe and long dagger; a long fur cloak hung from
his shoulders, mailed boots covered his feet and steel
gauntlets ringed with heavy faceted studs covered his
hands, in which a great two-handed sword stood bare.
Only mouth and chin were left clear of the metal, and the
set of the thin lips accorded well with the vicious mask
above. Like the statue of some war good brought to life
in that fell mist he seemed, or some deadly machine of
destruction. Even his voice was tinged with metal. ''They
grow bold indeed, those eaters of mansflesh. They amble
home, where once they would have fled.'' He paced forward, wrapping the cloak about him to muffle the ring of
the mail. ''Nevertheless they will be ready to fight quickly
enough, and they have one deadly way to meet our attack.
The very blades of their sweeps are set with steel edges,
and kept sharp, so they can be swung along the gunwales
of a foe alongside, with terrible effect. No boarding party
can pass—unless a way through is cut at once, before their
archers can muster. A murderous task, standing and hacking at those sweeps—for that you need a strong sword and
a stern will. I know, for I took that post in our last attacks,
and many perished because I could not lead the boarding
party. Will you now take it?''

Elof looked at him, and after a second he nodded.
''Where must I stand?'' he asked, his voice suddenly

hoarse. Kermorvan led him a little way aft, to where ten crewmen were gathering, bearing all manner of blades and axes, but wearing as armor only light steel caps and studded leather jerkins, many of Ekwesh type, and small round shields. He could see how many might die without a fully armed man to lead them aboard.

"We have armor for you, if you will—no? Then there's your post," the hard mouth whispered. "Up on the gunwales with you the moment we strike, and keep a hold on the for'ard shrouds here. Two sweeps at least we need cut away, a third if you can manage. Then follow us, or stay to fight off any who try to board us in turn. But hopefully we will keep them too busy for that little trick! So—we are ready. Hold tight now, all of you." The mask glared out into the mist, then aft to the tiller. "Are we within range of her, skipper? Very well, then. Rowers, to ramming speed."

The words were quiet, but there was a greater shout in them. The drumming on the deck grew louder, faster, and the rowers flung themselves forward on their oars, and back, gasping in great breaths as their backs strained, till the whole ship seemed to blow like one vast seabeast. It bounded forward, the serpent-head reared up at the prow in imitation of its terrible original, and the mist flew by them in shredded streamers. A mad exaltation seized Elof, and though he knew the risk, he sprang up to the gunwales, wrapping an arm round the deadeye, to see his bright ram-skeg go hissing across the water, like some vast arrow fired at the high inchoate wall of black and white that loomed up clearer and clearer ahead. Then the bow wave under it swelled suddenly and steepened, funneled between the two hulls—

The mist exploded upward, and a giant hand plucked at his legs and lifted him off the gunwales; the deck dropped away from under him like a gallows floor. For an instant he hung from the deadeye by one arm, frantically clutching his sword, then the deck swooped up to meet him again with a jarring, stinging impact. He reeled and saw a vast flat serpent-head rise and strike at him; he hewed wildly at its neck, there was a splintering of wood, and the sharp-edged sweep dropped away. He spun round on

the shroud, leaned out as far as he dared and hacked down
on the next sweep. The shaft cracked and was driven
downward to jam against the planks of the corsair ship,
splintering there as both vessels rose in the swell. He was
just swinging back to the other sweep when the shroud
was plucked like a harpstring in his hand and a figure
swept past him from above, leaping into the gap he had
opened and crashing down on the rail of the Ekwesh ship.
With a cry of *"Morvan morlanhal!"* Kermorvan swung
his huge blade, and Elof saw two black-clad bodies bounce
over the rail and slither down into the boiling water. Behind him grapples were flung, hooked on, and the corsairs
went swarming across to where he cleared a space. Then
the next sweep lanced violently forward, and Elof barely
managed to swing his legs up under him before it crashed
into the deck where they had been, planing great swaths
from the planking. His boots slammed down on the haft,
jamming the blade deep in the deck, and he severed the
head with a blow. On the Ekwesh rail above came a chorus
of yells and screams, and he stared up unbelieving as a
charge of Ekwesh warriors washed over the boarding party
and broke in eddies of disarray against Kermorvan's sword.
Now the masked figure was running forward, the boarders
behind him in an arrowhead, and against the huge sword
nothing stood, not shield or blade or the bodies of men;
Kermorvan cloved a clear path down the flank of the ship
to the stern, out of sight.

Elof saw an Ekwesh archer scramble up on the foredeck
for a clear mark, then be pitched overboard, skewered on
an arrow shot from the corsair's stern. But another arrow
sang down, one of the rowers coughed and sagged over
his oar, and the others ducked, still pulling away at their
killing pace. Archers were gathering behind the high rail,
ready to fan the corsair with arrows and cut off the boarders. "Time we was 'opping, sir smith!" bellowed the captain. He yelled something to his own archers and bounded
across the gap. He barely made it, hung by his hands; two
Ekwesh moved to shoot, and fell with arrows in their
throats as he clambered up.

Shocked as Elof was by the bloodshed, something boiled
over in him now; he scrabbled up the shroud till he was

above the milling Ekwesh deck, waited a moment as the ships rose and fell, then sprang. An arrow grazed his side as he leaped, he landed but fell askew and lost his sword. A dark-robed shape loomed up over him, he rolled aside and a blade clove the deck by his ear. He kicked out hard, the robe collapsed like a tent, and he had his sword and stabbed down hard. The robe doubled up around it, convulsed once with a dreadful choking yell and was still. He staggered up, staring appalled, fascinated at the gouts of scarlet on the black metal; he, he had shed it, here was his revenge! And then an Ekwesh with a spear was running at him; he saw the spear rise and fall in remembered butchery and cut violently at it. The spear flew asunder around him, its wielder stood an instant with a wide scarlet seam the length of his hide breastplate, then fell bubbling in a heap.

Torn between horror and exultation, Elof staggered drunkenly down the pitching deck; the Ekwesh ship was being driven relentlessly away from the rest of the fleet as the corsair rowers kept up their thrust, and more and more of the Ekwesh oarsmen had to leave their oars to fight. High on the sterncastle, bodies of archers strewn around him, stood Kermorvan now, a terrible figure in mail that ran scarlet, raining blows on the Ekwesh who came boiling up from below decks, to be hewn down before they could even join the struggle. Others clambered up through the rowing benches, but were caught by the corsairs as they reached the main deck. The air quivered with weapons clashing, the corsairs' hoarse warcries and the jarring howls of the Ekwesh. Blood pooled on the deck, greasy and slippery underfoot, and Elof saw the headless body of a warrior go skidding right across it and tumble through a hatchway; hysterical screaming erupted from beneath. Suddenly he was back in the ruins of Asenby, with the old Headman dead at his feet and the women howling around him, being weighed up by those terrible eyes—and then the eyes were there before him, yellow and blazing with insensate hatred. With a horror of madness he lashed out at them. Something bit burning into his shoulder, he saw a dark-robed figure go cartwheeling and spinning away down the deck, thin limbs flying in all directions, and only then knew he had struck down a real man, and no mere illusion. The sword that had grazed his shoulder clattered at his feet and went rolling after its wielder, who lay sprawled against the base of the sterncastle. Elof stumbled forward and reached the sterncastle just as Kermorvan came clattering down the ladders, brandishing his sword, broken halfway down the blade, and hailed him. "That's that! She's ours!"

Elof moved past him and turned over the figure of the man he had struck. The eyes glared back at him, wide open and alive for all the great cut that had disabled his leg. "A chieftain, by his robe," said Kermorvan, lifting it casually on his broken swordpoint. Something clattered at the man's belt, long as a dagger, and Elof stooped swiftly to snatch it away. But as the cold thing touched his fingers, he stared in utter amazement. A crook-headed shaft of bronze metal it was, a broad ring hooked through its lower end, the strange, rich patterns and characters on it half worn to glossy smoothness by the passage of many hands, many years. He knew it so well, yet saw it now with altered eyes. He clutched it tight, that well-remembered thing, and the wash of cold yellow flame within seemed to shine between his fingers, to tingle against them, so strong was it. Had the old Ekwesh also perceived something, and kept it for that, as something numinous?

"This . . ." gasped Elof. "It came from my town . . . he was the animal who sacked it!"

"And many others, no doubt. We'll bind this carrion and take him aboard alive, lads. I would have words with him, and we have no time now!"

"All 'ands to unloading!" roared the captain. "Move yer scuts, d'you want another shipload of these 'ere savages about our ears? Strip this rat-pit from stem to stern!"

The corsairs scuttled this way and that, picking up discarded weapons and armor, stripping the dead of ornaments and prising up the grilles that covered the hold hatchways. Kermorvan took no part in this, but went slowly to the rail, leaned on it and fumbled to unfasten his helm with blood-greased fingers. Elof, hooking the goad to his belt, undid the fastening for him, and Kermorvan sighed gratefully as he slid the mask off; it had left a deep bruised score in his face. "Kerys! That was sickening!" he said, licking dry lips.

"You looked to be enjoying yourself," muttered Elof, trying with trembling fingers to scrape the blood off his own sword.

"So might you in the exercise of your craft and mystery," said Kermorvan thinly, "forgetting for a moment where the sword you make may find a sheath! I am no berserk; I am glad to have returned these beast-folk their own physic in full measure, good weight, yes! But joy in it as they do, no. This is a larger ship than ever we have taken before, and more heavily crewed—by Hel, what's that?"

There was a sudden outbreak of noise from below decks, where most of the corsairs were forging, and Elof remembered the screams he had heard. But before either of them could reach the main hatch there was a trampling of feet, and a horde of women spilled on deck—fair-skinned women, evidently sothrans, with one or two children clutched among them. At the sight of Kermorvan in his gory armor they stopped short, almost toppling lastcomers back into the hold, shrieked again and huddled together. He looked almost as confused, gestured helplessly and began trying to explain to them that they were safe and would be taken back home. It was his red hair and clear voice that calmed them, more than anything he said, and the firm way he ordered the corsairs to look after them; they seemed almost as frightened of the corsairs as of the Ekwesh. At last all twenty-two women were lowered one by one into the corsair ship, some shrieking and struggling in the rope harness; they were simple folk from farming villages, and most had never been in a boat before the raiders had seized them. Great bales of plunder were lowered after them, and last of all the old chieftain; some of the bolder women mobbed him as he was bundled down, clawing, kicking and spitting. Then Kermorvan swung himself down into the corsair's bows. Two crewmen brought spearshafts forward; with them and Elof he levered the ram free of the shattered timbers, and the two ships bobbed apart.

"So easily freed!" he marveled. "But it bit deep as a

daggertooth! And not a mark on it, not a tine bent out of place—smith, may I never mock your mumblings again!"

But Elof was looking up at the Ekwesh deck, where a dull red glow was rising. The captain bellowed at the rowers, and they pulled away, but before they had gone two strokes' distance flames crackled into the Ekwesh rigging, burned around the mast and licked at the furled sail. They pulled harder for all their weariness, afraid of sparks in their own tarry rigging, and as the hulk retreated in the mist they saw the bindings flare and the high sail come crashing down, to vanish in an instant in a sheet of fire. "I hope the Devourer likes his meat cooked!" said Kermorvan drily. "I found fire burning in some kind of shrine upon the sterncastle, carefully enclosed in metal and brick. What smoked there as an offering I will leave unsaid. I kicked it over. Now let them search!"

"But you want other ships!" said Elof. "If you capture these—"

"I cannot use them, and nobody would buy such things. I might infiltrate a fleet more easily, but after the fighting I need smaller, faster craft like this—ten, fifteen oars a side, not thirty! Craft that can outrun the Ekwesh for short stretches, as we must do now, yet carry goods and men enough!" He grimaced. "And women. I foresee trouble, before all's done!"

But despite his misgivings, the women seemed to settle down well enough, more so perhaps because they had no homes to go back to. The corsairs, too, were quiet, for they had the exhaustion of battle and of rowing to keep them so. But great stores of supplies had been captured from the Ekwesh, and they were promising themselves a feast ashore. Six had been slain, another two had wounds they would die of, but the rest were luxuriating in the sheer joy of being yet alive. Kermorvan and Elof and the skipper took their turns at the oars with the rest, and they kept up a fair speed. They had to row for some hours through the mists, but at last these thinned and blew away, and they were able to hoist sail and make northward for another of their secret landings, a small hidden cove among the tall cliffs of a bay, invisible from seaward. Then Kermorvan called crewmen to take his oar and Elof's, and went aft to where the Ekwesh chief lay bound, guarded from the women's spite by a corsair too wounded to row: One woman plucked at Kermorvan's sleeve as he passed. "Sire, let us at him! Please! He . . ." She choked. "There was all our menfolk, even the little ones—took us off aship with our daughters—mine only ten—and then that one, he, he came and he took . . ."

Kermorvan looked at Elof. There was no girl of that age among the women, had been none anywhere on the ship. Gently he detached the sobbing woman's hand. "He lives only to tell what he knows. You have looked on horror enough; I am sorry. I will see justice done for you, as befits my station."

"I, or you," he added to Elof as they waved away the guard. "For you have a score also to settle with this creature."

Elof shook his head. "You may have the high justice; I do not. And, whatever else, I see a sick old man." He stooped over him to loosen his bonds, and was spat at for his pains.

"You—you I remember now!" He spoke the sothran tongue quite clearly, as if he had been taught. "Many years, but I forget not . . . Brat the great shaman took . . ." He leered horribly, and his breath wheezed in his throat. "Should—have slain you then, eaten your liver—and him also, may he rot! For he has brought me to this, me and my clan!"

"What," said Kermorvan in grim perplexity, "just by sparing this one's life?"

"No, fool!" gasped the old man. He seemed to seethe with his grievance, and be only too willing to spit the venom of it at any who would listen. "Great warrior, even you will learn! Face him, and learn . . . I am no fool! Would not have come south so far, so soon, but at his behest! Foolish counsel, while so much fat on bones of Northland! Too far, too soon, too little force . . ."

"Then why did you obey this man's behest?" asked Kermorvan quietly, kneeling down beside him. "Is he of a powerful clan?"

"Clans!" The laugh was like nails scratched on slate. "He destroys clans—lowers chieftains—brings old ways of

Aika' iya-wahsa down! Would have us unite with Otter, Eagle, Frog, our old foes, to crush by the force of many, like the Ice . . . Some will do it—I say never, many I speak for—till he wields his power, and then all is night, the heads bow before him . . . Fear none dare resist . . . Blade that never strikes a blow . . . My curse upon it, and the curses of all the ancestors of my clan, upon him, upon you, filth that you are—dung of the dog, beach carrion, couplers with animals—*Mai-yehsa' sekaw'hai* . . .'' The chieftain's voice cackled and crowed away into mumbling in his own tongue.

"Where was your fleet headed next?" demanded Kermorvan. "Straight for home?"

But the chief refused to speak any but his own tongue, even with Kermorvan's sword at his throat, though he still stared around at them all with quick turns of the head and fierce yellow eyes, exactly like an ancient buzzard. He had had his say, and turned stubborn and silent the moment he was asked a question. "Pain will not move this one!" said Kermorvan at last. "Better make an end of it now. Elof, you have no more to ask of this old serpent—Elof?"

Elof heard him, but he had sunk down in a heap on the deck.

"What's the matter with you?" barked Kermorvan.

"You heard him!" whispered Elof, clutching handfuls of empty air. "The man, the great shaman—fear none dare resist—blade that never strikes a blow—Kermorvan, he was my master! *And it was I made that blade!*"

The old chieftain heard and understood, for his cackling laughter rang high in the air. "Then may your own work skewer you! May the breasts of your daughters fill our cooking pots—" But Kermorvan was not a man to be trifled with. In a fury of loathing he spun round, and Elof heard the whistle and thud of the swordblade as it struck once, twice, again, and the laughter shrieked away into a whistling, gurgling scream, and was still. The women heard also, and raised a great clamoring cheer, and one voice shouted, "He didn't die easy!"

"Throw that offal over the rail!" barked Kermorvan, and he stooped to Elof and raised him up. "I do not understand all I heard, but obviously you do. You will tell me more later, when we can be apart. But I say this for now, I see no great evil in you. If something you have made finds an ill purpose—well, who better to unmake it? Think on that!''

It was two evenings after the attack that they wearily turned their bows in between the high cliffs of the northern cove, hauled its bows high on the silvery sand and sank down in utter relief. They built a great fire then, for the cliffs would hide the smoke, and the weary corsair crew slept while the women cooked food and mulled wine from the barrels the Ekwesh had taken. Then all ate and drank, the women with them, and their mood grew riotous. Elof, who would have sat apart, they embraced as a brother, and plied him with wine, praising his courage and great strokes that had cleared their way. He was the youngest of the crew, and well favored, and the women also made much of him, the younger ones fluttering around his neck or drawing him into the boisterous dancing around the fire. And he was nothing loth, for the wine had drowned his darker thoughts, and all his life he had known little of women. Kara's face danced before him a moment in the flames, but the arms round his neck he could feel, the lips against his own were warm, if not so fair, the bodies in his arms were firm, if not so slender. The fumes of the warm wine clouded his mind like breath on glass; he reeled, and two girls bore him up, one thin and red-headed, the other dark and plump, with merry eyes bright with promise. Wine held the whole camp in its grip, a potent wall against the terrors of the last days, and in its turn invoked a higher defense and refuge; the corsairs knew few restraints, the women had all but lost theirs in the shock of battle and abduction. Soon bodies lay sprawled across the warm sand, writhing in a different dance, blind to all except inner need. Elof staggered and reeled between the girls, giggling and breathless with excitement; they stumbled away up the beach to a shallow little cave between the cliffroots, and sank down gratefully on the dry sand of its floor. There clothes, torn and befouled by death in many forms, fell away, leaving only living flesh and blood yet flowing, and no barrier between them. Darkness and oblivion rushed in his veins, roared in his head, till all he

knew of was the warm flesh enfolding him, the soft damp
skin that trembled and fluttered against his body, the
breasts pressed flat against him or hanging like fair fruit
to his hungry lips. He turned from one to another, taking
and giving an animal comfort that blotted out all else; and
yet as breath grew fast and shallow, as the fire roared,
blazed, to its height and the hammerstroke struck searing
sparks to weld the linked bodies rigid, it was Kara he saw,
Kara he held, Kara was the vision in flames within, that
consumed him in an instant to darkly glowing embers, and
in the last to sleep.

He woke before dawn, slipped out from between the
girls, covering them with their clothes, and staggered down
to the beach to bathe. The shock of the cold water revived
him, and he came out feeling cleansed inside and out, but
mortally chill and hungry. He dressed in such of his clothes
as he could still bear to wear, found others among the
booty, and wine, bread and meat among the remains of
the orgy. As he strode back along the beach he came upon
Kermorvan, sitting with his back to a rock and throwing
pebbles out into the gray water, and greeted him merrily.
"I didn't see you enjoying yourself last night!"

Kermorvan gazed up at Elof with bleak eyes. "Enjoying
myself? In *that*?"

The weight of bitterness in his voice startled the smith.
"What ails the great warrior, then? Do you not like girls?"

"Of course!" said Kermorvan indignantly. "But not like
that!"

"Well, how, then?" demanded Elof, more than a little
nettled. "At your sword's point?"

In a flash Kermorvan was on his feet, his pale eyes
glaring down into Elof's and his fist bunched in the smith's
jerkin. "I was not raised to suffer any taunt lightly! Be
glad it is untrue, or I might find pleasure in proving it on
your hide."

"Well? You scorn me freely enough! Were you raised
to do that? Where's the harm in all that went on, rough-
grained though it be? I saw nobody taken against their
will."

Kermorvan subsided, muttering, "It profanes something sacred . . . Something vital between a man and a

woman that ought to be theirs alone—respect, regard, cherishing . . . Out on the sand like lust-ridden animals—but I am sorry I insulted you, smith. It is simply that you do not understand.''

"What makes you so sure of that?" inquired Elof drily. "I may be village-bred, but I love. I shall cherish her all my life, if I can only find her again. But she and I, we both inhabit bodies, they will have their needs. And those needs may be overwhelming, warrior. Especially in the face of what we lived through yesterday.'' He looked at the lines on the tall man's face, the shadows under his eyes. "You slept poorly last night, I would guess, if at all. But I slept, though I have seen less slaughter than you in the world.''

"Aye," sighed the other, "I have seen too much. And I fear you and I may live to see more. Forget my harsh words, if you can, for you may well be wiser than I. But tell me, you who were village-bred, you who were taken by this great shaman—what have *you* seen, in your time? What is this thing you made, this blade? Tell me, if you will, for I fear it concerns all who oppose the Ekwesh, and perhaps also the Ice.''

Elof studied the face before him, eager yet anxious, with the bright, direct eyes of an eagle. How much would he understand of what must be told? This man of justice, would he understand mercy? But he was right, inescapably right. Told it must be, and at whatever cost.

"Mylio!" was the swordsman's first reaction. "That name is of my people, but there is nothing else good of it. It was borne by nobles of the old north, some of whom yet lived on in Bryhaine—but the last was exiled in my father's day, I think. A scholar, but a wicked, ambitious man who maltreated his peasants beyond bearing. Is this his son?''

"Maybe. Or the man himself. There were treatises on the extending of life in his library—all on the forbidden wall.''

Kermorvan's brow darkened with sudden distrust. "Dark arts! I have never believed in them, not truly, but . . . But you have studied them.''

"I have," said Elof steadily. "Hear me out." Kermor-

van nodded, acknowledging that that was just. He hung
on every word, choking back the hundred questions that
hovered on his lips, until Elof told of the night-shapes, of
the bell and the strange warrior-party whose coming it had
heralded. "Kerys!" breathed the warrior. "Duergar—it
could only be . . . The cut trees also, and the minework-
ings. That explains much, very much."

"D-Duergar?" asked Elof, puzzled.

"Hear him!" breathed Kermorvan, almost laughing.
"He walks among marvels, and does not know them! You
have never heard of the Elders, the mountain-folk? Why,
they—but go on, finish your story."

Elof shrugged, and told of the sword's power unleashed,
his warning and his strange escape. "So you see, we had
been carried, somehow, further and faster than a horse
could have borne us, to an easy path down."

Kermorvan nodded. "You were taken by secret ways
through the mountains, not over them. Naturally that was
faster. But go on." His face was sympathetic as Elof told
of their troubled wanderings, his loss and his decision to
seek healing in the Marshlands. Kermorvan stared with
greater wonder at the sword when told of its origins, but
kept silent. It was only when Elof told of the strange rider
that he sat up sharply, as if arrow-struck. *'Raven!* You've
seen Raven!''

"I've seen many ravens. There were two that night—"

"I mean the man, the . . ." He swallowed, and looked
wildly around him. "Your visitor! You . . ." He shook
his head violently.

"You don't believe me, I see," said Elof sharply.
"Well, I cannot prove it. But who is this Raven character
anyhow? I could use a word or two with him—"

Kermorvan was making undignified stuttering sounds.
"Oh, I believe you," he managed to say at last. "You
would not say anything so ridiculous if it were not the
truth! But suppose I said I saw the maiden Saithana swimming up to join us here? Eh? Because it's about as likely!"

"What d'you mean?" cried Elof.

"I mean, you smith of strange marvels—" But then he
shook his head, and looked around uneasily. "I cannot
say. I have to think . . . Later, not now."

"Not now?" groaned Elof. "But I have to know what to do, now! You see what I have unleashed!"

Kermorvan visibly gathered his wits, and considered. "Yes. And I can find some counsel in what you have told me. What can be made, as I said, can be unmade. Or it can be countered. Make some other weapon, since this particular power of yours is with you once more, and go up against it."

"But how?" breathed Elof, "I lack the knowledge—"

"Which your former master has. A problem, yes. But do you not see that he also lacks something? The power! The art, or whatever you call it, or he would have made such a terrible thing himself, and never have entrusted it to an apprentice. Perhaps he did not expect it to come so powerful from your hands—but I wonder . . . That absence of his was so convenient; he may have been tempting you, to see what you might produce. He may even have planted the seed of that betrayal of your fellow apprentice in your mind, which would lift some of it from you. But whatever the reason, you have one great comfort, evidently—in this strange art of ours, you are more potent than he!"

Elof sat gaping like an idiot, as the clear cold voice hammered home its truths. Waves washed through him as they fell against the beach, and he felt something burgeon within him, rising from toe tip to the roots of his hair, so that it bristled and rose. His hand sank to the goad at his belt, closed around characters he had remembered. *"Yes!"* he breathed. "It must be so! He *knew* . . ."

"So! Then your problem is simple. Find yourself a better master, and learn what you need from him."

"But who? Most mastersmiths would have no truck with a vagrant like me—except old Hjoran, and he knows nothing of the kind of things I would need . . ."

"No masters among men, maybe—but there are others."

"Others?"

"Aye, and you have met them already, and that alone is like a meeting out of dreams to me, or a childhood fable. Again, your master has kept you ignorant of what might serve you in the world. For it has long been said that in the high mountains bordering both Northland and Southland dwell the Elder folk, the stunted ones that in your northern tongue are named the duergar.''

"In my tongue?'' asked Elof. "But before you used it, I never heard the name, not even as a childhood tale. Though I was not told many tales . . . no, not even then."

"Yet it is known even in our poor cloistered Southlands, where no legends ride abroad to smithy doors. In the wild lands on our inland marches, under the shadow of the mountains and the Great Forest, only a few dwell, hillmen and hunters—simple at best, more often cloven in mind. Some claim to have occasional meetings on the high slopes with the Elders of the mountains, and they revere them more than their own civilized lords.'' He shook his head. "It is said they are the greatest masters of smithcraft, and once taught our ancestors. It is said also that seeking them out is deadly peril.'' He sighed. "But our need is great. And you who are so powerful a smith might find welcome among them, for they are clearly no friends of the man you seek to counter, and once you saved them from him. Most important of all, you know what no others seem to— a region where they may actually dwell.''

"I do,'' mused Elof. "Though the aid I gave them is paid, surely, and it would be a long and dangerous journey alone . . .''

"So it would. But you need not go alone. I will come with you—if, after all I have said, you can tolerate me.''

"Tolerate you?'' Elof looked askance at the tall young man beside him, selecting another pebble to throw with deep care and concentration. He thought of a flying leap between ships in poor light, in armor that would drag a man down living into Amicac's jaws if he so much as slipped, all to save lives among his crew. "But you have a purpose here, among the corsairs—''

"My purpose is fighting the Ekwesh. That tore me from my home, and what shreds of prosperity and influence I yet enjoyed. I had hoped to lead this ship in time, to buy and recruit others and weld them into a real shielding force. But last night I saw finally that for all that butcher's work, all the lives lost, I had hardly scratched the surface of their armor! One ship—a thirtieth part of a tenth part of their present fleet, and that barely a tenth of what their force might be, if they are united under one banner! That above all I must fight. And I do firmly believe that you have been sent to me to do that. You, smith, you are my chance, and I must not fail it, or you. I ask again, will you go with me?"

"How old are you, Kermorvan?"

"Twenty-five years."

"You look older. I am only twenty, twenty-one at most, and hardly fit, it seems, to be running loose in this world. If you will tolerate me—why then, I'll go with you gladly."

CHAPTER SIX

On the Anvil

"A dark prospect, and a long journey on two feet," said Kermorvan, as he surveyed the evening landscape spread out before them. Below the hillcrest on which they stood the country fell away to great stretches of tangled woodland and empty plain, without sign of life or habitation; the wind howled across them unhindered. Only on the far horizon could the jagged peaks of mountains be made out, sullen and shadowed below an angry sunset. Never once, though, did he turn and look back to the hills through which they had come, and the bay that lay beyond.

He had insisted that they should slip away at once, before the corsairs awoke. "Or they may try to prevent us. They might even be foolish enough to try main force." He smiled. "Though I doubt if they could stand against you and I together."

"But . . . you don't think you're deserting them?"

"With so much loot? The rascals are richer now than they deserve to be, through me. And by returning these women they can buy off their outlawry and be quit, if they are wise. No, I owe them nothing—though I agree they might not see it in that fashion! So let us be gone!"

Thus they had hastily gathered gear and food together, and made their way out of the inlet and along the sandy shore of the bay to where its cliffs could more easily be climbed. Kermorvan, in addition to the single-handed sword he usually wore, bore a heavy pack that Elof guessed contained his war gear, but it seemed to slow him not at all as he bounded from rock to rock with an ease the smith's shorter limbs could not match. Through the rolling hills beyond, Kermorvan kept up a punishing pace, and stopped only as the sun fell toward the distant peaks.

"You see," he pointed out, "our search took us north of the marshes into the Debatable Lands—there they lie, that dark and hazy expanse! To the northeast there, already in the long mountain-shadow, is the southward way you and your friend took." Elof thought of Roc, as he often did, and wondered how he had fared among his own people. What would he make of this strange character, this corsair with lordly manners? They had one thing in common, beyond doubt, and that was a kinder heart than their outward selves suggested. "We, though, must seek a quicker way north," Kermorvan added. "Even if it is a whit more dangerous. So we will follow the High roads that run by the coast at first, and only later turn off toward the mountains." His look grew remote, as if he strove to see further than the eye alone could reach. "I will be glad to see them again, those mountains," he sighed. "They are noble places on their lower slopes, with green woodland and many fair lakes, and the heights had great majesty. I often wished to go higher, but deemed it rash to brave the Ice all alone. And now you tell me you lived there many a long year!"

"In a high house, and no doubt well fortified in more ways than one. But I didn't know you knew the mountains, Kermorvan! You're no northerner, are you?"

"Not I!" he said, laughing. "But when I left my home in the Southlands a few years past I traveled north with some merchants, for a brief season. I journeyed south again down the coast ways, and know something therefore of their broils and pitfalls—though doubt it not, they will have increased. Then it was I saw clear proof what the Ekwesh were about, and grew less blinkered than most of my kin. The little towns raided, they wounded my heart— the rooftrees yet smoldering, the fields laid barren, the bones of their defenders left to the sky to mourn and the scavenging beasts to bury."

Elof nodded. "Perhaps you saw Asenby, where I grew up, left so some seven springtimes gone."

"I saw many such, and no one living to tell me their

name. One looks much like another. Come! We have a long road ahead of us, the more we manage the lighter the morrow!''

"It's almost dark . . ."

"So it is. But would you sleep out on a barren hillside, when there is a fine firwood downhill, with branches to make a good shelter? I'll show you how. Come!''

And thus it was throughout most of the days that followed, with Kermorvan very much the leader of their little party. Elof did not resent this, for the sothran knew the way well, and was moreover a practiced woodsman and accomplished trapper and hunter. Elof thought how much more comfortable such skills would have made him and Roc on their wanderings, and strove to learn from him. That first night a few lopped fir sprays became a welcome roof against the trunk of a great tree. "The art," Kermorvan remarked as he wrapped himself in his great cloak of dark green, "is to make the roof steep enough to spill off rain, but not so high that the warmth of your body goes to heat a great pool of air overhead.'' He pillowed his head on his bundle, and muttered a curse as it clanked. "Not as snug as your smithy, perhaps, but it will serve.''

My smithy! Suddenly a great longing for it flooded over Elof, an overwhelming homesickness. For squalid as it was, it was the only home he had made himself, and he missed the security and peace he had found there, even the monotony that went with it. His precious tools still hung there, if they had not been stolen. Why had it all been wrested away from him? Why should he not simply make his way back there, do what he could, serve in his way? These duergar creatures—how human could they be, dwelling beneath the mountains? What did they live on? They had looked human enough, in their way—but strong and dangerous also, having little in common with ordinary human beings. Even the Mastersmith had feared them, till he had the sword. Seeking them out—a mad idea, forced on him like all the rest . . . He tossed and turned in a fit of resentment, hearing the pine needles whisper vague secrets beneath him. Why? And by whom? What power, what arrogance? He ground his teeth at the memory of that mocking smile, and glared at Kermorvan. In the

morning that one would tell what he knew of Raven, if it
had to be wrung out of him; Elof had to content himself
with that.

He did drowse at last, lulled by the rush of the wind in
the pines overhead and their heavy fragrance, undisturbed
by the owls that came to perch on them and the scurrying
of small things among the pine needles. He woke only
once, with a full moon in his face, and peeped out between the branches to see wide white wings flash across
its disc, once, and vanish. He sank back into sleep, and
dreamed of Kara.

Next day, as they marched down out of the woods and
out onto heathlands, he found Kermorvan still strangely
unwilling to talk outright about the dark visitor. "Somebody once told *you!*"

"I was not under his eye, then!"

"And I am? Then so are you, as long as we're together.
I'd better know something of him for my own protection,
hadn't I?"

"Protection?" Kermorvan sounded puzzled. "Raven is
not evil. Or, I should say, he who is called the Raven, for
it is only a given name; I have heard many others—
Wanderer, Hooded Man, Father of Storm, Lord of the
Battlefield. I know not which, if any, is truly his own.
Such a power is not so easily confined within a single
name."

"A power? A lord of the Ice?"

"Did I not say there were others? Powers that defend
life as the Ice seeks to destroy it? Though which of the
two is stronger, or whether they are equal, or whether both
serve a greater power yet, no one can agree. But such
powers there are, and my people have long revered them—
too long, perhaps, for they have faded into half-truth and
legend, figures on walls and banners, half-remembered
songs, no more. Saithana, if truly she exists, may be one.
But Raven certainly is! For know, smith, that you shod the
steed of a great power that night. If you like, a god!"

"He said as much!" Elof gasped. "But then . . . if this
is as you say, and it makes my head whirl worse than the
wine, he did indeed bring me to meet you . . . for what
purpose?"

Kermorvan shrugged. "Who can say? But purpose there was, and we are working it out with every stride we take. Do you see now why I have not cared to think too heavily about this? Every choice I make, every decision, affects our cause in many subtle ways. And not necessarily for the best! The Raven is not evil, but he does not take sides, they say. He is the defender of life, in all its forms, and human life most of all. He is, or was once, a great sign among us, but I have also heard that he is yet respected, at least, by many of the Ekwesh." He walked on a long way, letting Elof digest that. "And even if he does favor our cause, he may not give the help we would wish. For his is an enemy to sluggish stagnation, it is said, and favors change and growth even at the cost of strife. He will not allow men to become dependent on him, save perhaps to balance the enmity of the Ice. So he will stir their affairs about in strange and willful ways, in the guise of a trickster—as you have found!"

At length Elof said, "Now I come to understand much, and a wider world opens before me. But it is a confused one, and even more dangerous than I had thought it—not merely full of ordinary and unconnected dangers, but a very battleground of forces! Small wonder the Mastersmith denied me such knowledge, he who serves the Ice, seeking to turn me down its paths for his own purposes. But I remember nothing of such lore even from my far childhood in Asenby."

"Aye, such things came to be little thought of there, as the high wisdom of old slipped away and the people's concerns turned more to the harvests of soil and sea. Perhaps this secretive smithcraft of yours helped that dwindling, hoarding knowledge as its wealth, away from the common run of folk. That was one reason I never considered it more than a mere superstition, when first I met it. Now . . ." He gestured helplessly. "A wider world has opened to me also, and every bit as confusing. I held the view of most educated men—among my people, that is—believing the powers were something remote and impersonal, guiding our affairs from afar. I held tales of their appearance in human form parables at best, and at worst lies to the credulous. How after all could some such airy being don a human frame, like a cloak?''

"He seemed solid enough to me, that Raven!'' said Elof sourly. ''And that damned great beast he rode! Or was everything illusion?''

"Perhaps not,'' mused Kermorvan. ''I always found tales of the powers riding from place to place, or indulging in less dignified behavior, absurd or blasphemous. But I remember reading one philosopher who purported to explain them by holding that the powers assumed human form the better to understand us and influence us—sharing the ordinary joys and pains, strengths and hindrances of our bodies, and cloaking much of their awe and might. Another held that they could only affect this material world directly by taking some solid form in it, and that that form was more or less fixed, reflecting their absolute natures. You may guess I thought this feeble stuff then. But now . . .'' He shrugged eloquently. ''I am baffled. And that is not something I will ever readily admit.''

"But the horse rode faster than any normal horse might,'' said Elof thoughtfully. ''Or so it seemed . . .''

And so they made their way up through the wild country, talking and disputing, marveling at each other's wholly different brand of learning. At day's end they often found it had lightened their road, speeding them further on than they expected. In that first day they neared the margins of the Debatable Lands, and at the next day's dawning the High roads of the coast were already in sight.

"I have a little money,'' said Kermorvan thoughtfully. ''Enough, maybe, for a couple of horses, when we come to somewhere that will sell them.''

"Might it not be better kept for food?'' asked Elof.

"No, I think not. Speed will help us, at least for a time. If pressed, we can always sell the horses again. Or eat them,'' he added thoughtfully. Elof grimaced.

But it was long before they found anywhere to buy food or horses, for the first small town they came to along the roads lay in ruins, and the next also, and the next. They might perhaps have found some stored food the fire had missed, but neither man could bring himself to search. It had all happened some months since, but the stench of fire and decay hung over them yet, and unburied skulls still grinned among the fireweed in the blackened fields. These towns had lain between the roads and the sea; the next, Randeby, was inland, and built around a high bluff, and it stood, after a fashion, having driven off a heavy attack with loss. But there the fugitives from the other towns had come, eating up the already scant supplies. Famine and pestilence hung over its walls, and gaunt-cheeked men and women encamped at its gates swooped down on the travelers with savage shouts the moment they were seen. Kermorvan had to fell three to drive them off, and for all the rest of that day he was silent. "Human wolves!" he said at last. "Poor creatures! For the last small coin in our purses, or crust in our satchels."

"Or even the flesh on our bones," said Elof dourly. "So I read their taunts. Thus the Ekwesh drag us down to their level."

"And yet there is food all around them, for the hunting. But I will not risk staying to teach them the skill." He gave a wry laugh. "The Raven may have been kinder than you knew. There will be little enough traffic moving on the roads this year, even inland, if this is the rule."

Elof nodded. "I might have starved even as they do. I wish I could help them!"

"Rid them of the Ekwesh, then. For without that all lesser help is meaningless."

They slept in trees that night, and after, to put off any pursuers. But the day after that, as the road curved well away from the sea, they came to Tensborg, another and much larger town that had not been attacked or over-whelmed by fugitives, and found that though there was little food to spare there were horses in plenty, kept for the sothran traders who had not yet come this year. They bought two decent mounts at small cost, and thereafter made good time northward. For a month they rode up the High roads along the coast, seeing the northern country-side alter gradually around them. As the roads turned in-land, skirting a hilly region, they entered a changing woodland. The high redwoods and bristlecone pines be-came fewer; hemlocks, oaks, firs and spruces took their places, and the smaller dawn redwoods. The undergrowth, too, grew thinner; the high sword ferns disappeared, the anemones and rose rhododendrons, with their brilliant blooms, became gradually smaller and paler and finally all but vanished. But as the roads neared the sea once more, the woodlands themselves vanished among low hills topped with scrubby grass, and in the dunes only verbena and sea lavender showed bright. It was around the sea's margin that they saw yet more of the havoc the Ekwesh wrought among the little towns. "Always by the sea!" said Kermorvan coldly. "For the Ekwesh are not great horsemen, and have not mastered the act of fighting on horseback—you need proper stirrups for that! So they bring no horses with them, and will not roam far from their ships lest they be cut off."

Elof looked to the east, where rolling hills rich with grass and little patches of woodland stretched away into the dim distance. This was the country he had grown up in; he could not be so very far south of Asenby here. Yet it felt not in the least like home . . . "So the inland towns are safe?"

"No! Though they think they are, here and in the south. When those barbarians meet no resistance they will surely move further and further from their ships, bring or capture horses—oh, I have tried to tell so many men that, traders and farmers and fat little burgesses. And where has it got me? They don't *want* to believe! The Ekwesh are another man's problem, never theirs."

"But if it is the Mastersmith who drives them on, then besting him—"

The swordsman shook his head. "It may save the situation for a while, but not forever. He merely seizes his advantage, exploiting what his masters have already prepared, long before you forged that blade. Without him the Ekwesh would simply go on as they have been doing, and sooner or later they would have struck at the south. Other, stronger forces drive their empire on, and whether it is in our or any man's hands to best then, I do not know."

At length they came to a region where high hills and deep inlets blocked the coast way, and the roads turned away inland. Here they were in much worse repair, and the going was slower; it was weeks more before the travelers reached the feet of the mountains, and high summer blazed down upon them. It was the best and safest time to venture into the mountains, but as they did not mean to go by the well-trodden roads, or stay within the usual passes, the horses would be no use. They sold them at a little town Elof remembered from his first wanderings as reasonably honest, and with the proceeds bought food. But Elof held back a few coins to treat with the town smith for metal and the use of the forge. He took two strong staves and shod them with metal spikes and heavy beaked heads so well crafted that the smith suspected a plan to discredit him, and had to be persuaded otherwise at the point of Elof's blade. "At least that master of mine gave me some skill in the mountains! Picks like these may save our lives on the high slopes."

Kermorvan cocked an eyebrow at the fuming smith. "Then let us put them to the test at once! There is no safe bed for us here now, in any case. The mountains must provide!"

They slept that night in a small wood as they often did, a league or so above the town. But just as the moon was sinking they were rudely awakened by a sharp scuffling at their roof of branches, and springing up they found themselves face to muzzle with a vast bear. It sprang back at their sudden yells, and they had time to draw their swords. Moaning in anger, it reared up on its hind legs, twice as tall as Kermorvan, and cuffed its huge paws at them. The swordsman grabbed his pack and drew out his mailcoat, trailing it like a net ready to tangle its claws. But seeing them stand their ground the bear ducked down with a gruff snort and went crashing off into the wood. Kermorvan shivered. "I thought we would be safe, as we have been till now. Most beasts will flee a sleeping man, or ignore him."

"Indeed," mused Elof. "The smaller bears may be savage on occasion, but the giant breed who winter in the caves rarely eat meat, even carrion. What made him so aggressive?"

"Bears were ever fickle in their ways," shrugged Kermorvan. "Well, let us rebuild our shelter, and take turns on watch. I will take first turn, till moonset."

Elof nodded, but was silent. It seemed strange to him, that attack, like the symptom of some hidden sickness in the woods. He rolled in his cloak, now cool and unwelcoming, and did his best to sleep. But all through the next days, as they climbed through the steep hillside forests, the image of illness kept coming back to him, in the blighted trees, the weird phosphorescent fungus growths on the dead stumps, the huge patches of poison ivy that seemed to spring up at every turn. Vines and parasites trailed rootlets round their necks, creeps caught their ankles, thorns snagged their clothes and pricked their skins. Things of small moment, perhaps, but they were matched by the behavior of the beasts. More than once the travelers had to leap back as bronzen snakes struck rattling at their legs instead of slithering to escape. Kermorvan, gazing up at a strange sound in a twilit tree, almost lost an eye to a great horned owl that swooped upon him and was only with difficulty thrashed away. In the heat of the noon, flies came droning down the slanting sunbeams and would not let them rest an instant; toward evening the bloodsuckers hung about them in a whining cloud. All usual enough in woodlands, but not in such intensity. It seemed to Elof that some change, subtle and sinister, was taking place in the woodlands he had once roamed through on the Mastersmith's expeditions. All too often the blood-freezing yell of haunting daggertooth would send them hurrying on with drawn swords.

"How many of the brutes can there be?" panted Kermorvan. "So many in this small area would surely strip it of game in a week! Or is one persistent animal hunting us?"

Elof shrugged. They slept in a tree that night, lashing themselves to the boughs with the morse-hide ropes they had brought from the ship. Elof lay awake long on his perch, though it was not too uncomfortable, staring up at the pale glimmer over the mountains, at the edge of the night. He thought of the pent-up power it reflected. Was the spreading sickness, the new hostility of the wood, yet another kind of reflection? A chill breeze crept through his cloak; he shivered, and looked away. But before he was wholly asleep he heard a soft pattering on the leaves

over his head, and great round drops came trickling down
onto his face. He groaned, but there was no risking a
shelter on the ground now; he would have to suffer the
rain where he was.

The lower woodlands were hard enough to endure, but
as they neared the higher slopes worse was to come. They
had long since exhausted the food they carried, and it was
chiefly Kermorvan's skill at trapping that kept them alive;
they could find little enough game to hunt. "I almost wish
that daggertooth would come after us now!" muttered
Elof, worrying at the flesh of a small shrew-thing. "We
might see what his steaks taste like!"

"He could hardly be any tougher," agreed Kermorvan,
thrusting his portion back over the little fire to cook further. Then he sprang to his feet, overturning the meat,
stamped the flames to embers and whipped out his sword.
"Hau yma!" he whispered. *"What moves?"*

Faintly Elof heard it at first, a low soft crackle, the
sudden burst of a dead branch on the forest floor, bushes
rustling as they were thrust aside. Something was moving
indeed in the twilight, something slow but heavy. And yet
there seemed to be no rhythm in the sound, no separate
footfalls.

"It's . . . slithering . . ." he whispered.

"Aye . . ." muttered Kermorvan, and then suddenly he
thrust himself sideways into Elof, slamming them both
into the weeds behind the bole of a great tree. "Climb!"
he hissed, and sprang for a lower branch, while Elof was
still trying to collect his wits. Kermorvan saw him stagger
up, and swung back down to reach out a hand, just in
time. There was a sudden loud smashing in the bushes,
and with a rush something huge came sliding and slithering into the little ring of bushes. Gasping, they hung there
in the tree, Elof slung precariously between the branch
and Kermorvan's hand. From where they were they could
not see what had come at them, until there was a loud
rasping sniff and it moved forward. Then a great dark
flank slid into view. It rested on the ground like a serpent,
but it was larger by far than any serpent they had ever
seen, and a short stubby leg protruded from it. A long-
clawed foot crunched down on the embers of their fire,

and there was another loud sniffing sound, a rustle as of
scaly skin, a waft of putrid, musky stench. Elof's blood
ran cold, but his curiosity, as ever, overran it. Detaching
himself from Kermorvan's unwavering grip, he leaned forward, trying to make out what manner of beast it could
be. But unfortunately, perhaps, it was facing away from
them, and he saw only a thick hindleg, some twelve feet
behind the foreleg. Just in front of it lay their packs, with
so many things they could not spare—

Elof swung down on the branch, and hung an instant by
his hands. Then he swung back, kicked forward, and
dropped light as a feather on a bare patch of pine needles,
muffling his footfall. He bent, scooped up the packs, praying Kermorvan's would not clank again, and flung himself
into the weeds as the dark flank heaved and the leg thrust
out. But the thing had not noticed him. In another wave
of stench it slithered slowly forward, almost rowing itself
along with its short legs, and went snaking off downhill.
But it was a long time after the sound died away before
either man dared move.

Kermorvan swung himself down nimbly. "Kerys! That
was bravely done, my smith! What in the world was it?"

"Don't look at me for an answer! A dragon, perhaps?"

"I think not. I remember dragons on old tapestries in
our house, made by people who knew them only too well,
and none looked like that. Besides, that seemed a very
beast, a stupid one, and dragons are said to be—something
more. It moved like a wall lizard—a quick rush, then
rest."

"A lizard halfway to a snake, then, and as big around
as a horse. I have never seen or heard of anything such in
these woods."

"Then I'll wager it's something off the Ice, some beast
let loose to wreak havoc in its vanguard. Faugh! The foulness of it! Let's be far from here, for our dinner's ended
for tonight."

There were other encounters before they left the woods,
though none so close or fearful. Once as they made ready
to sleep they saw something dimly phosphorescent go hopping along between the tree trunks below, and where it
went even the faint night murmurs fell silent. And later,

as they were casting about for a way out to the slopes above, something came crashing and blundering across the path they had taken, away downhill; they could not see it, but from the threshing of the bushes it might be a man, if a very clumsy one. Neither curious enough to linger, they cut their way through onto the stony slopes with as little ado as possible.

"And yet here is no refuge," said Elof as they toiled up the rough hillside, the rock's bare bones showing between the thin coating of topsoil, scrubgrass and stunted shrubs. "For I remember this place, and we are now no more than a day or so south of the pass above the Mastersmith's house, and that means we take care; in clear weather he was often abroad. North of that, beyond his valley, he never took us; there the Ice thrusts glaciers deep among the mountains. Where those duergar creatures left us, that lies eastward around those peaks there, about two days' walk. That seems as good a place as any to search."

"Then we will climb to just below the snow line," said Kermorvan, "and make our way round."

Before long even the last traces of green died away beneath their feet, save for a few feeble plants in earthy crevices, and they were marching along great ridges of solid rock, or slipping and slithering across wide swaths of loose rock and scree, or scrambling up piled boulders. The wind had a bite to it now to match its howl, pressing their cloaks flat, plucking at their bags, lashing their faces till eyes grew gritty and nostrils burned. It was mustering the gray clouds like an army, piling them up in ranks around the northward peaks; Kermorvan looked up at them anxiously. He dragged out a scarf as long as his arms, and was binding it round his face when he realized Elof had none; at once he sliced it neatly on his half-drawn blade and handed over the remainder. Elof took it with a sober nod of thanks, for he could think of nothing to say.

But at last, late in the second day, they rounded the peak into the lee. Wind still eddied around them, but with less force, and they took a moment to rest. Elof looked about him at the mountainside, remembering those first dazed moments of a strange freedom. There were the lakes, the woods, but no longer as friendly as they had seemed. The bleak gray light did not help. He turned away to the ridge above. "Beyond there lie the glaciers. The duergars cannot have gone that way. It must have been somewhere on this slope they vanished. Or appeared to. It was dark, and they had the only lanterns."

Kermorvan kicked at a hefty boulder. "I did not realize the Ice was quite so close. That bodes ill. If they do have a door or gate here, something that could make that deep sound you heard, they will have disguised it with all their skill—too much, perhaps, for us. But we will search, all the same." He looked up at the sky again, the mustering of the clouds. "Let us hope we find it soon. For in these high places, even at this season, such a sky can mean snow."

Darkness was falling as they toiled up to the ridge, weary, chill and sick at heart. They had quartered the whole wide slope between them, and found no single boulder, no crack in the steep rock walls, no break in the scree, which seemed anything but natural. Only the very summit of the ridge remained, and it looked too bare to hide even a rathole, scoured flat by the relentless north wind. Beyond it, too, the stark glow seemed stronger than ever against the gray clouds, and shone like a warning even on the brief mist of their breath. *This too may be frozen. . . .*

Kermorvan, as usual, reached the rim a little ahead. And there Elof feared for him, for he saw the swordsman halt in his tracks, silhouetted against the glare, stand staring a moment and sink very slowly to one knee. Elof sprang to catch up, and himself came reckless over the rise, and stood transfixed at the sight spread out before him.

They had come to the rim of a deep valley in the mountains, a steep walled gouge like a swordblow among the peaks. Somewhere in his dazed mind Elof realized it must be directly opposite the Mastersmith's valley, stemming from the far slopes of the same peak. But that side was merely barren and cold. This side was in the grip of the Ice.

So it was that Elof first beheld the great Adversary, and he also sank down, daunted. It was a sight of awe and wonder, and what he had least of all expected, it was beautiful, so fair the marvel of it awoke coursing ice in his very veins. Far out into the distance below him stretched the glacier, infinitely far along the widening valley between dwindling peaks and out onto a vast expanse of softly glowing gray-white. The eastern walls of the mountains sank into it as if into a sea, overwhelmed; here and there, as if in mockery of former majesties, a remote peak protruded, blunted and crumbling like a slighted fortress. Beyond these pathetic remnants it stretched out into an infinite distance so featureless that the eye strained to focus on it and blurred painfully, finding no hold or reference. Even a horizon seemed to be lacking, perhaps because there were gray clouds there to merge with it. Whatever the truth of it, the sight filled Elof with the sudden chill feeling that he, that the whole warmly living world of earth and flowers and beasts and men and women were nothing but a very thin crust of dirt upon an infinity of cool sterile whiteness, a smear of filth on the chill beauty of a gem, at the mercy of its slightest movement or disturbance, utterly insignificant. Even when he shifted his gaze to the high peaks above him and across the valley, seeking comfort in their strength, they seemed things of slight and temporary moment, no more a barrier than their buried kin had been. It was simply a matter of time, and the Ice had already long spans of years frozen at its heart. What did man have?

Then suddenly he held his gaze, peering, questing into the gloom beyond the glow. He scrambled up, braving the wind that whipped at him, shielding his eyes with his hand till he was sure of what he saw. He turned and found Kermorvan at his side. The swordsman's face was pale and stern, full of awe and wonder, but no slightest trace of fear; it was set like flint, and the gleam in his eyes as they scanned the endless distances was a challenge returned. "You saw something?"

"I . . . think so! Out across the valley, among the high peaks beyond the end of it, see! *See—*"

Kermorvan rubbed his eyes, peered and shook his head. Then he turned back, blinking, and looked at one peak again. "I see . . . the faintest of orange glows . . ."

"You do indeed!"

Kermorvan eyed him doubtfully. "It could be many things . . ."

"So it could. But do you see any more hopeful sign?"

Kermorvan shook his head grimly. "I do not, for this slope below us seems as empty as the rest. Very well, let us be on our way, for it will be sore walking to bring us round all these mountains." He swung his pack back onto his shoulders, and was about to set off down the slope again when Elof caught him by the arm.

"Not that way," he said. "We dare not go round, I know that part of the mountains only too well. We would have to risk crossing the Mastersmith's road, and near his house!"

"Well then, what other way may we take?"

Elof bit his lip, and looked away, down into the valley far below. "There is only one. Across the Ice."

"*What!*" Kermorvan clapped a hand to his sword. "I'll take my chances with your accursed master—"

Again Elof held him back, this time with real force. "You fool! If he can compel the Ekwesh, could he not take you without a blow struck? And not simply slay you, but bend you to his will, and set you against all you now seek to preserve! Is *that* the chance you prefer?"

Kermorvan stood angry and irresolute, looking down the slope to the distant valley, and up toward the crest and the Ice glow. It was obvious which he preferred, but he could not escape the smith's logic. "I said I would go with you," he muttered. "Do not doubt me. But will we not be risking the same, or worse, upon the Ice?"

"It may not be so terrible, not here at its margins!" insisted Elof. "You saw as I did, nothing moved in that valley, nothing stirred. And it is not wide, we could easily be across in a night if we hurry—"

"A night—" began the swordsman, gazing back down the valley again, but then he caught Elof's arm, and pointed.

Far below, at the very margin of the nearest patch of woodland, something was slipping through the bushes, something big enough to make them rustle and quiver without showing itself. But then, as the bushes ended among high stones, it did emerge for an instant into the gleam of stars and Ice, slipping across an open patch to take cover behind a great jagged rock. It was man-shaped, but chillingly unlike a man, huge and heavier in the shoulders and high-crowned head, with long arms that swung at its side as it loped along.

"*Kerys!*" breathed the swordsman. "Think you that's what was on our trail in the woods?"

"It moved in much the same fashion—but listen!" A little way along the line of bushes something else was rustling its way forward, and there were other sounds from deeper in the wood, a soft guttural grunting. "A whole pack of them!" said Elof quietly. "Well, warrior, are you still for going back that way?"

"Suddenly the Ice acquires a certain appeal," admitted Kermorvan drily. "But might those things not be set to drive us onto it?"

"Perhaps. But only at our last extremity, frightened, slow and unwilling. They might not expect a sudden bold dash . . ."

"I would not call twelve hours' fast marching a dash, however bold. But you have the right of it, smith! Lead on!"

Together they strode back up to the crest and, as lightly and quietly as possible, began to descend the far slope. "This isn't too hard!" whispered Elof.

"No more is the path to the River, they say," countered Kermorvan gloomily. "One way."

"Ach, save your encouragement for the Ice, we'll surely need it there!" Surprisingly, Kermorvan chuckled, and climbed with a lighter step thenceforward.

At first sight, from high above, the distant Ice had looked glass-smooth and dazzling white, but as they clambered down the steep slopes the glacier that filled the valley seemed grayer and more marked. Elof could see that in fact it was not at all smooth, and only anything like white in the center; along either edge ran great striations, almost as dark as the rock they clashed with. As they came closer these resolved into dark uneven ridges streaked along the surface of the Ice like sediment in a frozen river. "I have heard them talked of," said Kermorvan, "and called *moraines*. They are made of rock and debris the Ice has ground away in its passage, freed when a little of the surface melts in warmer weather. No doubt many a proud mountaintop lies before you there. And they will not make our path any easier.''

The moraines lay the length of the valley, but there were other, finer markings lying across the surface, cross-hatched in places and deepened by long shadows. ''They look like wrinkled skin,'' said Elof. ''Ancient skin, withered and grimy. And see there where the valley bends, they deepen and come together as they might at an elbow! As if the glacier were the limb of some horrible beast-thing . . .''

''Those would be crevasses, I fear,'' said Kermorvan. ''Thicker and deeper at the elbow, as you say. Let us keep well away from there! They will be hard enough to avoid as it is!''

And indeed, when they at last drew near the margins of the glacier, Elof wondered if he had not led them astray, so rough did their way look, and so fearsome the moaning of the wind among the moraines. A frozen film, clear, hard and treacherous, lay over all the lower rocks, and slippery pockets of dirty snow lay frozen between the stones. One last step from the rim, he stumbled badly, almost fell, and halted, wavering. Then, cautiously, he took his first step onto the Great Ice.

For a moment he thought crazily he was back in his forge, and had trodden on a hot iron coulter. The searing blaze in his worn boots was cold, not flame, but the sensation was the same, a fearful burning that mounted to his calves. He hopped with the agony, scrambled up onto some stones to find a moment's relief, but it was as if ice was touched to his bare nerves. He hesitated, gasping, desperate to spring back to the rocks. A longer time he might have stood there, perhaps to his own destruction, had Kermorvan not plunged straight out among the frozen debris at the moraine's edge without so much as breaking stride. That took away Elof's choices; he could only set his teeth in his lip, and stumble after.

He was startled to see Kermorvan hurrying along, choosing his way carefully in the twilight, but swinging his pickstaff and bounding from stone to Ice and back again with all his usual energy. It struck Elof just how bold this man was, marching out to confront a thing that had probably been a childhood bogey, and in manhood had come to embody the powers he hated. There might be tremors in his mind, but in his stride none, nor did he fail to turn back to help the smith when he slipped noisily down a high ridge in the uncertain dusk. By then, an hour on, numbness had dulled the pain enough to let Elof speak. "Don't you feel it?"

Kermorvan crouched down beside him among the debris of shattered rock. "Feel what?" It was obvious he did not. Elof wondered, but did not explain. Kermorvan drew his cloak about him. "The wind, yes! And cursedly exposed, out there in the open, with so much light around us. It might be harder going in the dark, but I would be less worried about unfriendly eyes. May those clouds come south before moonrise, and blot out the stars also!"

But he was not to have his wish, for though the clouds mounted into immense black ramparts on the northern horizon, the wind died, the chill air fell still and silent. The sky over the valley remained open and bitterly clear, and the stars as they came out looked down on their warped reflections in the Ice.

There came a sudden shimmer in the air high overhead, as if a vast invisible curtain had been momentarily twitched across it from one horizon to the other. Kermorvan, rising to his feet, gasped and ducked down, and Elof beside him. A sound grew in the silence, a faint angry crackle at the edge of hearing. The curtain twitched again, this time a pale rippling flicker of reds and greens, growing ever more intense; blues and purples shone only a second before the dark sky swallowed them. Pale yellow streaks of light arced across the darkness and diminished. A corona of cold fire, impossibly vast, rippled across the stars and shamed them, a vision of piercing splendor.

"What sight is this?" breathed the sothran, shielding his eyes.

"The North Lights!" whispered Elof, feasting his gaze. Another streak crossed behind them. "And a rain of starstones to go with them! I have seen them before, but from a distance, and never so gigantic, never . . .''

"What could it portend?"

"Nothing, that I know of," answered the smith. "And yet . . . The Mastersmith did once say that they might herald some meeting of forces—what more, I can't imagine."

"A meeting!" muttered Kermorvan grimly. "Then let us not be caught in the middle!" Half-crouching, hiding from watchful eyes, they began to creep forward along the moraine until they were opposite the nearest part of the far slope. "Now there is nothing for it but the open, between the crevasses," added the swordsman tautly. "And the longest part of our way. Come!"

And so they made their way across the whiter open area of the glacier, striding along broad ridges, creeping across narrower ones on all fours with deadened fingers that could barely grasp their staves, hearing little gouts of half-solid snow fall away from under their feet and go slipping down into the deep crevasses at either side. They landed with a soft echoing splash, suggesting that hard-edged ice awaited them down there if they fell, and not soft snow. The cold fire overhead beat down on them, setting strange livid hues in their faces, lending shadows a faint flickering animation that made finding their footing doubly difficult, filling the distance with sinister promises of movement. Strange forms took shape and danced among the patches of clear ice; once Elof seemed to see Kara's face in the reflections, gazing at him in fear and warning, and later he saw Kermorvan rub his eyes and mutter, "The Gate! The High Gate . . ." No way among the crevasses was ever as clear as it had seemed at first, and they had to be forever spying out new ones. But these seemed always to drive them up the valley, away from the wall, and they became acutely aware that precious hours were passing. Kermorvan hugged chill hands; Elof, scanning the open distances of the valley, flexed his numbed limbs and remembered all he had heard of the dangers of frostburn. All of a sudden Kermorvan came to a halt, so suddenly they almost collided, and stood peering down the valley. Then he shook his head impatiently and was about to move on when Elof tugged him back. "No! I see it too!"

With one accord they sank down in the soft snow of a low drift, and watched. A fleck of shadow seemed to detach itself from the far side of the valley and come gliding out across the black length of moraine, as smoothly as if it was a polished floor. With a slow bobbing movement the shadow drifted toward the clear center of the Ice, gliding over the crevasses as if they were not there. It had man's shape, as an empty cloak left hanging has it, but drawn out, spider-thin and gray. Swiftly it advanced to the center and seemed to hang there, floating like a frond in a still pool, the high hood bobbing gently from side to side. Slowly it turned, the travelers ducked down, but it stopped and hung there swaying once again. It seemed to be facing southward, to the Valley's end and the furthest extremity of the Ice.

Fearing to stir under the thin cloak of snow, Elof slowly turned his head and stared into the distance. For long minutes there was nothing, then he thought he saw a flicker of movement. It was like a shadow growing thicker, darker, coagulating into solid form. His scalp prickled. He was seeing something take shape there, out of the empty air, a figure forming on the Ice where an instant before there was nothing. It was there now, and coming forward. But it seemed small and clumsy, like an insect stumbling over rocks compared to the thing that hung there, not two thousand paces distant. He risked a glance at Kermorvan; he also was looking south, and grimly. If they moved on, the cloaked thing might not spy them, but the newcomer surely would. They could only wait like stones, and hope to be taken for them.

Slowly, awkwardly, the new figure approached with none of the other's eerie grace. It seemed shapeless, inchoate, topped with a dully gleaming carapace, like an insect's head. It took Elof a moment to see it was human, and in fact striding over rough terrain with unusual ease. The shapelessness was a wide dark cloak or robe, the carapace a metal headpiece, a helm.

Elof choked. His heart faltered, then thundered against his ribs till it seemed the valley wall must resound as

loudly. There was no mistaking that helm, richly ornamented, mailed, masked, though little he had dreamed of
the true power worked into it. *Of moving swiftly, and unseen* . . . And the walk he knew no less well, the sharp,
measured stride that set the robes fluttering like dark pen-
nants in the still air. Just opposite them, two hundred paces
at most, the figure stooped, the helm's malign eyes turned
this way and that, uneasily. Towering above, the hooded
shape swayed patiently, waiting. Then the mail of the mask
was swung back, the helm lifted in gloved hands, dark
hair that seemed frosted streamed down around wide
shoulders, and Elof looked once more on the pale proud
features of his former master. Again the Mastersmith
glanced from side to side, as if he felt burning eyes upon
him, but then he looked up, straight into the smoke-dark
shadow of that swaying hood. He gazed a moment, and
then, very solemnly, he bowed.

A flash overhead, sudden and startling, tore Elof's gaze
away. The starstones were raining thicker and faster now,
darting through the paths of the stars like mocking children, streaking the night sky with orange and red until
they rivaled the Lights. But then these also blazed out,
with a power that charged the air till it cracked like a forest
fire and the travelers felt the hair lift and bristle on their
heads. Behind the Lights the stars seemed to leap and
dance in the distorted air, bent into a mighty corona with
its heart among the Lights. They rippled once, twice, three
times, even more violently, and then it was as if they folded
in on themselves and became solid, like a mantle falling
to earth. A great cone of bright radiance hung in the air
above the heart of the Ice, pulsating like a heart, and the
man and man-shape alike turned to face it. Within that
mantle a form took shape, stately, cloud-tall, pale as pearl,
thin as smoke, its own light shining through it. A woman's
shape, unclad, arms outstretched and long hair streaming
out behind her as in some unfelt wind. Slowly, solemnly,
the gray hood inclined. But the man bowed deep, deeper,
till he sank down upon his knees, and forward still till, arms
outthrust, his forehead rested in abject adoration upon the
glittering Ice.

"Now!" hissed Kermorvan, for the eyes were turned

away. "Now, for your life!" He swept out his sword, then gasped in horror as green phosphorescence leaped and wavered on its point and trickled crackling down the blade.

A mighty gust of panic surged through Elof. He seized the glaring swordblade and quenched the balefire under his clenched fingers; Kermorvan slammed it back in its scabbard, and they turned to run. Down the drift they slithered, crouching like apes to stay in the scant cover, bounding along on their staves, stumbling and falling into deeper patches of snow, never caring for the crevasses that gaped hungry on every flank. Neither dared look back, but ran and ran till every breath came like fire in a raw throat and their limbs were knotted with pain. Once they went slipping and sliding away down into one of the crevasses, but the snow they carried before them broke their fall; they scrambled up and went stumbling on in the shelter of its high walls. Climbing out at the end was less easy. They had to hack steps in an overhanging wall, but when they managed it, and lay gasping on the brink, the radiance at the heart of the Ice lay far behind them, no more now than a cool, distant glare through which no detail could be seen.

At length the two travelers picked themselves up, shaken and trembling, and without a word they turned and went trudging off toward the dark lines of the moraines. Every now and again Kermorvan would turn and look back to be sure nothing was on their trail, but only once, as they crested a heaped moraine, did he clutch Elof's arm, and point. They threw themselves down in the snow. A long shadow wavered across the glacier, but the figure that cast it against the nacreous light was small, striding away southward once again. It seemed to Elof that his head was bare, though it was too far to be sure. When they looked back once again, he had not vanished; shrunken by distance, a tiny figure still labored on across the rubble of the glacier. "Your late master, I presume?" inquired Kermorvan sardonically, though there was a catch in his voice. "I wonder why he does not use the helm once more?"

Elof shrugged, and walked onward.

The way was less far than it seemed, for the moraines on the glacier's northern flank were closer together than on the south, and lower. They crossed them easily in an hour or two, and were glad of their shelter; a wind was rising now, and when they looked up at the sky the stars were still, and vanishing behind the clouds' swift onrush. Beneath them the Ice glittered empty and lifeless once more.

At long last the day dawned, though bleak and gray, with no sun visible. Kermorvan shook his head like a man awaking from a dream. Ahead of them now the peaks rose, and even their stern barrenness seemed more wholesome than the Ice. Only two hours after dawn they stepped off it as they might off a ship. When his foot left its surface the cold fire drained at once from Elof's legs, so immediately he all but staggered and fell with the relief; only a chill, normal and endurable, remained. Kermorvan again seemed to sense nothing unusual. Instead he was gazing up at the clouds and sniffing the air. "Snow indeed!" he muttered. "When it cannot shield us any longer, and we have no way but to climb! Elof, my smith, pray that we may find your mysterious light soon, or it may be the death of us! Come!"

The wind moaned around them as they climbed the valley wall. It was steeper here than on the south side, and they had to keep their arms free to climb, so their cloaks could not protect them against the biting wind. The rock, though hard, was cracked in many places by the bitter cold of the Ice, and more than once what seemed a sturdy ledge would go sliding out from under their probing feet and rattle away in a shower of little stones to crash down at the rim of the glacier. "And reveal where we are, if any follow," grunted Kermorvan. "But at least the slope seems to be growing gentler. Here comes the snow!"

The first few flakes were indeed swirling around them, and more came streaming down along the wind, striking the cliff on either side and swirling in their faces as they toiled on up and came at last to a long slope leading up the peak they sought. Soon the snow was lying in their path, great fat flakes that melted only at the edges, that fused together into hard ice underfoot, coating the stone like glass. Elof had to take care not to tread in Kermorvan's steps. By the time they came on an easier part of the slope, it was already deep in snow. Their boots picked it up as a hard shell and grew heavy, so they must needs break it away with the staves. "If this gets any thicker we may miss our way," said Kermorvan anxiously, "and in the mountains that is deadly! But we are not so far below where you saw that light, now. The clearest way up would be to follow this rockwall here—" He touched it, and pulled away his hand with a cry of surprise. "It's warm! At least, warmer than it should be! And see, at the top there, those cracks like great vents—and smoke is rising! Earthfires!" He slammed his staff down furiously. "So that is what the glow must have been! Nothing would live underground where the fires are strong! We have doomed ourselves, and for nothing!"

"Do not be so sure!" said Elof sharply, though he, too, felt a cold qualm of doubt. "The Mastersmith's house was built over just such a place, and harnessed the fires for the forge! Might not the duergar do the same?"

Kermorvan started to shake his head, shrugged and picked up his staff. A curtain of gusting snow swept down the slope, piling what had already fallen into deeper drifts. "It makes no odds!" he shouted over the sudden roar of wind. "We may as well die looking—"

A huge shadow reared up in the snow. A vast arm outthrust clutched at his throat. It was as sudden as that, and he was hurled spinning against the rock. But Elof had time to duck, and the thing went blundering past him, toward the cliff. Rock splintered and fell away, and there was a bellowing yell of pain and rage. Elof bent down, grabbed Kermorvan and dragged him away from the wall and a little way up the slope. He lay gasping; Elof stood over him, drew his sword and hefted his pick in his left hand. But after only a moment Kermorvan was struggling and cursing back to his feet. "What was that?" he demanded, fumbling with his scabbard.

"A snow-troll, I think," said Elof tautly, "though I've never seen one. Gray fur, black claws and the size—" He licked dry lips, and felt the cracks in them sting. "I think it was what followed us in the forest; they go there sometimes—" The snow swirled, there was another bellow and a sudden rush from behind them. Elof turned, slipped and fell flat. A huge shadow swooped down over him—and then whipped back, with a jarring shriek of rage. Something hot and stinking sprayed across Elof's jerkin, and when he scrambled up he saw a great spatter of red in the snow, and Kermorvan standing with smoking blade. "Back to back!" he yelled, "and we'll hold them! *Morvan morlanhal!*"

A chorus of shrieks answered him, and dreadful shapes loomed up in the whiteness, closing in around them. Arms swept out, and Elof hewed at them; dark blood fountained, and a huge hand fell writhing into the snow. Behind him it sounded as if an axe smote solid wood, a metallic snapping clang, and Kermorvan staggered back into him as a huge body fell flat in the snow. Off balance, Elof saw a terrible face arise, a snarling, snow-encrusted mask like a fearful parody of a man's, and above it a jagged boulder clasped in black claws. He dropped down past a leg like a gray tree trunk, and even as the stone thudded where he had been he hewed at the monstrous calf. The thing convulsed and toppled, shrieking horribly, and he struggled up and passed his sword through its body. Then he sprang forward into blindness, to where Kermorvan had stood, but was no longer. A gray heap lay sprawled there with a sword-shard glinting in its skull. Troll-shapes loomed around the rock face, three at least, and the warrior was backed up against it, one shoulder streaked with blood, striking out with the splintered stump of his blade. Elof snatched up his pick and hurled it at the broad backs, shrieking mad words of challenge against the wind. One squealed, they turned to face him, and he scythed his sword at them two-handed, the black blade thrumming as it clove the stormblast. He took a step, and astonishingly they fell back; again, and another one loomed up, and was barged aside as once more they gave way. Then as Kermorvan came skidding down the slope Elof sprang forward and hewed in earnest, and they turned and fled. His blade skipped slashing down the straggler's back, and a trail of shrill yelps faded into the snow. "Well fought, smith!" yelled Kermorvan. "But they'll be back, when they're over their fright! Alas, one took my sword in this thick skull!'' He was fumbling furiously in his pack with his wounded arm. ''A dagger—''

''Forget it! Drop that, and come on! If they're coming back we've got to climb! *Climb,* d'you understand me? Those vents—maybe we can find one that's safe! They'll be warm, at least!''

Kermorvan nodded, but clutched the pack protectively to him. Elof gave up and went hurrying up the rock face; Kermorvan stayed on his heels with no apparent difficulty. Rime crusted white on their brows and around their scarved faces, where it melted in their breath and sent little damp trickles down their cheeks. The wind yelled, and the snow lashed and stung their eyes till they could hardly even see the wall they followed. But all of a sudden a new wall was looming up in their path, and in it dim shadows appearing and fading as gusts blew across them, the only dark things in a world lost to whiteness. Eagerly they staggered forward into the wide mouth of the vent, feeling the stone warm indeed under their hands, until Elof collided with a rock face. ''It's blocked!'' he called. ''Try for another!''

''Too late!'' cried Kermorvan. ''They are out there now!'' A yammering cry answered him, as if in mockery. Elof ran his hands desperately over the smooth stone; was he dreaming, or could he still feel air moving around him, air warm as a spring breeze?

Kermorvan was bracing himself, clutching his absurd stump of a sword. ''Try and get to the next one,'' he said calmly. ''Or away altogether, if you can, while they're busy on me. For busy they'll be . . .''

''No, madman!'' barked Elof. ''At least wait! There's something strange here—'' His hand slipped across an outcrop of the rock, and his fingers closed under it. It was thin, too thin—and the shape of it . . . He ducked down and peered through it. Warm air, stale and strange-scented, played over his face, melting the rime of his brows and hair, so he hardly knew whether it was water or tears that came trickling down. ''It's metal! The wall is a casting!''

''*What?*''

''See for yourself! Gridwork, in the rock, sculpted to

look like it! Angled so cunningly you can scarce see
through!''

"Can you open it? They are coming, those out there!"

"Here, take my sword! And give me yours—" Elof ran
knowing fingers over the metal, rapped it and listened to
it ring. It was beautiful, cunning work, but the weakness
of such a casting was that it must look like the rock it was
set in; that strange shape would create uneven points,
stresses . . . He rapped again, and again, listening, and
finally rang the sword pommel against it. "Quickly, if
ever!" hissed Kermorvan. Elof hesitated, dry-mouthed. A
low, gloating cry came from the cave mouth. He jabbed
the blade stump deep into a slot and with all his great
strength bore down on it in one single effort. He felt the
ruined sword bend, creak beneath him. Then there was a
sudden sharp clang, a glint of bright metal, and one small
bar of the grid snapped and bent outward. It was not
enough. In utter desperation he set his fingers in the gap
and heaved, felt it give slightly, braced his feet against the
wall and pushed till the sinews cracked in his broad back.

Kermorvan spun round startled at the grinding squeal
of metal against stone. "Kerys! A gate!" But the moment
his gaze turned there was a rush and rumble at the cave-
mouth, and a great form blocked out the snowlight. Kermorvan whirled and plunged straight at it, Elof's blade
outthrust with spearing force. A bubbling yell cut off suddenly, and Kermorvan fell back, freeing the sword with a
vicious twist as a huge body slithered noisily down the
wall. Without breaking stride he tossed Elof the reeking
blade, snatched up his bundle, and before the smith could
stop him he plunged like a diver through the narrow slot
of darkness, beyond which might lie anything. There was
a crash, a slithering sound, the rattle of loose rocks dropping down into emptiness. Elof groaned, and dived after
him, only to be caught by an iron arm behind the door.

"Easy, my smith! There's a drop of some kind just beyond! Now let the mice stop their hole again, before the
cats recover." Together they dug fingers into the slots and
pulled, feet sliding among the rubble, until the gate,
screeching and protesting, ground home against the rock.

Elof wedged the runners with such chips of rock as lay around.

From outside came sounds of movement, something slithering over the metal, growls and snuffles. Elof clutched his sword tight. Were the things man-wise? Would they find the broken bar? They were strong enough to slide back the gate . . . He felt a great weight press against it, then a sudden ringing impact that almost overset him. But this work was made to withstand crude assaults, and agonized brute yelping trailed away, lost in the wind.

He heard Kermorvan chuckle in the blackness. "Somebody has earned a sore toe, I'll wager. Kicking the wall like a brat over a lost treat." The swordsman shifted painfully. "We have had a sore journey, you and I. Now my fine sword that came from my old home must lie and rot on the mountain. My broadsword was already broken, so now I have none, and that is a worse laming to me than this shoulder. But at least we seem to have come to the right place!"

"Cunning work!" sighed Elof gratefully.

"And a keen mind that saw through it! Now look around you again, my smith!"

"Look?" said Elof doubtfully, but he turned.

After the noise and whirling whiteness outside, darkness and quiet seemed to press in on him like a stifling weight. But his eyes were growing accustomed. There *was* a faint glimmer, a pool of dim radiance spread out before him. He reached out, but Kermorvan held his arm. "Do you hear?"

Now, as soon as he turned his mind to it he did indeed hear, and feel, for the low, slow throbbing came up through the rock under them. He thought of the wheels turning in the Mastersmith's forge, and the hammers that shook the house. He realized then, remembering the rattling stones, that the light-pool was in truth an opening, a shaft into unknown depths. "A steep drop," said Kermorvan, scrambling forward. "But see there, those regular shadows! Those must be handholds, some carved in the rock, others iron rungs. We can climb down, though our ropes are lost."

"Should we not call down first, to herald ourselves and let them know we come peacefully?"

"Would they heed such a shout? Or even understand it? It is said they do not care for human guests, peaceful or otherwise. We would be too vulnerable on those rungs, they might fill us with arrows and never find out their mistake. Soon enough to explain ourselves when we are on firm ground again."

"I take your meaning," admitted Elof. "Can you climb with your shoulder as it is?"

"Easily, it is a scratch. Though I will be happier the sooner it is washed and tended; who knows what filth was on those claws? But let us be on our way."

The shaft was steep, but far enough from the vertical to make the going quite easy. This was fortunate, for they were both more exhausted than they had realized. Their limbs trembled, and Kermorvan's shoulder tired quickly. "But at least the handholds are firm and well placed—no worse than a steep ladder. One can stop to rest. I had been afraid they might be too small and weak if the little people made them—"

"They may not be as little as you seem to think," Elof warned him. "I could ill judge the height of the ones I saw, but they seemed—well, solid. We would do best to use them with respect."

"Naturally, for they are perilous to rouse, it is said."

"I meant more than that . . ." Elof began, but gave up. Kermorvan talked of these duergar as things other than human, but Elof could not forget that ring of faces, strange in their features but vibrant and alive and wholly human in their feelings. Hopefully he would see for himself soon enough, for they were almost at the base of the shaft now. It seemed to be widening around then, opening out into a broad and shadowy chamber with what looked like an earthen floor. "A few steps," gasped Kermorvan, "and then you may hail to your heart's content. I, I am going to rest—"

A shrill whistle sounded. There was a flicker of movement, a sound like a great wing beating in the air between them, and Kermorvan vanished. Metal clashed and jangled as if a forge roof had fallen in, and he sprawled on the chamber floor entangled in a glinting net; dark figures rushed in on him. Something lashed painfully round Elof's legs and tore them away from the rungs; the rung he held bent under the strain, then his fingers were pulled free and he dropped hard onto the floor and lay winded. A heavy net fell over him, he tore at it and found linked metal rods resisting his efforts. Harsh shouts echoed in the shaft, strong hands seized him and coiled ropes round the net, and he was hoisted up and borne forward. Lights danced and flickered around him, earth thumped under heavy feet and they gave way to the hollower drumming of wooden planking, behind it the rush of running water. Abruptly he was flung forward and landed with a crash in what felt like a wooden cart. He could hear Kermorvan cursing weakly somewhere in front of him.

Wild anger woke in Elof, and drowned all his caution. He had come all this way, through wide lands, hard weathers and the terrors of the Ice, all to be netted like some wild beast, without a word spoken or question asked. Well, let them listen now! He dug his fingers into the net, bunched it into two huge handfuls and tore it free against the ropes; they snapped and fell away, and he sprang to his feet, shouting, "Wait—"

But then he stopped, and his mouth fell open. He stood, not in a cart, but in the center of a long boat moored at a high wooden wharf, lined with glowing globes of light on posts richly carved; beyond it, a street of housefronts whose warm-lit windows glinted on the cobbled road. And all around him, the sound of a wide, rushing river—

A torrent of red exploded in his head. Dazed, he fell to his knees, saw the planks rise up to meet him and rolled over into darkness.

CHAPTER SEVEN

Stone and Steel

The sounds grew louder, the bellows roaring, hammers pounding, the heat and the light so fierce he could hardly approach the forge. Yet struggle nearer he must, braving the pain and the shriveling heat, to grasp the scorching metal, and hammer, hammer out the thing that must be made—

He struggled up on one elbow, grasping and shaking his head as if he could somehow displace the ringing ache. The light hurt his eyes so much, he did not at first notice it was dim. The first thing he saw was a goblet on the floor beside him, and the sight of it awoke a terrible taste in his mouth. He caught it up and sipped tentatively, then gulped down the strong wine in a draft, coughing as the bitter residue of herbs caught his throat. Blood roared a moment in his temples, his stomach lurched and then suddenly the room swung into clarity. Sitting across from him, his back against a huge heap of old chests and baskets, was Kermorvan, looking somewhat battered and pale, but with his shoulder neatly bandaged. He met Elof's look with a wry cold smile, and lifted one foot slightly. There was a ring and clink of chain. Elof looked down at his own feet; they, too, were fettered through on the grimy floor. Memory spilled back, and he was about to burst out in angry questions when he saw Kermorvan roll his eyes meaningfully sideways. He cast a casual glance that way, and found that they were not alone. They were indeed in the hands of the duergar, and evidently in their dungeons also.

A single one of them was guarding the travelers. Elof

grew less surprised at this the more he weighted up the sturdy figure sitting comfortably in the corner by a door as low and wide as himself. He wore no mail, only jerkin and baggy trousers, but a solid helm covered all his head and most of his face, save a squat bulbous nose and a bushy tangle of a beard and behind the t-shaped slit in the visor eyes glinted; they seemed to meet the smith's gaze and return it with the same even scrutiny. That, and the tending of their ills, was an encouraging enough sign in its way. Across the guard's knees, however, lay a formidable billheaded spear, one gnarled fist almost negligently around its axis, where a single twist could swing it to stabbing height.

Elof turned back to Kermorvan. "Have you told them anything of our quest?"

"Only that we came in peace, and in opposition to the Ice. But I might as well have been talking to one of your anvils, for all the answer I had. I thought it better to say no more then till you were awake again. I think we are to be sent before someone. We were many long hours in that barge, and though I could make out little, trussed and dazed as I was, I believe they brought us to a place far from where we first—"

He stopped, for the guard had risen suddenly. He looked at them for a moment, then thrust open the door and ducked out. "A fine dungeon!" laughed Kermorvan. "No lock on the door. Though it is dirty enough, in all conscience, and these fetters adequate. Had I my sword—"

"It would avail you little," said Elof, tracing the bluish sheen of the metal bands around his ankles. "This is strong work, and new-looking, the fastenings also. As if this place had been made into a dungeon from the storeroom it looks to be—"

Kermorvan arched his brows. "Why? Because they've never before needed one? Surely not!"

The door creaked back, the guard reappeared as suddenly as he had gone. He marched over, swatted Elof's hand aside and undid the band. Elof sprang up on unsteady legs, but more helmeted figures appeared now in the doorway. They gestured him forward, but kept spears leveled at his chest. Behind him he heard Kermorvan's fetters clatter to the floor, and together they ducked awkwardly through the door and cautiously into the corridor beyond. The sight of it made him shudder. Grim and bare as it was, he could not think why, till he realized it was made in the same fashion exactly as the corridors of the Mastersmith's tower. Understanding that, other things began to slip together in his memory. But he was given no more time to think, for spear-butts at their backs urged them on; Kermorvan glared angrily, though he had the wit to stay calm. They were hurried along and round a corner, then up a flight of steep steps and through low heavy doors. Smooth paving replaced flagstones under their feet. The room beyond was as gloomy as the cell and passage, and little wider, but its ceiling was high enough to be invisible in the shadows; even the tops of the high dark doors in the far wall could not be seen. Guards took station beside these and the doors they had come through, grounded their spears and stood waiting. In the sudden hush Elof could hear a low buzz of voices from the room beyond.

Kermorvan nodded. "So," he whispered, "we are indeed being brought before somebody of importance. Let us at least hope he will give us a hearing!"

"How can you be so sure?" asked Elof. "Can you understand what they say?"

Kermorvan chuckled sourly. "No indeed. But courts, it seems, do not change overmuch, whether it is men that hold them or not. This antechamber, the sentinels, the hubbub, all unmistakable."

Then three great strokes boomed on the high doors, and the guards sprang to haul them open. Smoky red light flooded in, the travelers were thrust forward into it, and the doors slammed solidly shut behind them.

Blinded at first by the strange glare, they saw nothing, but heard the babble, smelled the strong scent of an excited crowd around them. It was a hostile babble, and the smell was not that of ordinary human bodies. To Elof it was strange and unsettling, though in itself more wholesome than a human crowd, more like the clean sweet smell of the cattle he had tended. But Kermorvan held his head high and wrinkled his nose fastidiously. As their eyes

cleared they gazed upon what they had endured so much
to find, the court of the duergar.

A high hall it was they found themselves in, the highest
indeed that ever Elof had seen. Yet he might have thought
himself under the roots of some impossibly vast tree, for
so the columns of the walls were carved, gnarled straggling shapes that closed together in shadowy vaultings far
overhead. The air under this strange roof seemed at once
fresh and smoky, like a late autumn afternoon; the reddish
glow came from torchlike objects set high on the walls
and burning steadier than any torch. The light danced
about the gilded carvings covering the doors, glowed on
the sharp-edged patterns set in the polished stone of walls
and floor, where flakes of pink granite and green dolerite,
purple quartz and ruddy sandstone vied with strange and
rare minerals. Shapes or characters they made, hard and
enigmatic, save on the far wall, above the heads of the
dimly-seen throng. An image was there, so striking that
Elof forgot all else in contemplating it, a high silhouette
seen from below, like a man through the eyes of ants, a
broad figure haloed in glittering flame and with a hammer
raised in one firm hand. Before him was an anvil, and he
hammered at something held upon it, something shining
and jagged. It might have been a short, burly man, that
figure, or one of the stranger shapes that now closed in
around him.

"Well, men?" a cold harsh voice demanded, speaking
the northern tongue. "Feast your eyes as you will. You
came to find the wealth of the duergar, through many perils, no doubt. We would not grudge you one brief glimpse
of it."

They were not, as Elof had warned, so very small. The
tallest, rising on their toes to see, were less than a head
shorter than he, though many were much smaller. It was
their shape that made them look stunted, wider than most
men, with heavy arms on broad sloping shoulders and thick
neck. The faces, though, seemed stranger than he remembered, for now not one of them was smiling. The mass of
them, the adults, looked carved from old, well-seasoned
wood, and carved deeply at that, for almost all were a
mass of lines; those framed with white hair might have

been made of bunches of cords. But it was the beardless faces, the younger faces, that were the most disturbing. There the unhuman mold showed stark beneath the skin, bared of the trappings common to man and duergh. The forehead was low and sloping, partly hidden by the bushy brows that rode the arched ridges above the eyes; but it was those eyes, huge, wide and deep-set, that banished any trace of the bestial in the face. The noses were almost all large and slightly snubbed, but varied as much as those of men. Below them, though, the duergar face fell away in a great curve to wide thin lips, and below those to a heavy clean-edged jawline with no trace of a projecting chin. High cheekbones and thick jaw muscles hollowed the cheeks; the ears were large, lobeless, curled at the top into a slight suggestion of a point. If they seemed to be set rather far back, that was because the head itself was longer and wider than a man's. All of these things Elof noticed, and yet in the same instant he saw men who were handsome and girls who were pretty—or might have been, had they smiled. But it was not smiles that bared the large teeth, or kindly curiosity that had them milling forward around the travelers.

An angry buzz filled the hall as the voice spoke, and guards sprang forward to clear a path with their spear-shafts. Elof saw then that the hall was a shallow amphitheater centering on a narrow platform, below the vast image. The dais stood head-high to the duergar, with many solid figures seated about its base, their very attitudes at once proclaiming their importance. Kermorvan was right; some things did not change. But more impressive by far, though he lacked their dark-sheened robes and rich furs, was the speaker. He sat atop the dais, in a chair of plain gray stone. Its arched back, upon which thin lines of gold traced out a single straight character, was high enough to diminish the tallest of men. He who sat beneath was not the tallest of duergar, withered and bent with age unguessable, but it diminished him not a bit. The stone around could not have been harder than his voice.

"Your coming, you see, was known at once. The rivers bring us messages, and the air, the cave breezes—but most of all the stone." His fingers caressed the rough gray chair arm, almost tenderly. "Always the stone. Our northern outposts are few now, but they are ever alert; they must be, for they watch the Ice! And so you were taken. You—*men*." The word hung bitter on his tongue. "Men. May the day perish on which first we took pity on your kind! Upon which we, the Elders, first sought to raise you up from your animal estate, as we ourselves had been raised long since! Every time we have aided you, misery and pain have repaid us. Across half a world we have fled you, and yet still you leave us no peace. By luck or design you have fallen among us, where no man should, and awoken greater fear and disquiet than I looked to see in my lifetime. I would know why." Angrily he tugged the plain robe of silver fur closer round his thin limbs. "I am Andvar, lord of all the duergar folk in these mountains. I am half tempted to kill you at once and have done. But I will not have it said that I stoop to the level of your folk. Speak, then."

Kermorvan's face colored with anger, but he kept his peace and looked to Elof, who stepped forward. "I thank you, lord, and I think you will not regret hearing us. We are sorry to have alarmed you; the way we came, we were driven to by sore necessity and fell pursuers off the Ice. But we came to these mountains in search of the duergar. We came to gain your aid, not your riches."

There was a rumble of sardonic laughter, and even Andvar's dark lips twisted. "Aid also may be stolen, as we have learned. What is your quest?"

Elof met his gaze. "A quest vital to all who oppose the advance of the Ice, and the Ekwesh its champions. And though I have never spoken with any of your folk, I have once at least proven myself no enemy, and been treated in turn as a friend." A stir of interest ran through the great hall, and Elof held up a hand. "I ask only that you hear my whole tale, before making your judgment."

Andvar waved a wide leathery hand, brushed a straggly lock of gray hair out of his eyes, and settled back on his bleak throne. "So be it. All here will understand your tongue well enough, and fairly you speak it. But I usually know the names of my friends."

"Of course, lord," said Elof uncomfortably. "This is

Kermorvan, a great warrior from the Southlands, my companion.'' Kermorvan bowed, though with a strange smile on his lips, as if there was something sadly lacking in the description. ''My name is Elof—''

Derisive laughter hooted through the hall. ''A modest name, indeed!'' barked Andvar. ''That ancient title, The Smith, know that we give it only to one who is truly One Alone.'' He gestured up to the mighty image above.

''If you are offended, I am sorry!'' breathed Elof in utter dismay. ''I chose it in all innocence, for I was a nameless foundling, and I am a smith among men. For I was chosen as a boy by the Mastersmith Mylio—''

He stopped, sensing the sudden chill hush in the hall. Andvar's eyes narrowed, and his fingers tapped on the arm of the throne. ''That name is no longer any bridge to our favor.''

''So much the better for me!'' said Elof defiantly. ''Will you keep your word, and hear?''

Andvar sat rigid with anger against the stone. ''Say on, then. Be silent, all.''

From that moment the listening duergar might have been carved from the rock, until Elof told of the forging of the test pieces. Then the whole atmosphere in the vast stone chamber changed, and the stillness grew charged, as before thunder. When Elof finished telling of the forging of the sword, it was Andvar who broke his own command. ''You forged *that* thing, boy? *You?*'' A long finger crooked at him. ''Come here, smith among men. Let me look at you more closely!''

Elof stepped forward to the base of the dais. The duergar lords there rose, leaning on tall staves, and drew closer, their wide eyes staring through and through him. He stepped up on unsteady legs, and the wrinkled face of the duergar lord bent over him. Ancient eyes, yellowed but clear, met his; he held the gaze, and was startled to see a reddish flicker deep in the huge pupils that was no reflection of the torches.

After many minutes Andvar sat back in his throne. ''It could be!'' he said, and his tone was thoughtful. ''It could be. The crafts of man and duergh are very different things. Those are strange fires burning in you, but hot enough, indeed—'' Then the wrath in him overran his curiosity, and he slumped back, knotting his hands. "And what claims on our mercy does such a feat give you, then? How shall we best reward the making of so evil a thing? At least I shall not now think your end unjust, for there are lives of our folk to pay for, and that one of your own whom you betrayed. An apt pupil you were, of that master! He was our friend at first, and of service to us, and when he sought to settle in our ancient watchtower we agreed, won over by pity for one exiled from among men! *Pity!* We even helped him build his forge, and shared our wisdom freely! And then when we found him delving in our mines, and dealing with uncanny folk, we warned him, sought to have him leave freely. He delayed us for long months with endless pleas and promises, and at last even threats. Even in the end, when we had to send a force to dispossess him, we gave fair warning—and do you know how it was met?''

"I do," said Elof. "I was there, because I was fleeing him, and the thing I had done. I sought to warn your folk, shouting from the hillside above. I am sorry I could not do more. Then I fled myself, in panic as I thought—but I see now that it must have been the sword, its effects tempered by distance. Some of your folk, I believe the survivors of your force, found me and my then companion, and took us to freedom by underground ways. They judged that I was their friend, and I am grateful to them. Will you gainsay them now?''

Andvar stared at him in astonishment, but before he could speak, one of the lords sprang up onto the dais, caught Elof by the shoulder and whirled him round. A hard-planed face, neither old nor young, stared into his a moment from an almost equal height. A band of gold, finely worked, gleamed round his thick neck. Then Elof was clapped on the shoulder with staggering strength. "What he says is true, this man-smith!" barked the duergh. "He has changed, but I would not forget him. He saved most of that party, me and my girl Ils among them, so we got him away through the underhills. He earned that much help, and more, say I.''

"That's right!'' shouted a female voice from the crowd, amid a growing rumble of dissent.

Andvar raised a hand to quell the hubbub. "You were ever generous to men, Ansker. I will not say you did wrong, in that instance. But what this man-smith has unleashed—and why has it taken him well-nigh two years to seek our aid? If there is more to tell, man, you had better do so!"

A bitter despair rose in Elof's throat, though Kermorvan was gesturing to him to go on. Whatever he told them, would this malign old creature ever agree to help a human? Not by the will of his folk, it seemed, unless perhaps this Ansker. He stole a glance at him. It was met by an encouraging nod, and the dark-haired duergar girl Ansker was talking to waggled her eyebrows slightly, and grinned, so that he remembered her also. He grinned back, and took heart.

His words spilled out into silence, like a stone into a deep pit, till he told of the strange rider at his door. Ansker sat up then with a sharp hiss of disbelief, but the lords around him drew back, and the crowd muttered unrebuked. When Elof had finished, the duergar overlord looked at him long and silent, and when he spoke his voice was deeply troubled. "What then would you ask of us?"

Elof held up his hands. "A key! A key to unlock the power that lies here! I unleashed this evil, as you rightly say. You cannot yourselves counter it, or you would have! Who else, then? Surely I have the power, if anyone—but I lack the knowledge! I have made master's work, but I am an apprentice still, and masterless. Be you my masters now!"

The silence broke like a floodwall, and the duergar voices rose in a great roar to the high roof, disturbing bats there that flittered forth like living echoes. A spate of argument broke out, furious jabbering both in the northern tongue and a sonorous, rolling speech, and many surged down around the throne, milling and jostling. Kermorvan they almost ignored; it was Elof the row was about, and it looked to be savage. One or two of them came charging up the steps of the dais, and had to be thrust back. Andvar's looks grew blacker by the moment, until he sat suddenly straight and gestured to Ansker and the other lords.

Their staffs hammered down on the dais in an echoing drumroll that washed away the contentious voices from the hall. Andvar smiled grimly into the sudden quiet. "So! Humans may be a rare sight, but that is no warrant for imitating them! We will hear my counselors on this, Ansker first who has walked most among men."

Ansker bowed to Andvar, and turned to face the hall. The gold collar shone like a token of the authority in the lean face above, and the rich voice.

"Lord Andvar, we should help him. We have to!" The hall droned like a nest of angry wasps, many muttering but not daring to raise their voices against their lord's fierce glare. "Think of it!" shouted the great duergh fiercely. "You've all heard what the creature Mylio is up to with the sword now—raising those savages up to assault the human lands—"

Andvar shrugged. "How should that concern us, my good Ansker? Are we likely to see the Ekwesh galleys sailing along our mountain streams, laying waste to our deep wharves? Let man kill man, and we may sleep at our ease in the mountains once again."

"May you indeed?" shouted Kermorvan suddenly, and the anger in his clear voice was startling. "Lord of the duergar, does your wisdom sleep? I have heard such words in the mouths of fat burghers in my own land, when I told them of the threat to the north. Nay, I have heard them from northerners even, who knew that the devourers could never come far enough south to menace *them*. And these last weeks I have seen their bones and their children's bleach under the sky! So I ask you this—when both northern and southern realms of men have fallen before this Mastersmith, what then should shield you? He knows you are here, he knows your ways, he covets your wealth and surely he hates your challenge to his will! And most of all, he is not driven only by his own greed, which might know a boundary, but by the powers of the Ice; what restraint have they ever known? So be your wharves aboveground or below, will he not be bound to seek them out sooner or later? Take heed it is not sooner than you think!" He paused, and from his great height cast a gold glance around the duergar court. "And consider this also. This man-smith, as you term him, Raven himself came to his aid. You can see as I could that he does not lie. Will you refuse to give what the powers themselves offer freely?''

The hard words echoed out into a silence as absolute as any Andvar had commanded. Anger still simmered through it, but shot through now with doubt and apprehension. Heads turned to their lord as he sat slumped in his great chair.

''My wisdom does not sleep,'' said Andvar at last, icily. ''I do not fear any of them, Ekwesh, Mastersmith, even the Raven-Wanderer. You do not know the power of our mountain fastnesses, man.''

''I do,'' said Kermorvan calmly. ''I am here.''

''With help!'' barked the old lord over the rising disquiet. ''And you were known and caught at once! As for Raven, even allowing the tale true, we may honor him, but we do not march in his steps!'' He gestured up to the image that towered over his throne, and Elof could see now that it was rich beyond price, the flames alone made with many gems and rich metals. ''We owe allegiance to one power only, and that is Ilmarinen the Smith, who alone of all the ancient powers keeps true to his trust! He shaped us our refuges of old from the coming of men, and he will not desert us now!''

Then Elof saw the jagged work of silver upon the anvil, and understood. ''He shaped you the mountains, then, to preserve your folk, and their wisdom? I for one am glad, for I have learned to value great craft, and I revere those who use it well. But lord of the duergar, have you ever thought *why* your folk were preserved? Was it simply that you should all grow inward and apart, here below, and contribute nothing to the world outside? I know little of the powers, but I cannot believe they would waste riches thus. Was it not rather for such a day as this, when the dark arts of the Ice we both hate may be countered by your ancient good?''

''That's telling!'' shouted a clear voice, and the girl bounced up onto the dais beside him. ''That's the word!'' To his surprise, other voices echoed her, and were not shouted down. There was a shuffling in the hall, a sound of taut unease.

Andvar, staring open-mouthed, recovered himself and glared. "Do we then need humans and children to teach us our purposes?"

"It seems we do," said Ansker quietly. "The powers do not tolerate stagnation forever, we know that. Lord, we have been complacent too long already. I hold myself as responsible as the rest. We must begin to act, and where better than here?" The buzz of voices swelled, and Elof felt a shiver of excitement at the change in it. Andvar was turning this way and that to his other counselors in a debate that grew more heated by the minute.

"So!" he said at last, and the silence fell again. "As I said, my wisdom does not sleep, and I fear no outside assault, whether by its minions or the Ice itself. But this man-smith shapes doubt as skillfully as evil weapons, and sets my folk against my will. Well, have your way, then. Ansker, you hold yourself responsible, you say? Then I will, also. Hear my decree! You may take this creature and teach him what you will, for two years at most. That is time enough for us to judge him, and see whether we may safely let him go, knowing as much of us as he does. But we must meanwhile be sure of him. For that length of time he will never, upon pain of death, set foot beyond your dwelling and forge. Well, are you satisfied?"

Behind him Elof heard Kermorvan utter some exclamation under his breath. He was dismayed himself. Two years, without open air, light of moon and star . . . And in that time what would be happening in the world outside? But what he had come for, he had found. He bowed low to Andvar, and to Ansker. "If Ansker will have me, I am honored."

Ansker smiled. "Have you some work of yours about you, lad?"

"I . . . fear not, my lord. Except the hilt of my sword, which was taken from me at my capture."

Andvar gestured, and a guard came forward bearing his blade and Kermorvan's two broken ones. Ansker unhesitatingly picked out the dark blade. "The others are sothran work," he said absently, and sniffed. He peered at the hilt, rubbed his finger up and down it, and tilted it to the light. "What virtue did you set in this?" he demanded.

"I do not know, lord. I made it when I was . . . unwell
. . . and did not try to give it any." Ansker's mouth
twitched, and he turned to the girl. "Look upon this, Ils!"
Together they pored over it a moment, and then suddenly
they burst out laughing. "Oh, it has a virtue all right!"
chuckled Ansker. "But you did not make the blade?"

"No. I found it, in the marshes of the Debatable
Lands."

"Ah," breathed Ankser, nodding. "It is a strange thing.
But the hilt is fine work for a human, sir apprentice."

"Then it is settled," said Andvar grimly. "And I suppose we must extend our forbearance to this sothran his
companion."

"Your magnanimity honors me, lord," said Kermorvan
coolly, and bowed. "But warm as was your reception, I
have no wish to stay. So by your leave—"

"I give you none," said Andvar thinly.

"Your pardon, lord!" said Kermorvan more heatedly,
"but what is the good of imprisoning me here? I am no
smith, there is little I can do in your land, and much of
moment awaiting me in the world outside. I came only to
guard and guide my friend over a difficult road—"

"Nevertheless, you came! And as for guarding and
guiding, you would not get far if you tried to return without your friend to shield you—"

"But *he* was shielding *me!*" said Elof confusedly.

"Do you really think so?" smiled Andvar contemptuously. "Do you imagine light is so easily seen from our
airshafts, or the gates on them so lightly protected? There
is a virtue in them, that they cannot be told from the stone
in which they are set, save by our people. And yet you,
Elof, saw the light from afar, your friend only saw how it
might be broken. What else, I wonder, have you all un-
knowingly found throughout your travels, what menaces
has the power in you held at bay?" Elof gaped, shaken to
his core. "But as for you, fellow, no more debate. You
leave us, if at all, when he does. Though I agree we have
little use for you. A human warrior!" He sniffed. "I would
not trust such a one bearing arms for me. Still, we shall
find some useful employment for you. The mines, perhaps—"

"Do you mock me, Lord Andvar?" Kermorvan's face had turned pure white, save dashes of red that burned in his cheeks, and his eyes as empty as the sea. Towering over the duergar, he strode forward. Guards clashed their spears together in front of him, and they were thrust aside like stalks of grass; the blades leveled at his back, but he paid them no head. "Keep me here, if that is your will. Have me rot in your dungeons, if that suits your whim! But do not try to make me your slave or your beast of burden! I was not born to such usage, though I will endure any hardship in this world, be it only honorable. I would sooner walk from here to the River than lift the lightest burden of a slave!"

The crowd growled, and Elof suddenly felt very alone among them, for he did not understand the wrath that had come over his friend. "Don't be an idiot!" hissed Elof. "You worked on the ram with me—"

"That was necessary, a soldier's task!" said Kermorvan frostily.

"Well, this—"

But Kermorvan was deaf to all else, and his voice rang clear as the hammered silver on the wall. "Hear me, Andvar, and consider well! For I am no common man. My forefathers through many generations have sat in judgment as you do now, upon a chair of stone, robed with the authority of the law and the will of their folk. They have condemned men as the law dictated, to prison or to death— but never to be a beast of burden! If they had, so it was held among us, they themselves would have borne greater disgrace, and their rightful authority would have fallen from them like a tattered cloak. And so it may from you, lord and king. For will you have it said that you stoop not only to our level, but far, far below it?"

No duergh stirred or spoke. Kermorvan stood tall among them, like a tree against a stormy sky, his face set hard as their palest marble. Elof stared, for he had never seen the man so. Time hung round him like a heavy mantle. Andvar seemed old, his halls ancient, and yet Kermorvan who was young bore as great an air of antiquity, as if he were only a link in a great chain that stretched unbroken away into the deeps of time. The lordly, even condescending,

manners had hardened into something immensely strong
and ageless, like statues he had read about of ancient kings,
and the wrath that had blazed in the gray eyes had frozen
into a bleak, terrible justice. And before those eyes even
the lord of duergar seemed daunted and cast down.

When he spoke his voice sounded quivering, almost
querulous, after the ringing music of Kermorvan's. "I
meant neither disgrace nor mockery," he muttered. "Labor in the mines is esteemed a work of solid worth to us
all, those who undertake it hardy and strong."

"And courageous!" added the girl Ils, firmly. Elof eyed
her; he detected something in her voice, something left
unsaid, and he could guess what. Mines would suit the
bravest, true—but only those who could offer no better
skill of mind or hand. Among these worshipers of skill
they would be little esteemed. Kermorvan, though, appeared not to see that, because abruptly he stepped back
and bowed stiffly to Ils, and again, less deeply, to Andvar.

"I thank you, lady," he said. "And I accept your given
word, Lord Andvar. Since that is so, though the task is
very strange to me, I may accept it with honor."

The sudden release of tension in the hall was almost
tangible, but Elof was torn for a moment between common sense and his duty to his friend. He did not wish to
see Kermorvan made a fool of, but if he told, then all was
awry again. Worse, though, might follow, if that fearsome
warrior worked it out for himself. In desperation he looked
at Kermorvan—and saw a rueful twinkle in those chilly
eyes, that both startled him and lightened his spirits. Kermorvan knew very well what had not been said—and was
pretending he did not. Elof sprang down from the dais,
and wrung his friend's hand. "Don't think I don't know
what you're doing for me!"

Kermorvan shrugged in slight embarrassment, surprised at himself. "Not only for you. For the first time I
find it better bending to a wind than falling altogether; too
much is at stake. I am sure my ancestors would understand. Let it pass, you have what you need; let us hope
two years will be enough."

"They had better be. Let us hope the Mastersmith does
not strike against your land before then."

"Yes. It depends whether he chooses to overrun the north completely first. But if I were he, I would not, for the real threat to him lies in my land now."

"And ours!" said Ils cheerfully. Kermorvan bowed again, but Elof looked her up and down with rank curiosity. The strange duergar face looked well on her; in fact, she was more than comely in anyone's eyes. Her black hair, cut short and very curly, came almost to her brows; her wide, intelligent eyes were very clear and brown, her nose pert and snubbed over an enormous, infectious grin. She wore boots, a short heavy kilt and a dark tunic, sleeveless and caught in at the waist with a richly ornamented belt of leather and mail, on which hung a long sheathed knife and various less recognizable things. The tunic, baring large areas of white skin, made her look startlingly buxom to human eyes, but also revealed the play of hard muscles in her arms and shoulders. She returned Elof's look with equal frankness, and suddenly reached out, tweaked his upper arm and jabbed him in the ribs. "Not as weak as most humans, just underfed! Well, we'll look after you—"

"Be sure that you do!" said Andvar harshly. "For mark you, I hold you both answerable. The warrior you will take down to the wharf and there commit to the custody of Bayls of the mines. But this one is your responsibility! And on you, man-smith, I lay one further charge. We may let you return to your kind, one day. Say what you will of us then, good or ill, we care not! But we alone may share our wisdom. Swear by your very craft that you will never reveal its secrets! Now take them from my sight! And blindfold, that they learn not the ways!"

Kermorvan snorted contemptuously, but Elof swore his oath, and then they went forth from the hall. Guards led them hooded through long corridors, and through heavy-sounding doors into a wide space where the air was fresher and cooler, and sound less confined. Over cobbles they walked, and the sound of running water grew ever louder, until their feet drummed on some surface of planking that creaked against stone. There the guards handed over Elof to the care of Ansker and Ils, and Kermorvan to Bayls, who was harsh and curt of voice, and ordered him aboard ship at once. The warrior laughed. "So it begins. Bear up, my smith, and learn well! Don't flatten your thumbs on the anvil! Make it all worth our whiles!"

"I will!" said Elof fervently, wishing he could find better than that to promise. "And you, have a care of that high head of yours on the roofs!" Ils helped them shake hands, and Kermorvan was led aboard. Elof stood listening to the light flapping of sails and creak of hull and cordage as the boat was made ready, feeling once more alone and adrift, blaming himself for his friend's plight. Suddenly he felt the hood being tugged up over his head.

"No guards around to tattle, so away with that foolishness!" said Ils firmly.

"Well," said Ansker indulgently, "since we must pen you up, it would be a shame indeed not to have at least one sight of the duergar realm. Behold, then!"

Elof, blinking, looked from him to Ils, and then, slowly and unbelievingly, around him. It had felt so exactly like the open air on a cool summer's evening that he had not stopped to think just where they might be. He stood on a wide river wharf full of bustle and movement, a well-made work of wood upon a stone slope; white sails were being unfurled, flapping in the brisk breeze that was rising along the stream. But that stream flowed in through a dark cavern mouth in one of the walls, and only a little way further on it vanished again into another wall. Elof's eyes followed that wall, up, up, expecting to see a strip of the sky over high valley walls. But sky there was none, and he had to fight not to shrink down under the weight that oppressed his mind, beside which all the works of man looked small. For above the wharf rose steep streets of houses, small but solid, their windows glowing in the dusk light, and above them in turn, cresting the hills, the walls and turrets of a strong citadel, lowering in the stone. Its many circles of walls, so smooth they might have been hewn entire from the stone, dwarfed both the houses and the strong towers and galleries that ringed the surrounding walls. But great as it was, that citadel was dwarfed in its turn. For the little town and all around stood within the bounds of a vast cavern in the living stone, a wide hollow hill as it seemed, and overhead was stone unbroken save for small channels and crannies whence came the scant light, dimmer than the lanterns by the river. He thought of where that river must lead, of other wharves in other caverns under the high hills. And the realm and power of the duergar loomed very great before him, like some vast beast which has lain sleeping and all but forgotten for long ages under the earth, but might yet arise to awe the very daylight.

"You see," said Ansker, without appearing to notice how the sight affected him, "the heat of the earth at these depths warms the air; this wars constantly with the cold air of the mountains, and so is in constant motion throughout the long caverns of our realm. Thus the air is kept flowing and fresh, and gives us breezes on which our ships may sail."

Elof shook his head in awe. "I wonder if we were not foolish, Kermorvan and I, with our bold words to your lord. How could Ekwesh or Ice ever threaten you in such a fastness as this?"

Ils shook her head vehemently. "Foolish? Never say so! First bit of sense anyone's talked in council this century. Did me good to hear. Andvar's getting on, that's all, and he doesn't like men much. Remembers when they were pushing into our farmlands and hunting grounds."

"For we grow most of our food aboveground as you do," said Ansker, "on high mountain terraces. And so we are just as vulnerable to the Ice in that way. And in other ways. The Ice can wear away even a mountain, little by little. Have you never heard stone splitting in the cold nights, and the grind of the glacier against the rock? But it need not even do that, there is a faster way to overwhelm us. If it can fix the cold around us, keep our winters harsh and drain some of the warmth of summer by sending cold winds and fogs and freezing water in the rivers, then every mountain's cap of snow will start to grow, extending the snow line downward and spreading chill before it. Very soon it will become a glacier in its own right—and one with no more mountains between it and your westward lands. And beyond them, only the sea. Thus the Ice may breed, in mockery of the life it so despises."

"And the duergar?" asked Elof hoarsely. "Master Ansker, what would happen to your folk then?"

"Burial," said the elder duergh solemnly. "Utter entombment—our airways choked, our rivers frozen. The blood and breath of our realm cut off, and our high pastures and fields no doubt laid waste by the cold or the fell things the Ice unleashes. But that will be slow to happen, for the Ice moves most easily where heart and spirit will not stand against it, where knowledge and craft cannot flourish, and only strife, oppression and bloodshed prosper."

Elof nodded slowly. "I remember things the Mastersmith said, when first he showed me the Iceglow in the sky—how it mortified the body and strengthened the mind, seeking to freeze away animal passions and leave pure thought. Perhaps normal humans—and duergar—are offensive to it; perhaps it truly cannot abide the presence of a great mass of beings who both think and feel. So it can only come against us when we are already weakened and scattered."

Ansker nodded. "And so turns man against man, and perhaps man against duergar. It were well that our old strife were forgotten, and our still more ancient kinship was renewed. May this be the first step on that stair! For though we must confine you, yet you are our honored guest. Come now!"

The wharf stretched all along the riverbank, its sides lined with immense stone blocks like those in the Mastersmith's tower. At intervals along it were tall columns bearing torchlights, their reflections gleaming red-gold in the still dark water, and below these were ladders and stairs leading down to the waterside. All these were made of dark metal most curiously and beautifully wrought.

"Stone and metal," remarked Ansker, "our foundation, and the dual nature of our kind. Andvar now, he was a worker of stone, and shares its virtues, to be hard, dependable, enduring. But Ils and I and many of us, we are metal; we are strong in our way, perhaps, but flexible also, able to change and be shaped by time and events."

Ils chuckled. "And yet to keep enough spring to find

something of our former shape when needed. You, I think you also are metal, and your friend in his way.''

"I pray that he is!" said Elof, looking down at the boat, which was ready to depart. It was a strange craft, long and narrow and smooth-sided, with a low mast and wide square sail, very lightly rigged. He waved, though he did not expect to be seen. But to his surprise a tall figure turned on the deck and waved in return.

Ansker chuckled. "Bayls of the mines is not as hard as he makes himself out to be; he would not leave anyone blindfolded longer than need be. I do not think you need fear too much for your friend.''

Elof sighed. "That comforts me!" The gentle cavewind bellied out the sails, and the craft glided out onto the glassy black river, leaving scarcely a ripple, like a dream. The crew were singing in their deep voices, a merry-sounding song in the duergar tongue, which Elof cannot then have known. Yet a version of a song in the northern speech is here preserved in the chronicles, and it may well be the one.

> *Deep under stone the breeze is rising,*
> *Hoist the sails, for we'd soon be gone.*
> *Bid goodbye to your bright-eyed judies,*
> *We'll sail where gold outshines the sun!*
>
> *Deep in the caves the river's running,*
> *To your oars, for there's rapids soon,*
> *They'll have a jump your girl won't give you,*
> *We'll sail where silver outshines the moon!*
>
> *Deep under mountains dark is closing,*
> *Light the lamps, keep a watch afar!*
> *Rock grow fangs in the narrow channels,*
> *We'll sail where a jewel outshines a star!*

Little is recorded of the things Elof learned in his months of study under the smith Ansker, for such wisdom was not commonly committed to records that all might read, and least of all by Elof; he kept his oath, as he kept all, faithfully. It is known, though, that much of what he learned concerned the natural properties of things, and how they were related, rather than of arcane craft. "For that is in most ways a shadow," Ansker is recorded as saying, "of the power that lies in you yourself—a subtle and intricate way of shaping and channeling what flows from you to your work. This you have seen. When your guilt hung heavy about you, you could set all the signs you wished upon simple work, but no virtue took root in it, for you feared in your heart of hearts to release any, and all unknowing sought to stifle the gift within you. But upon this sword hilt you set no sign at all, and yet it is rich with craft."

"What is the virtue in it, then, that you and Ils saw?" asked Elof. "And why did you laugh so?"

Ansker chuckled again. "Because, my lad, you could have brought nothing better calculated to make us trust you. Ils! Look again, and tell him."

She caught the sword lightly, handling the sharp blade with care, and turned it to the light. "I see no definite virtue, truly you left it formless, a song without words." She gave him a mischievous smile. "I see *you!* Or . . . or an aspect of you. You as you became in the Marshlands. Your purposes . . . the things you wish to fight. And to defend." She looked at him, past the hilt. "By not directing your power, you've made this sword . . . part of yourself, almost. That may happen sometimes, with things we make and use for long. They take on an air, an aura of their owner, as a dog may of its master. But never so strongly!" She shook her head in surprise. "You've mirrored your living will in this sword, so strongly it could almost speak. Even now it may make a fair sound as you wield it, a kind of singing—am I right?"

Elof blinked. "I have wielded it only amid great noise, in a seafight and a storm—but yes, at the last it hummed, a deep note . . ."

Ansker frowned. "The sword? Surely you mean the hilt only, for the blade's no work of his . . ."

"See then!" she said, and laid it down.

Ansker's fingers glided over the metal, following the elusive gleam in its blackness. "You are right!" he said at last. "It resides in the hilt, but has spread to the blade.

How ever could that be? Perhaps there is some old spell in it which meshes with your power—but so strongly!'' He sighed, and looked at his apprentice keenly. "Elof, you must take care. You have deep wells of craft in you, and you seem always to pour more into your work than you expect. Doubtless the Mastersmith hoped only for a weapon that would sway his enemies, or at best cow them—not drive them shrieking in droves! Be warned.''

"But if that's so . . .'' Elof stopped. He was thinking of the bracelet, and the virtues that lay on it. If he had made that as powerful . . . if *she* only knew, might it not serve to break the hold Louhi had on her? He became aware that Ils was looking at him a little strangely, and remembered she had seen things he wished to fight—and to defend. How clear had her vision been?

He shook his head in bewilderment. "How can I ever learn to control something I don't even understand?''

"Learn to control the materials you work with. Learn their properties, what they can and cannot do, and apply your craft accordingly. When it is this powerful you may use it as a cutting edge rather than a bludgeon, and so aim it more accurately. Less craft, more skill!''

So Elof turned back to his anvil, and many a long month he slaved there, struggling with metals he had once thought easy to work, and many other substances also. He learned the subtle arts of alloying that could make something chiefly of gold or silver almost as durable as steel; he learned how to make things of steel as light almost as wood by crafting cunning edges, honeycombs or webs whose strength lay in their shape alone. He learned how to work strange light metals that would not normally take shape under the hammer, or would burn like a starstone at the first touch of the flames. Ansker taught him much lore of minerals, crystals and jewels, which the Mastersmith had never made much use of. But strangest of all, it is recorded that he learned from the duergar smith how to look deep into the structure of the metal itself, so see the shock of each hammer blow travel through it as clearly as ripples through a pond, and how the next blow or heating or quenching would affect what he worked. He even, it is said, came to know the many shapes and forms and structures that the very crystals of which all metal is made might take, and none in more detail than iron. That was a metal he had almost come to scorn, because it was so easy to work; but of all the mistakes he had made, he came to believe that this was the greatest. For with the initial ease went infinite variety, especially in the alloying and shaping, and much of this required almost an infinity of skill and patience. But it was at this difficult work that he was to become most accomplished of all.

To learn so much he drove himself very hard, and rarely had leisure to resent his confinement to Ansker's forge and halls. These were in a cavern chain of their own, high in the mountain that was the duergar capital. "It is an ancient place," the smith said, "and so hallowed—the forge has served my line since the duergar first settled in these mountains, many an age past. There are virtues of many kinds to be gained simply from working in such a spot, and it is always best to have your own settled forge, when you can."

Elof stared into the rich flames. "And I do not even know who my parents were. I am a wanderer in this world, nowhere at home for long. Would that I might find such a place! But my heart misgives me, when I think of it."

"May you never have cause to rue it, then," said Ils softly.

But where Elof stayed in one place, Kermorvan did not. Ils, who traveled widely, brought him news of his friend whenever she could, and it grew ever better. Set to labor in the mines, he impressed the duergar first with his unrelenting endurance, which matched their own, and later with his great valor and prowess. Dark things stalked the mines, for there were old workings which ran out under the Ice, and guarding them was no easy task. Once his party had to face a great snow-troll, of the kind that had hunted him and Elof into the mountains. Armed only with a pick, Kermorvan held the passage against it till guards could come, and struck its deathblow in the fight, a feat that won him great honor. For that, against the will of Andvar, he was himself made a guard, and at last was being sent the length and breadth of the duergar realm, helping to guard the miners and the precious trains of ore.

It is said, though, that he always pined in this world of twilight for the sun and open air, and seized every chance he could get of duty that took him near the open, even in the depths of winter. But though far enough south at times to be within reach of his own land, he never broke his trust and stayed to serve the duergar faithfully. For that, perhaps, they honored him most of all. He was never permitted, though, to speak with Elof. Ils took word to him, however, and no less encouraging. Elof's burgeoning craft amazed the duergar, who had never suspected humans were capable of such skill. Many called upon Ansker to see and sneer, and went away marveling.

So both men prospered in their way, and won the regard of some, at least, of a secretive and suspicious folk. But one thing tormented them both, and that was the lack of word from the world outside. Most duergar cared little for the affairs of men and avoided any contact. The only word came from outlivers of both peoples who might occasionally meet by chance in the wild lands around the mountains, and since they were equally solitary and eccentric their word was not to be relied on. Once some young and adventurous spirits able to pass for men had walked briefly among them; Ansker had been the most daring of these now living. But Andvar had long forbidden any such practice. The best Elof and Kermorvan could glean was that the Ekwesh, though powerful in the north, had not yet made any decisive strike southward, and with that they had to be content.

But there came a day when Kermorvan was taken from his post, and told he was summoned to the capital. And as he took ship northward, he reckoned up the days, of which lately he had lost track, and realized with a thrill that their allotted time was almost up. A great excitement and a cold fear swelled up within him then, all too closely mingled. He was glad when he came to the door of Ansker's forge, a vast cluttered cavern hall strewn with anvils, benches and weird devices, and saw his friend's bulky shadow on the rough rock wall, hammering away at something on a small anvil with strokes that fell heavy but minutely judged. Only when he had finished did Elof lay down his hammer and look up.

"Kermorvan!" They shouted with laughter, and wrung each other's hands. "Welcome, wanderer! You great fool, what kept you hovering there? You should have called out!"

Kermorvan smiled wryly. "I know better now than to interrupt a smith at his work. These duergar folk are an education; the mildest of them might cleave your skull for that. I feared you might have picked up their habits—and in truth, you have something of their look about you now! Leaner, more lines on your face, and the only color in it the forge-tan, heat and smoke."

"And his eyes," smiled Ils. "How they take the fire now, eh?"

Kermorvan, smiling, turned to bow, then froze, blanched slightly and whirled away to eye some pieces of armor lying on the side bench. Ils shrugged, and turned her back. Elof strove to conceal his amusement; it was only reasonable that in this heat she should work as he and Ansker did, stripped to the waist. But to spare his friend he changed the subject. "Well, I won't say you've not changed since we last met. Didn't think you could look much harder, but you do! And how'd you come by that color under hill, eh?"

Kermorvan laughed. "They thought I could use some open air, so they sent me south to their mountain pastures this spring. I've been guarding the herds and the fields on the mountain terraces. Me, guarding goats and deer and herdsmen! But it was welcome work, for all that. You could have used it, by the pale face on you!"

Elof nodded, and his broad shoulders sagged a little. He slackened the band of cloth round his forehead. "It seems a lifetime since last I saw the sky. And I have missed so much the seawind among trees, the birds singing! Few find their way down here, where only the bats are happy." Then he straightened again, and the flames danced in his eyes. "But it was worth it! For I have been hard at work—and not without result!"

Kermorvan's face grew tense. "You've learned something?"

"Learned much, many things. And not only learned them, but put them to good use. Which reminds me—"

He turned suddenly and went to the anvil where he had been working. There he bent over something, wiped it with a cloth, and stood up with a dark-bladed sword in his hand. He tossed it hilt-first to Kermorvan, who caught it neatly, hefted it approvingly, and gazed in wonder at the blade. The metal was not bright, but gray with an odd golden sheen, and as he looked closer Kermorvan could see it was marked with a pattern of minutely fine dark lines that flowed shimmering like water through the metal.

"What magecraft is this," he exclaimed, "to make a sword blade out of silk, water-shot silk?" Then his fingers danced on it, as if it was hot to the touch. "Is this another one of these patterned spell-bound monstrosities?"

Elof smiled tolerantly, and shook his head. "Neither silk nor spellbound, and you may handle it safely. None more safely, in fact, for I made it for you."

"Oh," said Kermorvan. "Ah . . ."

Elof repressed a smile. Here was the man looking embarrassed again, at his unintentional rudeness! "Well, I owed you one, I thought, since you'd broken both yours, and one in helping me. I had no time to make two, so this is a hand-and-a-half blade. I was only finishing fitting the pommel as you came in just now. But you need not feel uncomfortable with it; there is no magic in it, as I knew you would prefer."

Ils chuckled. "Nothing you would know as magic, in any event. That pattern comes not from twisted ropes of metal, as in the mindsword, but from tiny amounts of flame-pure charcoal in the steel, lending it great strength."

"Charcoal?" said Kermorvan, startled. "Would that not weaken metal? Or is that not some magic? It seems a fine and fair bale—"

"Yes indeed!" said Ansker's voice from behind them. The smith strolled down the steps and held out a hand. "Welcome, Kermorvan; I am glad the message found you so promptly. You'll honor us by accepting a stoup of ale? I thought you might. Ils, stir your stumps, girl, before we die of thirst! So, a fine sword it is, and hard in the making; but there's no spell in that. The charcoal's cooked into the metal as it's drawn living from the ore, and lodges in the very crystals of it. That makes it hard, but brittle—almost like stone. The real art lies in breaking down just enough of the crystals to a springier kind, more like common steel, so you can balance the qualities. A powerful lot of forging that takes, strong heating, hard hammering, slow cooling and quick quenching—a great labor. See how the lines run the length of the blade, but here and here and all the way up they fold in across it; that's where the hammer last struck, tempering the stony metal against the springy. Our dual nature again, stone and steel. But few if any among duergar smiths living could craft you a finer blade than that one.''

''High praise indeed for sword and swordsmith!'' breathed Kermorvan, and looked at it with new wonder. ''And a great gift, Elof, for any warrior among men. My thanks, good friend, and may it repay them in the hand!'' He swished it through the air in one hand, then in two. ''Or hands, for as you said, it is a perfect hand-and-a-half length for me. I'll wager this one won't break in a troll's pate!''

''True enough!'' agreed Ils as she reappeared. To Kermorvan's evident relief she had donned a patterned brown tunic, and bore two large stone tankards in each hand. ''But for proof,'' she added as she passed them around, ''you could try it on your own pate! Not having a troll handy.'' She sat down on the large anvil, and sipped delicately at her own ale.

''No proof is needed,'' said Kermorvan stiffly, and Elof smiled to himself again. Ils seemed to unnerve this stiff-necked sothran more than a mountain full of trolls. ''It bears witness to your teaching, and Elof's skill.''

''Aye, it's passable,'' said Ils, with a curious expression. ''But there's better witness than that! Hasn't he shown you yet?''

Kermorvan looked sharply at Elof. ''You've made another weapon? Something you can use against the Mastersmith?''

Elof nodded. ''Maybe. Worth trying, anyhow.''

Ils leaned over, and there was no mistaking the excitement in her eyes. ''He made your sword in the times he had to wait for this! While he was waiting for the crystals to grow—''

Elof motioned her to silence. "Better we show you," he muttered. "You are the warrior, after all. Tell me what you think of this as a weapon." He strode over to a cluttered workbench, and picked up one of the various pieces of armor Kermorvan had been looking at. A great lefthand gauntlet of mail and jointed plate it was, long enough to cover an arm to the shoulder; no joint, no seam in it, but was covered and blocked by finest mesh mail. Every finger was a masterpiece of minute armory, molded in bright smooth steel, and covered in the strange lined characters of the duergar and the swirling archaic script of the north, the joints sealed by welded ringmail as fine as cloth. Heavy as the gauntlet looked, Elof donned it with ease and flexed the fingers as he might his own. Kermorvan peered at the hand as he did, and saw set in the palm what looked like a great white jewel, cut flat, upon which the fingers closed. Elof glanced around the forge, bit his lip, and walked over to the fire. With his free hand he pumped the small handbellows till they gasped like a hunted animal and the coals at its heart glowed red-white under leaping blue flames. Ils caught her breath, and Kermorvan stared unbelieving as he saw his friend reach out, shielding his face, and plunge his mailed arm downward.

"No!" The swordsman was on his feet in an instant, but he was too late, too far to stop those steel-sheathed fingers dipping deep into the dragon-glare. A sickened look on his face, he watched the hand rise clenched from the flames, like the fist of Surtur stirring under the earth. Fire dripped from it, and the steel of the fingers bore a baleful glow. Then, very slightly at first, they unclenched.

It was like opening a furnace door. Fire roared in the hand, as if somehow still fed there by the bellows blast. A glow spread between the fingers, flames arose and licked around them, and yet the metal itself showed no sign of heat. Slowly, very slowly, the fingers steepled, and a thin cone of flame roared and trembled at their apex. With a grin on his face, tense, taut, triumphant, Elof swung round and thrust out his mailed arm in a defiant gesture. The fingers spread wide. A tongue of fire darted across the forge, licked a scorched circle on the wall, and vanished into nothing. Kermorvan sat dazedly staring at the circle, for though among the duergar he had heard much of smith-craft, he had never before seen its power so clearly.

"A remarkable thing," said Ansker calmly. "It is made in something the same fashion as our lanterns. But in all our long years of craft and learning we duergar have never achieved anything quite like it."

"You see," said Elof in a slightly shaky voice, "it has virtues on it of catching, containing, binding. It could do as much with the sunlight, or the wind, running water, the sound of a voice—any force, anything that has heat or motion it can grasp, gather and turn back."

"Including the force that turns men's minds?" demanded Kermorvan sharply.

"I . . . think so, I hope so. Ansker and Ils could teach me little about it, even when I showed them that strange goad, and the symbols I took from it; the duergar have never sought to learn the skills of domination, not even to withstand them. But I have, to my sorrow. I know something must pass out of that mindsword, to strike so many at once. As I have felt, its power is diminished by distance, exactly like a lamp's light or a voice, or the flight of an arrow. So is it not also some kind of force?"

"A dark light, a voice speaking fell things, an arrow of the mind," said Ansker. "So I felt it. So it laid its hand on me even as I fled."

"And I," said Ils, and the light faded in her wide eyes a moment. She shivered in the forge's heat. "I do not wish to face that ever again. It was terrible."

Kermorvan looked doubtfully at Elof. "You think, you hope, it may work. But you will not know, will you, till you go up against your enemy? Can you risk such a thing? I expected—I cannot say—another sword, perhaps? To meet fire with fire?"

"Such means are not mine to use!" said Elof bitterly. "I cannot play with fear and terror, to thrust the minds of men one way while the Mastersmith drives them another. For what then would happen to those minds, caught between two such powers? Would they not crack and shatter like nutshells between stones? Or would you have me drive an army of my own against the Ekwesh, and set them on to slaughtering each other?" He stared bleakly into the distance. "How long must such a struggle endure, when the only real combatants hide behind their forces like human walls? For years, for generations of slaughter and death? Madness and ruin, both, and our only reward the cold pleasure of the Ice. Or worse. If I set myself to driving men like shoals before the shark, year after year—then even suppose I defeated my late master, would I not in the driving grow too much like him, and step into his place?" His voice dimmed with anguish. "It has come close to happening before. He chose me, and he was not wholly wrong. We are too much akin, he and I."

"Folly!" said Kermorvan sharply, twisting his new sword nervously in his long fingers. "That gauntlet cannot possibly match the power of the sword! At best it is a defense. You should have made some weapon of attack!"

Elof shook his head. "No. I cannot turn the craft in me to such ends, not now. It would rebel against me, as once already it has. This—" He hefted the gauntlet. "You misread my purpose. This cannot strike of itself. It can only gather or return what is sent against it, and with only such force as is used. It can collect that force, bind it, even concentrate it. But it can add nothing of its own."

Kermorvan clutched the sword to him, and bleak despair settled in his eyes. "It's not enough!" he insisted. "Kerys, it couldn't be! A toy, a trick—"

Elof laughed softly, and held it out, palm open. Kermorvan's scornful words came echoing back at him, and he flinched. Elof looked at him sardonically. "Are you so sure? Maybe you deserve a better proof. Stand, and be answered!" Kermorvan rose awkwardly, and Ils also, with a look of deep concern in her eyes. But Ansker drew her aside.

"Now," said Elof, unmoving. "Take that fine new sword of yours. Lift it high, yes, like that. Then when I give the word, you may strike me down."

"What?" cried Kermorvan, faltering.

"Do as I say!" snapped Elof. "Bring the blade down on my head, and with all your strength, mind! Then we shall see how the trick is played!"

"Elof!" gulped Kermorvan dazedly. "I am sorry! I did not mean to—"

But Elof held up his mailed hand. "Mind you aim straight! That is all. Are you ready? *Strike!*"

Kermorvan had gone white, caught between anger and shame and alarm at what he might do. He hesitated an endless few seconds, veins bulging at his temples, then brought the blade down upon the unprotected head of his friend. He struck with neither his full strength nor speed and so might, perhaps, have been able to turn the blow aside before it fell. But he was never given the chance. The mailed hand rose to the blow, palm open, and the blade smote down upon the pale jewel at its heart. But as they met there was no sound at all, and the stroke, though it might easily have lopped an oak branch, did not so much as cause the hand to waver. The steel fingers clamped tight round the blade. For a single heartbeat they held it rigid, while Kermorvan's eyes bulged in disbelief, and Elof easily thrust it aside and down. Then the fingers flew open.

Kermorvan's sword was wrenched out of his grasp, with force enough to spin him round and throw him to the ground. Across the forge it arced, almost too fast to see, and with a deafening clang it struck against the huge anvil, sprang high in the air and clattered to the ground.

"My!" breathed Ils. "Glad I wasn't still sitting there!" Kermorvan could only stare, and even Elof seemed taken aback.

"I am taught," said Kermorvan hoarsely, as Ansker went to help him up. "Elof, will you forgive my doubts? It is a mighty weapon you have made—as mighty, it seems, as its mightiest opponent!"

Elof looked troubled. "Rather you should forgive me, for I never expected the reaction to be so violent. Is your sword unharmed?"

"It is!" said Kermorvan, still stunned. "It is the anvil that is chipped! And you say there is no magic in this? It is an awesome thing!"

"In the right hands," said Elof. "But believe me, I too have doubts. That fell sword was shaped by the Master-smith, even if the hand and the power were mine. It was hammered out in his will, with knowledge that came to him from darker sources. You are right to doubt if I can counter that. It was forged, ultimately, upon the Anvil of the Ice.''

"Yes," said Kermorvan. "But it is he who wields it. He seems to me to take all he has from others. He has, then, less of his own, and that should count in your favor.''

"You speak truly," said Ansker. "I have met him, talked with him, weighed him up. Though he has strong craft of his own, for a man, it flows less richly and freely than yours. That Ekwesh mask-magic of his that blasted your old sorcerer, he had to dance himself in their fashion almost to exhaustion to unleash it, did he not? So. Few mastersmiths among men could pour power as you have into two such creations, let alone one.''

Kermorvan smiled. "So? Is Elof not doubly a mastersmith now? Even a sword that can bite iron unscathed is surely a masterwork of itself!''

Elof shook his head, a little sadly. "Ansker has shown me. Journeyman, that is a single bridge for all to cross, but not so mastership. That is achieved only when the smith masters himself, when he can control and direct whatever power he has; without that the craft alone means nothing. And at that I am only competent, no more. Two years could not bring mastership.'' He snorted. "Perhaps I should be able to make a sword that cleaves anvils, not scratches them!''

"I have something for you, nonetheless," said Ansker gravely. "I remember the fashion in which such things were made, among your people. They may find the sign on it strange, for it is mine, but your skills they cannot challenge. The seal of a duergar mastersmith might be of help to you, one day.'' He held out a thin chain, and looped upon it a seal of black stone set in gold.

"The stamp of a journeyman!" laughed Elof, and fell to one knee. "Master, I thank you!''

Ansker hung it round his neck. "Do so, by achieving mastership!''

"That must come soon!" smiled Ils.

"Perhaps!" said Elof. "But my need is now!" His eyes screwed up, as if in pain. "When I think of those patterns on the sword—I remember them so clearly, they haunt me—it's somehow vital I understand them . . . And something else is needed from me, something vastly important—I can see that—but I don't know what!'' His voice wandered away into a whisper.

"There I cannot yet help you,'' said Ansker gravely. "And there is no more time left you now. That is why I called you here, Kermorvan. Only two months or so remain of your two years, and you should be ready to leave. But it may not be so easy.''

"What do you mean?'' asked both men together.

"I mean that Andvar may not allow it. He has always hated allowing you to live, let alone learn among us, and still worse is the prospect of letting you free once again, knowing what you do about us. He regrets being forced to do as he did, and though you have won many friends, there are yet more who still distrust all mankind; with their support he can afford to ignore the council. I fear he may seek to delay you, even forbid you altogether. And delay you he must not! Word reaches us from the world outside, where spring moves toward summer once again. The Ekwesh raid no longer southward, but mass in force on the northern coasts. It is as if they await something. And some weeks since, our watchers saw the Mastersmith quit his high house in dead of night, and set off toward the west, toward the sea. Surely he goes to join them. The assault on the Southlands begins!''

CHAPTER EIGHT

The Wind Beneath the Earth

Kermorvan's breath shuddered in his throat. "You are sure?" he demanded. "So many rumors—"

"These are no rumors," said Ansker firmly. "Your coming here stirred the whole duergar nation to alarm, the more so as you came through our northern outpost, that closest to the Ice. Strange stirrings have been noted there of late, and the fell things roaming the mountains have greatly increased, so now no northern pass is safe. We have been keeping a special watch lest some assault on our realm also is brewing, and even wrung permission out of Andvar for some scouts to venture afield. They now report that this winter and last some of the Ekwesh have not sailed homeward, but have remained on the northern lands they have wasted, levying tribute from your inland towns under threat of assault. We hear that they even build longhouses and bring in thralls to farm the lands for them. Evil times! Those ravening creatures are worse even than the east-men who first overran our lands!" Kermorvan twitched with anger, and the duergar smith made a conciliatory gesture. "They were your kin, I know. And not all behaved evilly to us. But most did, driving us from lands we had mined and farmed freely for many lifetimes, calling us vermin and slaying us out of hand, with a price on our skins—"

"Surely not!" cried Kermorvan.

"It was so, I assure you," said Ansker calmly, "though

227

I am not old enough to remember those times. Even Andvar is not, not quite. But his father was. I cannot wholly blame him for his distrust of men." Kermorvan glared down into his ale. "But that is of no matter now. Our concern is to get you away from here and back to your folk as soon as may be. And that means before Lord Andvar can prevent you."

Kermorvan looked thoughtful. "That will not be easy. This is a mighty warren you have here, and well guarded—"

"But we will help you," put in Ils. "We, and others of like mind, we have been laying our plans . . ."

"You should not take such a risk!" said Elof, Kermorvan nodding his agreement. "If Andvar should find out—"

"What can he do?" smiled Ansker. "Very little, to us, for all his bluster; there are too many of us, and we are not without influence. It is you who are in danger, and you should go at once, before word can reach him! Once out of the capital, Andvar will have difficulty in bringing you back. So, we have arranged that there will be a boat waiting for you at the quay, small and fast as suits your need. It should be there an hour from now, well supplied for a long voyage. You may sail southward, and leave from one of our southern gates, now little in use."

"This is generous, Master Ansker!" cried Kermorvan. "And I have some skill in boats, myself—"

"But not below ground!" said Ils. "You'd dent that high brainpan of yours on a passing stalactite! And you don't know our waterways. Me, I've played courier to the south often enough, and ridden the odd rapid or two for the sport. So I shall be going along."

"But—" began Kermorvan.

"For that and other reasons," said Ansker inexorably. "We who favor aiding you men, we must have better reports of what passes in your lands, in Suderney most of all. We hear some tidings from the Children of Tapiau, and one or two outlivers, but they are odd even for men. A clearer eye is needed—one that is happier in the hard light of the sun than most of us. As I was once, but I have dwelt below ground now for many a long year. And it must be someone who will find acceptance among men he meets, also."

Elof laughed. "Ils will find that readily enough—eh, Kermorvan?"

Ils fixed the swordsman with an eye of black steel, and fingered the half of a heavy axe at her belt. "Why—er, yes, I . . . suppose so," he managed. "In her way."

"Truly?" said Ansker. "There are times when even I despair of understanding your folk. But it is settled, then." He sniffed severely. "Now perhaps I may have some peace here! It has been noisy enough with one young person, growing restless and wanting to see the world, but with two . . . Ah well. Perhaps it will seem too quiet, then." The wide eyes of the great duergh scanned them over the edge of the ale mug. "Do you take care, Ils. And you also, you men, for we have learned to value you both. Elof, because he is so like us, more than I had ever thought a human could be. Perhaps you have a strain of us in your ancestry."

Elof laughed. "I'm flattered! I might think more highly of my parents, if that were true!"

"Is is possible?" demanded Kermorvan. "You are different races—"

Ansker shook his head. "Simply two aspects of one. As alike a facets of the same jewel—"

"As alike," grinned Ils, "as dog and wolf . . . *if* you will forgive the comparison!"

They laughed. "But do not think it is only kinship that counts, warrior," Ansker added. "Though you have not been so happy among us, you have stinted nothing; that we will not forget."

Kermorvan rose and bowed. "Lord Ansker, I thank you. It seems you have been kinder to us than we deserve, and I shall strive to be worthy of it. If anything yet lives of the southern realm when all is done, better days may come between it and the mountain folk."

"Let us hope so," nodded Ansker. "But for now you must depart. The boat should be there any minute, and you must take it at once. The southward winds are strongest soon, within the first hours of the evening, so prepare yourselves. There is a scabbard there to fit your new sword, Kermorvan; you have your other gear? Good. And you, Elof, yours?"

"All but this huge hammer!" said Elof, rolling it in oilcloth in his bag of tools. "These are not the least prize I carry away, Kermorvan! Finer they are by far than the ones I left to molder in the Marshlands, free of any taint and full of Ansker's wisdom. No smith among men has better!"

"Or deserves them more, I think," said Kermorvan. "Well, master, is there some secret way we must take?"

Ansker looked surprised. "Hardly. We may simply walk down to the wharf; none would hinder you if you are with me. We shall say our farewells there!"

Nevertheless Ansker paused as they crossed the great gallery poised like a watchtower over the northern entrance of the river, and took care to scan the streets spread out on the slopes below. "There are few folk about, and no guards on the Long Wharf. It looks safe enough. Let us hasten!"

Elof shivered as they made their way down the cobbled streets. The air of the great cavern felt dank and cool after the fierce glare of the forge, the light dim. It might have been that that made him nervous, but he noticed that Ansker, for all his casual words, stopped and looked around carefully at every corner, and most of all at the southern gallery, now almost overhead. "We must be wary here, for that watchtower is a favorite perch of Andvar's, now he grows aged. Like an old eagle on his eyrie—"

"An ancient bat in his belfry!" commented Ils. "Well, there's our craft, just making ready by the Long Wharf there. Trim little thing, isn't she?"

A mast rose by the wharfside, taller than most of the trading craft, and differently rigged. The hull below it was long and lean, some thirty feet from stem to stern and slender of beam, with a blunt vertical bow ending in a high carved post, and a long tiller stretching forward over the stern. It was fully decked, with a companionway aft and a covered hatchway to the hold just behind the mast. This bore two spars instead of one, a short one near the masthead and a wider one not far below, from which duergar crewmen were already unfurling a mainsail that flared out widely at its base. "A topsail also!" said Kermorvan, surprised. "I hope the rigging is stronger than your wont, even in these light airs!"

Ils sniffed. "Strong enough, warrior! It's a stepped mast, so you can lower it at need, and that takes firm stays anyway. Just you sit tight and let me do the sailing, I've handled these courier boats before."

"I doubt it not," muttered Kermorvan gloomily to Elof. "How would a mere boat dare misbehave?"

Ansker chuckled. "Well, my lads, all your needs are aboard, and so must you be. I'll not make a long farewell of it, but—"

A sudden shout sounded from above, a hoarse command in the duergar tongue and then in the northern, *"You below there! Stand!"*

As one they looked up at the low battlements of the gallery, and Ansker cursed. There stood Andvar, and not on his own; a cluster of grim-faced guards gathered around him. His rage was almost visible, and it quivered in his rasping voice. "Has it come to this, then, that one of my trusted counselors will stoop to conspiracy with foes and usurpers? Did you imagine I would not hear word of such a thing, that all were as disloyal to our folk as you? We had only to catch you in the act!"

Ansker growled his disgust, and glanced down at the wharf. "There is always some fool . . . Listen, lads, Ils, do you make a run for the boat while they're still out of bowshot!"

Elof shook his head. "And leave you here, to face—"

"To face nothing! He'd shoot you gladly, but he'll never dare touch me!"

"He's right!" hissed Ils. "Come—"

But before they had clattered ten paces down the steep slope Andvar jerked his stick in the air, and with a low rumble something slid forward over the outmost end of the battlements, a fearsome thrusting beak of a device that was unmistakably a weapon. Andvar tugged angrily at his beard. "Stay where you are!" he cried, his voice cracking and shrill. "Till the guards come! Or we will shatter you and your boat together!"

"He's taken leave of his wits!" hissed Ils, as they came

to a skidding halt "Look at the guards, they don't like this!"

"But they may still fire upon us," said Elof. "If they believe your people's survival rests on it—and you can be sure Andvar has chosen his most loyal followers."

"Are you gone mad, lord?" shouted Ansker furiously. "My daughter is with them—"

"The worse for her! Upon her own head is any harm, if she will dally with men! And I will have a reckoning for this upon you both, for all the council may say! You betray your land and people to a—"

His words were cut short by a sudden sound, high and distant, cleaving the still air like a blade. In the northward tunnel the steely rant of a trumpet was ringing echoes off the rock. The echoes took form and became other trumpets, louder, nearer, blasting out an alarm along the dark river. Ils cried out and pointed, and they saw flashes and flickers of light awaken in the tunnel blackness. High on the towers of the citadel a wide concave mirror swung round to catch and relay the light, and from the town behind came a rising outcry, doors slamming and feet running. A deep bell tolled in the citadel, and from across the town, high in the cavern walls, another pealed in discordant answer.

"The watch is calling!" puffed Ansker, trotting down to join them. "The last they signaled thus, it heralded your coming! But what can this be now? Ils, read me the message!"

The lights danced in her large eyes. Her lips moved, spelling out the letters in the flickering light. "It comes from the far north . . . *moving on the mountain wall—some assault preparing . . .*" They looked at each other, as the flickering slowed and stopped. For three breaths they waited, and then it began again. "*Attack!*" said Ils between clenched teeth. "*They come!*" Then she cried out. They all saw it as it happened. The furthest, dimmest light in the tunnel flared suddenly and grew bright, blazed out red like an ember in the sudden blast. The firelight leaped from it an instant to all the other lights, capered red in the high mirror above, then went out.

A sound came rolling out of the darkness, flanked and

distorted by its own echoes, a booming, bestial rumble.
Behind rode a wind that whistled and pulsed as if the
blackness itself gasped for breath, and on it a stink of sour
musk, of hot metal, of burning meat. The boat's half-
lowered sail threshed and beat like the wings of a terrified
bird, and fell with the boom of canvas as the startled crew
let go the sheets. Again the sound drummed and rolled,
the lights flickered again, the trumpet notes blared to a
scream against a distant clamor of voices, and a streak of
red leaped in the dark. The wind throbbed hot on the
watchers' faces, and out of the tunnel glided two huge
shadows.

Voices rose in panic from the town; the boat crew sprang
ashore and bolted. For a moment Elof and Kermorvan
could make out only the beat of huge wings in the gloom,
and between them dancing points of dark iridescence on
something long and writhing. High they soared, flitting
through the shadows of the roof, and then one shape
swooped and fell away on thrashing wings, straight down
toward the rooftops of the town.

From the gallery above came Andvar's voice in hoarse
command, and the war machine began to swing round and
up. But it was slow, too slow, for the shape arrowed down
now upon the gallery itself.

From all sides came a single terrified shout, and the
rumble of running feet. But Andvar had just time enough
to draw himself upright and erect, lift the staff he no longer
leaned on high over his head and brandish it fiercely at the
swooping shadow. Then a spurt of fire spat downward and
streaked along the battlements. The lord of the duergar
stood still, a dark silhouette defiant against the racing
flame, but it rolled over him and he was gone. Small black
figures scuttled this way and that, sprang in desperation
even over the battlements, only to blaze in midair and
streak down like starstones onto the huddled roofs beneath. In the redoubled glare the beating wings showed
transparent, the long serpentine body hanging below glittered and sparkled, its short legs raking at the air like a
hunting cat clawing its prey. But among the lines of flame,
shapes struggled with the war machine, there was a loud
metallic bang and snap, and the beast lurched away from

its play and tumbled in the air, leaving smoking streaks of cracked stone across the gallery. That rumbling roar shook the air, and Elof and the others instinctively ducked as the shape fell toward them, wings booming and clapping. It was immense; it seemed to fill the cavern roof—then it flattened out into a glide. The wharfside lights glittered a second on scales like small shields, then shattered before the wind of its passage. Liquid fire beat and boiled through the streets ahead; the rumble of running feet was lost in howls and screams. War machines spat from the citadel walls, and a shower of harpoons came rattling down. One dropped smoking from the air and stuck quivering in the deck of the boat. Down from the roof dived the second shadow, greater than the first, to strike at the citadel, and strange shadows capered before its spattering flame.

"Dragons!" gasped Ansker, struggling to his feet. "We must get to the citadel, if we yet can! A grown pair of that size has not been seen in the world in my memory, nor so bold an attack! They have passed all our northern towns, to strike straight at the heart of our land! Come!"

"We cannot," said Kermorvan, and drew his sword. In the streets ahead a wingtip flicked briefly over a roof, there came the sound of a wall crumbling and hoarse screaming suddenly drowned in the belching rumble. A light spurt of fire shot up, racing along a street like a fast-flowing river, kindling flames on either hand. The smaller shadow coursed overhead, twisted gracefully up the cavern wall, across the roof and sped back down across the housetops once again.

"The worm plays with our people!" said Ils thinly. "The filthy brute has got between half the town and the citadel, while its fellow engages the defenses; now he may clean it out as pleases him! Father, what can we do?"

"We? Hope it tires of its play, leaves a way clear, even for a few moments. That would let most folk still in the town find safety—if the citadel gates may be opened. Those beasts must not get in! They would hunt us out of it, settle there and breed where we could not easily come against them—"

The noise above was deafening, the deep rumbling dragon-cries shaking stones from the high roof, to crash down upon the town. Under the clangor of the bells, the cries and hammering of weapons, it was an effort to think, easy to panic. At the far end of the wharf a heavy trading barge suddenly spread sail and swept out into the middle of the river, passing them as it made for the southward gate. Down like a stone from the roof dropped the greater shadow, long tail sinking, down between the boat and the gate. The craft looked tiny against it. A catapult twanged above, and again the watchers ducked as a heavy bolt bearing a thick blue-flamed charge plunged down past them, narrowly missing their boat at the wharf. It splashed hissing into the river, and a blue glow still burned as it sank. The tail of the creature swung up, and then lashed down upon the hapless barge, cracking like a whip on the water. It struck the flanks of the barge with a dull boom, figures fell on the deck, the mast whipped, cracked and toppled into the water. The barge, holed, rolled over and drifted to one side, cries coming to the wharf as its crew struggled around it in the river. Overhead, wings beat, the long head ducked down and the thin jaws parted. A single gout of flame dropped onto the water and spattered into a ring of floating fire; the hulk blazed and the cries fell silent. The beast swept upward again, against a shower of darts.

"So, no escape by boat!" muttered Kermorvan. "Where has the smaller brute gone now? It no longer quarters the town—"

"The main street there is clear," panted Ils, and drew the axe from her belt. "We might make a run . . ."

"I see no better way!" said Ansker.

"Come then, Elof—Elof?"

"Go on!" gasped Elof, struggling with his pack. "I'll follow straight!" The others hesitated, but he waved them away, and they ran. He stumbled after them, still wrestling with the straps.

The shadows of the cobbles danced underfoot in the changing patterns of fire and thrashing wings overhead. One street went by, and then another, empty, and the slope steepened. Ahead of them lay the corner they must turn to reach the gate, but many minutes of running still lay between when the lesser dragon stepped slithering round it, and faced them.

Kermorvan, as he stumbled to a halt, was first to see the look in those eyes as it turned to them, and knew that it had been waiting deliberately for any seeking to escape that way. They were appalling eyes, as huge in proportion as a bird's, and brighter, wickeder. They blinked once, slowly, as a snake does, a thick clear scale sliding like a shutter; and when it dropped they were aglow with de-lighted malice. The wings rose and rustled like ancient leather, spanning the street's width, then foiled again in a waft of musky stench; oily greenish scales rattled between legs and body as it paced forward, lightly, almost minc-ing, wholly unlike the ungainly beat in the forest. The hooked claws scored the cobbles.

Elof, coming up behind, saw Kermorvan stand his ground as the thing advanced, hefting the new sword al-most regretfully, like one contemplating some foolish ex-travagance. The head tossed, the nostrils flared and steamed. Then Elof plunged past Ansker and Ils, and el-bowed his friend fiercely aside. The same movement of the arm drew on the gauntlet, and as the meshed teeth parted he thrust it out in, as he realized, the self-same gesture as Andvar's.

The street vanished into roar and flame. It roiled and swirled in front of him, filling his sight with dazzling in-tensity, yet he felt nothing. Wonderingly, almost absently, he remembered to close his fingers. The fire swirled and died, and beyond it, half-blinded, he met the maddened stare of the dragon. Between them the cobbles were slick with something yellowish and oily; a foully acrid stench caught at his throat. He reeled, fist bunched tight against something that shook and quivered, saw the huge eyes glit-ter, the beast's head toss again and come thrusting for-ward, and as the serrated teeth gaped Elof flung his hand out wide, as if to leap down its very throat.

The world puffed outward in light and noise, a great hand seemed to brush him aside. Then sight returned, and he was sprawling on the cobbles, with awful sounds in his ears. Past him dashed a tall figure, and as he picked him-self up he saw Kermorvan plunge into the threshing, coil-ing mass, raise his sword high and hew down at the struggling thing. There was a deafening yell, and fire spurted upward. He picked himself up, drew his own sword and hobbled forward. The huge head twisted in front of him, scorched sooty black, its jaw hanging, an eye in sunken ruin. Kermorvan hacked again at the upturned throat, and flame ran across the seam. The body convulsed, he was hurled aside, and the living eye glared up at Elof. Clasping the black sword in both hands, armored left and bare right, he smote at the outstretched neck where Kermorvan had struck. The blade rang on cobbles beneath, agony spattered like hot metal across his hand, and the head sagged; two axe-blades thudded into the gap, then Kermorvan's sword, and the head dropped. They staggered back from the convulsing corpse. Flame spurted among the blood and filth that pooled in the street, and flickered suddenly on their fouled blades. Elof's forgework had hardened him to ignore most burns, but abruptly he winced and brought his scorched hand to his mouth. A weirdly bitter taste polluted his tongue, and he spat hastily.

"It burns from within!" shouted Kermorvan in disgust, scraping his blade clean against a stone. "What manner of beast can live thus?"

"None!" gasped Ansker breathlessly, holding his side. "Elof caught its first fire . . . and lit the foul stuff it spews . . . while yet in its mouth—"

"Guard yourselves!" shouted Ils. Overhead they saw the other beast swing away from the defenses, and hover high under the roof, wings thrashing, as it saw what had become of its fellow. For a moment they thought it would swoop upon them, but then a long blackened tube thrust out over the citadel's high walls. There was a sudden spitting roar, louder even than the dragon's; a ball of blue fire lanced across the height at the beast's wing, so it had to fall awkwardly aside. Up into its path curved a shower of darts, and a great cheer went up from all around. A long ship had come gliding out of the northward tunnel, with many more war engines upon its decks, and behind it spread the sails of another. The dragon plunged aside toward the far side of the cave.

"From the north!" said Ansker, recovering his breath in deep relief. "They have held off any further assault, then, and come to our aid. Ils, my love, and you lads, now's your chance! Into your boat and away!''

Kermorvan and Elof looked uncertainly at each other.

''Don't be such damned fools of men!'' roared Ansker. ''Think we can't cope now with one little dragon? But suppose you lads get hurt, or our precious weapon spoilt? Who'll save your city then?''

''But you—'' said Elof, clenching his fingers.

''I can reach the citadel now, can't I? Well, will you stand blathering while Kerbryhaine burns?''

Kermorvan's sword clanged back into his scabbard. ''Fare you well, then! And our thanks!'' Ils blew her father a kiss.

''Take care!'' he called. ''Send word when you can! And may the good will of the mountain folk go with you!''

Elof raised his hand, unclenching the fingers, and captured light sparkled a moment from the jewel as he waved. Ansker's way was lit clear. The duergh turned and went stumping up the slope toward the citadel. Ils was already running, but as they reached the wharf he saw her stop once, look back, and run on, and knew that the high carved gate had opened.

The deck of the little boat boomed and swayed as they sprang down onto it. Kermorvan swore; a plume of smoke rose from where the dart had fallen, heated by dragonfire. Elof ran to it at once and began hacking at the planking, leaving Kermorvan and Ils, who knew what they were doing, to seize the flapping sheets and halyards and secure the sail. Suddenly he laughed, and closed his armored left fist around the dart; the fire died at once, and he was able to wrench it out and toss it overboard. A light spurt of flame danced on his palm and was gone.

''Well done, my smith!'' laughed Kermorvan as he ran to cast off. ''It has other uses, your little toy, than giving firedrakes a taste of their own!'' They laughed, slightly giddy with the sudden release. Kermorvan clapped him on the back. ''It was bravely done, that! You may call yourself a mighty warrior now, and no mistake!''

''I do not wish to!'' said Elof, as Kermorvan thrust a pole into his hands. Ils leaned hard on the tiller, and together they pushed the bows out into the stream. He looked around at the mess of smoke and flame on shore, the carnage and the noise of battle. "A smith is all I wish to be, and at peace!"

"Time enough when you're old!" called Ils from the stern, angling the tiller delicately as the tunnelmouth gaped wider ahead. "Kermorvan! Take you the halyard and hoist the topsail, if you want to live that long!"

Kermorvan cursed under his breath, but sprang to obey. With the topsail up the little craft gathered speed rapidly, cleaving the dark water cleanly under its keel. They slipped slowly under the high arches, and darkness folded over them. The tunnelmouth became a patch of flickering light, dwindling behind them, and the sounds of conflict dispersed into echoing rumbles in the unseen roof. "The lanterns—" began Ils, and then said, more softly, "no. Better we go as far as we can without them. I can see enough, for now. This part of our way is well-traveled and deep, we have only to keep with the current."

"Will boats not be coming from the southern towns also?"

"Yes, but not for some time yet. The cavewinds are against them for now, and going against the wind is a long haul on a narrow river. They will row until the wind changes, and not reach this stretch till morning. By that time I think the dragon will be slain, or have fled, if it can. We have dealt with such attacks before, though none so powerful."

They sat silent for long, their exhausted bodies ringing with the fury of the last hour, while the boat glided on peacefully and the row of battle died away. A feeling of peace settled around Elof in that cool darkness, and yet he found himself resenting it. "I don't know why!" he muttered, groping his way across the deck. "My hand was burned by that brute's blood, it pains me. But there is something else . . ."

"Does that gauntlet gall you?" suggested Kermorvan. "Take it off, man, and relax!"

"Not I! And your hand yet lay on your sword, the last I saw it!" said Elof sharply.

"Kerys!" barked the swordsman. "I cannot rest either,

after all that. My heart halts in this murk, it tells me all's not yet past. The lanterns, girl!''

"As you wish," said Ils, "I can lower their covers from here." The familiar smoky red glow flickered slowly to life at either side of bows and stern, and at the masthead. "It feels as if the breeze is freshening, anyway. As well to see our way clear. Hasn't it fallen silent back there?" And as she spoke, a cool gusty wind did indeed billow out the sail, and the small ship bobbed and bounded ahead.

All of a sudden Elof sprang up. "Silent indeed!" he hissed, seized a lantern from the rail and bounded high onto the stern, clutching the carved post. He hung there a few breaths, peering; was he imagining things? The wind's chill fingers ruffled his sweat-soaked hair—*the wind!* He shouted, and swept out his sword, "Kermorvan! To me! The brute is on our heels!"

Ils sprang up with a cry. Kermorvan came stumbling along the deck and up to where Elof stood. "What? I see nothing—"

"The wind! And the fighting has stilled back there! Feel how it gusts and freshens!"

"But why—" began Ils.

"Its wings!" shouted Elof, and then there was no more arguing. A low coughing rumble echoed out of the darkness, a great blast of the dragon-stench swept about them, and it was as if the shadows beyond the stern folded down and fell. A firebolt struck the water only just astern, burst and scattered across the dark surface in a hiss of steam. Pale eyeless fish leaped in alarm and fell back dying. Gobbets of flame floated flaring upon the water, and the tunnel was filled with firelight. A pulsing, snaking shadow, the second dragon came gliding across the roof.

Downward it swung toward the little boat. But as it came, the sails boomed tight, the rigging thrummed and the boat gave a great leap forward, its lean bows lifting on a sudden foamcrest. The dragon, aiming for where it had been, plunged down astern, flailing its wings desperately to avoid the cold blackness beneath. The boat shuddered and ran before the blast, and Ils had to slacken the straining mainsail lest it burst. She shouted with laughter, "He's driving us along!"

It was true. Unfolded, the wings of the beast were vast, many times greater than the sails, and the wind of them that had heralded its coming was enclosed in this narrow passage. The more it strained to catch up, the faster it drove them, though the blast was gusty and hard to handle. But at last it seemed to see what it was doing. As they came out into a wider, higher stretch of the river, it rose suddenly, wheeled away, and with wings outspread sank slowly downward toward the deck.

Barely in time did Elof raise his hand, for the blast of fire was better aimed this time, and again the mist of flame billowed around him. Then it was gone, and an iridescent pool settled on the river, flickering into flame as it touched the rest. Elof closed his fingers as if around some invisible sword hilt, and a blade of fire roared from the hollow of his palm, too quickly for the beast to escape in this narrow space. There was a shriek of pain, a gap appeared in the edge of one membranous wing, and the beast tumbled awkwardly aside.

Kermorvan's voice echoed defiantly under the roof. "Save your spark, worm! We've the match of it here!"

And it was as if the creature understood him, for without another blast of fire it rolled over in the air and fell hawklike upon them. Down across the stern it swooped, long jaw hanging as if to rake the blind fish from the water on its crest of teeth. Ils slammed the tiller toward the wind, the two men swung round, and blades gray-gold and black swept up to meet the dragon. Elof, clinging to the backstay, reeled in stench and windrush, heard Kermorvan shout *"Morvan morlanhal!"* and himself struck out blindly at the vast arrowing mass as it flashed past, eyes glinting, jaws snapping. Elof heard a crash, felt the backstay leap and thrum against his arm, and then it was gone, past, rising away. Kermorvan was sprawled on the deck, but already picking himself up. Dark drops slid steaming from his blade, and Elof saw the like on the point of his own. He looked up at the dragon, saw it circling, pawing frantically at great welling slashes along its muzzle.

"One more swipe like that and he'll fetch down the mast!" yelled Ils. "He'll be back any minute! Hold on! There are old side channels along here—"

She leaned on the tiller and kicked the sheet winch rattling free. The sails flapped, the boat lurched and heeled slowly to port and swept in between two rising spears of rock that stood like sentinels from the water. The gunwale scraped and splintered along the rock, and the hull bounced as something underneath chewed at it. The high mast rattled and bent among hanging teeth of rock; some snapped and fell spearlike toward the deck, and then they were through. Sails flapping slack, the goat glided over a surface that shone green and scummy under the lamps, a stagnant pool, and stopped with a gentle jolt and low booming sound against something in their path.

"Ils, it's blocked!" shouted Elof, running for the bows, where something bulky protruded from the water.

"Idiot!" shouted the duergar girl, bouncing from her seat. "Haven't you ever seen a lock before? Kermorvan, grab a pole and shut the gates behind us!"

Looking astern, Elof saw the high posts protruding from the water, the system of chains and pulleys leading to what must be massive counterweights overhead. Kermorvan, who had evidently seen these things used before, reached out with a boat pole and tripped a mechanism. The weights fell clicking downward, and the scummy water swirled as submerged gates swung shut. From beyond the bows came a sudden trickle of water, growing to a spilling fall. But across the water astern flame licked, and a great streak of it came splashing between the high rocks. One splintered at its narrow top as a spear-tipped tail swung against it, then the dragon was climbing away again.

"He'll be through next time!" called Kermorvan, looking at the reflection that writhed and scudded over the disturbed river.

"Can't wait for the basin to empty!" Ils yelled. "Elof, your sword! Cut the counterweights free—"

Elof looked up. In the light of the bow lanterns, he saw another set of chains and weights above the forward gates. Sword in hand, he hoisted himself up on the forestay, swung out as far as he could, and chopped at the hanging loops of chain.

Even the blade he had made for Kermorvan might not have served, for this was duergar steel of vast and ancient age, and there was set on it a great virtue of neither corroding nor growing brittle; time had but tempered it. But older yet was the black blade, and it sheared screaming through one chain to starboard, and then to port. Slowly, majestically, like the redwood trunks they were shaped to represent, the counterweights toppled forward. One fell into the dark beyond the gates with only a sullen splash, but the other dropped upon the gate beneath and knocked it sagging on its hinges. Elof had the barest instant to drop back into the boat. Water gushed and swirled through the gap, the gates were thrust aside in its rush and the little boat was flung forward into the dark upon a toppling cascade of foam and a last great blast of air. High above, fire spurted into the blackness and splashed along the cavern roof, dripping a blazing drizzle into the ruined lock. The travelers, clinging to what they could in their heeling craft, had a last glimpse of a long wicked head thrust baffled into the narrow space, where its wings could not be spread to their full, and heard a final shriek of rage ring jagged along the walls. It was an animal sound, and yet Elof could almost believe he heard words in it, though he could only guess at their meaning.

He saw Ils wrestling with the tiller, Kermorvan hauling on the mainsheet and unable to help, and as the bows lurched upward he took his chance and went sliding down the deck to her. They seized upon the jerking, lurching bar, forced it down between the teeth of its retaining rack and leaned on it, clinging together and grinning foolishly at each other. If felt good, very good, in the first relief of escape. Ils's wide eyes were brighter than ever under her wet tousled hair, her bare arms warm against his, and there was a heedless exhilaration in this mad rush down into the dark, a joy in being alive among noise and spray and turmoil and cool air rushing by.

Kermorvan was less happy. The sail had backed violently, forced against the mast by the sudden rush, and only his quickness in freeing the sheets had saved it from tearing, or even dismasting them. But now he was hanging onto the flailing mainsheet with all his weight, and seeing himself slide nearer the gunwale every time the little boat lurched.

"We've got to stop her heeling!" he shouted. "This keel-less little cockleshell, she will capsize!"

"It's all right!" shouted Ils. "Any moment now the channel grows wider, the outrush will slow down soon enough!"

And even as she spoke its momentum faded, quite suddenly, like a rough child losing interest in the toy it shakes. The boat bobbed and bounced sickeningly for a few minutes, swayed dangerously under the jagged outcroppings of the low roof, and suddenly was straight and upright once again, gliding calm as a swan down the center of the new stream.

Ils and Elof sank down on either side of the tiller, gasping, and then clambered up to help Kermorvan rein in the gently flapping sail. "Kerys!" he said, massaging his arms and looking back into the shadows. "That was a well-turned escape, Ils. Bad fortune on us that the brute chose to flee south instead of north."

"Bad fortune?" asked Elof, to Kermorvan's surprise.

"What else?"

"Only that it was also bad fortune that the other brute also lay in wait for us, when it had the whole town at its feet."

Kermorvan and Ils stared at him, and at each other. Finally the warrior shrugged. "Well, I see no sign of the creature now, so it would seem we have truly escaped it, this time. But I would we could have slain the thing, as we did its fellow, whether it was hunting us or not! I do not like it left free in your people's realm, Ils. Surely there are many places under the mountains it may hide . . ."

"None where we may not hunt it down!" said Ils grimly, and the heavy bones of her face stood out. "Have no fear of that! Do we not have old Andvar to avenge, and many more, our homes and our forges left ruined and ashen? My folk will harry that thing without ceasing, if we have to hunt it from end to end of the hills and back, until it lies smoking in its own fires before us, or quenched in our deep waters. Its mate slain, it can breed no others to help it. We will have it!" She looked up at the roof and the walls around. "As for us, we have other concerns more urgent."

"Why?" asked Elof. "Do you not know where we are?"

"I believe I know well enough, though I must check on our charts. It is where we may go that worries me, and how we may come to our destination. This is an old channel that has lain unused for longer than I have lived, and I would not have taken it save in desperation. It will take us some way south, but not as the main ones do to our southern lands and their gates. Instead it turns southwest, without branch or tributary that may be sailed, and leads out under the lower hills, coming at last to their cliffs on the coast, north of the Debatable Lands." She bit her lip. "Somewhere there it ends in a way out; so much is marked on the chart. But where, or how, I have never heard."

Kermorvan peered at her in blank dismay. "Can we not go back?"

"Not through that broken lock," said Elof. "Unless we abandon the boat, and climb the walls. And then? Would you make your way along that narrow riverbank on foot, with the dragon still sniffing around after us?"

"No, indeed," said the swordsman ruefully. "Not now that it has learned better than to use fire! Very well, our path must be dark, in every sense. It was a sorer blow that beast-thing smote us than it knew. May we still get there in time! How far have we to go?" Ils was hauling a mass of rolled charts from the locker. Keeping a weather eye on the tunnel ahead, she spread out one on the deck, and the men gathered round to see.

"How far?" she said. "Seven days' sailing, perhaps, if we could sail all the way. It is marked here as a good fast flow, fed by many small springs and without silting or other hazard, save when the roof grows low on leaving the mountains. Then we must lower the mast at times, and drift so it may take a little longer."

"In this stifling blackness!" sighed Kermorvan. "With nothing to see beyond the light of our lanterns, not even a one of your towns to pass through. Seven days sunless! How shall we mark their passing?"

Elof shrugged. "I am sorry for you, my friend. But we have seen little enough of the sun for two long years; a few days more will surely make little difference. If nothing else, we have plenty of time to rest and think.''

"And drink!" said Ils, turning from the chart locker to another. "And sing! Here is wine to wash the dragon-reek from our throats, and put a merrier light on our journey!"

They settled down in the stern with food and drink, though always within reach of tiller and winches. Kermorvan took the heavy flagon he was offered, twisted out the cork in powerful fingers, sniffed, raised his light eyebrows, tilted it to his lips and drank deep. Then he lowered it, and drew a long breath. "There is sothran sunlight in that wine, summer sunlight spilled warm across a hillside. And song, and the clash of arms in honorable contest, and the stirring of blood. With that, and in such company, I could almost be happy, even here. But my heart will not cease its yearning for my Southlands, and its deep unquiet. Bryhaine!" he cried aloud, and the echoes rolled under the stone. "Kerbryhaine! How close are the raiders upon you? How strong now your walls, how fast your gates? But be they hard as the mountains, as immovable, a power comes that will strike at where you are weakest, I know. How firm holds your soul, my city?" And he sat beside Ils at the tiller, and softly he began to sing, to an old tune, but with hard and bitter words.

> *Kerbryhaine! Your Seven Towers stand gilded by the sun,*
> *Beneath your walls the fields lie green, the tree-lined waters run.*
> *Yet in your heart what light is there, what grows and comes to flower?*
> *Does mind grow cold, do weakened hands slip their ancient power?*
>
> *Kerbryhaine! I see you now, once noble, high, and fair,*
> *Your greatness gone, your wealth dispersed, as empty as the air.*
> *What wasting sickness struck so at the flesh beneath the skin,*

Took might and honor at a stroke, and withered from
*   within?*

Kerbryhaine! A sapling tall, but one that dies, not
*   grows!*
The greater tree you left to fall, but now your own
*   sap slows!*
The winter comes to all that lives, the Ice that slays
*   the root—*
If Spring shall ever shine again, will you still bear a
*   shoot?*

Kerbryhaine! If worth remain, if aught is left to show,
The smallest leaf, the slightest bud from ancient bark
*   to grow,*
The gain is worth the sacrifice, the battle worth the
*   slain—*
But will your spirit yet endure the healing stroke of
*   pain?*

When his song was ended, Kermorvan smiled apologetically. He drank again when the bottle came back to him, and appeared to grow happier, and joined in the songs Ils and Elof sang. Ils sang in her low sour-sweet voice, strange old songs of the dwellers under stone, rendering the words into northern speech for the men.

Cold, cold the winds through caverns blowing,
Dark the waters as under stone they run,
But soft is the glow of the lamps at journey's ending
And the gold is warmer than the sun.

Fade, fade the leaves upon the branches,
As the winter comes, till there are none.
But deep under earth the stone is ever fruitful,
And the gold is brighter than the sun.

Fall, fall the suns as summer passes,
Short there is life and love grows cold.
But here far below a love need know no season,
For her eyes are brighter than the gold.

Elof in his turn sang a few songs as they drifted through the darkness, though to him his deep voice sounded rougher and less pleasing than theirs. He taught them the old round songs he remembered from his childhood, simple boisterous songs of herding and fishing, and a few strange snatches he had come upon in his wanderings.

So they made merry on their lightless road, not guarding their lanterns or laughter or song, for in that dark vein of the duergar realm there could be none to hear, save the many small things that scuttled away before the light, and the bats their voices scared out of the roof. They were young, as their different folk counted youth, and they were gliding day by day from danger to danger, but for now they were at peace. They only excitement came at the times when they saw the rock ahead close down like the gullet of some great beast, and must stand ready by sweeps and fending poles. But as the seventh day, by their rough reckoning, wore on into the eighth, Kermorvan, who was on watch, began to grow more and more uneasy, scanning as much of the shore as he could with the lanterns. At last he awoke the others, who in the close air preferred to sleep out on the deck.

"This had better be good!" growled Ils from within her blankets.

"Hush!" said Kermorvan. "You who grew up here below, do you not feel it? A change in the air . . ."

Ils sat up. "It grows cooler, indeed. And yes, it moves!" She looked at them. "We may be drawing near the end of the journey, at last."

"What then? Do we simply leap ashore? I have seen no likely place among the teeth of these rocks for a good three leagues gone. Or would your folk have set a proper landing stage in a safe corner?"

"That, surely," muttered Ils. "But I see no sign of one anywhere near, and there is a sound growing I do not like. Almost I feel it, a deep rumbling sound—"

"Rapids?" growled Kermorvan.

"No. That sound I know, none better . . . this is smoother, steadier, with none of the chatter and roar. And we have no room to raise the mast!" She stood, still wreathed in blankets, and looked anxiously around. "I feel something may have changed, or been changed. We must be ready to escape if we can.''

Elof looked about him. ''Where to? I see no bank to land on, no cave or crevice even in these walls. And we are drifting quite fast—''

''You are right!'' barked Kermorvan. ''Much faster than a minute past. The current is drawing us along . . . and that sound—Ils, do whirlpools ever form in your rivers?''

''In no channel we have cleared! Nor has it the deep thunder of a fall. Truly strange it sounds . . . We shall know soon enough, at all events!''

So in haste and worry they gathered together their most precious gear, and a few of the sealed casks the boat carried as floats. That done, they readied the heavy sweeps, knowing they could not hold the boat back against this current; at most they might steer it past rocks, or fend them off. And then they waited, for that was all they could do, while they were drawn faster and faster on through a passage that grew more menacing by the moment, high rocks seeming to spring from the water like teeth around them. Yet the channel still seemed well chosen, for they were swept safely by and on into the depths of the cavern.

Then Ils stood on tiptoe and shouted to Elof, who had taken station in the bows, ''Light! I see light! Do you?''

Kermorvan ran forward to join him. ''I see nothing . . . black as pitch.''

''But her eyes are the duergar's, and like a cat's!'' Elof reminded him. ''And I, too, think there is something ahead . . . a glimmer . . .''

Then the boat bucked under him, and he was all but flung overboard. Kermorvan grabbed at him, and would have gone over instead had he not caught the lantern staff. The roof seemed dropping to meet them, a giant's fury bellowed in their ears, and Ils shrieked in fear and delight. A sweep jerked upward, dropped and splintered against some unseen obstacle. Beyond the bows a tiny disk of light swelled in an instant as the boat was pitched at it like an arrow at a target, and seemed to burst around them. They sailed out into the very air, and tilted downward on a leaping, foaming hillside of water. For a mad moment Elof, sprawling on the deck, thought he was back in the

lock, then the boat evened out once more and he saw that
though there were still fangs of rock overhead, a gray light
shone between them and mocked them with fantastic shadows. He heard Ils cry out for help, and saw her bent over
the tiller with an arm across her eyes. He staggered aft,
and a line swept down the deck with him, like a clear wave
washing the grayness from the wood, dimming the lanterns to feeble embers and setting blinding highlights in
the metal. As he reached Ils he saw astern the impossibly
tiny cavernmouth that had spewed them out, the chute of
water that had borne them, all so natural but no doubt
cunningly contrived. As, surely, were the high walls they
were gliding between, and the great stone slabs, irregular
and dangerous-looking, that formed a roof. Or had formed
it, for they were there no longer, and he knew, though he
dared not look direct lest he be dazzled like Ils, that above
them was only the open sky.

A wind whipped around him, and he shivered, though
once he would not have thought it cold. On the scents and
sounds that rode it a host of memories came flooding back,
the smell of salt and wrack, the gull cries echoing into
emptiness, the endless beat of the ocean pulse. The walls
widened suddenly, the wind grew fresher and the little
boat was bouncing and bucking out into a wider body of
water, a small fjord whose steep cliff walls plunged straight
down into deep water on either side, without beach or
bank or any other break, however small. The wind was at
their bow, but lacking mast or sail they were easily swept
down a fast current toward the mouth of the channel, not
far ahead. And beyond it, vast and ominous, Elof saw the
rolling grayness that was the open sea.

Quickly he helped Ils away from the tiller, but turned
at Kermorvan's shout. The swordsman, who had spent
most time aboveground recently, was already wrestling
with the sweeps. "You can see?" he grated. "Good! Rack
the tiller, then, and leave it. A lee shore! Wind blowing
toward the land, and only our good fortune that it is quite
light! We will need all our sinews against the swell!"

Ils blinked blearily about, her huge eyes narrowed.
"What are you thinking of?" she cried shakily. "We can't
take a boat like this out to sea!"

"What else remains?" demanded Elof. "There is nowhere we can land! This place both hides that seagate and defends it. Your ancestors must have chosen it for that—"

"Aye, or shaped it so!" said Ils, and Elof looked up at the high weathered walls in sudden awe. "They would have expected any of our folk coming that way to have a seaworthy ship."

"But we must risk heading out regardless," said Kermorvan, "or be dashed back among the rocks—if we stay upright so long! We might get out under sail, on a close reach, but without a keel we would capsize for certain! Unless—" He stared ahead a moment. "The mast!" he cried then. "Ship the sweeps! We must raise it at once!"

Swiftly they stepped and raised the mast, hauling on stay and halyard till their muscles cracked. Kermorvan kept casting anxious glances at the approaching sea as they made fast the last halyard. "You must keep her headed into the wind a while," he said. "As I remember, they carry plenty of spare gear, these caveboats." He turned and went clattering down the hatchway into the open hold.

"What now!" demanded Ils angrily. "I had sooner we risked it with the sweeps than chance whatever he plans! If I could only *see!* I am hardier than the old folk, I can endure even the bright sun in time . . . but I feel so helpless now—"

"By Kerys' Gate!" echoed Kermorvan's voice from the hold. "That may do it!" He came bounding up on deck dragging with him a great length of wood, four stout planks some twelve feet long bound together with iron. Lashed to this with many turns of the duergar's strong cable was the shank of the broken sweep.

Ils blinked. "The cargo plank? What would you with that?"

For answer Kermorvan called, "Help me, Elof!" and together they manhandled the clumsy planking over the gunwale aft of the mast. Elof held it while Kermorvan bound the shank of the sweep into a rowlock, and wound lashings round the planking itself. Then he let it swing downward into the water beneath, which was already churning as the current warred with the wind-driven sea. Quickly he lashed the plank firm against the rail, and turned to the mast. "Mainsail only, till we learn the proper trim! That board may take some getting used to!"

Quickly they lowered the mainsail, and Kermorvan ran aft to reeve the sheets. "Elof! To the bows, and watch! Keep you a firm hold, she may heel badly yet! Ils, how may I use these winding devices?"

Elof heard the clank and rattle of the winches as he stumbled forward, the creak of the yard swinging around and the boom of the tautening sail. Suddenly the boat seemed to come alive beneath him, leaping forward through the creamy water, heeling slowly away from the wind and then back into it as Kermorvan fought to trim the sail. The water ahead seemed clear; he risked a look astern, and saw how Kermorvan was fighting to hold the little craft steady. He was playing the sail as one might a difficult fish, edging closer and closer to the wind till the boat threatened to heel, but never allowing it to go far over; his wooden planking thrummed and trembled in its lashing as if great forces strained against it, but seemed to be holding. They were coming out from between the cliffs now, and the wind was suddenly fresher, the sea more lively. The swell was higher, capped by brisk white crests that hissed angrily at the cutting bow beneath him, and slapped hollowly against the boat's lean flanks.

"We are through!" called Kermorvan. "Deep water under us! How does the board hold?"

"Well, I'd say!" Elof called back. "That was a timely idea, friend!"

Kermorvan shrugged. "I should have remembered sooner. It is only a simple leeboard, such as my people use on smaller boats that must pass through shallows yet sail well in deeper waters. They mount theirs on pivots, one on either flank, so that they may be raised or lowered at need."

Ils slapped her hands together. "Of course! I have heard we used such a device on our few seagoing boats, but mounted in the center of the hull, the better to mimic a keel. I have never seen one, though, let alone sailed it."

"If it handles no better than this, I would not pine! Still, it has brought us this far, and that will serve. Do you see anywhere we might come ashore, Elof?"

But Elof, already scanning the cliffs, was shaking his head in dismay. This was a rough and craggy coast, its cliffs raw and steep in their newness, its beaches few and far between, save in deep bays where rivers might lay them down. Kermorvan twisted round to look, and cocked his head. "I know this part of the coast! There are places to land in the marches, a little way south. We are far enough out now; I'll bring her about and we can turn that way. Hold on, and keep watching!"

Elof felt the boat's way slacken as her bow moved to meet the wind head-on. For a moment she bounced helpless in the waves, then the yard creaked about, the sail thrummed again, and she swung slowly round and set off more sedately southward, wallowing against the waves. As soon as she was stable he clambered up on the rail for a better view, and stood clutching the carved stempost, wet now with salty spray. So they were at the north of the marshes now! He smiled, a little grimly, and rubbed his unshaven chin. It had been a long time, in his young life. Somewhere over to his left, then, if it still stood, was a tumbledown house by the Causeway, its hearth cold, its store of tools left free for any who came by. Had Kara, perhaps, passed by again, found the door banging loose in the damp wind, and looked in, to find only desolation? But he had seen her, if it was her, pass south on some mysterious errand that might or might not be her own, and in the Southlands he would start his search. A thought settled upon him, and blackened his vision. *This you must first do . . .*

He remembered the Mastersmith as a scared boy had seen him, a vision of power and mystery, and part of him still quailed before it. He searched for something to set against it, and found Ansker, sturdy, plain of speech and manner, and yet cloaked about in a mystery far greater than the Mastersmith's or any mere man's, the inheritance of a secret, ancient folk. He could count Ansker and Ils his true friends, he was surer of nothing else, and yet in all his time of living with them he had never, he knew, been able to look beneath the surface of the duergar people; he had seen only what in them was akin to human, not what was alien. Perhaps he had not had enough time, for what is two years to beings who might live through four lives of men or more? Or perhaps their strangeness was simply too alien to be seen from a human viewpoint, as blank as the cliffs he scanned now. From farther out to sea their narrow openings might be more apparent, the chinks in the armor. But from here they appeared a wall of grayness as solid as the dark line of shadow on the horizon.

But as his eye settled on that, he forgot about all else, duergar, beaches, cliffs, and stood where he was, staring out into the dim afternoon light as if it still blinded him. When a hand tugged at his leg the shock almost overbalanced him.

"What is it, Elof?" yelled Ils hoarsely, and he realized his friends must have been shouting to him already. But all he could do, at first, was point. "What?" she shouted. "There's nothing I can make out but a black streak on the sky, miles off. Does it mean a storm?"

"It does!" said Elof curtly, and sprang down. "Kermorvan, do you see that?"

"I do, though my eyes still dazzle. It seems almost to hang above the horizon, like the black fume of earthfires. But the wind drives it far south of us, it cannot harm—"

"Can it not then?" cried Elof. "Are you also grown blind under the earth, to see it as a cloud? Look again!"

Kermorvan rose and stared, and then looked quickly to Elof. "It cannot be! Not stretching so far as that!"

"It is, I tell you! Do you think I do not know that sight? Black sails, black hulls, mastheads, pennons fluttering halfway from here to sunset, and more ahead! You know their fleets—have you ever seen a greater?"

"Not since first I took sword in hand against them!" groaned Kermorvan. "The assault is launched at last, the final blow! And we come too late!" For an instant it seemed he would let fall the tiller and all else. But even as Ils made to grab the tiller from him, his back stiffened; spots of scarlet blazed in his cheeks as he measured the black line on the horizon, weighing up its distance and its numbers. "Not too late! Not yet! They cannot overwhelm Kerbryhaine the City in a day, in a week even, with or without the Mastersmith's weaponry. And beyond that lies all of the Southland.''

"But we're north of the marshes! It would take us weeks on end to work our way south from there!''

Kermorvan nodded. "I think we must keep to the water as long as we can.''

Ils looked at him, shielding her eyes. "You know the sea, I do not. But how long will these light timbers hold out? Not long, I think. Already they complain at the rough play these high waves give them.''

"Yes. And this is light weather enough. But I can see no other way. A few hours, a few days, a week, even— we must grasp at whatever time we can save, great or small.''

Elof flexed his fingers, thinking of the gauntlet stowed carefully in his pack. "We risk losing everything, our lives included. But what good will any of it do, if we arrive too late?'' He thought of Kara, caged in by the shadow of fear, and clenched his fist. "You be the judge.''

Ils nodded wryly. "Anyway, it's rare weather for a dip.''

Kermorvan settled down by the tiller once more, and stretched out his long legs with a contented sigh. "Then we sail on,'' he said calmly, and the cold glitter of the waves shone in his eyes.

CHAPTER NINE

The Voices

The Chronicles say then that they set course southward, and on the horizon before them rode the dark line of sails. But the great warships of the Ekwesh were far fleeter than the little caveboat, and before night on the first day the line had vanished.

"They are into Southland waters now," muttered Kermorvan bleakly. "They will sail on as fast as they may, through day and night, allowing no ship of ours time to spread the alarm. And so must we!"

"But there are only two of us!" protested Ils, who was taking the tiller as darkness came, when she could see better. "And I am little used to this harsh sea sailing. We must beach her sometimes if we are to rest!"

Kermorvan shook his head. "Beach this cockleshell? We dare not. We might never be able to launch her again. It will be weary labor, but we must endure it—"

"Teach me!" said Elof. "I cannot simply sit by and let you two exhaust yourselves!"

Kermorvan wagged his head doubtfully. "You would not find this crazed little boat easy to learn on . . ."

"Better a novice than nobody!" insisted Elof. "I can share your watches at first, and then take the helm on my own when you feel I am ready."

So it was that Elof joined Ils on watch, and first learned the handling of a boat. He must have been an apt pupil, for he could be trusted with the helm almost at once, and was very soon left on his own. He took watches in the uncertain hours between light and darkness, for he seemed

256

to see better then than either of his companions. Like them, he would sit for long hours bowed over the tiller arm, not only watching, but listening, feeling, alert with all his senses for the changes in wind or water that constantly threatened to upset the unstable little craft, to split the light sail or snap the mast. Most of all, though, he had to learn to listen to the rush and slap of the ocean under the thin planks, and how they groaned and creaked in response, wary for the faintest sound of yielding joints or splitting timbers. It was an unnerving sound, for it brought home to them all how fragile was the barrier between them and the envious sea. "But the very lightness of the boat aids us," said Kermorvan, "for feel how it flexes and twists! It moves with the water, like a living thing, instead of against it, and so the force of the waves does not war against it. But that cannot last. Every twist loosens the seams a little more, we take in a few drops more water. If once a seam goes altogether, we can do little to bail a craft this size. The number of our days at sea is already written, though we cannot read it. We dare not sail too far from the coast."

And yet that in itself was a hazard, as he explained to Elof, for there were immediate dangers in sailing too close in. Rocks, reefs and hidden surfless shoals rose up too readily from deep water, and anything high up, cliffs, hillsides, even clumps of woodland, played mad games with the wind. Whatever landsmen might think, most sailors found it safer to stay well away from shore. For now they would have to strike a balance, and keep alert to the perils of the coast. In the end, though, it was out of the open sea that their greatest danger came to them, and it was heralded in Elof's watch, in the dark moonless hour before the dawn.

It was the twelfth day of their sail, and he was well used to his post by then. The wind, as it often did, had slackened at that hour, the air grew still and warm, and the sea as nearly calm as he had ever seen it, a slow, heavy, oily swell. It heaved and surged under the slow-moving hull with sluggish weight, and made little sound. But in the unaccustomed silence Elof heard another noise. It was faint at first, as if coming from a great distance, but it made the hair bristle on his head. At first he thought Ils must be having some evil dream, for it seemed a woman's voice, sobbing in desperate grief. But then without break it slid downward below the range of any human throat, deepening, becoming a low, dull, throbbing moan, as if the waves themselves groaned under the burden of the hull, under all the sorrows of the world. Another voice broke in above it, a high keening croon that sounded mad, or foolish, or utterly unhuman, and another, a dark pulse, throbbing, humming, like the beat of some enormous heart. Elof listened a moment, holding his breath so as to hear more clearly. It seemed to him that the voices were getting louder. And there was something else in them . . .

He slammed the tiller into its rack, and vaulted down to the deck to shake Kermorvan's sleeping form. As always, the swordsman was awake at once.

"What threatens? Is it the hull?"

"No. A sound . . . a strange sound, a frightening one. Like cries, high and deep, all together."

"It could be seals," shrugged Kermorvan. "They grow large, here in the south."

Elof shook his head violently. "I grew up by the sea, I have many times heard seals, sea lions, even the great morses and weed-browsers. Listen and tell me if this is like them!"

Kermorvan listened, and his eyes widened. Before he could say anything Ils erupted out of the fo'c'sle. "Do you hear that?" she hissed. "The whole hull's aquiver with it!"

"I hear," whispered Kermorvan, puzzled. "Like nothing I have heard—unless . . . Ils, do they sound louder down below? Under the waterline?"

"Why . . . aye, they do! Then they're coming up through the very sea itself?"

The sounds were growing louder, and it was as if there were more of them now. To Elof, rapt between wonder and fear, they seemed to blend like some strange inhuman choir, sounding strange harmonies that shifted and swirled like the shades of the North Lights. And the feeling grew on him that there was indeed something more, that the

eerie chords were forming other sounds, separate syllables
of some vast distorted voice, speech drawn out, elongated,
smeared as ink is by a careless hand. A word, a single
word stretched out and repeated over and over with gigantic, timeless slowness; a word he could understand only
too clearly. He gasped, and clutched at Kermorvan's arm.
"Do you hear?"

"I said I did! What ails you, man?"

"Not only the cries! Do you not hear it—hear the . . .
the word in it?"

"The word?" barked Kermorvan, and listened again,
frowning. "No word! Just . . . cries, strange cries . . . no
more . . ." He turned, as if struck by a thought, and
peered out over the shadowed water astern.

"No more," echoed Ils. "Elof, what is it you hear?"

Elof heard his own voice sink to a harsh whisper. "My
name."

"Your *name?*" Ils stood dumbfounded as the sound
grew and swelled around them. The whole ship shook to
a soft booming growl, far deeper than any beast they knew
of could ever produce: a high crooning tone rattled loose
metal fittings, and even seemed to shiver in their teeth.
Suddenly Kermorvan gave a great shout, and pointed. In
the swell astern something sprang up, glistening and flicking in the air, and toppled back with a loud smack. Further
off to seaward came other such sounds, a strange turmoil
in the calm water. Another sprang up, close enough to be
seen as a great barb-finned fish little smaller in the body
than a man. But even as it smacked back into the waves,
something rose up that dwarfed it utterly, a great dark
hummock, lumpy and gray-mottled, edged with white
foam. Forward it plunged, vanishing into the slope of the
next leaden wave only to burst out of its nearer flank in a
great scatter of spray.

"Hounds of Niarad!" shouted Kermorvan, bounding
over to the mast and seizing a sweep from the rack beneath
it. Another high hummock came arching up no more than
twenty yards to starboard. He stood poised with the great
oar across his shoulders, straddling the center of the little
craft, ready to leap to one or the other flank. "You two,

to the tiller! Hold your course till I call; be ready to go about at once!''

Ils and Elof reached the tiller, but as they seized it spray flicked up a little way astern, and one of the fish leaped in the air, higher than their stern-tree. But it did not land. From the wave beneath, with almost leisurely grace, a vast head arose, foam-streaked, to intercept the heavy fish as it fell. Long spearhead jaws slid smoothly open, closed, the fish vanished without struggle or snap and the mottled body plunged down in a great solid cascade that seemed to go on and on. A flattened half-moon blade of tail thrashed at the surface, and vanished.

''The brute's twice as long as us!'' whispered Ils. ''Or more! And look!'' She peered out into the first gray glimmer of dawn, too dim as yet for Elof to see far. ''There must be hundreds of them! All spread out across the sea— Kermorvan, what are these things?''

He hesitated a moment. *''Valfis* is what Elof's folk call them, I think.''

''Whales?'' breathed Elof, staring into the gloom. Then he laughed. ''But whales aren't dangerous, unless you actually hunt them or sail across their path! Every fisherlad in my village knew that!''

''Then they didn't know Niarad's Pack! These are not the wise great whales, nor orcas even! Look at the head on them, narrow and sharp like the tip on an arrow! These are ancient, deadly brutes, with wit enough for anger and malice, little else. They are his sentinels, and his hunters! And may he draw them from us now!''

''They called my name . . .'' whispered Elof. There was a sound like an explosion, acrid spray fountained all over them and great gaping jaws, wide enough to take in a man, breached only feet from the aft gunwale. The teeth were few and wide-spaced but huge, many-crowned as mountains of stained ice, glinting cold as the eyes above them, set larger and higher than any common whale's. Behind them rose the body, and the mottled grayness of it was not skin but scaly armor, great heavy rows of shield-shaped scutes stuck in the leathery skin. It was like some vast serpent in armor, as large around as the boat and nearly three times its length.

It lay there a moment, not hunting like its fellows, but rolling lazily in the swell. It twisted half on its side, exposing a naked white underbelly and long white fins, and the wide cold eye glared up at the watchers on the deck. Then it rolled level again, and from nostrils halfway up its snout it blew great blasts of misty vapor, acrid and stinking, and ducked its head beneath the surface, slipping sideways—

"It's going under the hull!" gasped Ils.

Kermorvan nodded jerkily, but did not move from his spot. "Do nothing! We may not anger it. It is far too powerful . . ."

The boat rose on the swell, the sea-hill of the back slid beneath, and for a moment Elof thought it would pass without harm. Then the little boat juddered, vibrated, groaned, and splintering sounds echoed up out of the open hold and fo'c'scle. The vessel bounced along the immense back like a child's toy dragged over cobbles; the tiller leaped out of the rack and swung wildly, the sail spilled its air and thumped tight again, the improvised leeboard groaned in protest as it was scraped.

"The brute's scratching its foul hide!" groaned Ils, running to the port side.

"Is that all it wants with us, I wonder?" muttered Elof, grabbing the swinging tiller.

But the others did not hear him, for at that moment came a violent cracking buffet to starboard, and the whole length of the creature seemed to come surging out of the sea. It scraped upward against the hull, rolling it till the rail dipped into the frothing water. Quickly, lightly, Kermorvan rested the butt end of the oar against the scutes and fended the boat off as gently as he could. "It may not notice—" he began, and then the tail flicked up and the boat bucked violently, flinging him sprawling on the sea-washed deck. A loud snap echoed hollowly out of the hold, and the rush and churn of water grew suddenly louder. For a moment it seemed as if the beat had dived back into the swirling sea. But then Ils cried out, a great turmoil grew in the water, and it breached once more, its whole forepart arrowing upward, curving over as if to come crashing down upon the deck, staving the side in if not splintering the little boat altogether. Elof staggered down the soaking planks, tugging the black sword free from his belt, and it whined an angry song as it matched edges with the rising wind.

"Did you call me, brute? Did you sing my name? I come, then! *Elof is here!*"

In the moment of its falling the huge body convulsed, twisted aside and toppled awkwardly down into the water. It landed with a thunderclap, a massive fountaining of water that fell in sleeting walls across the deck. The wave caught all three of them, flung them up and dropped them sickeningly. Elof went sprawling against the rail, barely keeping hold of his sword. The boat lay wallowing in the trough of the wave, floating at a crazy angle. Kermorvan hauled himself up by the mast. "We're shipping water! Steer for the shore!" Slithering and sliding, grabbing on where he could, he made his way astern to where Ils was fighting with the tiller. Together they threw their weight on it, he kicked out at one winch and the yardarm creaked about as the sea beneath them steadied. Dawn glimmered in the soaked rigging, spilled highlights across the swimming deck. The freshening breeze tugged at the soaking sail and rattled the topsail as Ils raised it. Out to sea, surging and sporting after the fish that leaped now like jewels in the sunlight, the leviathans surged on, and paid the listing craft no heed as it came rattling and creaking about in a last desperate race for the shore.

Looking around, Elof was startled at how close to the land they were. It loomed over them, dark and featureless as yet against the glowing sky. The clash with the seabeast had somehow driven them far further in than they had been, and already he could hear the distant rumble of breakers. But louder yet was the hollow booming of the water washing around beneath the deck, and he turned and ran across the heeling deck toward the fo'c'sle. All their gear was stored there, and most important of all the gauntlet; water could not hurt it, but might easily hide it. Fortunately the sea had barely reached there yet, though he could hear it thudding against the bulkhead to the hold as he hastily made up their packs, bundling up as much of their remaining food as he could. He resisted the temptation to put on the gauntlet; he could do many things with it, but not swim. Instead he strapped it tight inside his jerkin, and scrambled back up on deck, hoisting the baggage with him.

It was already grown worse there, in the brief time he had been below. The little craft was still held on a broad reach, angling in toward the shore, but she rode low in the wavecrests now, and at every dip a little spray of water leaped from the hold. "Good work, my friend!" shouted Kermorvan, as he made fast the packs to the sweep rack. "Now get you for'ard and spy us out somewhere to land! We must needs bear away shoreward any minute!"

Elof needed no urging. He was already at the stempost, squinting out into the half-light to the jagged shadow of the land. There was something, it seemed . . . "A beach!" he yelled.

"Where away?"

"Straight in . . . but 'ware breakers, there are shoals around it!"

"No help for that!" called Kermorvan. "Even now she splits! We bear away!"

For one sickening moment, as the bow bounced and plunged into the waves, Elof thought they would capsize. The shoals hissed and thundered on either side as he stumbled aft; they lurched a moment, almost checked as something tore shrieking to the bows, but then the next wave lifted them over and past it, and they were running before the wind, running through water that became rougher, choppier, full of foamy streaks and floating masses of weed, toward a narrow spit of shingle standing out from the foot of a high dark slope. There was a sudden smash, the boat lurched as the leeboard ground into some soft obstruction.

"Cut it loose!" shouted Kermorvan, and Elof's sword crashed down through rail and planks and lashings, once, twice, and it was torn free and bobbing in their wake. Then a monster growled and seized the boat in its jaws, tipped up the bow and crushed it splintering inward. The rigging sang a discord and snapped, sail and yard crumpled downward and the mast broke in its step and toppled across the deck. They were all hurled flat on the planking.

After that moment of shock and stunning confusion, what followed seemed like sudden, reverberating silence. It was only as Elof lifted his head cautiously that he began to make out sounds again, and sensation. The sounds were ominous, the wash and rumble of surf upon stone, the sea flogging a hull no longer light and resonant but dull, congested, full. And the sensation under him was no more of riding the waves but of being ridden by them, rocking and rising only a little, and constantly slipping, falling away. He tried to scramble up, and found the deck tilted to starboard at an impossible angle, and fixed there. He could see waves washing under the rail, looking strangely steady. "We're aground!" he said.

"We are beached, is what you would say." Kermorvan, bleeding from a scraped brow, was handing himself along the port rail above. "At least the bows are, and split open like a rotten fruit. There is water enough here for the stern to sink, though, and perhaps pull us off. Better we get ashore at once." Elof nodded, and picked himself up more carefully. The stern dipped alarmingly as he stood, and barely rose again. Ils, less easily overbalanced, stood braced on sturdy legs at the sweep rack, untying the packs. They grabbed them and stumbled for'ard, clutching at rails, cleats or any likely handhold. One sprung plank came loose in Ils's hand, and she seemed about to go slithering down into the water, but Elof was fast enough to catch her. The bows were resting on a shingle bank some twenty feet from the beach, and they had to scramble down the splintered planks and half wade, half swim to the stony beach, holding their gear clear of the water. They stumbled up above the wave line and collapsed onto the rounded pebbles, gasping with effort, feeling the land they had not touched for two weeks seem to heave beneath them, so used were their bodies now to the movement of the boat. After a while Kermorvan rolled over and sat up, gazing at the wreck of the boat. And as he watched, the waves took it at last, dragging it from its weak hold upon the bank. Away it slid, its ruined bows rising upward a moment before they dipped and disappeared. "It let us down," he said bitterly. "All this way it bore us, and then

failed at the last. We must still be far from Kerbryhaine.
If it could only have lasted another day, another two . . .''

"You yourself said it was never meant for such a voyage," said Elof. "Call it rather a miracle that it lasted as
long as it did, and sailed as well. Though your skill and
Ils's played an equal part in that, I am sure."

"A miracle?" said Ils. "Not so, not altogether. The
boats of the duergar are loyal, there are great virtues set
in them, of fair voyaging and safe landing. It did what it
could."

"Yes," said Elof. "It would have sailed on happily
enough, I doubt not, had we not been driven ashore."

"Driven? Deliberately?"

Elof nodded somberly. "There was a will behind those
creatures. They herded us as they were herding their prey,
into the shallows."

"How are you so sure of that? Because you thought one
called your name?"

"Not one," said Elof. "All, together. As if the cries
of the whole pack merged into one greater voice . . . I
can say no more. Do we know where we are?"

"I hope so," said Kermorvan unhappily. "I had time
to make out something of the land. If we are on the southern side of these hills behind us, there is yet hope; if not
. . . But we will have to climb them to be sure."

"Aye," said Ils sourly. "But not before we've dried
ourselves out."

"And breakfast!" said Elof, rummaging in his sack.
"So much I learned from a friend called Roc, that the
worst world may look better from the other side of a meal.

> *"Hope or despair mean little to the starving dead,*
> *Hope may sustain a man—but better yet is bread!"*

They built a fire of driftwood against a boulder, though
Kermorvan was worried about the smoke being noticed.
But Elof put on his gauntlet and drew out the force of its
rising, so that it rolled sluggishly away down the stones
and over the water, like morning mist. Food and fire did
indeed hearten them all, and so when they were rested,

and their boots no longer squelched as they walked, they set out to climb the slope that led up from the beach.

It was a long road, for there was no path; the grass and undergrowth grew lush around their feet, and the sun was very hot. Small birds, blue as sapphires, whirled and screeched impudence among the blades and bushes. The trees were tall but widely scattered, giving little shade; many more were old stumps half hidden in the long grass, which hissed at the travelers in the hot breeze. They could take off their cloaks and jerkins, but not the burden of their packs. "So this is the Southlands!" panted Elof. "A wonder any man can live here!"

"Aye, no wonder they've got themselves red hair," said Ils thickly, shading her eyes. "Mine's like to catch flame any minute!"

"You should go further south yet," said Kermorvan with a grim smile, "for there the brilliance of the sun turns the soil hard and brown and parched, and yellows the grass even as it grows. And beyond that there are terrible scorched deserts of stone and sand, a barrier no man may pass, it is said. Sure it is that many have died trying to reach the far south, Brasayhal the Lesser."

"Strange!" smiled Elof. "Could they not simply sail there?"

Kermorvan shook his head. "At sea they call that region Niarad's Oven. The wind will drive ships there, only to vanish and leave them hanging becalmed, while their water runs out and their crews die terribly of thirst. None care now to risk that!"

Elof shuddered. "I cannot blame them. But who is this Niarad they name so often?"

"Do you not know?" exclaimed Kermorvan. "But of course, you would not. Well . . ." He paused, and looked back at the waves washing far below. "He is a power, a great power by sea. You might perhaps call him a cousin of your friend the Raven."

Ils shook her head decisively. "We hold otherwise, that they are of very different kinds and orders, those two! For one thing, Niarad is said to be much more ancient than Raven, being more akin to the wilder powers like Tapiau. For another, Raven is a wanderer, but Niarad's realm is the sea alone; it is said he *is* the sea, for he dwells always within it and seldom takes anymore bodily form, having little favor for any life beyond its bounds."

"Yet it is told that he appeared in man's form at the founding of our great cities!" said Kermorvan sharply. "And he is revered among us by many statues in that shape, and no other."

Ils shrugged. "Perhaps he did. Who can be sure, with the powers? Their nature is not yours or ours, their purposes seldom clear. Happy those who can avoid getting entangled in them."

"But that does not seem to be my fate," said Elof. And through the remainder of the climb he thought long and hard about that voice, and the name only he had heard.

But when at last they came to the summit he forgot it in an instant. At first concern drove it from his mind. Kermorvan had been looking around anxiously with a look of dawning recognition on his face, and abruptly he ran forward, his long hunter's stride carrying him up the hill well ahead of the others. And when he reached the crest, and looked out into the distance beyond, they saw him clench his fists and raise them to the skies, and shout something in a terrible voice. Startled and alarmed, they struggled and panted up the steep grassy slope to join him. He turned to face them as Elof crested the rise. "Damn that seabeast and all its kind to death and the Ice eternal! We're still *north* of the hills!" He turned, and stopped dead. "And look—by the Gates of Kerys, *look*—"

But Elof hardly heard him, for from here he could see beyond these grassy hills, and immediately he was lost in wonder at the lands that were spread out before him.

The Northlands had their richness also, and he had seen much of them in his roamings. But the north, even at its green best, still looked wild. The land beyond the hills was something he had never before seen, a country shaped in its wholeness by man. It was a land of little rivers, each a sparkling silver thread running through its own broad plain between long low hillsides. The plains were a patchwork of fields, green and brown and yellow, the hill slopes strung with terraced gardens and vineyards, or little clumps of well-tended woodland. Here and there in the nearer valleys he could almost make out groups of buildings that might be large estates or very small villages, never anything much larger. It looked intensely inhabited, that land; he felt it ought somehow to be quivering with the activity of the thousands of careful hands it must have taken to make and keep it that way. It was a vision of mastery, of prosperity, of a people who had turned all that lives and grows to serve them. Even the grass he stood among on this uncared-for hill seemed more regular, more even than it would be in the north. Nowhere did he see a trace of raw nature untamed, till he at last tore his eyes away from the amazing vista, to look down the steep slopes below into the deep dale that opened at his feet.

All along this lay a long arm of forest, like a dark mantle; of all he saw, it alone looked stern, wild, unmastered, a tangle of warring growth. It was taller than any woodlands of the cold northern realms, though it had no greater majesty. But as the dale neared the southern coast it diminished and grew shallower, and there at the last, within sight of the sea, the dark wall of the trees dwindled also, and stretched no further.

"It is fair, this Southland of yours," said Elof softly, and Ils, standing beside him, nodded agreement.

"Fair, aye, a noble stem! But how fares the flower?" Kermorvan's clear voice trembled. He took Elof by the shoulders, and twisted him round to look toward the southern coast. "See there! Look upon Kerbryhaine-in-Bryhaine, Kerbryhaine the City, the Fair!" His voice fell, almost to a whisper in the wind. "And look well, for you may never see more. We are come too late."

And Elof looked, in deep wonder and delight, upon the mightiest work of man that he had ever seen. At this far distance, brilliant in the hazy light, it might have been some minute toy or trinket he had shaped on his smallest anvil, carved out in his finest vise, some delicate brooch of polished gray-green rings, inlaid with fine flecks of ivory and topped at its rising heart with bronze and gold, tipped with silver at the water's edge. But now the silver seemed tarnished, and there was a darkness in the air, a somber reek that hung over the lands around like the smoke of many great fires.

"Battle is joined!" whispered Kermorvan, almost voiceless with anguish. "And I not with them!"

"Bear up!" said Ils sympathetically. "We'll get there soon enough . . ."

"Soon enough?" cried Kermorvan, in a frenzy. "If that boat had lasted we would have been there in only a day or two more! Now we have a week's march or worse!"

"Surely not!" exclaimed Ils. "It cannot be much above twelve leagues' distant, this great burg of yours, and over such fat easy country, for the most part! Cannot such hard doers as we are traverse that in three days?"

"Of course!" said Elof. "The coast curves out, we would have had to sail a long way round. But by land we need not follow it, we can go straight as the arrow flies. Once through that forest, what else—"

"We cannot go through that forest!" said Kermorvan in black anger, and sat down heavily in the grass. "We dare not!"

Elof stared down at his friend. "What's this? Dare not? The man who cut down half an Ekwesh war crew single-handed? Who took on a whole pack of snow-trolls, and tried to elbow a hunting whale aside?"

"Aye, and was ready to face down a dragon!" chimed in Ils. "Frightened of a few moldy trees, even to save his own city?"

Kermorvan's mouth twisted in disgust. "I am not afraid, as you mean it! Save of failure! Would you leap down a precipice to save going around it? Those are no ordinary trees. What you see below you there stretches back unbroken to the end of your mountains, Ils, and through the lands there, out to the east."

Ils sucked in her breath. "Part of the Great Forest, then? I had heard it ran still almost to the sea, but I did not know it was here."

"Aye, the Forest, Tapiau'la-an-Aithen, the black heart of the whole land. And we would be doing scant service to any of our homelands, north, south, or underground, if we vanished, never to appear again."

"Vanished?" said Elof.

"Indeed, and without trace. So do all who stray over

the fences of that shadowy realm. Do they not keep the tales of the Tree Realm, even, in the north?''

"Some," said Elof. "But surely, here . . .''

Kermorvan shook his head. "Once it was much larger, spreading some way down all the valleys you saw southward, and those margins of it were less shadowed than the rest. In the days of our strength, when we had suffered too much loss from that forest, my people rose against it as they would against an invader or oppressor, and cleared it back for many a league. But this glen we could never clear, and to this day we shun it, save for a few foolhardy ones. And they never trespass more than once.''

"They are too frightened to adventure a second attempt?''

"They never return from the first.''

Ils sniffed disdainfully. "This is a foolishness, my lads. The duergar walk at need in the margins of the Great Forest itself. Oh, it has its perils in plenty, yes. What part of Tapiau's realm would not? But nothing so absolute, so final, that we could not venture it—not even the Children of Tapiau. I can tell you now, I'd sooner risk crossing this little valley than see my homeland fall to the maneaters.''

"So you think me fool and coward that I dare not?'' said Kermorvan bitterly.

She rested a plump hand on his arm. "I think those who vanished, Kermorvan, were not such men as you. Or you, Elof. If the whales knew your name, perhaps the trees will know it too.''

Kermorvan visibly gathered himself together. He sat for a moment, hugging his knees and glaring out at the dark fumes that rose around his home. He shivered, for all the warmth of the sun. "So you both would venture it, for a land that is not your own?''

"You know what my true concern is," said Elof, and he, too, looked out to sea as once he had, in years that were past. "But if I wait till your city is overwhelmed, it will fail anyway. And other sothrans than you have been my friends. For them, for you, for my quest, yes, I would risk it.''

Ils chuckled. "That master of yours all but tipped Ansker and me into a crevasse like the others. That's one score to settle, beside all else with the Ice he serves. Aye, I'll risk it.''

Kermorvan gave a calm smile, as one whose troubles have been suddenly settled, and he sprang lightly to his feet. ''Then I cannot honorably do any less! Come! A river runs before the forest fence, we shall eat and drink there, and spy out our best road through. Come along! What do you stay for?'' And he strode purposefully away down the slope.

Ils grinned at Elof, but he found it hard to return her amusement. Fear and courage were things he must come face to face with, soon enough, and he marveled at how little he had understood them. On the Ekwesh ship and often since he had seen Kermorvan do bold deeds, and thought him simply unafraid, as little aware of perils as Elof himself might be of forgeburns in the heat of some great labor. Elof had admired that, but felt it was something inhuman, remote, nothing he could ever hope to imitate. But here, now Kermorvan had shown his fear. He had balked at what was evidently the worst peril he knew, a fear he had learned from childhood, and still he was walking, quite calmly as it appeared, into the shadow of it. How had he achieved that? Perhaps by finding—no, by creating a greater fear than that of the forest, the fear of dishonor. Elof sighed. What greater fear could he find in himself than of confronting his old master, armed with the very fruit and prize of Elof's own worst deed? In turning it against him, the Mastersmith, whatever ill he intended, would be doing no more than justice. What could he fear more than that?

The dark peaks of the trees seemed to thrust up at them from below. The travelers came level with them long before they had reached the valley floor, marveling at their great height, and the thickness of the roof of foliage they spread across the valley. ''You could almost walk over that!'' exclaimed Ils.

''It would be hardly less safe,'' said Kermorvan drily. By then, though it was yet early afternoon, the sun was dipping behind the steep valley walls, and an ancient gloom seemed to drape itself like a shadow-veil around the forest. To the bare lower tree trunks it clung, muffling sound, baffling the sight. Only at the margins did the trees glow light green in the sunlight; the bulk of the forest reared behind them like a wall of darkness. But as they stopped to eat under the shade of the outmost trees, rows of leaning alders along the riverside, it appeared quiet and peaceful enough. "And it cannot be very far through, at this point!" said Elof encouragingly, as they finished their scanty meal. He stooped to fill their leather waterbottles from the river as it came tumbling down the slope beside them, clear and shallow, to fall rumbling into its own deep-cut channel between the roots of tall firs like gateposts. Kermorvan, chewing an end of smoked meat, said nothing. "A few miles at most," Elof added. "And beyond that an easy way through the hills, by the look of it. We should be out by nightfall."

"If our way is straight," said Kermorvan, and rose. "Well, we have naught to gain by delay. Are we all prepared? Very well then. But Kerys! If it were not the only way . . ." And turning, he plunged between the alders into the gloom of the forest as a diver into deep water, and to the others, only a little way behind, he was as swiftly swallowed up.

Hastily they scrambled after him, and found the undergrowth tangling thick about them, sword ferns, wood ferns, five-finger ferns, tall horsetails gaudily ringed red and brown and green, tangled bushes of huckleberry, clumps of iris and many others they did not recognize. Low branches of hazel, maple and mountain lilac swept at their faces. But Kermorvan, only a few steps ahead, was gliding between them with the ease of great woodcraft, and by following him they found the clearer ways. Ils had least trouble of all, being the shortest, but Elof, wiping pollen from streaming eyes, tugged at his sword, yearning to hack his way clear; he remembered, though, the woodcraft he had learned from Kermorvan, and forbore. No need to make his trail any easier to follow, if followers there might be. He became acutely aware that the ground was sloping away beneath them, the walls of the dale turning steeply downward once more, and when he looked back the forest edge was high above his head, the afternoon light shining through it as over a high wall, split into smoky beams among the tree trunks. "There must be deep places in here where the sun never reaches, where no light ever shines!" He spoke softly, and shivered a little. Even the wind among the leaves seemed high overhead, and below here it was strangely still.

"Indeed there must!" laughed Ils. "And what would you do if you had not got one of the duergar with you, then? Eh? My eyes feel eased as they have not done since I was carried off by you squint-eyed men! In this fine shade I can see patterns on plant and stone that you cannot. I can see the small things as they stir among the leaves. The very fungi on the rotting wood glow with light for me to see by! Now say, have I not the better of you strong swordsmen?"

"You always had!" chuckled Elof. He was suddenly almost achingly glad she was here, with her sardonic good cheer and stonelike steadiness. In a rush of sudden affection he reached out and hugged her. She drove a bunched fist into his diaphragm, not especially hard.

"Hands off, you smelly young human! At least till you've had a bath in something better than seawater!"

He laughed, unoffended. They had been friends since their first day together in Ansker's forge. He had always found it easy to like Ils, to forget she was of a different, alien kind, one that held men in no great esteem, and that she was undoubtedly far older in years than he. Now, though, she had reminded him of that, in a roundabout, half-joking way. He did not mind, but nor, then, did he stop to think she might have been reminding herself.

Kermorvan's harsh whisper broke in on them. "Cease, you two! Are you on a country stroll?" They knew he was right, and fell silent. There were sounds in the forest they should be paying attention to, the hollow music of tumbling water, the rush of swaying branches, the rustle of leaf mold and snap of twigs on the forest floor, the patter and scurry of small things among them, the cries of birds. It was in these, in their sudden change or cessation, that they might find their only warnings of trouble, if trouble there came.

Elof listened then, and as he listened he became more and more aware of the size of the forest. The sounds of it seemed to stretch away into infinity, to drown any faint murmur from the world outside. A difficult patch of bush brought him breathless among a stand of redwood trunks; he leaned for a moment on a wide bole, looked upward and stood rigid with amazement. Up they soared over him, those ragged trunks, to an immense height, as if they were pillars supporting the sky. They were even taller, growing from this steep slope, than they had looked from the hillside. The smallest of them was as large as the largest in the northern forests he knew, and they grew closer together. The thick branches bristled out from the upper trunks to link and mesh into a roof so thick that only a shifting dapple of light fell to the damp floor beneath, and in some places less than that. Elof understood the tangle of growth he saw around him, plant climbing upon plant, all clustering like frantic children around the boles of the high trees, redwoods chiefly, but with firs and cypresses among them almost as tall. It was all a struggle toward the sun, a slow fierce war of jostling growth whose intensity, once perceived, was almost alarming. It was like walking among statues in attitudes of battle, and seeing blood flow. The forest seemed suddenly a less peaceful place, full of jealous, malign vitality, and he scurried on to keep up with the others, feeling he understood Kermorvan a little better now.

More time passed, another half-hour perhaps, and they were still going downhill. The light overhead seemed dimmer and grayer, the trees if anything even taller and more overpowering. Ils glared into the dimness. "How far down does this dale go? I cannot even see the further slope yet!"

Kermorvan nodded. "We will not be through before nightfall, I fear, Elof—"

But Elof gestured him to silence, and they stood very still. The birds had fallen almost silent. The sound of rushing water was louder now below them, but there was another very similar note above it, a new sound of rushing and pattering and splashing. Kermorvan looked up, and water dripped down upon his face. "Rain!" he said. "Well, we have shelter of a kind down here, no one place better than another. As well to press on." So they donned their cloaks, pulled their hoods out to shield their faces and walked on. The wind rocked the treetops and drove last autumn's skeletal leaves dancing across the forest floor, but the mighty branches above them scarcely stirred. The smell of the mold grew richer, stronger, heavier, almost stupefying. The ceiling of foliage did indeed stop the rain, but only to pass it on as slower, heavier drops, or a haze of spray which worked its way in everywhere. They were soaked in minutes, and deaf to everything save the sharp relentless pattering, a sound which lulled the mind and numbed it. Then it came upon them.

Elof heard only a sudden windrush, moaning like a great horn, and a creak of branches above him before something seemed to smash down onto his shoulders. He twisted, tried to reach his sword and instead found himself grappling with a tall figure, clawing at smooth bare skin, slick with rain. Then abruptly he was sprawling winded on the ground, a weight on his back and hard rod or staff pinioning his arms and head, driving his gasping mouth down into the mold. Beside him he could hear Ils thrashing and cursing; frantically he heaved upward, caught a glimpse of Kermorvan still on his feet, sword drawn, standing off a ring of indistinct shapes. A blow rang on his scalp, and he sank down stunned. Dimly he heard a rush, clanging, shouts and a thud as something heavy toppled down on the ground. Then he was hauled roughly to his feet and hurried stumbling to one side, unseen arms pinioning his hands behind him.

Through blurred eyes he made out Ils, disheveled and furious-looking but otherwise unharmed, similarly held in front of him. "Don't struggle!" she hissed. "Deadly danger! Tapiau's Children!"

Only then did he notice clearly the strange figures who held her. They were not a comforting sight. They looked human, but they were inhumanly tall and slender, nearly twice Ils's height and very long-limbed, with skin the color of light honey. It showed, for they wore little, and looked to him more savage than the Ekwesh. That much he had time to notice before the furious struggle around Kermorvan spilled over. A body slammed against him, the grip on his arms broke and he tumbled forward into the path of another running figure, who leaped over him without stopping and vanished into the bushes. Shouts rang out, a scream; he sprang up, swept the black sword from its scabbard with a cold whistle, and fell upon the figures holding Ils. They dropped her arms and danced back; one flung a javelin, he swung his sword at it and it exploded in flinders. Then, quite suddenly, they were gone. There was no trampling in the thick undergrowth, not a sound of flight; it was as if earth and tree-shadow had swallowed them up.

Ils bounced to her feet and pointed. Elof spun round and saw Kermorvan, breathing hard, with a great splash of blood across his cloak, and more along his blade. And at his feet, twisting, lay one of the strange creatures. Elof stepped closer, and gaped with astonishment. Under its dusty harness of metal-studded leather, it was unmistakably a woman.

"What forest demons have we here?" panted Kermorvan. He looked deeply troubled. The woman's long arm was deeply gashed, and a puddle of blood was soaking into the mold around the shattered fragments of what had been a vicious-looking hooked pike. He and Elof looked at each other in momentary helplessness; this was an enemy, but could they let her bleed to death in front of them? They themselves had only been held, not stabbed as they could have been. And she could be some surety for them. Suddenly, without a word spoken, Kermorvan was on his knees, pinching the wound shut with his wiry fingers, and Elof and Ils were rummaging in their packs for bandages and salves.

"This should be sewn up," growled Kermorvan, "but we cannot take time for that. A bandage is only a minute's work and will bar the blood enough for now; let us hope her friends have the skill. Elof, do you stop her twisting her arm, thus. Ils, do you keep a watch. What are these half-men, anyway?"

Elof took the long arm in his lap, and barely managed not to drop it as he saw the hand. It was half again as long as his own, and weirdly unlike it. It was as if an ordinary hand had been taken and stretched, but without growing any thinner. The four main bones and the fingers beyond them were all far longer, and in repose they curled inward like a hook, meeting the palm. The thumb, by contrast, was little larger than his own, and set more to the side of the hand. But the muscles and tendons stood out around it as they did around the fingers, with an impression of wiry strength. He imagined trying to do fine smithying with such a hand, and shook his head. No wonder they were so primitive! But something jarred within his mind, and he looked again at the harness, and wondered. It was not the crude breechclout he had first thought at her thighs, but a shaped strip of soft leather bound round her hips with a broad belt of the same stuff. Not a bad garment, if all its wearer cared about was protection, not modesty, and there seemed to be patterns worked on the leather. There definitely were on the broad studded strips that ran from the belt to cover her breasts, restraining them and acting as light armor. Protection again, but no undue concealment. It looked like fighting gear for a scout or fast skirmisher, cut down to the absolute minimum. But she would still need boots. He looked down at her feet, and felt cold. They were bare, and they were shaped as weirdly as the hand. But there, somehow, it looked even worse. What then of her face? It was hidden by a tangled mat of brownish hair; hesitantly he brushed it aside and this time did jump. The eyes were a glitter of icy green, wide, wild, slanted like an animal's, the face around them drawn back in taut snarling lines, lips stretched transparent over grinding teeth. It looked so like an animal, he expected her to fly at him, but then he knew it for a grimace of terror on features that were essentially as human as his own. He opened his hand reassuringly, drew it back and saw her relax. Kermorvan finished his bandaging, reached up and swiftly bound the bent arm to her body. "That will stop the wound opening again, for now. We had best be on our way now, and her with us."

"Is that wise?" asked Ils drily. "Is taking hostages honorable?"

Kermorvan winced. "It is necessary. Helping her was right, but it has cost us the minutes we gained putting them to flight. Anyway, she is no hostage, I will not harm her. But they are not to know that. Come!"

Another windrush moaned among the trees, and a sudden spattering of rain fell about them. There was a loud rustle of leaves. "Too late!" said Elof through clenched teeth, and he cursed himself. It was obvious now how the other creatures had vanished so quickly. He of all of them should have seen it: that hand had been ideally shaped for tree-climbing as he would shape his forge-tools. Now they had come back, with others, moving with the wind so they would not be heard, and swung down from all sides. They stood now in a wide ring, alert and menacing. They had bows now, and more spears poised to hurl, and even Kermorvan made no attempt to move.

Elof could see their faces clearly then, and they surprised him. Men and women both were much alike, long fair faces, clean-lined and clear-skinned, with high cheekbones and square jaws. There was little expression in them but anger flickered about their mouths. The woman staggered to her feet and stumbled over to them, clutching her bandaged arm.

"If that'd been a man," growled Ils disgustedly, "you'd just have left him!"

"Of course," said Kermorvan absently, then looked slightly puzzled. Elof held up his hand impatiently; the woman had been saying something to the others, and it seemed to him that he almost understood it. He tensed as one man stepped forward, spear poised to stab, and looked at the three of them. He stood with his legs apart, shoulders bowed, but even so he seemed far taller than any normal man, looming over them all. Then he said something, and his voice was deep, but soft and gusty. Elof cocked his head, and the man repeated it.

"Er' Aika' iya-wahsa?"

"He's asking us if we're Ekwesh!" exclaimed Elof. Ils gave a snort of disgust, and Kermorvan a rare peal of laughter. "No! Not Ekwesh!" barked Elof, hoping he would be understood as easily. "Ekwesh—" He clenched his fist, and made a gesture of hurling something aside. "Do you understand?"

"Tapiau's Children you called them, Ils," said Kermorvan softly. "Didn't I hear Ansker say you trade news with these folk?"

"More than news," said Ils tautly. "Those are duergar

bows and blades—small comfort! But there is little contact, they are strange folk, and the duergar do not have the
freedom of their realm. I have never before seen them
myself, and I do not know their tongue. Indeed I am surprised to find them here, for they dwell mostly deep within
the forest to the east.'' The woodman stepped forward,
spear still poised, and stooped down to peer at her. "She
is of the duergar, the lady Ils," said Elof, slowly and
clearly.

The woodsman turned to Kermorvan, who stood very
straight, with folded arms. "I am a warrior of the Southlands," he said calmly, "by name Kermorvan." The
woodman stiffened slightly, but made no hostile move.
Momentarily a strange, remote look shaded his eyes.

"And I am from the north," said Elof, pointing uphill.
"A smith. Called Elof." He tapped his chest, because the
woodman had looked at him so blankly. "Elof."

Abruptly the woodman grounded his spear, and called
out an order. The bows were lowered, but the woodfolk
swarmed forward, so quickly the travelers were caught off
guard. Before they knew what was happening they were
again pinioned in huge hands, strong enough, as Elof now
knew, to sustain a heavy body swinging through branches.
He felt his feet leave the ground, legs dangling, and then
the forest seemed to rush at him as the woodfolk charged
into the trees. He flinched, but nothing struck him, though
he seemed surrounded by rushing walls of green; he could
not tell who carried him, whether the others were with
him, whether he was on the ground still or up among the
branches. The mad whirl seemed to last minutes only, but
when his sight steadied he was moving through a totally
different part of the forest. Around him was deep gloom,
and when he looked up there was nothing more, no trace
of sky or light of any kind. Somewhere beyond his sight
water ran hollow and deep. A sound of wind in branches
seemed a distant thing, high up and far off; over his head
the branches scarcely stirred, as if the wind from the world
outside could hardly reach them. He could have been lost
in the deepest delvings of the duergar, and the few immense boles that were gradually becoming visible in the

gloom only some carved pillars, stout enough to be a mountain's roots. *"Ils?"* he called. *"Kermorvan?"*

"Here!" cried voices some way off, and then they stopped. A hand shook him roughly, and he said no more. Ahead of him a glimmer of light was growing, and he saw that his captors were moving across a forest floor now clear and almost bare of anything save leaf mold, fallen branches and strange fungi; small wonder at that, where no sunlight could reach. But ahead of it was a shaft of brightness, of dazzling brightness, a clearing in the deepest wood. Nothing grew in it higher than grass studded with small gold flowers, save at its heart a vast red trunk, alone and unsupported, glowing in the rich light of afternoon. Toward this he was rushed, half expecting to be tied to it. But instead they stretched out his arms and rested his palms flat against the bark. Then, almost reverently, they set him down and stepped back. He half turned to look up at them, taking one hand away. One, a woman, reached out an arm that seemed too long, like a spider's, and pressed the hand back, flat. Then she stepped away once more.

Bewildered, he turned to face the tree. He smelled the faint aroma of the sun-warmed wood and found it pleasant. It felt much as any other redwood, fibrous, flaky bark on a heavily ridged bole, softly rough to the touch. That, too, he found more pleasant than usual; it felt positive, as it did touching an animal with a soft coat, one of his old cattle perhaps, feeling the quickening of life beneath the skin, the play of muscle, the bloodpulse in the veins. Here, somehow, he seemed to feel the life of the tree, the moving sap, the sunning leaves, the drinking roots, the slow rhythm of unhurried, unhindered growth. It was a strange, a unique, exciting feeling, and he thought of a whole forest that pulsed with life like this, his mind racing from tree to tree, to shrub, stalk, fern, grassblade, seed, fungus, spore. And there too among them, darting like the very sparkles of the sunbeam, were patches of quicker, hotter vitality that enlivened the whole, spice that made a sweet dish more than bland—animal life among the plants. He felt his weariness, his shock, fade in the sun's warmth, the thirst in him melt away, almost as if he also could put

down roots to tap the Earth. That struggle for existence
he had noted now seemed more like a dance, a piece of
music made of many themes in which each won itself a
place, a time, and dared not outstay it without discord. It
would fade when it was done, but grow again. He saw, in
its totality, the interlinking, interwoven life of the forest,
and the greater whole that its parts made up. A leaf trembled, a tree creaked, a hawk stooped, ants scuttled; in a
clearing, startled by nothing, a bright-eyed deer leaped
and sprang away. A thought awoke. And he understood.

Why have you come here?

"Why?" He stared wildly around, but he knew he had
not heard that voice in his ears. It was a vast sound, and
cold, like a great shout from afar. It had a strange wild
note in it, waxing and waning like the gusty wind, like
the clear horns of the village hunters he remembered,
blowing in the distance near dusk. "My name is Elof—"

I know your name. Why do you trespass in my domain?

"I . . . I seek to reach the . . . the great city of the
southmen. The Ekwesh besiege it now."

*I have had tidings. What would you there, you and your
friends?*

Elof looked nervously at the tree, staring up toward its
lowest branches, high above. He noticed then that its summit was sharp, not rounded as so many tall trees were by
strikes of lightning. Kermorvan had said the forest was his
people's foe; did he dare risk telling it, this voice that
seemed already to know so much, about his weapon, his
quest? "I . . . and my companions . . . we bring help to
them, that is all."

Three against thousands? They will scarcely miss you.

Elof pushed his lips against a bitter retort. "Do you
favor the Ekwesh, then?"

The light seemed to be fading, and looking up Elof saw
that the sun had sunk below the rim of the ring of trees.
Gray clouds were drifting across the circle of sky above.
Far distant in the wood a wolf howled, a sound of distant
anguish and pain.

*I? I do not favor the Aika' iya-wahsa, nor he who drives
them on, Louhi's huntsman. Do you not know me?*

"No!" said Elof, angry at being toyed with, yet wondering even so if he spoke the truth. The wind rose, the trees shook and rustled, bending before it as if in obedience.

I am Tapiau.

Elof's fingers dug into the soft bark. "I know no more of you than that name."

Do you not? There was almost a note of amusement in the words. A great cloud of pigeons flew up, whirred around, settled among the branches once again. *Know this, then. One Alone. That I am a power among these trees, that this is my domain, and I gave you no leave to tread within it. You should have chosen some other way south.*

"We did!" barked Elof, angry and shaken. "We tried to go by sea, but were forced ashore by whales!"

Even so? Then Niarad also will not have you within his domain. But I will be merciful. Go, take your companions, and retrace your steps!

"But this is vital!" pleaded Elof desperately. "We bear . . . something of great import. If we do not reach the southburg within a few days we will be too late!"

Wind whipped at him, the leaves crackled. He looked up, around. Gray cloud now blanketed the sky, and sunset was near. Drops pattered down among the leaves once more. No word was spoken, but Elof felt at once that wall of shadow he had first seen, an immense indifference. He beat his fist on the bark, but knew as he did so that it was useless. The voice was not in the tree; the voice was in the whole forest around him, stretching out to its remotest, unguessed-at distances. The tree was a focus only, a local one, like a window, a door. And now it was closed, barred, shuttered. The forest had turned away from him.

He bowed his head, and his hands sank down on the tree. He was about to take them away when he heard a harsh cry from above, saw a flickering speck of black out of the corner of his eye. He looked up again. The sky shivered with light, and there was a distant crackle of thunder. There were two of them, tossing and swirling around the blasts of the upper air, riding the coming storm as if for sport. Down they came, circling, spiraling, cawing carelessly to each other in tones he seemed almost to understand. Squawking and flapping, they burst in among the branches of the great tree, scattering a rain of dry scaly needles and cones down upon Elof's unprotected head, and with a final insolent caw they settled on a low thick branch that bent alarmingly under their weight.

One cocked its head and regarded him with beady amusement. *"Thinking!"* it croaked. He heard the word clearly.

"Remembering!" croaked the other.

"Delay!" said the first, and ruffled his wings.

"Danger!" said the second, and in high alarmed tones added *"Help!"* It rattled its long black beak loudly, and wiped it along the bark.

"Storm!" said the first.

"Fly!" croaked the second, and they took off in a thrashing flurry of wings. Thunder rumbled again, startlingly near, and again the sky was lit pale. Into the middle of it they vanished, dwindling to dark specks, and were no more seen.

"I could understand them!" said Elof aloud, staring after them.

Those who have tasted the blood of the worm may come to understand much, in time.

"You again!" gasped Elof. "What now?"

I spoke in haste. You did not say enough of your errand. It is important, and I will not hinder you. But still you may not walk freely in this land, nor linger a moment longer than you must. My folk will bear you to its southern borders faster than you could go yourself.

"Thank you, Lord of the Forest!" breathed Elof.

Do you call me that? I thank you, and for thanks, be warned. The trees creaked softly. *That which you bear is not enough. More is needed.*

"More, lord?" breathed Elof, flooded suddenly with despair. "I have no more to give . . ."

Not yet. But I would aid your quest somewhat. Hold still. There was a sharp, snapping crack, and something fell slithering down the great trunk, to land with a crash beside him. He looked, and saw that it was a small branch, a twig really, but thickly covered in the scaly redwood needles. *Take that, and guard it well. While there are needles on it, even withered and dead, something of the*

*virtue of forests will cling to it. It will not shield you in
the brightness of day, nor in the clear moonlight, nor
among the cold stoneworks of men, but among nature, in
times of twilight and shadow it will help you pass unseen.*

Elof stooped to take it, and bowed his head. "We will
use it well, lord, and acknowledge the power of your
realm. But what else must I . . ."

*It is nothing I can give. You will know it, I think, when
most you need it. Now go!*

Again Elof felt his arms seized, found himself whirled
round, and saw the trees come rushing at him. The stormy
air whistled around him, the branches swung and nodded
wildly, and now the movement did not stop, but went on
and on, a great giddy rush that left him breathless, barely
able to think. Then it ended. The onrush dropped suddenly, sickeningly downward, then the grip on his arms
was released, foliage whirled about him, and he tumbled
with a rustling crash into a drift of rotten leaves. He sat
there a moment, winded, shaking his head in utter confusion. But still clasped in his hand was a long sprig of
redwood.

"Elof!" shouted Ils, and as he picked himself up, dust-
ing away damp fragments of decay, he saw his friends
rushing through the trees toward him. Ils made it first,
and caught him in a hug that strained his ribs. "Where'd
you get to, idiot? All we knew is that they whisked us off,
we heard you shout, and then we were swung here!"

"And dropped," said Kermorvan, flexing his arm gingerly. "But they left us all our gear. I begin to think I was
not so foolish, tending that witchwoman."

"They are a strange people," said Ils.

"Surely, if they are stranger than the mountain-folk,"
grunted Kermorvan, as they turned to the pile of gear, and
began to gather it up. "At a hazard, Elof, you were taken
to their chieftain?"

"Say instead, their father," said Elof.

"What?"

"Later," said Elof, unnerved. He turned to ease the
redwood sprig carefully into a pocket of his pack, and
strap it on. "Ask me later, if at all. We must leave here
at once."

Kermorvan shrugged. "Easily done. We have come right across the dale, and are almost at the southern fence of the trees. A pass opens between the hills only an hour or two's walk east of here."

Ils shivered. "But the weather! Can't we settle down for the night here in the shelter of the trees, rather than out there on the windy hills—"

The sound that stilled her was not loud, but it was very large, as if many trees and bushes rustled all at once. They turned, and became aware of the shadow that moved slowly among the thicker green behind them. It looked like a moving wall behind the leaves. Hands crept to sword and axe as it lurched slowly closer, then fell away in dismay as they saw the true size of the thing. The bulky body rose to more than twice Kermorvan's height above the ground, on four legs that rivaled the redwood trunks around them in both girth and appearance, for the whole brute was covered in sparse but shaggy brown hair, thinnest on its small triangular ears. Small red-rimmed eyes, glinting with a mildly wicked merriment, gleamed out from the bony, high-crowned skull, and below them, weirdest of all, two vast curving blades of yellowish-white horn or tooth. Longer even than the very forelimbs of the beast, they crossed at the tips, and between them rose an immense flexible snout that browsed and ruffled among the thick foliage.

"Mammut!" whispered Ils. "But a kind greater than any I have heard of, that's sure." It looked absurd, that snout, until they saw it pull down a huge branch with casual strength to shame the arm of a troll. Not far away among the trees came another, similar, crash and rustle. Then the travelers backed away as one, very slowly.

"Would you still linger?" hissed Elof. "Tapiau bids us begone!"

"I know well enough when I've outstayed my welcome!" Ils muttered. "Yon hill takes on a strange allure." So they caught up the last of their gear, and wrapping their dark cloaks about them they moved silently away among the trees, until they came at last out into the cloudy dusk. The hillside beyond was steep, the grass and bushes tangled, but they did not stay to rest, clambering up it as fast as they could go. A blaring call, trumpeting derision, sounded at their backs, but only Elof stopped and turned, looking back across the dull sheen of the leaf-roof, to where it parted a little around the pinnacle of the tallest tree, and touched for a moment the rough outline of the sprig within his pack. Then Ils called him, and he hurried on.

CHAPTER TEN

The Tempering

So it was that same night that the three travelers crossed the southern slopes of the high hills, and came at last down into the fair land of Bryhaine. They found the pass without trouble, and came through it into country that Kermorvan knew well. Even in the dark, with only a faint moon glimmering through the heavy clouds, he was able to guide them along many little winding paths on the hillsides, and lead them so well that when they at last made camp by the mouth of a narrow dale, the hills lay behind them. Beside their camp a small swift stream disappeared downhill in a stairway of falls and deep pools, and at dawn next day, having bathed in the pools, they followed it on its way. It wound away between little stands of trees, across patches of green meadow, and came at last to a low stone wall which marked the edge of a vineyard. Already the fruit hung heavy on the vines as they passed. "A good vintage this year, by the look of it!" said Ils.

"But who will harvest it, I wonder?" said Elof. "Listen!"

"I hear nothing!" said Ils, puzzled.

"Nothing indeed!" said Elof. "Beyond the vines lie fields, a farm. And yet these farmers are surely not greater sluggards than the northerners I knew. Some at least should be up and at work now. Do you hear the clink of hoes, the cackle of fowl, the call of animals driven to pasture or to milking?"

"Nothing," said Ils, and so it was. It was now high summer, and those lands were at their richest, the corn

287

ripening all across the broad plains, the fruit swelling on the orchard boughs. Yet the only sound of man in them was the rumor of distant war, and it echoed in emptiness. All the folk had fled.

"A few, perhaps, will have gone inland," said Kermorvan as they walked down to the first river ford. "Westward toward the wild land around the roots of the mountains, where I suppose the duergar gates are, Ils. But that to us is rough and dubious country. Most of them will now be within the walls of the city, eating up its store of supplies, draining its wells and crowding it out so sickness spreads. I would not have admitted the peasants, but the syndics will."

"It seems the kinder course," said Elof doubtfully.

"Kind for the moment, unkind for the future. They will hinder and weaken our defenses, and perhaps bring doom upon everyone, when they would have been as safe or safer inland."

"Even so," said Ils, "could you drive them clamoring from the gate?"

"I would never have let them reach the gate to begin with, but made preparations, issued commands against any emergency, and seen that they were understood. As they would be, were the need made clear. How else may a realm be defended? But this the syndics will not do, lest they alarm the poor tender people. Well, I'll wager they are alarmed now!"

And he strode splashing fiercely across the ford, checking his pace not the least against the strong current that tugged at their ankles.

To three hardened travelers this was an easy country, its paths and rutted roadways a great luxury; they made a fast pace, and it was not yet noon when they crested the first range of hills between them and the city. Now it was only some five or six leagues distant, and much clearer to see, though the air shimmered with the midday heat. From a brooch it had grown to a great shield-shape, set upon a checkered blazon of fields and with high-crowned towers for its boss, atop a stone hill from which the ivory walls ran outward as ripples spread in water. A fair sight it would have been in days of peace, but now both blazon and shield bore the strokes and scars of war. Smoke arose in great wreathing coils from many of the blazoned fields, brown as the scars of some spreading disease among the rich greens and yellows of summer. The sea, too, was stained, its tarnish clear now as innumerable black flecks of sails. Many as there were, the high walls dwarfed them, and from within these no smoke came. But it was clear the city now stood encircled, and the siege had begun.

It was a great sight and a terrible one, that beleaguered burg. Kermorvan took one horrified look, and would look no longer, but strode down the slope into the vale beyond. Elof and Ils looked at one another, and ran after him.

The valley below was wider and its floor less even, but Kermorvan went striding across the lands like a man within yards of his own threshold and a storm coming on. The others had to hold him back almost forcibly, and remind him that it would do no good to arrive at the city exhausted and without due care. It was as well they were heeded, for in crossing a small farm they rounded a corner and came suddenly upon a foraging party of Ekwesh, nine in all, lolling at their ease among the arbors. For a heartbeat their stern copper faces were blank with astonishment, then Kermorvan was among them before they could drop their looted wineskins and snatch up their spears; he fell upon them like a howling wind. Three he slew with two great slashing strokes even as they scrambled up, and two he felled in a breath when they stood to fight. Elof and Ils, caught up then and engaged the rest, and the dark sword sang in the light as it shattered their spears. Ils with her axe hewed the legs from one, Elof thrust through another who sought to stab her, and the last two turned to flee. But Kermorvan caught them by the farmhouse wall, knocked one sprawling and cut down the other among the splintered debris of the door. The fallen warrior sprang up with a long knife poised to throw, but Ils's axe struck him between the shoulders and he fell. Kermorvan drove his sword through him. "For none," he said, "must escape to give the alarm, or we would be hunted down in hours. I doubt not the land here is alive with them, for with so large a force they cannot have brought much provender. We must go carefully. Well, they have a few less mouths to feed now, and ere long, I hope, fewer yet. Let them dine on these their friends, if they find them!''

For all Kermorvan's words of caution, he still led them at great speed across the country, only taking more care around estates and dwellings. These were few, and scattered. ''Does Bryhaine not have any other towns?'' Elof asked Kermorvan.

''Only three of any size, a port to the south named Bryhannec and two inland towns. Our ports to the north are smaller, about the size of your large Northland towns. Most people prefer to dwell within one great center; a legacy, perhaps, of the days when we first came to this land across the eastern ocean, and were alone among immense forests and mountains vaster than aught we had left behind us. Even now we still cleave to the coast, wherever we settle.''

They saw three other Ekwesh parties before they left the valley, but only at a distance; they were sauntering along, evidently not expecting trouble, so it was safe to assume the others had not yet been missed. As night fell the travelers came into the first slopes of the hills, and made a comfortable camp in a shepherd's empty hut; they ate well, though they lit no fire.

''Our food is all but gone,'' said Ils sleepily.

''What of it?'' said Kermorvan, already wrapping himself in his stained cloak. ''Tomorrow we will win through to the city, or have no cares about food thereafter. As well keep up our strength.''

''Tomorrow,'' thought Elof as he sought the sleep he felt he would never find. ''Tomorrow the city—and what then? Will I find it then, that one more thing I need? Can I possibly find it in time?'' But then sleep stole on him unbidden and he walked through uneasy dreams. Faces swirled before him, translucent against darkness like moonlit clouds, faces of Ils, Kermorvan, Roc and ever of Kara. But behind them all came the sword, its fell patterns no longer fixed but swirling like oil on water, changing so he could read them like script, and he knew with mounting excitement that it was about to reveal to him the secret he needed to know. Then it shimmered, shook, swirled again and the pattern twisted into hateful faces that leered and mocked at him. And still the sword advanced, swelled and grew gigantic, till it struck at him with a crash and a rumble like a falling mountain, and he was cloven to the heart.

"What was that?" he cried, sitting bolt upright. Then he realized he had been dreaming, and yet it seemed to him that faint echoes of his dream still shivered through the cool dawn air.

"A single thunderbolt," said Kermorvan softly from his place by the doorway. "The flash awoke me. Yet such a thing is rare in our summer storms. Strange. Still, the awakening came timely. We must be on our way!"

Elof and Ils rose, grumbling a little, and made a hearty breakfast on the last of their stores, while Kermorvan fumed and fretted and would hardly touch a morsel. He even grudged them minutes to splash water on their faces at the nearby spring before setting off up the hill, but now he kept a more cautious pace, an eye on the land around and great care that they should not show themselves. This close to the city they dared not cross the hillcrests and be seen against the sky, but walked a weaving path between the slopes, ever alert for sign or sound of danger. It was late afternoon, therefore, when they made their way into a little coppice of trees that skirted the last and lowest slope. Elof knew they could not be far now, for the sound of the sea was faint in his ears, and he could taste it on the breeze. But there were other sounds and taints also, and less welcome. "Here we may rest a while, and scout out our way," said Kermorvan. "The far end of this looks out upon the city."

They came to a line of trees linked by a great bank of bushes and tall ferns; cautiously he parted them, and peered out. Then Elof heard him catch his breath, and it sounded like a sob, whether of rage or sorrow or despair he could not tell. He pushed forward also, and looked out, and he, too, caught his breath at the sight before him. "It reminds me of my own village!" he said softly, and choked. "You will think that foolish! When it could have fitted into a tiny corner of this great burg . . ."

Kermorvan shook his head firmly, though his face was gray. "No! Never foolish. The lesser must be free of this slaughter, or how shall the great endure? It is the same, and as evil, be it writ large or small.''

"He is right," said Ils. She unslung her pack, and pulled from it a bright shirt of fine mail. "Your folk, mine, his— their deaths weigh every bit as heavily in the scale, and the balance is a fearful one. This must stop!"

They were no more than a half-league now from the city walls, on a level with its highest towers, and it lay spread out before them. To Elof's eyes it seemed to spill outward from a central hill, outward across the flatter lands to either side. A great encircling wall, fronting the harbor and running from there inland in a horseshoe shape, seemed barely able to contain such a vast sprawling scatter of rooftops, all shades of slate, gray-green and weathered ivory. It seemed to Elof that his village and every other village and town he had ever seen, whether of men or duergar, might be dropped among them all together, and never noticed. Ivory also were the high walls which meandered here and there between the rooftops, setting off one section of the city from another in a way that looked at first meaningless, till he realized he was seeing the history of its growth, outward like the rings which mark the passage of seasons in a tree. In their way these rings were also a mark of time and growth. When, every few generations, the community dwelling beyond the walls had grown too large to defend from within, they would simply build another section of wall, or even an entire new encircling wall, round it. Sometimes the wall behind might be demolished, but most often it was left as an extra line of defense. Elof traced these walls inward, and marveled at the great number of them. This city was an ancient place.

And no part of it seemed more ancient, or more noble, than what he saw at its heart, wellspring of all that growth. The heart of the brooch, the shield-boss, was a rising promontory of rock, a gentle slope on its narrow landward side but dropping as a sheer cliff to the waters of the harbor. Atop this, like a high crest on a helm, it bore up a great fortress of seven high towers. Gray were the lower slopes of the citadel, for they were carved whole from the living rock. But above them the towers were of ivory stone, as also the walls and roofs that ran between them. They stood like a diadem on the brow of the rock, the tallest of them rising straight up from the cliff face above the waters. And the tops of the towers glowed under the noon sun, more brightly even than the sea which lay beyond them, for they were roofed all with bronze, and crowned in bright gold.

So much Elof would have seen if he had first gazed upon Kerbryhaine the City in the days of its peace. There might perhaps have been great ships stirring in the harbor, white sails spread, or a thin wisp of smoke arising from some great cooking fire in the citadel, where an evening's banquet was being prepared. But now there was much, much more. The sun still shone mellow upon the tower tops, the many-hued banners they bore swirling proudly in the wind from the sea. But against them rose banners greater and more telling, dark reeks that heralded no feast fit for men, the high plumes of black smoke from the ruined lands around.

From here the devastation worked upon those lands was all too clear, the scatter of camps, emplacements, trenches and hasty fortifications, and the files of black-clad warriors that flowed among them like ants from a nest. What had once been buildings beyond the walls were but blackened shells now; what had been fields and pastures and parks were trampled down and strewn about with litter of war gear, loot and debris. What must once have been pleasant groves beneath the walls had been hewn down and stacked against the gates, or made into great laddered platforms to be pushed on rollers against the walls, and spill warriors inside.

The harbor, too, was despoiled, its waters choked now with the skeletal remains of ships, some beached, some thrust up out of the polluted water. Beyond the seawall the sails that crowded shore and sea around, like a spreading stain, were every one of them black. The grim hulls of the Ekwesh rode at anchor, the livid faces painted along their flanks menacing the city with gaping jaws. From their decks, as from the land, catapults raked the ramparts with terrible volleys of arrows and harpoons and shot of metal and stone.

But it was not only from field and sea that the banners of destruction arose, for new fires had sprung up. The ruin outside had entered. The outermost encircling wall, that only the day before had stood a stern bulwark against the spreading reek, now bore a terrible wound in its northern flank, a great jagged collapse of stone, scarred black and ashen as if by blasting heat. Into it, like a plague, streamed the black and white banners of the Ekwesh. Beyond it rooftops of gray and cream lay broken, and among them danced triumphant fires. Through the shattered streets figures of men flickered back and forth in bitter conflict, darting and dodging among the buildings, and on parts of the wall above, defenders still strove to turn back the enemy, lest they be pinioned from both sides. But the banners pressed even further and further on, and more advanced from outside. It was like a blight that had settled on a fair flower and now was creeping inward by degrees, toward the heat. Already the somber ensigns flew above a high round tower at the harbor end of the wall, and behind its battlements of sea-whitened stone robed figures were gathering. The first wall was breached; overwhelmed, futile, the first circle taken. The Ekwesh had overwhelmed the outer defenses, and were within the city.

"How?" whispered Kermorvan in anguish. "That wall should have held many days yet, even against this force. Yet already they stand atop Vayde's Tower! They dare . . . What sorcery has done this?"

Elof looked long and hard at that blasted gap, and in his memory embers burst into sudden flame. Suddenly he was back on another hillside, above another town, with the echoes of another thunderbolt yet ringing in his ears.

"Sorcery indeed!" he breathed, and a black anger awoke in him. "For so my town was taken. If there was any doubt it ends now! *He* is here! For he has woken the lightning to break your walls."

"Is that then what we heard?" muttered Kermorvan, shaking his head. "But the outer wall only has fallen. The inner ones are in less good repair. Why should he not strike them at once?"

"Because the spell exhausts him. He must dance himself to a frenzy in heavy costume and mask, and put forth great power—greater here than he used against Asenby, where he had only to strike down a man, not a wall. He will not do that again this day! But tomorrow . . ."

"By tomorrow's dawn," grated Kermorvan, "his dance will be still forever. Look there!"

Kermorvan's keen eyes narrowed, he was staring across to the roof of the captured tower, almost level with them now. Elof followed his look. Even at this distance the figures were distinct in the clear light; some bore spears and black and white armor, most wore the robes and hats of chieftains, but among them walked one whose robes were plain black and without ornament, though he bore some great crested headdress. To the ramparts he came, mounted them and leaned over with arm outstretched. And as he did so, as trumpets brazened rising discord, the smoky sunlight flashed sullen and strange from the blade he swept in a wide arc, like some terrible scythe of the unseen. One of the crude siege platforms was hauled rumbling forward against the defended end of the wall. The first warriors were poised ready to spring down, when grapples were flung from the ramparts, and a smoking barrel of oil or tar was rolled out and down into its heart. It blazed at once like a gigantic torch, and shadows capered in the flame and fell from its ladders, ants caught in a bonfire. Then the grapples were hauled back, and the whole ramshackle structure lurched, tilted, folded inward and collapsed upon the fleeing Ekwesh beneath. But even as it crashed in ruin, banners dipped and signaled from the tower, and catapults, mangonels and other engines were drawn up to harry the wall anew. Boulders drummed upon the stonework, smashed the turrets, sent crenellations flying in deadly splinters. Darts hailed down on the parapets, and stricken men toppled over onto the heads of their foes. Another platform was pushed forward, files of men gathering around it, but they seemed to falter a moment in their advance as they came within range of the burning tower. Again the sword scythed out into the air, the invaders' battle line blurred, blended and streamed together like the orderly traffic of an anthill stirred by a child's stick. The new assault washed forward through the flaming ruin of the last as if it were not there. Onto the plat-

form men crowded as it was thrust forward, and even
before it crashed and swayed against the wall they were
hurling themselves down upon the very spearpoints of the
defenders, overwhelming them in a tumbling, insane wave.
Flame raced among the dry fields from the fallen tower,
and smoke hid the scene.

Elof turned away, hand to his mouth. A great emptiness
seemed to open up inside, a chill void in which thought
and feeling alike were swallowed up. Kermorvan looked
at him fiercely, questioningly. Elof nodded once, and felt
a bitter, salty taste flood his mouth, a sickening, bloody
taint. He spat into the bushes at his feet, and it was blood,
and there was a sudden sting in the back of his hand; he
had bitten deep into his finger without noticing.

"Then all that remains is to bring you to him," said
Kermorvan calmly. His cold eyes met Elof's, and his face
was as bleak as his words. "For this I have passed over
Ice and sea and many other perils, and I will not now fail.
Will you?"

Numbly Elof shook his head.

"Very well, then. We will wait here until dark, and then
I will bring you to the city and tower through the Ekwesh
lines. But you, lady," he added, turning to Ils, "you have
come further with us than you meant. You will best stay
here for now, where you may yet turn for home should
things go ill."

She glared at him. "Skulk here when things are just
getting interesting? Do you think you'd have got this far
without me? No, my lad, I come also. Or do you fear they
will not welcome me in that fine burg of yours?"

"They will," said Kermorvan grimly, "since you are
with me. But later there may be many old errors to be set
right."

Many times that day they saw the sword sweep out over
the city, and watched visions of fear and horror take form
in its shadow. Men made mad were driven against their
adversaries like chaff in a wind, till blood ran in dark
streams down the warm stone. Sometimes the sword would
be brandished out toward the harbor, and more of the dark
ships would come crowding ever closer in among the
hulks, sweeps threshing in the narrow channels as if to

waken the drowned who lay below. At last one small ship dared to sail right in under the shadow of the high tower, tilting its bow catapult skyward. A harpoon-sized bolt struck into a tower window with a wide gallery beneath, a rope was hauled up by its cord, and up this swarmed Ekwesh with bows and spears slung at their backs. Half dangling by their hands, half walking up the rock face, they were almost at the gallery, some sixty feet above the harbor, when the next window opened, a pikehead caught in the rope against the rock and severed it. The climbers had never a chance, but fell away with it, to land shattered against deck or water. The oars began to back water frantically, but then some thing of great size and weight was tilted over the gallery rail. It fell spinning straight down upon the hapless ship, clove its foredeck and smashed through the planking. Water fountained upward, the ship lurched and listed, the mast toppled, and bodies spilled into the water on either side. The defenders leaned over the gallery with jeers of triumph. But the stern catapult was still manned, and a hail of heavy shot pounded all around the window. The great gallery cracked, fell away from the wall and crashed down in ruin upon the sinking vessel and the swimmers around it, bringing defenders and attackers alike to a common end. Sickened, Elof rested his head in his hands; only the sounds could he not shut out.

As dusk gathered, these slowly stilled, and it was smaller fires that sprang up in the gloom, the attackers retreating to their camps. But there was no peace in the quiet that settled over the beleaguered city then. It was a taut, watchful quiet, the desperate stillness of the wounded beast shivering in its retreat. And over the camp was the quiet of the hunter, watching, waiting, with the blood scent already in the wind. The three travelers could sense that watchfulness as they slipped out from among the trees. There was a faint glow of moonlight; they made their way slowly, from bush to bush, from tree-shadow to line of hedgerow or fence and across the fields these guarded. But the fields bore no crop now save ashes, and among them many bones of those who had not had time to reach shelter, men and animals both. The first onslaught had been

sudden, the city ill-prepared, that much was obvious, and
Kermorvan ground his teeth as they passed. Many of the
human skulls were small. "It will be paid for!" he muttered. "And not only by the Ekwesh, if I have my way."

It was two hours, perhaps, before they came within sight
of the besiegers' outer lines, and found just beyond them
a wide chain of picket camps, with many men patrolling
the darkness between their fires. "They are alert," muttered Kermorvan, as they crouched in the shadow of a
tumbled wall, by the blackened skeleton of a tree. "Vic-
tory or defeat must hang on a hair now. Tomorrow morning . . ." He said no more, but they knew. Tomorrow
would bring a bolt to shatter another wall, and perhaps
with it the flagging will of the city. "And that alertness
will make our task the harder. To reach the tower we must
enter the city somehow, and that will mean getting past
the guards at the beach—see their fires?—and slinking
through the streets. A slow and perilous task that will be!
It would be quicker simply to cut around the top of the
walls, but—"

Elof coughed hesitantly. "There is something that might
make it easier—at least as far as the walls. I am not
sure . . . a token . . . I had it from the forest." He reached
into his pack, and pulled out the sprig of wood.

The others eyed it uneasily. "A token, you say?" whispered Ils. "But how will that serve . . ."

She was answered as the scent reached them, a warm
smell, resinous, heavy, heady. It seemed to flood the mind
and sing there like the thin song of insects in a warm still
twilight. Elof held up the sprig, and it was as if the dead
tree above them awoke, summoned up the ghosts of its
leaf-heavy limbs and set them swaying in the strange
breeze, casting their old wide shadow in the pale light.
Then Elof turned the sprig, and it seemed that the shadow
spread outward from his arm, flowing and pooling in the
darkness like blood from a secret slaying. And through it
ran that heady heaviness, rich with soft rustle of a quiet
forest, a safe place to rest one's weary limbs, to forget
one's troubles and fears, to let one's leaden head nod a
moment and find peace.

Through the gloom moved the travelers, and it seemed

to them that light leaf mold rustled beneath their feet, that the sounds of harsh voices and the clink of weapons and armory and even the sound of the sea faded into the small night noises of any woodland; that the smells of cooking, of blood, of death vanished among the many strong scents of trees. Not the sharp evergreens of Tapiau's forests, these, but the blossoming fruit trees that must till recently have flourished here. So perhaps they also were revenged upon their slayers, for the travelers slipped like ghosts themselves among the lines of picket and sentry, moved between the trenches and the fosses and the tents of dark hide. Kermorvan had noted each position of the enemy, each obstacle on their path; at any given moment, though he could not see far ahead, he knew what must lie there. When he was in any doubt Ils, to whom the dark was no greater than that of the duergar's delvings, could set them aright. But always as he turned and twisted the little bough Elof felt a light pattering on his hand, as a few more needles fell away.

So they passed through the lines of the enemy, and came at length to the wide breach in the wall, like the outline of a great blazing spearhead that had struck down into the stone, splintering, shattering, melting to nothing. The black-armored sentinels squatting there nodded and bowed their heads, dreamed perhaps of the dank chill forests of their harsh homeland, while their watchfire flickered and sank under the wood-shadow. Death hovered over them in those few seconds of passing gloom and they never knew it, nor paid any heed to the slight choking sound, half anguish, half fury, instantly stifled as Kermorvan caught rein of his temper. There were only a few faint scufflings among the rubble then, that might be rats climbing after carrion, and they too faded and were gone.

In the darkness the wall seemed to go on upward forever. Elof moved almost in a daze, hardly able to believe the clifflike heights he scaled were the work of men. The massive stone blocks he clambered over, as great almost as those of the Mastersmith's tower, must rather have been hewn and raised by the creatures, human and animal, who stood as carved pillars on the houses below. Very fair those houses had been in the days of their pride, but pitiless gleams of passing moonlight revealed them like hollow teeth, crownless now, jagged, blackened, empty windows agape or yet smoldering, pitiful as the skulls in the fields. Bodies lay unburied on the rubble at their bases, or found a grave of sorts beneath it, only a limb thrust grotesquely out, or simply a smear of blood across the paving, dust-gilded already and trampled in by many feet. It was a mixture of wonder and horror too rich for the smith, too much the nightmare of his youth writ grotesquely large; he wrapped the darkness he carried tight around himself, to see no more than he must. Kermorvan clambered on, thin-lipped, without looking back. Only Ils seemed little impressed with the city of the carnage, except to shake her head wonderingly at the foolish strife among men.

When they reached the top of the wall, clambering over the rubble of the blasted parapet, she stopped and shivered. "I feel very high up here. And out in the open. Is that shadow-thing of yours fading?"

Elof looked around, and nodded. "It has lost many needles, amid too much stone."

"Then save it!" said Kermorvan. "Do you bestow it safely, for we may need its last powers yet. Up here behind the battlements we should be able to pass without it, if only we tread silently."

They moved then like sentinel spirits above the shattered streets, agleam with Ekwesh watchfires. The battlements were broken in many places by catapult shot, and the flagstones of the parapet cracked; here and there the wallhead had fallen away, leaving gaps they had to jump across. Many of the defenders who had fallen on the ramparts yet lay there, in places so thick it was hard to step among them, white faces and wide eyes yet staring up at the travelers as they passed. To Elof they seemed to be asking why he had come so late, and from Kermorvan's expression he felt much the same. It seemed like a century, though it cannot have been more than an hour, before they reached the southern flank of the outer wall, and found their path blocked.

Here, as in other places where outer wall drew close to inner, a short bridge had been built between them, defended at either end by a high gatehouse, turreted and galleried, straddling the parapet in front of them. Tall gates of iron, blank and featureless, barred the way along the wall. Elof looked hard at them, wondering about their weak spots, but knew he could not break them silently enough to avoid an alarm.

"Tread softly here!" whispered Kermorvan. "For we do not know who holds this part of the outer wall, and dare not simply knock. I have no wish to be quilled through by my own folk, if they are too hasty to challenge before shooting. We must see them first. So I rely on your eyes, Ils!"

She peered into the deep shadow beneath the turret. "I see nobody on the gallery at this side, nor on the bridge, nor at the windows. If there are sentries, they must be watching the outward side. But how can you hope to get past?"

"Climb across to the bridge, of course," said Kermorvan, and padded forward, unwinding a rope from his pack, while the others gaped in disbelief. "And from thence to the far rampart. The outward side of the tower is featureless to discourage grapnels, but on the inward side there is guttering. I will go first, and hold you, if the rope will reach." With long swift fingers he knotted it round his waist and sprang swiftly up onto the top of the battlements, crouching so as not to be seen against the sky. When he reached the guttering he straightened up swiftly and inched his way out spiderwise, long limbs outstretched, face flat to the stone. The others heard his taut whisper. "The rope . . . too short! Follow as best you can—Ils, then you, Elof!"

Ils swallowed audibly, but managed to clamber up with Elof's help. He heaved himself after her, steadfastly refusing to look down, but when he reached the corner of the gatehouse he found her frozen in the way, her face leaden in the moonlight. "Be bold!" he whispered. "Your mountainsides are higher, delvings deeper!" But not so open, he guessed, nor without a single handhold, and he felt his own palms go moist at the thought.

"*Kerys!*" hissed Kermorvan. "Come on, you fools!" Elof swallowed, detached an arm from the rope and caught Ils round the waist to steady her. With that encouragement

she began to shuffle forward again, a little unsteadily, but
gaining ground as she went. Elof saw that her eyes were
tight shut. He inched along after her, sword slapping awkwardly at his legs, wondering if he really could hold her;
short of stature she was, but solid. But at last there was
Kermorvan, balanced on a waterspout, reaching down to
help her over the rim of the battlements onto the parapet
behind. In helping her up Elof staggered and for one
nightmare moment looked down into the shadowed pit of
rooftops beneath. Then Kermorvan's hand reached out to
him also, and he was tumbling over the ramparts onto the
grimy stone.

They lay there a moment in the deep shadow of the
gatehouse, in a gasping heap, catching their breath, sa-
voring a sudden release from tension. Then Kermorvan
chivvied them afoot in fierce whispers, and turned to climb
the far side of the bridge. But just as Elof scrambled up,
the swordsman spoke in his ear. "Hsst! What's that?"

They stared. In the shadows at the far end of the bridge
something glinted, shifted, shimmered, became clearer.
A tall figure took shape, clad in bright mail covered by a
dark surcoat. He was busy removing his helm, like a weary
sentry coming off watch. He looked up, started violently and
swept out a great sword. Kermorvan made no move to draw,
but stood calmly watching. The armed man hesitated.

"Who goes?" he demanded. His speech was like Kermorvan's but gruffer and less precise. "Speak, or I'll—"

"Has the moon gone to your head, then, that you do
not know me, Bryhon?" demanded Kermorvan in return.

The newcomer stopped dead, stiffening with evident
amazement. The moonlight shone clearly on his face now,
and Elof all but choked. He was very tall, taller even than
Kermorvan and more broadly built, certainly older. His
hair was jet black, long and waving glossily around his
neck, though only a few strands straggled across the top
of his pink scalp; his beard was equally thick and glossy,
with the same stiff wave in it, the eyes heavy-lidded and
still, the nose long, straight but slightly bulbous. It was a
well-made face in its way, but to Elof, for a moment, it
seemed very terrible. There was no fine resemblance, but
the overall likeness of cast and coloring was so strong that,

just for a minute, he had mistaken the man called Bryhon for the Mastersmith.

Bryhon took one jerky step forward. "You!" he barked, and his sword flashed up. Within the inner gate there was a soft clatter of arms, a scuffle of heavy boots and four mailed men came spilling out onto the bridge, looking from him to the newcomers with cold, alarmed eyes. Three had short bows drawn ready in their hands, the fourth an arbalest, and their surcoats bore the same claw device as Bryhon's. The dark man cocked a shaggy head at the travelers. "Do you look at this, then, lads, and believe it if you will! My lord Kermorvan, come swarming up walls in the watches of the night!"

"Kermorvan?" croaked one of the men, and gaped. Kermorvan, who had made no move to draw his own blade, inclined his head slightly, as if acknowledging a salute.

"Now why do you suppose he was doing such a thing?" said Bryhon icily. "And at such a time? He might, of course, be risking breaking his banishment—"

"I was never banished, Bryhon," said Kermorvan evenly. "You cannot banish a man in his absence."

"Which is why you left so abruptly," smiled Bryhon. "How do you know the law has not been altered?"

"Because the people are not yet so foolish, Bryhon."

Bryhon shrugged. "I'll not bandy follies with you. In all but name you were banished, and the last we heard you'd fallen in with just such a pack of sea raiders as we find baying at our gates the now." He shook his head grimly. "And only this day were all the syndics wondering how a crew of savages could plumb our defenses so well. Now we know, I fear."

Kermorvan's whole face seemed to narrow, eyes and nostrils pinched tight with fury, and yet he still laid no hand to his sword, and spoke coldly. "At another hour you might regret that, Bryhon. But it was forgetting all old wrongs and enmities I came back, bringing a great help in our need—"

"An army, then? And did you lose it along the way? I see nothing about you but a pair of thralls as ragged as yourself—"

"I am no thrall!" growled Elof, straining to copy the swordsman's measured coldness. "My name is Elof, I am a journeyman smith out of the Northlands. And this is the lady Ils of the duergar. We serve no man save as friends!"

"How fortunate a man of his high station," said Bryhon, without once appearing to notice Elof, "to count as his friends vagrant blacksmiths and vermin." He shook his head and smiled as in quiet satisfaction; good humor smoothed his voice. "No, my lord. Even if all you said was true, still we could not have you coming back at such a time, sowing discord among the weak-willed and undermining the authority of the syndics. In the people's interest, it cannot be tolerated—"

"You invoke the people so readily, Bryhon," said Kermorvan, his voice still calm but taut beneath, as if he could barely believe what he heard. "Why not ask them?"

The dark man shook his head again, and there was now no mistaking the cool gloating in his tone. "Alas indeed, that we will not be able to do! But you might confuse enough of them, to begin with. Even the rumor of your coming would split the city in strife. Better that they hear no more of you, or blame the Ekwesh if you are found—"

Kermorvan's sword hissed from its scabbard, and Elof's came snarling in its wake; Ils hefted her axe for a cast. But the bows were already leveled, the distance too wide. Elof knew that however fast Kermorvan was, he could not outrun an arbalest bolt. Bitterness welled up in him as he tensed for the last useless spring. To have come this far, this hard, to lose all to some infantile squabble . . .

"*Halt!*"

The voice that echoed along the parapet had none of Bryhon's suavity, but it was commanding enough to match him. "Halt there! Put up those bows! First man looses is cannibal meat! What in all the pits of Hella's afoot here?"

Bryhon turned on the burly figure in mail and helm who came stumping round the gallery of the gatehouse above, then looked warily as the inner gates opened upon a cluster of men armored alike. "Who are you, to countermand my orders? Do you not know who I am?"

"Aye, syndic, I do," said the newcomer firmly. "Just a citizen like anyone else, as you're always telling us. Not

even in command of this quarter. As to who I am, I'm a
sergeant of the Guard. Mind telling me what you and your
followers are doing up here at this hour? Not had enough
fighting today that you must be about the ramparts all hours
of the night?''

"As well that I was, with you guardsmen asleep!" said
Bryhon venomously. "I caught these traitors sneaking up
here—"

"Aye, so I saw, sir. *And* being a guard, like, and all
wide-awake. Seemed a mite hasty, *if* you'll pardon me,
sir . . .''

"Look you here, sergeant, we are besieged, we cannot
waste time on trials! These creatures are our enemies—"

The sergeant shook his head. "Can't agree with you
there, sir. See, it's like this—the long one and the plump
lass I can't avouch, but there's one I know is no friend of
the Ekwesh, 'cause he's a good mate of mine—eh, Alv?"
And he turned to Elof and pulled off his helmet, spilling
out a shaggy mass of red hair, a hot red face beneath. "Or
what was it I heard you called yourself now? *Ey-lof?*"

Elof stumbled forward in utter confusion and delight.
"Roc! Roc, you son of a smith—"

The former forgeboy gave him a polite but dignified
salute, and turned to Bryhon. "Anyhow, sir, this comes
under the hand of the syndics captaining this quarter. I've
sent for one, and he'll be along any time. You can take
the matter up with him if you care to—no? Then I'd be
obliged if you and yours'd clear the ramparts before the
reivers hear the row and loose off a catapult, just for
laughs—eh?''

Bryhon looked at him a moment with blank resentful
eyes. "I'll remember this," he said quietly, gestured to
his men and stalked past the guardsmen into the gate. The
sound of boots on stairs rang away into distance and depth.

"Ach, go shake your ears," muttered Roc, and held up
a hand to check Elof's eager questions. "Better wait a
moment, wait for the syndic. I'll handle this!"

After the tension of the wall and the meeting with Bryhon, the delay was agony. The travelers fidgeted in silence
under the eyes of the guards, though it was mostly at Kermorvan they stared, with, it seemed to Elof, a strange

mixture of fear and reverence. His kinship here was obvious; many had his cast of features, though less fine, even
those with hair that was red or black or that strange golden
shade that reminded Elof uncomfortably of Louhi.

It was perhaps half an hour before they heard more feet
approaching, among them a noticeably lumbering step.
More guardsmen came crowding out of the gate, and in
their wake a burly man of some height, dressed in a rich
but rumpled fur-lined robe, who glared sleepily at the
travelers. "Now then, Roc, what River-spawn are these
that cannot wait till morning for me to look them over?"
Then he peered closer, and his jaw dropped till his red
beard blended with the fur of his collar. "Kerys' Gate!
It's Kermorvan!" Then he turned, peered at Elof and
roared with laughter. "And by the black arse of Amicac,
he's got the Causeway smith in tow! And we thought the
bogeys had carried you off!"

Roc grinned. "The look of him now, sir, he'd scare the
bogeys!"

"Well, be thankful he's on our side, then! Bring them
up, lad! Bring them up!"

Kermorvan smiled wryly down at Elof, as they were
ushered up into the tower guardroom. "It seems you are
as well known in my homeland as I! And better liked, it
may be . . ."

Elof chuckled. "Lucky, at all events, that I fell upon
the only two friends I have here!"

"Lucky?" rasped Roc. "Still don't credit me with a
brain in my skull, do you? Had your description posted
with the City Marshals for two years now, on the off chance
you might wander in! Price on your head, attached only.
Not that large but they remembered. Lucky I wasn't far!"

Elof whistled. "Yes, or Bryhon might've wasted our
coming!"

"Oh, they'd've stopped him. I think. Anyway, you're
here, and Kathel's a powerful friend to have, as I've
found."

Kathel grinned toothily at Elof. "You need money to
be a syndic, lad! Some inherit it, like Bryhon, but I made
it on that last trip; I'll not be forgetting them who helped
me then, him or you." He looked at Ils, subsiding wearily

into a chair, and at Kermorvan. It was a look of wary disapproval, but not outright hostility. "But then there's this . . . lady. And there's you. Why do you come back? Come to crow that you were right all along? To turn out us syndics, in the middle of all this? What is it brought you?"

"The need of my city," said Kermorvan gravely. "And Elof. He had better explain."

The tale took less time in the telling than Elof had feared, for Kathel had already heard much from Roc. "He's my armorer now, y'know? Has his own little forge, but keeps my housecarls in tinplate. When he isn't too busy mending the kitchenmaid's kettles!" He laughed uproariously for a moment, then grew serious. "So you're telling me it's this misbegotten Mylio's the one we see stirring the savages up?"

"They are more than savages," said Kermorvan grimly. "They have a great realm, after their fashion, and it grows crowded. They would have come here anyway, at first to raid, later to settle. Mylio has merely brought them sooner, before they are truly ready."

"If you say so. And with that sword-thing, eh? From Vayde's Tower, too, the bastard get of a sea hag!"

"It is not where I would choose," agreed Kermorvan, looking at his friends. "I heard many tales about that place when I was young, and some were very dark. It was a small palace once, and is still rich inside. The Mariner's Guild maintained it when I was a boy, and in days of peace still burn a beacon on its roof to guide ships. But no man has lived there for many generations; it is not a favored place to sleep."

"We've seen lights there after dark," said Kathel. "So it looks like he doesn't mind!"

Kermorvan smiled thinly. "Perhaps the Ekwesh like to brave such things, or Mylio feels at home among them. But if Vayde walks there yet, they will find him restless company! Let them beware!"

Kathel pulled his robe tight about him. "That's no fit jest! I wish Vayde would return, alive or . . . otherwise. He'd settle this whole filthy crew, mindsword or no. But you seem to think you've a parry to it?"

When that was answered Kathel looked at Elof, and glanced uneasily at Ils, dozing in her chair. "From duergar teaching . . . And you'd trust such uncanny stuff as that?"

Ils opened an eye and glared at him. "This place is a madhouse! We come to help them, and they call us vermin, treat us like foes or worse—"

Kathel shook his head. "These are hard times . . . lady. And confusing ones, for a man who's just trying to do what's best for his city. An hour ago I wasn't even sure there *were* such folk as you! And the last I saw young Keryn Kermorvan, he and his factions were mobbing the Syndicacy steps against Bryhon's bunch, breaking every pate they could reach and calling down curses on the rest. Can't help but leave scars, that, on more than pates. Though I'll admit he was younger then, and that the times have proved him more than half right. Question is, what in the fires of Hella do I do now?" He stood up and walked over to the window, though it was boarded over. "By rights I should hold you for the Marshals of the city to examine, and refer what you've told me to the Syndicacy. All of which, with things as they are, would take another day, at least—"

"Do you think you've got another damned day?" demanded Ils.

Kathel looked at her. "No. No, in truth I do not. My heart misgives me; another wall down and there will be panic, for who can fight the storm?"

"We can!" said Ils, and her face was as proud and hard as the stone of the city. "We three!"

"We four!" rumbled Roc. "By your leave, syndic, these wild folk need looking after. And I've a word or two to say to my late master. We four!" Kermorvan smiled coldly, but he nodded.

Kathel looked long and narrowly at Ils, at Roc, at the smith and the swordsman, and tugged at his beard. The eyes of a merchant weighed them up, but the spirit of the rover burned behind them. "By the Sun Ascending, I believe you. You folk, if anybody! Out of the olden times you are come, it seems, and the hero-lays. Men of prowess and power and wizardry, such as I had never hoped to see.

Such as I doubted could exist! Old and fat and fond of my life, me, but if I could in duty come, even to bear your spears, then into the open jaws of Amicac I would!'' He sighed. ''But I am sworn here, where folk depend on me. And war brooks no delaying. So, this I will venture and take upon myself, to set you free, and to give you rest, food, arms, any help you need.'' He drew a deep breath, as one who has crossed a threshold he fears. ''Use it well!''

Kermorvan rose swiftly. ''I thank you, syndic! The food we will take, but no rest; it is now fast upon midnight, and we must make our move soon. Nor do we need arms; Ils wears mail, Elof will wear none save that gauntlet, and I have carried my own mail over land and sea for this hour.'' He tore at his ragged pack, and a heavy parcel of oil leather spilled onto the table. He unfolded the dully gleaming mail and helm, and took from inside it a smaller package, equally well wrapped. ''Now let us eat.''

It was a hasty meal, and a quiet one. Elof and Roc tried to chaff each other as befitted old friends at last free to talk, but what lay ahead stood as a barrier between them, deadening merriment. Ils seemed disturbed by this city of men, gazing uneasily around the walls, sniffing suspiciously at the food, taking only what others tasted, though it was common fare enough. Kermorvan, already clad in his mail, ate in silence that was not his usual calm, fingering over the small package, and when Kathel's summons came he sprang up at once and left his plate half full.

Fresh clothes awaited them, chosen in dark colors, and black cloaks to go over them. Ils found some dark wax to rub on her bright mailshirt, but Elof left his gauntlet as it was, wrapping a fold of his cloak round it. Roc had a long knife in his belt, and swung a heavy mace from his wrist. ''Better than a sword for a man of sound figure such as me. Powers, what a fearsome crew we look! Any Ekwesh that see us'll die of fright!''

''Or laughter, my lad, if he sees you first,'' said Kathel, as he led them out of the guardroom. ''As well there'll not be too many people about at this hour, or the sight of you'd lower their spirits.''

But there were folk about, for when Kathel led the little party out onto the bridge again a murmur went up from the inner walls around, and arose from the streets beneath, where many lanterns and torches ate away shadow. It was a rushing, rustling sound, like the wind running among reeds, a word repeated from one to another among a great crowd, a name. *Kermorvan.*

"News travels fast!" growled Roc, in an undertone. "But then, that is what half the city's been praying for since the black sails first showed on the horizon."

"And the other half has been blaming me for it, no doubt, as Bryhon did." Kermorvan looked around anxiously. The noise was growing louder, threatening to become a shout.

"Is it Kermorvan? Is it? Is it?"

"Save us, lord!" shouted an old woman. "Down with the syndics!"

"No, up!" shouted a coarse voice. "A rope for their necks, a rope for the fat syndics!"

"A rope!"

"It's their doing—"

"Save us, lord! Scatter the savages—"

Kathel, pale with fury, was trying to bellow above the row, futilely. More and more people were gathering along the ramparts, sorry creatures many of them in flame-scarred clothes and soiled bandages. They did not look poor or underfed, but all the more desperate for that, sudden orphans from a secure daily life. Elof heard Kermorvan curse, saw him swiftly unroll the package and strap something between the shoulder plates of his mail. Kathel's breath hissed between his teeth.

"Hold up a lantern!" Kermorvan barked at the guardsmen, and stepped forward into the pool of light. The warm glow gilded his bronze hair, his pale proud face with its hollow cheeks under high cheekbones, and set a chilly flame in his shadowed eyes. A gasp went up from the crowd on the wall, and then a rising rumble of excitement. He flung up his arms suddenly, with greater effect than if he had shouted, for the lantern light glistened upon the breastplate he had added to his mail. Dull black it was, darker than the rest, but damasked in gold upon its surface was a strange pattern. An image it was in an intricate style, of a blazing sun, and before it, rising with open beak, a great raven with the eyes of a man. The silence was so immediate that Elof could hear the ripple of his mailshirt; then came a long sigh from the crowd. Kermorvan looked around him, unsmiling, and spoke in that quiet voice of his which was yet like distant trumpets. "Save your acclaim! Make no noise, none at all, or you will alert the enemy! But as you see, I am lord Keryn Kermorvan of Morvan. I have come back as I said I would, and I will do what I can in the defense of Bryhaine. All of Bryhaine! For never did we need to stand together more than now! So, no more of this talk of ropes; the syndics never sought my life, whatever others may have wished. For now, follow them, follow this man Kathel! And any whom he names in his turn! For there is virtue yet among the syndics, like gold—since one must often delve deep for it!" Laughter rippled, and the mood was turned. He drew his cloak over the emblem. "Now go, and my blessing with you! Go in peace!"

As quickly as it had gathered, the crowd began to disperse. He turned to Kathel. "What little peace yet remains to them, poor wretches! Are you content?"

Kathel nodded soberly. "It seems gold is commoner than I thought it. Yes, I am."

"Then do you take it upon yourself to make ready sortie and assault! Give me a horn such as the guardsmen use, and when you hear it from the tower . . . And perhaps the Raven should fly also from the fortress."

Kathel opened his mouth to protest, and then said nothing. "All right!" he managed at last. "No small favors you ask, you heroes! I'll risk this. But afterward?"

Kermorvan shrugged quickly. "There will be more voices in that than yours and mine. Come, we waste time!"

The doors of the outer gatehouse were opened for them, and at once shut softly behind. They were where they had sought to come, on the last stretch of the outer wall, that led straight to the harbor and the Tower of Vayde. Roc looked uneasily at Elof. "Don't like this! Our dear master's bad enough, but what else's in that tower—well, my blood runs icy just thinking!''

''But I thought Vayde was one of your great heroes!'' said Ils. ''Wouldn't he be on our side?''

''A hero, of a sort,'' grunted Roc. ''But they say he built that tower beyond the city walls, as was then, 'cause— well, he kept odd company . . .''

The tower loomed ahead of them, immense in girth and height, featureless, lightless, darker than the darkness and as inescapable. There was no feeling of emptiness about that grim silhouette, none at all; rather, its fullness seemed to spill over, mingle with the dark, tinge it with menace. It drew the eyes, that tower; to look away from it too long was to fill the mind with strange fears of what might have appeared there meanwhile, some watching, questing apparition. But looking too long served only to people it with the flickering phantoms tired eyes create, and to risk breaking your neck on the shattered and rubble-strewn rampart into the bargain. It was hard going, worst for Ils with her short limbs, having to clamber where Kermorvan could bound; Roc was in little better ease, and weighed down by full mail. But when Elof, balancing a moment on tilting stone blocks, was tipped over by the gauntlet's weight and almost fell, it was their strong hands that bore him up. Roc and Ils. . . .

Friends. He had never had friends when he was a boy. He felt suddenly like sending them back, like ordering them back, instead of casting them away in this mad enterprise of his own making. Kermorvan too, who should only be asked to fight against an ordinary foe, and not the unnatural wiles of smithcraft. Let mage take mage, cancel out both, let the normal folk, the unstained, untainted folk go on to lead their normal lives, as was their right. But not his. Upon the Anvil of Ice he had met his forging, and the stamp of it he would never quite lose. What if he succeeded here? What would he be then? Where would he go?

Picking his way around ruin and slain, he could find no answer. Here the fighting had been fiercest, the city folk rallying under the warrior-hero's memorial. How many of these bodies sprawled here had died calling on that name, wondered Elof, looking with dimming eyes for his return? And what name would he call on, when his turn came to join them?

Suddenly, Kermorvan, leading with drawn blade, thrust out his arm and fell to a crouch. Elof saw then what lay ahead. As they had expected, there was a rough barrier thrown between intact battlements, and behind it an emberglow lit the forms of Ekwesh guards, nodding wearily. They had settled how to deal with this, and as Ils and Roc drew level they sat a moment to get their breath. Then Elof drew the black sword, ready to muffle its strange voice, but it was a soundless thrilling tremor in his hand. Ils hefted her axe, and Roc twirled the mace into his hand by its wriststrap. Kermorvan waited a moment longer, snapped down his visor and sprang away, bounding from stone to stone with his cloak blowing like some vast bat, up on the battlements and across the barricade before its sleepy sentries could rouse. There were ten Ekwesh there, but they were swept down as by a wind before they could utter a sound, stricken where they stood or hewn over the wall onto the ravaged roofs beneath. Then the travelers were dashing along the last length of the wall, heading for the dark arch of the door that led into the tower.

It was not locked, for its lock had been smashed out from within, no doubt when the Ekwesh took the tower. Beyond it Elof saw at first only a wide hall, lit by a single guttering lamp, and a few doors ajar on darkness. It was the smell of the place that struck him first, a smell of still air, heavy with age and dust, and the peculiar scent of damp heavy cloth. He realized then that the strange bulky shadows in the corners were great gathered swaths of tapestry, a material so heavy and so dusty that it looked like stone in the half-light, its colors faded, its pictures reduced to meaningless swirls. Cobwebs, equally dusty, hung around it as if in mockery, and from the great octagonal table at the center of the room. But around this the dust had been quite tracked away by the passing of many feet. At the far side, one wide double door opened onto a wide flight of stairs, lit by moonlight flooding through high casements in the tower wall. On these the dust was less disturbed, so that individual footprints could still be seen.

"He'd come here," whispered Roc softly. "Seem like home to him, it would. But which way? Up or down?"

"On the floors below lie the public rooms, halls and audience chambers, and below them butteries and servants' quarters," Kermorvan whispered. "Those stairs serve the private apartments, only four floors of those, two to a floor and one on top, with a great open gallery. I am certain now there is somebody living in them. The Ekwesh would normally ransack a place like this, looking for gold thread in the tapestries, if nothing else; this has been kept undisturbed. So it will surely be someone not of their people who is up there."

"Then let's be searching!" said Ils cheerfully. "I'll spy out your way, save you blundering into the furniture, right?"

In single file they made their way across the wide stone floor, treading with infinite care lest a boot scrape too loudly. Roc found that most difficult of all, and more than once he staggered and almost overbalanced against the table. But in the half-light on the stairs it again proved to be Elof who saw best, and he took the lead. It was a wide spiral staircase, as in the Mastersmith's tower; three could walk up it arm in arm, and its roof was high and vaulted, hung about with shadow. More tapestry lined the walls, less dusty; Elof could make out whole scenes in the fitful moonlight, lines of wagons, battle and slaughter under trees, and once on a great plain. It was an uncanny place such as he had never before been in, and he sensed that his friends liked it no better. He felt a strange deep chill run through the middle of his body, from chest to groin, and his feet felt numb and weak. What had this Vayde been like, who might yet walk here? He could imagine hearing footsteps high above, strong heavy feet marching inexorably down through the dark on this staircase, where they could only go over you, or *through* . . . And yet that somehow failed to chill him. He felt a different terror in this place, a clinging sense of anguish, sadness, ultimate loss, and somewhere beneath it a consuming anger that seemed to echo around the walls like an ancient cry of resentment. That frightened him, because it so closely matched something in himself. If he failed here and was

broken or struck down, would he too become part of that?
Would the voice of his misery also echo down the long
years?

He stopped. They had come to a landing, a wide corridor running down between rows of doors, some small
and plain, some high and ornate; one in particular on each
side rose above the others, double doors with an ornate
transom window above them. But the dust of the corridor
was undisturbed. They looked at each other, and Elof gestured up the stairs. Kermorvan nodded, and they moved
on. The next floor was the same, the same corridor, the
same undisturbed dust, and the next also, and Elof began
to wonder if they were being foolish, if the Mastersmith
were not peacefully asleep in one of the very tents they
had passed by out there in the twilight. He turned, hesitantly, wondering if he should not go down at once, while
time yet remained. But it was then, if ever, that he felt a
true presence in the tower. The darkness rang like a bell,
like a voice, a vast wordless forbidding note. He looked
wildly at the others, but they only looked doubtfully back
at him. They had heard nothing, that was clear. What could
he, but shrug and lead on?

And on the next floor, the last before the top, lines in
the dust led down the long corridor together to the high
doors, where they divided, one turning into each. Elof
flexed the fingers of his gauntlet. Kermorvan added grimly,
and hefted his sword. "Roc! Ils!" he mouthed, in the
faintest of whispers. "Best that someone guards the
stairs—till we are sure—" They looked sulky at that, but
nodded. Kermorvan arched his eyebrows questioningly,
and waved his sword from left to right. Elof shrugged and
gestured to the lefthand door. Carefully, minutely, he
picked his way down the corridor on silent feet. The door
was unlatched; he put his ear to the crack, and heard a
sound of breathing, soft, even asleep. He nodded to Kermorvan, bit his lip, and very gently pressed the door a
little way open, enough to see dimness and dark inside,
and slip his fingers round the edge, lifting the heavy wood
slightly and so moving it without the hinges creaking. Then
he held up a hand for Kermorvan to wait, pointing to his
eyes; it was ill-lit in there, and he could see better. Ker-

morvan's mouth narrowed, but he nodded in return. Elof peered cautiously through the narrow opening.

He found himself looking across a large gloomy room and through another set of doors, standing open, into a wide, high-ceilinged chamber. It was lighter than it had first appeared, for two tall casements flanked the curved wall opposite, set in deep bays with an upholstered seat beneath each. Between them, almost to the high ceiling, rose the pillars of a great bed, carved with tracery, and hung about the tapestry less gray than that below. It was gathered back, so he could see that in the bed a figure lay, and that the hair against the white pillow was black. He swallowed hard and stepped forward, half crouching, gauntlet outstretched with the fingers wide, sword clenching tightly in his other hand. One step, two, three—light, careful strides that carried him across the open expanse of the room, between the pools of moonlight that the pale sky spilled through the windows. He had all but reached the end of the bed when something caught his eye, a light shape draped carefully across one of the windowseats—a garment, a mantle, all in white. He gasped involuntarily, and in a sudden whirl of fabric the figure in the bed sat up. He saw the bedclothes fall away from a slender body. It was a woman, the moonlight bathing her small breasts, showing him her face. It was well for him his dry throat strangled his startled cry. He tried again, and could whisper no more than her name.

"Kara!"

She started, peered into the dark. "Who . . ." And then she gave a little gasping shriek and rose on her knees, the armring gleaming under the moon, as he flung himself onto the bed and into her arms. He gathered her up against him, marveling at the warmth, the slightness, the sweet scent of her, the startling strength of the arms round him. They babbled at each other, foolish incomplete words, their cheeks ran wet and they knew not nor cared who it was wept; their lips met but could not cling for lack of breath. He let fall his sword, his hand caressed her back, hers his, and the two acts were as one, the product of a single will.

"It's all right," he whispered breathlessly. "It's all

right . . .'' he repeated, without knowing whether anything would ever be right again.

"*Elof*—"

He held her at arm's length suddenly. "How did you know? How did you know my new name?"

"*Louhi!*" breathed Kara, shivering violently. "She knows it! She's here! In the other room—"

Suddenly she gasped and broke away from him, looking past him to the door. In the middle of the room stood Kermorvan, his face so utterly void of expression that it contrasted weirdly with his ready stance and blade. He swallowed convulsively and was about to speak when Elof furiously waved him out. "And beware the other door!" he hissed. "I'll follow! Get out!" He turned to her. "He's a friend, he meant no harm . . ."

"Then bid him for his own good go far from here!" said Kara bitterly, and then anxiously, "Oh, Elof, be careful! You're in terrible danger! I've heard her talk to the Mastersmith about you—"

"And he is here too."

She nodded, and shut her eyes as at some sudden pain. "I tried to escape! I did try, on a journey southward! I broke free! But—" She brought up her legs from beneath the covers. Round each ankle wound a strangely coiled ring of silver, and they were bound together by a thin, intricate chain that was the length of a short stride only. To Elof's narrowed eyes a gleam coursed through it that was not of the moonlight. An anger to match his own flashed into her eyes. "She caught me. And at her behest, he did that!"

In a rush of fury Elof caught the chain up in his fingers, as if to twist it apart, but he could not, nor would even the black blade do more than scratch the metal. "A forge!" he growled. "We will get you to one, and see then whose will is the stronger! And Louhi, she dies this minute—"

"No!" gasped Kara. "No, you must leave, she will destroy you! She will call him upon you! Think! If she can hold even him in thrall—"

"I will cast him down first," said Elof between dry lips. "Then we will see, she and I! Where does he sleep, do you know that?"

She pointed upward. "The highest floor, the great chamber. There he dwells, but sleep? I do not think he sleeps. He is changed, grown even stranger than he was. I think she does that to those she holds—"

"But she is not changing you?"

Kara took his hand and held it to her breast, and he felt the heart leap beneath. "I am of no common sort," she whispered, and smiled through her tears. "And a stronger chain than any he can forge was already upon me. I will not change!"

He nodded. "Nor I!" She kissed him again then, more solemnly. "Now get dressed, you must come—"

She shook her head, and pointed to her ankles. "I cannot."

"I am not leaving you here alone! Not now that I've found you again—"

"You must! Does your friend not wait?" She stared out of the casement, to where the pale moon sank. "But listen, love, life, if ever any chance or power parts us anymore, follow the dawn! Seek to the east! And I, if I win free, shall quest westward for you, in the path of the moon! I swear it! By all that I am!"

He nodded, for he could not speak, touched her lips once more, and rose, catching up his sword. He looked at her there, watching him, and felt his heart blaze up within him, as if her gaze kindled it to flame. But as he backed away, and she sank and dwindled into the shadow, so the flame died, faded, till only the darkest ember remained. With a last glance back he stepped through the open door— and almost trod down Ils, standing rock-still in the middle of the corridor with a terrible look on her face. He glanced anxiously at the far door, but it was undisturbed, and he waved her angrily away.

The others were gathered on the stairs. "Who is she?" demanded Kermorvan. "Can we trust . . ." He met Elof's eyes, and said no word more.

Roc nodded. "I've seen her, once, and I know A—Elof. If he trusts her, why should not we?"

"Fair question!" asserted Ils. "She is this Louhi's and not yours, that much I heard. Remember, our lives and many others depend on it. If he is not up there, if meanwhile she raises the alarm, then we are cut off. We cannot fly off this tower!''

"He is there!" said Elof coldly, and gazed about him. "I should never have doubted it, I felt it on the stairs. The very stones cry out in protest, every metal fastening rings alarm in my mind. She warned me, wishing me to escape."

Kermorvan eyed Elof anxiously. "You grow strange to me, in this strange place. I would not trust what that lithe little creature said, with the bonds that lie on her soul. But I fear we have no choice. We must venture it now."

Ils bowed her head. "Yes, you are right. We are at her mercy, then. Lead on!"

The night hung deep across the last staircase, for the moon had set now. Elof clambered on, step after step, and the warning of the forest rang over and over in his mind, *Something more!* Something he would know when most he needed it. Fear, the chill fear of failure, fanned the dying ember at his heart. *Tapiau, Raven, you unknowns, you mocking powers, when else will I most need it, if not now? I am within my enemy's walls, he holds the girl I love in thrall, I go to face him with a weapon he may brush aside in scorn—when if not now?*

He rounded the last corner, and stepped up into sudden light.

It was no ordinary light of lamp or fire, no healthy glow but a bluish sea-deep gloom, the daylight of drowned men. It came spilling down the stairs through the wide ceiling trap in which they ended, fantastically shadowed by the wrought railing to either side. He stepped cautiously up till his eyes were level with the floor above, and peered quickly around. The apartments here stretched the whole width of the tower, a great central chamber leading out onto a wide curved balcony. Around the walls of the chamber, behind a circle of carved pillars, were various other doors, all closed, and there seemed to be nobody visible. The chamber itself was a mess, a clutter of old furnishings and dusty hangings like the tower below, but intermingled with newer things that lay strewn in heaps about, rich things for the most part, vessels of precious metals, rich garments and hangings, arms and armor well

decorated, bright jewels and ornaments, carvings, paintings. By the balcony, against a pillar, stood a robed statue
of some white stone, a hideous mask of Ekwesh fashion
tilted casually atop it. A chest of coin stood open against
the far wall, and above it a faceted globe of glass in a
curiously wrought stand, from which the strange light
came. And everywhere lay books, heaps of books, stacked
scrolls and bound boards laid in eccentric piles. Trenchers
of food lay here and there atop them, half-eaten. The air
was heavy and stale, with a hint of foulness, as if some
beast had laired there awhile. But in all the confusion
nothing stirred.

Slowly, carefully, Elof mounted the last steps, and Kermorvan behind him. The warrior's face darkened with anger as he took in the scene; the creamings, this, of the
loot of the city, the small part so far captured. Elof knew
the warrior must be seeing not only the worth of it, but
the bloodshed, the shattered homes and ruined lives that
were the price each piece bore. Kermorvan looked around
and nodded jerkily, clearly thinking this a likely enough
lair for the Mastersmith. So too did Ils, by her face. But
Roc dared to whisper a doubt that mirrored Elof's own.
"He was ever so damned particular! Would he dwell in
such a sty now?"

"Kara said he had changed! Perhaps this is what she
meant . . ."

"Perhaps indeed!" said a thin smooth voice, though
they had scarcely breathed their words in each other's ears.
As one they turned to look across the room, to the black
gap of the balcony. And there the statue, too, as they had
all thought it, turned to face them. "But I am sorry if you
find fault! These are the hardships of a campaign among
allies largely uncivilized. Though I confess I grow more
forgetful of the common things of every day, the temporary impurities of life, the fouled soil in which thought
must for the moment grow."

Elof and Roc, who had known the man before, could
only gape. The voice, once resonant, had thinned to a dry
metallic edge, and the rest of him had withered to match
it. The skin on his hands was white and featureless as the
smooth swath of gown he wore, the strands of his hair,

once lustrous black and curling, could now have been the fibers from which the gown was woven, lying lank about his face. And as they watched he tilted back the long-beaked mask of the Thunderbird from his face, and it too was white, the beard shrunk to blanched wisps. Even now it might still have been a statue's face, or more properly a death mask, for the same placid calm rested upon the closed eyelids and faintly smiling mouth. Then the eyes snapped open, and they also were white, clouded and milky behind lashless lids.

"Looks like a cave-slug!" muttered Ils. "Slimy, pale and eyeless, never a drop of red blood in him!"

But the Mastersmith smiled courteously to her, and to each of them in turn, as if to demonstrate that he was not blind. "Welcome, Lady Ils, Lord Keryn Kermorvan. And to you, my boys, Roc and Elof, who is yet the Alv I knew. You see, I know you all. Your coming was not unheralded."

Ils glared at Elof. "Not by Kara," he said quickly. "She did not know who was with me, or our names. This comes from within the city."

"Not unheralded, as I said. You are an innocent, boy, adrift in a world you do not comprehend, the play of forces beyond your perception, and beyond your childish concepts of good and evil, of rights and wrongs. Does not the storm drown many a mariner? And yet the selfsame wind will drive the ships of many more to safe and prosperous haven. You cannot have one without the other, a fair wind in one corner of the ocean must be fierce in the other. The world is a single great interplay, a linked chain you cannot even begin to envisage, of which even I have only been permitted to grasp a small portion. If great suffering is occasioned here, yet it is only in the cause of ridding life of all its merely animal horrors, that the rule of pure mind be restored in a world cleansed, a fair monument wiped clean of filth scrawled on it by fools, purified by the power of the Ice."

Kermorvan snarled something and pushed forward, but Elof held him back. "Throughout my growing years I heard this and much like it from you. Fine words! Fine enough, almost, to dignify a lust for wealth and power, bought even at the expense of your own humanity, I see. Almost, but not quite. The snare that caught me then, I will not step into a second time. But even if all you said were true, I still would prefer my childish notions, and my duty to those who have befriended me. I will never sacrifice them to some invisible future good, some fair wind elsewhere. Where the storm threatens, let it beware!''

The Mastersmith's blank face twisted a moment. ''You have sacrificed them anyway. They who would fight the storm must endure its wrath!'' And reaching swiftly among the heavy folds of the robe, he caught hold of a scabbard and hilt. So it was that out of the deeps of the years, the most fell work of Elof's own hands arose to confront him.

It gleamed in the wintry light, that sword, its flowing, enigmatic patterns bright as the day when he had deemed his work done, and exulted without a thought for what might thereafter befall. And as it shone before his eyes it seemed to him independent of he who brandished it. He saw it more as he would his own face distorted in a mirror crazed and shattered, a facet of himself malformed and twisted. It was in revulsion only that he thrust the gauntlet up to blot it from his sight, but that served him well. For no greater fear or horror descended upon him, yet Kermorvan, barely within the blade's influence, was convulsed as by a bolt of lightning. The gray-gold sword twisted aimlessly in his hand. His limbs jerked, his spine snapped rigid, arching his head back, and from wide-stretched lips he shrieked aloud, terribly loud, a racking, tearing sound of animal terror and agony. He stumbled back, clutching at his head as if hot metal ran through it, utterly unmanned; he blundered into the wall and rebounded against Ils and Roc, so perhaps shielding them somewhat, though they cowered away as one would from the sudden opening of a furnace door. But they caught the tall man as he fell, bore him up swiftly and dragged him kicking back to the steps. His scream had done its work, nonetheless, for from the dark below echoed shouts, slamming of doors, the ring of steel-shod feet upon the stair.

The sword shifted its direction, wavered away from Elof and toward his friends, Kermorvan gray-faced and furious, struggling to rise. But Elof sprang forward after it, keeping himself between it and them, and shouted back over his shoulder, "Get you below, and him with you! You might yet make the door—"

"No chance!" shouted Ils. "They come! We will help you—"

"You cannot! Hold the stair, cut your way out if you can! This is for me alone!" He saw her nod and swing herself down the steps, Kermorvan stumbling after her, and from below there came the sound of blade on blade, and Roc's angry bellow.

Now the sword swung no longer, but pointed straight at Elof, and he felt the sheer power of it pour about him as if it were a rapid he was fording, ever threatening to sweep him off his feet. Desperately he closed his fingers in an attempt to catch it in, but there was too much, too strong a flow, it spilled between his fingers and poured its frothing waves of fear and horror into him. His hair bristled, his heart hammered, it seemed that the floor split at his feet and an abyss gaped there, himself swaying on its brink, hearing the shrieks that echoed upward. He struggled against the current, gasping, choking like a drowning swimmer, and his sight began to dim. Images of terror swirled up before his eyes, shapeless at first, then shadows that gathered and coalesced, flying at him like dark wings riding a stormwind.

He flung his own sword up against them, and for a moment it too became a thing of horror in his hand, dripping with marsh-slime that became the foulness of a corpse split open, rotting and reeking down across his hand, pooling about his ankles, bogging down his steps. But only for an instant. Another image rose up around the marsh-blade, the hand that had first wielded it and clutched it down into a mighty death, that hand no longer blackened and shrivelled but strong, fell, resolute, the hand of a man hewing foes down in droves before him even as his life ebbed and the marsh ensnared his limbs. Elof had taken that blade as his, set himself within it, and with it he had, all unknowing, taken on him its weighty inheritance. He could not now dishonor it by doing less.

He fought forward, thrusting himself into the heart of

the terror he faced. He dimly heard the sounds echoing in the stairwell, hoarse shouts, the dull hammering of arms, the harsh rasping gargle of a life flowing away. All the black dreams he had dreamed came flooding back against him then, all the visions his fever had conjured up, sweating there among the soot of his forge upon the Marshlands—the clawed fingers, the bodies in the wagon, Ingar crumbling away under his hand, Kara a mocking wraith, all mingling into one fearful shape of death and decay, and endless liquescence of life.

He felt as if he could endure no more, as if his heart and mind and will were tendons in a tortured hand, stretched to their limits and beyond, only waiting the last vicious twist to snap in consummate agony. But in none of the fearful things did he find that final force. They came not new to him, as they might have. In his trials and suffering he had faced them, and the worst of him they embodied, once before. And though they still clawed at the very depths of him, yet he found he could face them now. In grief and regret he leaned forward against them as he might into a gale, and like leaves they scattered around him, stuck a moment and were whirled away. He could acknowledge the guilt that was in him, and balance it against what else he found there. He could guess at a price to be paid, make a clear decision. He was sure of himself at last.

Something more?

He struck forward still like a swimmer, on, on, and felt the rush of horror falter an instant, the darkness ebb. His eyes cleared suddenly, and he found himself staring almost into the Mastersmith's face. Beneath the weird mask's frame it was its own gray mask of fear, that Elof should win so close. The pale man staggered back, waving the sword wildly to fend him off, and then in a paroxysm of utter panic and desperation he swung up the patterned sword and struck with all the force in his smith's arm, straight at Elof's unshielded body below his breastbone's end. And thrust him through.

Elof folded forward around the surge of icy, incredible agony, staring foolishly down at the thing that invaded his body. Detached by pain, his mind floated free, watching his own red blood spill out along the blade as an idle spectacle, an interesting exercise, seeing it flow among the patterns he himself had set there, linking them, uniting them at last into a script he could read, a pattern he could understand, that leaped fully formed into his mind. He knew at last the whole meaning of the symbols he had set in the sword.

And dimly, through his roaring ears, he heard an exultant yell from the stairs, a cry of sheer joy from Ils's powerful lungs, and the sound of a body clattering down steps. Roc too was shouting, and above all there rose like a vengeful trump the bitter cry *"Morvan morlanhal!"*

Then he was convulsed again by agony as the sword was jerked free of him, with a cruel twist to it that seemed to tear him asunder. Yet he laughed, laughed aloud as he clutched his hand against the wound, feeling the blood run warm across the gauntlet. There came the sound of many running feet, and cries of fear cut short, and the noise of more who fell and, toppling their fellows, went tumbling away into the depths, a panic, or rout.

"The biter is bitten!" he gasped, and staggered back against the wall. "The thief is robbed, and by his own hand! Do you hear, Mylio, do you hear? Something more was needed, he told me, and now I know what, indeed! You, master that you are, must needs be greater yet, and steal a power that you did not understand! You would have a sword to cleave the mind, to set a man's own fears against himself and drown his reason in its own black depths! But the edge that would cut the spirit is blunted by grosser things, a sword of the mind may not also strike the body! Yet you have made it do so—*and what is it now?"*

The Mastersmith leveled the sword at him, and Elof laughed only the louder. The gray man turned, ran to the stairs, recoiled and pointed it into the dark gap, jabbing desperately at the air as if to drive something back from the opening. But out of it, step by measured step, inexorable as fate, rose the terrible figure of Kermorvan. No longer did that fearsome warrior falter or fall. He had lost his helm, he was wounded in face and leg, but the blood that sprayed in gouts across his mail, that steeped his sword and sword arm scarlet from point to shoulder, was not his own, nor did it shine brighter than the wrath that sprang glittering uselessly with the sword, and Elof wept weakly with the pain of his mirth. "Where are your guards, Mylio? Call them back, bid them slay your foes for you now. Why do they flee? What is it that has gone out of them?"

Then the Mastersmith whirled, and with the speed of madness he hurled himself upon Elof, the sword that was now no more than a sword upraised to strike him down in a last hopeless vengeance. But Elof swept up his own sword, as the hand in his vision had done. Then, with the arm of a smith who had proved mightier, half falling forward, he hammered it down to meet the thing he had made. With a cry like an eagle, black blade stooped clashing upon patterned metal, struck through unstaying and past, down through the painted wood of the Thunderbird mask, through the blue-steel death's head within, through the softer skull beneath and on, on, down, to cleave the Mastersmith Mylio nearly in two.

A husk, a spilled thing, was dashed to the grimy stone of the floor. The halves of the patterned sword dropping spattering among the blood, and as Kermorvan ran up, horrified, they twisted and flexed there like some unclean beast severed, till little by little the cords of metal sprung, split, separated, unwound and writhed apart.

Up the stairs now, yelling exultantly, came Ils, one arm black with blood, bearing up Roc who was gashed badly in the leg and shoulder. But she fell silent as she saw the body of the Mastersmith, though she looked on it unmoved and snorted, "Surprised the thing still bleeds red."

Then they saw Elof, and stumbled toward him, forgetting their own ills. But he waved them back, hugging his own pain to himself. Kermorvan stooped, seized the shattered body and swiftly dragged it out onto the balcony. He looked out, and saw below him on the riven wall blackclad men mustering, slow and reluctant, tall chiefs and shamans in patterned robes screaming at them in furious exhortation. Then Kermorvan laughed aloud, a bitter laugh and cold, and blew a great blast on the horn he bore, and it went out and echoed across the rooftops, among the towers. Other horns answered it, horns that sounded many different tones, silver and gold, brass and steel, the dour blaring of steerhorns. For the alarm had spread, and many waited and watched. And he raised up in his arms, high over his head, the grim thing that had been their chiefest enemy, and the bloodrun seemed to stain the very sky red with dawning.

Many cries arose then from the wall below, but from beyond the untaken walls a solemn fanfare sounded, and the first faint light glinted back a thousandfold from moving files and blades bright-burnished. And atop the golden crown of the highest tower a small bundle rose up the mast, broke and fluttered wide. It was a battle pennant all of sable, with upon it a sunburst in gold and a raven rising to seize it. Kermorvan cried out in a voice that echoed about the walls of the city, that leaped across the scaled roofs and quivered in the very windows of the crowned towers, *"Morvan morlanhal!* Morvan shall arise! Up, Bryhaine, and strike them down! For see you, see! *They fall!"*

And with a heave he hurled the body of the Mastersmith out over the balcony, to plummet limply down upon the broken wall below, and at the very feet of his driven chieftains, held by the power he had long usurped, to be dashed there into shapelessness. Awesome it seemed to them, and terrible beyond words, that what they had deemed so powerful should be so suddenly cast down. They fell back, and their clansmen with them, scraping frantically at the blood that bespattered their robes lest it carry with it some taint of that fearful reverse.

"Kathel has kept his word!" said Kermorvan. "And now, Elof, we must get you—" But where Elof had stood there lay only the black sword, sadly wrung and twisted in a pool of bright blood, and from it a trail that led them to the stairs.

Down that last flight Elof stumbled, sick with agony, coughing down the blood that bubbled in his throat. From the streets below came the first clash of arms as the men of the city, heartened anew, cast off the night and swarmed out to engage their oppressors. And from the Ekwesh camps came stuttering drums, urgent now and uncertain. But Elof paid them little heed, for they and all else seemed to reach him now from behind a thick, a stifling gray curtain, and he yearned to cast it off, to be free. Only there was Kara, still Kara, he saw her all the more clearly when all else had faded, and he knew he must reach her room. He found it by staggering along the walls, almost falling against the door he had left ajar. But even as he plunged through he saw the bed empty and the high windows crashing open in the wind, and he dragged himself across to them. Below him the Ekwesh, neither a driven force nor a coherent army any longer, were streaming away through the streets they had lately taken. Under the fluttering ensign of Raven and Sun the men of the city fell upon them without let or restraint. Even women and children snatched up the weapons of their fallen enemies and harried them as they ran, hewing without mercy any who fell or were cornered. The few who stood to fight were overborne and trampled before their weapons could bite, shieldwalls broken before they could form. No longer driven to attack, no longer held in concord with their ancient rivals, riven of the will that had led them so far into this venture, of the sorcery that had smashed the walls before them, and witness to its last fearful fall, the reiver chieftains broke, panicked and turned to run. Under banner after banner sounded the call to retreat, to regain the ships and the freedom of the sea where they might yet be secure. Rout and riot overtook them amid the rattle of the drums, and those who were yet within the city saw their own ships being pushed half-manned from the beaches, being cut from their anchors and sails frantically unfurled. So it was that at last none sought anything but the harbor and the escape, rather than face the wrath of the folk of Kerbryhaine. And to their own lands they carried a fearful rumor of that wrath, but also of shame unshriven, dishonor unavenged, a smart and fester worse than the wounds they bore.

But Elof did not look upon what he had brought about, for he was staring eastward, into the golden light that poured now across the distant hilltops, bathing the land as if to cleanse it of the stain of war. Circling there, vanishing into it with great slow wingbeats, flew two huge swans, one white, one black. And about the feet of the black one there shone a gleam of silver.

Then Elof's weakness overwhelmed him at last, and he

sank down, away, onto the seat where the mantle had rested. His hand, now black and stiff with blood, sank away from his chest. And there stood Ils, and Roc, and Kermorvan, staring at him in pity and horror, but also in a strange dismay. He looked down, and tore suddenly at the ragged edges of his jerkin, laying bare his flesh beneath. No more than a faint line marked it, and it faded even as they watched. His wound had closed.

Thus it was that Elof came to the true end of his apprenticeship, and the warrior-servants of the Ice were for a time driven back from the Southland. So concludes the volume of the Winter Chronicles named the Book of the Sword. But it records that Elof was to lie ill, despite his strange healing, for many long months, till spring was come again, and the beat of swan wings across the sky. Only then, as the Book of the Helm recounts, did he set off on his journeyman's travels, that were to bring him in the end great understanding, great suffering, great love and the name of Elof Valantor, Elof of the Skilled Hand, mightiest of all magesmiths amid the dark days of the ancient Winter of the World.

Appendix

*Of the land of Brasayhal, its form,
nature and climate, and of its peoples
and their several histories, such as are set
forth in that volume of the Winter
Chronicles called the Book of the Sword.*

The authors of the Winter Chronicles were writing, as men must, for their own times; they left much unexplained that we no longer know, and less often explained at length matters we would today take for granted. Also, they were quite rightly concerned with setting down living experience, and not merely telling a coherent tale. In reducing the Book of the Sword to the fashion of such a tale, therefore, much detail has had to be added—often by guesswork, however informed—and much omitted. This account cannot replace what is lost, but may at least round out the picture. Only what is most relevant to the immediate tale is included; other matters, such as the nature of the Ekwesh society, must wait until more appropriate points in the narrative.

THE LAND

In the years of the Long Winter the extent of the land of Brasayhal was very great, a vast continent that stretched at its widest some thousand leagues from ocean to ocean across the northern world, and from the margins of the Ice to the all but impassable southern deserts some six or seven hundred leagues. Within this expanse were many

realms, and those of the men the least. The events of the
Book of the Sword here recounted took place wholly along
its western seaboard, in the relatively narrow strip of
country—some hundred and thirty leagues at its widest—
between Meneth Scahas, the Shield-Range, and the sea.
This was then the furthest-flung settlement of the peoples
of Kerys, and the newest, being little over one thousand
years old. A natural division to this western strip was the
delta of a once great river, now fenland so flat that the
sea's influence was felt many leagues inland; while out-
flowing streams remained fresh, stagnant or pooled water
soon became brackish, turning the area into a vast saltmarsh. To the south of it stretched out country that was
for the most part open and low-lying, much of it fertile
grassland with only one main hilly region along the coast,
and few large areas of woodland save around the foothills
of the Shield-Range. Warm and well-watered, it was ideal
land for both grain and livestock, and in the drier, hotter
country further south grew many kinds of fruit in profu-
sion. The sea was fished little, and served chiefly for travel.
With this the first settlers, as described by Kermorvan in
Chapter 5, were well content, since it made possible the
city-centered culture they had known in the east; the lands
north of the marshes seemed too wild to suit them. These
were not only colder but higher and more hilly, sloping
up more steeply to join the mountains, and broke up with
thick woodland disturbingly like Tapiau'la-an-Aithen, the
Great Forest of evil memory; save in the valleys, the soil
was much poorer than in the Southlands. Much of the tree
and plant life was different, seeming smaller and less rich,
and there were many more wild and ferocious animals.
For the time being, therefore, it was left little settled and
explored, save by solitaries and outlaws. But when the
later refugees were hounded from the south, they found
the Northlands more to their taste, the people being chiefly
of a northern strain in their homeland and less fond of
large cities. The weather, though cooler, was milder and
moister in summer, and if the grainland was less, there
were rich hill pastures for livestock and as much game as
their hunters could wish. Also the seas were as rich or

richer than in the south, and small fishing communities sprang up along the coast. Less fruit was grown, save in the southernmost valleys around Thuneborg, but gradual clearing of the forests provided valuable wood and more farming land, without ever becoming widespread enough to disrupt the natural balance. In general the northern settlers, both the first-comers and the later brown-skinned peoples from across the Ice, adapted to the land rather than mastered it, as in the south. Their population remained therefore smaller and more scattered, and the country between their towns and villages much wilder, even along the High roads.

In both north and south, settlement was at its thinnest in the country directly against the mountain slopes, though this was once good land enough and well wooded. In the south the first settlers had disputed this land with the duergar, often bloodily, and driven them out. But few who won it prospered, and many a townlet sank into gradual depopulation and decay. In the north there was less dispute, for the settlers were not so hungry for land and the duergar now wary of confronting them, but the spreading influence of the Ice across the Nordenberg ranges had the same effect.

This, then, was the fashion of Brasayhal's western lands at this time. Of its other and yet greater lands more is told in later books. But vast as it was, a region as vast again lay on its northern boundary, and this was the realm of the Great Ice.

THE LONG WINTER

It may seem strange that the land of Brasayhal could remain so habitable and fertile, even in the north, so close to the margins of the Ice. The popular image of an Ice Age is of a period of eternal winter, a chill world blanketed in perpetual snow and ice, without sun or season. In fact, in the many times of glaciation that have oppressed the world, nothing like this has ever come about. Few living things could long survive such a terrible climate, however well adapted. At the height of such glaciations the world as a whole did indeed become colder, but only by a few degrees, on average over a period of time; even where the grip of the Ice was hardest the seasons would still come and go. We know also of the most recent Ice Ages that temperatures fell by very different degrees in different parts of the world. The consequences would therefore vary greatly, and the changes they wrought thus be subtler and more gradual.

One such would be a drop in sea level, laying bare much new land, since so much water was now frozen, and the consequent disruption of the cycle of water between air and river and ocean. This in turn would change the patterns of wind and clouds, and the cycles of rainfall that depend upon them. In many places this would cause or worsen droughts, so that hot but lush and well-watered lands might lose much of their water, but, being far from the ice, little of their heat. They would then become parched, and the deserts spread; this might explain why the equatorial lands of Brasayhal became uninhabitable, impassable deserts, with corresponding zones of calm at sea.

But, contrary to what one might expect, the changes wrought in northern lands could easily have been less severe. The lands immediately bordering the glaciers would soon be reduced to the frozen wastelands called tundra, as did indeed happen in the heartland beyond the Shield-Range. But even there this did not spread as far south of the Ice as the modern tundra, no more than one hundred and fifty leagues at its fullest extent. This was probably because the glaciers thrust forward beyond the colder northern latitudes into warmer, lower lands, where a stalemate developed between their chill and the original climate. Where there was a natural barrier such as the Nordenberg ranges to hold back the glaciers, their effect seems to have been even less drastic. The temperate Northlands suffered severer winters, but spring and summer, though shorter, still came in much of their former warmth. Also, it has been shown that a great mass of ice tends to deflect cyclonic storms southward. The weather may have become stormier, therefore, but rainfall increased, making the land richer for plant life. Certainly a kind of rainforest grew in the north at this time, like that in southern lands but made up of different, temperate vegetation. And it is known that some barren desert lands grew green and wooded.

All in all, it seems that the glaciers had not then so much overrun warmer zones, as squeezed them closer together and heightened their extremes, reducing the distance between the coldest and hottest zones. One could travel from ice-bound lands through cool temperate forests to warm grainlands and subtropical orchards in a much shorter time.

But that is not to minimize the menace of the Ice. The balance of the world is delicate, and needs no immense fall in its mean temperature to wreak havoc on all living things. Such may have been the first intention of the Ice. But there was a worse one, for ice breeds ice, in many ways. A great mass of it must increase the world's whiteness, mirroring back much of the heat of the sun and gradually cooling the air around and ahead of it. If that air becomes too cold, as in the depths of a hard winter, it allows the glaciers to spread further, and chills the icecaps of mountains in their path till they too grow and become glaciers, as Ansker accurately describes; he may have seen it happen, over a succession of winters. Those glaciers would in turn link up with the greater Ice, to reflect more heat and repeat the cycle further ahead, an exponential process with only one logical end. In that process there must be a single, crucial point at which it becomes self-sustaining, where so much heat is being reflected that even high summer in either hemisphere cannot raise the temperature of the world enough to drive back the Ice, and it begins to spread without seasonal check. No improvement in the climate would then be possible, and in a very short time an imprisoning shell of ice would close from both poles to the equator, and the popular picture of an Ice Age come fatally and permanently true.

That crucial point, obviously, has not so far been passed. But in these years of the Winter Chronicles, all unknown to Elof, it was drawing very near.

THE PEOPLES

THE PEOPLE OF THE SOUTHLANDS

The first men who came to the Southlands were rovers from the eastern colonies, many of them landless and outlaws. It was they who first clashed with the duergar of the region, who had formerly roamed at will in that rich country without any thought of claiming it for themselves. But the newcomers were bold and ruthless men, who had survived the many perils of the Forest, and were little disposed to favor any save themselves. A few small settlements were founded, but were destroyed in a generation or less, by either the duergar or internal strife. A few survivors only straggled back eastward, but with tales of the fine land that awaited proper settlement.

Understandably, however, none were too eager to risk such a venture until the Ice began to menace the eastern colonies, and the climate grew colder. The majority of the colonists were descended from the southern race of Kerys, the Penruthya (Arauthar in the northern tongue), and kept their forefathers' preference for a warmer clime, which suited the farming they knew best. A desire grew among them to risk the journey southwestward, but this their kings resisted; they knew that only a strong realm could hope to withstand to the Ice. Nevertheless dissension grew, swelled perhaps by secret votaries of the Ice, as its sinister glitter drew ever nearer the horizon. Conspiracies were formed, to plan flight—or escape, as they called it—and all through one late summer and autumn whole communities left their land and straggled off by one route or other westward. The then king, Keryn IV, might have prevented it with his soldiers, who remained largely loyal, but he was unwilling to start strife that could only aid the Ice.

The fate of such ignorant and ill-planned expeditions in the perilous heartland of Brasayhal can be imagined. Little more than one-third of those who set out won through to the coast. But these were principally the best organized and led, and their settlement this time was well chosen and established, a natural harbor among rich and varied country. This they called Bryhaine, the Land of Freedom, its heart their walled city. But they cast aside all the traditions of Kerys, for the men of wealth and power who had led the expeditions rejected any kind of kingship and established themselves as a governing body, the Syndicacy, membership of which was governed by contributions to the public coffers. The Syndicacy then went further, and made Kerbryhaine a purely Penruthya settlement, where their tongue alone could be spoken. However, they did not otherwise persecute those of northern stock who had come with them. Such was the founding of Bryhaine, and from the very beginning it prospered.

THE PEOPLE OF THE NORTHLANDS

The race that came from the northern lands of Kerys called themselves Svarhath, but were named by sothrans Runduathya. They looked much like their southern cousins, but ran rather to dark hair than to red, and to breadth rather than great height. By nature they were more taciturn and secretive, wise and deep-delving rather than merry and outgoing. They tended to mysticism and deep study, at their worst to fanaticism, treason and stratagem, but at their best to great loyalty, wisdom and strength of will. Thus it was that the majority of them held fast by their lord against the advancing Ice. But Keryn V could not or would not see that his realm was now too weak, and would not spare what resources remained to prepare any refuge. So when at last the Ice rolled over the east, most of those who were not slain fled westward in as poor a state, or worse, than the earlier fugitives. A few held fast, determined to defend the remaining smaller towns of their realm though king and city had fallen. By good fortune those who fled found a leader, though an unwilling one, in the great hero Vayde, who had lately won his way to them over the ocean from Kerys, one of the last to do so. He it was brought them across Brasayhal with small loss, and at last to Bryhaine. But there they found scant welcome, and as the years passed anger grew between the two peoples, swelling at last to terrible strife. Vayde, already old beyond the common years of men, engineered his people's escape northward across the Marshlands at the cost of many lives, including, it is said, his own.

So the realm of Nordeney began in blood, and this,

perhaps, was why it never became a truly sound country. Vayde, had he lived, might have united it, but without him men drifted apart, weary and distrustful, seeking only to live their own lives in peace. Small towns sprang up everywhere, generally around the households of wealthy men and chieftains, but they were small and scattered. The realm might well have been too weak to hold together long, but some hundred and fifty years after the first settlements, a new people began to drift into the northern territories, a strong, sturdy folk with strange-set eyes, black hair and skin the color of dark leather. They came chiefly in boats, from crude skin craft to huge black-hulled galleys, sailing westward along the dangerous margins of the Ice in search of new lands to settle. For they too were refugees from the Ice, which was overrunning their western homeland, and from the growing power of a strange cruel nation which was profiting from the disorder. The northerners, remembering their own misfortunes, and with plenty of land to spare, made them welcome. They were well repaid, for the newcomers, a lively and industrious people, well used to living in cool lands not far from the Ice, swiftly learned the ways and the tongue of the people of Kerys and joined with them in increasing the worth and strength of the land, and the wealth of the townships. Some grew quite large, though never to a fraction the size and stature of Kerbryhaine. Without the newcomers Nordeney might not have survived. In time they so mingled with the first settlers that a pure white skin became a rarity (and sometimes ill thought of), especially in the most northerly lands.

It was mutual trade and the demands of trade that came to hold the Northland towns together, and the guild systems, inherited from the east, became of signal importance. Within a generation too, there was trade with Bryhaine, which, no longer threatened, may have felt some shame and remorse for its former harshness. As the years passed into centuries the two realms settled into mutual acceptance, though the bonds of friendship that had created the strength of Kerys were never renewed. Strong links were forged by the traveling traders, and these lasted for many hundreds of years. But otherwise the two realms lived lives apart, neither knowing nor caring much about the other save as it affected their trade. So it was that neither saw the slow decaying that settled on them both, which a union of their sundered strengths might have helped resist.

THE LAWMAKERS AND THE GUILDS

The guilds were almost the only authorities common to Northland and Southland, and even that link was tenuous. They had common roots in both realms, and before that in the Lost Lands of the east, but by Elof's time they had grown far apart, most notably in the influence they enjoyed.

Rule and order in the north were clearly left to each town to sort out for itself; in larger towns some kind of elected council usually directed day-to-day affairs, but in smaller towns it was commonest to find a more or less autocratic headman, either hereditary or chosen by a council of elders. Law was therefore a strictly local matter, but the rules and standards set by the guilds, which the townships had to enforce, provided an element of continuity; as these covered such matters as fair trading, quality, weights and measures, contract enforcement, employment and apprenticeship, they concerned almost every aspect of life, and were a strong stabilizing influence. The guilds therefore wielded great political power, becoming the nearest thing to a government in Nordeney; they encouraged the leaguing of towns for mutual defense and the protection of trade.

In the Southlands, by contrast, power lay squarely in the hands of the Syndicacy. In peacetime it was principally a law-making council, usually dominated by one or two powerful personalities who were the city Marshals, commanders of the Guard, an armed constabulary. In emergencies such as the Ekwesh invasion, however, the Guard became the nucleus of a citizen army, and the syndics became commanders under the guidance of the Marshals, directing the actual fighting if they were warriors, supervising watch-keeping, firefighting and food rationing if they were not. Otherwise, individual syndics enjoyed prestige and influence, especially if they sat as magistrates in the city courts, but no personal power. Exceptions to this were the Marchwardens, syndics from the warrior class charged with defending the borders; in practice this usually meant suppressing bands of outlaws and corsairs, rather than actual war. As the Syndicacy grew complacent and corrupt, strong Marchwardens could often make themselves all-powerful within their domain.

In Bryhaine, therefore, the guilds were no more than trade and craft organizations, even their rules subject to ratification by the Syndicacy. Their political power was slight, save when members would band together to finance a representative for the Syndicacy. Kathel Kataihan was one such, for though his personal wealth was instrumental, he could not have managed all the high contributions on his own. Sometimes a powerful guild might put pressure on the Syndicacy; the Farmers' Guild had some prestige, for many landowning syndics were members, and the Mariners' Guild, directly descended from that of Kerys itself, jealously maintained the privilege of legislating sea traffic. But there was never any doubt where the ultimate authority lay.

Once only did the guilds of both lands work together, and that was in the early days when enmities had faded, both realms were wealthy and trade was expanding. Then they came together, with the guarded blessings of the Syndicacy and the larger northern towns, and built the great Causeway across the Marshlands, replacing the former crazy mix of half-flooded trails, short stretches of embanked wagon track and rickety bridges. They also began the extension of the High roads into Nordeney, but this was completed in later years by the north alone.

THE DUERGAR

The duergar race is so hedged about with mystery that it is hard to form a clear picture of their ultimate origins, though more is said about their history in later books. Their strange subterranean way of life, their great wisdom and craft, their long lifespans, diminished form and secretive natures are matters of legend, and in the days of their power few besides Elof and Kermorvan were privileged to see beyond that. But despite the accretions of myth, there is no doubt that they were an ancient offshoot of the same mortal stock as men. They often named themselves the Elders, and angrily rued the coming of humans as one would the growth of ungrateful and unruly children. Some clues may also be found in the detailed physical descriptions in the Chronicles. These reflect an anatomical pattern consistent with one particular race of men whose limb bones are characteristically short and slightly bowed, with very strongly marked points of muscle attachment, indicating a stocky build and remarkable strength. Their skulls appear low-vaulted, giving a sloping forehead, but the average brain capacity is actually larger. The heavy jaw and straightlined chin, neither receding nor protruding, are also characteristic of later forms of the only accepted subspecies of man, *Homo sapiens soloensis* or *neanderthalensis*.

The popular picture of Neanderthal man is still seriously distorted by early studies of the first remains identified, which suffered from the preconceptions of the scientists and their failure to see that the bones were those of an old man crippled with arthritis. The brain capacity alone should have alerted them, but the image of a shambling caveman they produced has proved hard to dispel. In actual fact a Neanderthal man would look little more unusual among later men than an Eskimo, and many Neanderthal skull and facial features can still be found as individual variations of *Homo sapiens sapiens*—except, that is, for the larger brain. Interestingly enough, many authorities regard Neanderthal characteristics as specialized adaptations to an unusually cold climate.

If such an identification is possible, it is an important factor in dating the Chronicles, and something of a problem. Neanderthalers vanished as a separate type some 40,000 to 35,000 years ago, in the middle phase of the last glaciation. Some theories suggest they were exterminated by *Homo sapiens*, others that they interbred with him—a view that surviving traits, such as a low bump at the rear curve of the skull, would support. A third possibility, indicated by the little the duergar would reveal of their own traditions, is that their own ancient civilization was of old assailed by the Ice and the coming of men, and only preserved by the intervention of Ilmarinen, whom they revered, in making their refuges in the hollow hills. As later books of the Chronicles indicate, there is probably some truth in all three.

At the time of the Chronicles the duergar way of life, as indicated in Chapters 7 and 8, suggests a relatively small population, widely scattered. But the sheer size of their underground realm, running the entire length of the Shield-Range, equally suggests a much larger population, and there is little doubt that in their isolation the duergar were in decline. Why this was is uncertain. Their food supplies were undoubtedly plentiful; they grew food on inaccessible mountain terraces not unlike those around Inca cities, whose entire topsoil was hauled up the high slopes on the backs of porters. Some livestock, including strains of mountain goat, was raised there also, but meat did not play a large part in their diet; it was not unlike the traditional Chinese fare, strongly based on grain, vegetables and the fish in which their rivers abounded, and generally well balanced. The health of the duergar was naturally good, and their knowledge of healing deep; there are no records of plagues or recurrent disease. The cause of their decline seems to have been spiritual rather than physical, and very probably Elof caught it exactly when he questioned their purpose in the world. Many duergar seem to have felt the lack of a purpose, and yet so mistrusted the outside world that they could not bring themselves to seek it. Ansker was unusual in his understanding of men, and undoubtedly he and Ils strove to appear as natural to them as they could; the commoner duergar personality seems to have been much stranger and more remote.

OTHERS

Such were the chief peoples of western Brasayhal at this time. There were many others on its borders, such as the Children of Tapiau, whose true home was elsewhere in the land, and the Ekwesh, at this time still sailing back to their homelands across the western oceans. More is said of these later in the Chronicles. But it is possible that there should be one more addition to the races of men. These are the snow-trolls, for, strange and monstrous as they were, they wore man's shape in a land where no ape has ever come.

But since they were creatures of the Ice, it is possible that they were borne from the far west, the harsh homelands of the Ekwesh along the margins of the Ice. Certainly some remains have been found there, principally enormous teeth, of a vast creature that must have stood half again as tall as a man, and with far greater bulk. Significantly, it has been suggested that the huge growth of these creatures, called *Gigantopithecus,* was another kind of adaptation to the Ice. And although such remains as have been found date from an earlier season of the Long Winter, it may be equally significant that legends of similar creatures yet persist on both sides of the Western Ocean, and in the same areas.

LANGUAGES OF THE TWO LANDS

Original texts of the Winter Chronicles are written in the ideographic script of Kerys, which was largely common to both northern and southern tongues. Because each word is depicted by an ideograph, and not actually spelled out, it is not always possible to tell which of the two tongues is being spoken in the text. I have tried to suggest this, though, where the context permits.

More seriously, it is not always known how words sounded, even though their meaning is known; direct equivalents cannot easily be traced in a living tongue, as was done with Egyptian hieroglyphs and Coptic, and this creates a problem. Each tongue has its own strongly individual character. One, the Svarhath, was distinctly ''northern'' in character, being somewhat hard-edged and harsh; the southern tongue, Penruthya, was softer and more rolling, and at the same time more elaborately formal. The names and terms we do know in these tongues make it certain that they were broadly ancestral to the Indo-European families, especially those strains which were to develop into the various languages of northwestern Europe (sometimes defined as the *kentum* tongues, from the common term for one hundred); in particular, they were remarkably close to the Germanic (or Scandinavian) and Celtic families respectively. So, to preserve their individuality, the spellings of names and other words have Scandinavian or Celtic flavors, as appropriate. It is important to remember, though, that they were not as different as this suggests; Scandinavian and German would be a better example in that respect. More than half their vocabulary came from similar roots, though differently developed and pronounced, and the grammatical structure was broadly similar. Not so the final effect; Penruthya speakers found Svarhath "furry" and somewhat uncouth, Svarhath speakers thought Penruthya clear but inexpressive. But neither found the other's tongue especially hard to learn, especially in written form, since the same ideographs served for both languages; this is probably why the various alphabetical scripts that existed never entered common usage, and were thought of almost as codes or cryptograms. Probably many of the Mastersmith's books were written in alphabetical characters.

It is interesting that at one point in the Book of the Sword, Kermorvan, through modesty or caution, very definitely talks in Svarhath when the subject would suggest his native tongue. This is his brief account of the fall of the great eastern city, in which he uses the northern form of its name, the Strandenburg, here rendered City by the Waters. His reasons are made clear in the Book of the Helm.

OTHER TONGUES

Little can be said about these at this stage. Most duergar knew the northern tongue; Andvar spoke an old and rather literary form of it. But it is noticeable that most other duergar spoke in a broad, colloquial fashion, suggesting a preference for informality in their own tongue. Elof and Kermorvan did undoubtedly learn some of the difficult duergar language, but very little of it is preserved; it looks at first sight almost Slavic, but has an inescapable resemblance to Finno-Ugrian tongues. More is said of this, and of the Ekwesh tongues, in later books.

SHIPS

Descriptions of three different types appear in the Book of the Sword. From these and occasional marginal illustrations and illumination (reconstructed on the maps at the beginning of the book) it is possible to make reasonably informed reconstructions.

EKWESH GALLEYS

The Ekwesh raiding ships were the most feared warships of their day. As the vessels described in Chapter 1 do not appear to have been bireme types—which would probably not have been very seaworthy in an open ocean—it is possible to make a rough estimate of their length from the number of oars per side. To be used freely, these would have had to be about three feet apart, but in a fast raiding vessel no more than that; a length of one hundred feet would not be unreasonable. Also, to be as hard to see as they were, the ships must have ridden quite low in the water. We know also that they were relatively sleek and narrow-beamed, and had at most partial decking to cover the cargo. All this fits a recognizable pattern. These vessels, like many "primitive" warships, were extreme sophistications of the war-canoe form, but given great speed and carrying capacity by the addition of a sail. This, as in most other ships of the time, was a simple square. Descriptions in the Chronicles, and details such as the heavy tarred-cord reinforcements, suggest that the Ekwesh had mastered the use of it across the wind, and even in some cases against it. Illumination and marginal illustrations, though stylized, bear this out.

The warships described in Chapter 1 seem to have been typical of the earlier days of Ekwesh expansion. It is significant, though, that they are definitely smaller than the ones described in Chapter 5. Even when laden with booty these ride substantially higher in the water than the corsair craft, and are described as being at least half again as long—probably something of an understatement. They have full decking and some kind of sterncastle, and holds big enough for prisoners and booty. Evidently the Ekwesh had begun to build larger and more sophisticated vessels to carry larger raiding parties, and richer pickings. Some of this may have been the Mastersmith's influence, but there is little doubt that it would have happened anyway.

THE CORSAIR CRAFT

This seems to have been a typical small war craft of Bryhaine. The spiked ram was characteristic, a useful weapon that could not only penetrate an enemy's planking, but hold to it for boarding, unlike most Ekwesh ships which rammed only to sink, having either reinforced lower bows or using a heavy beam with metal sheathing, which often glanced off springy planking. The corsairs' tally of oars suggests a length of around sixty feet, possibly more. It was probably more strongly built than Ekwesh vessels, somewhat broader in the beam and less subtly shaped, relying on its smaller size and proportionally larger sail area for any advantage in speed. It seems to have had very little decking, save platforms at bow and stern to cover the cargo, and the journey back with twenty-two women on board, described in Chapter 5, must have been somewhat arduous—though no doubt preferable to the Ekwesh holds.

DUERGAR COURIER BOAT

Although this was built only for fast sailing on calm underground waterways, it seems to have been of very advanced construction for the time, and this no doubt is why the one carrying Kermorvan, Ils and Elof was able to survive in the open sea for as long as it did. Under thirty feet long, it seems to have had the narrow hull typical of waterway boats, but with a sharp vertical bow, and, fortunately, a somewhat deeper draft; being fully decked, with bulkheaded compartments beneath, probably strengthened it. Its rig was unusual, the sail area much larger and baggier than normal to catch the gentle breezes of the tunnel system, and having a small extra topsail; this was not normally furled, but lowered against the mainsail, as on Norwegian *femboring* craft. Remarks in the text suggest that larger duergar craft normally had multiple sails, and perhaps quite complex rigs, though no doubt of a very specialized kind. Other unusual features of the courier boat were a pivoted rudder rather than a steering oar, and the use of winches to allow one person to sail the craft from the tiller, possibly aided by some spring or counterweight mechanism. Without these it might not have been possible to control such a sail in any strong sea wind. In fact, even with the leeboard improvised by Kermorvan (a feature still seen on traditional Netherlands designs) it is remarkable that the little craft carried the three travelers as far as it did without a capsize.

FLORA AND FAUNA

It is an indication of the slow effect of the Ice, despite the "compression" of climatic zones mentioned earlier, that so much of the life in these lands was little different from recent forms—except that in many ways it was richer. What the Ice could not do, the settlements of men have achieved. So, many plants and animals mentioned in the Chronicles are easily identified and need no comment; they are much the same as modern forms inhabiting these areas, or similar areas elsewhere. This last is particularly true of regions like the Marshlands, whose sharp and sinister black rushes (*Juncus gerardii* and *roemerianus*) survive to torment walkers in many modern saltmarshes. But even a slightly colder climate can dramatically alter habitats, and many strange creatures found places among these lands that now dwell elsewhere, or have vanished altogether.

THE CREATURES OF THE ICE

As to the strange and fearful beasts unleashed by the Ice, little can be said with certainty. If they were not created by it, they were distorted and ruined, a living mockery and vengeance upon life itself. It is significant that the Chronicles give them names in the tongue of the duergar, who knew them of old; the dragon they called *arachek,* the giant lizard-thing *akszawan.* It is some witness to the terror they wielded that recognizable images of both name and beast yet survive in the folklore of what were once the Northlands. The same, let it be said, is true of Amicac, the Sea Devourer; but terror though he was, he was no servant of the Ice.

DOMESTICATED PLANTS AND ANIMALS

The Chronicles give us relatively little detail about most of these—whether the "goats" on the duergar's mountain pastures were some kind of mountain goat or sheep, for example. But in one or two cases it is possible to say more.

HORSES These may have been a breed imported from Kerys, which did not survive the great changes that were to come. But a reference in one place to a stiff mane, and elsewhere to a small size, suggests that some, at least, were the primitive native breed, which probably resembled Przewalski's horse; it spread through these lands and into the far south, but became wholly extinct before modern times.

CATTLE (CHAPTER 1) The cattle the boy Alv herded resembled no modern breed. Indeed, their immense size and span of horns suggest that they were a very early domestication of the giant wild cattle, the aurochs; this only became extinct in 1627, and all domestic cattle are descended from it. It is interesting that the rare semi-wild cattle of the Chillingham breed, though much smaller, are this same off-white color; they are also so fierce as to be barely manageable without, perhaps, such a goad.

WILD ANIMALS

CARNIVORES (CHAPTER 2) The beasts that attacked the Mastersmith's party cannot be identified for certain. The description does not fit the commonest carnivores of the period, *Canis dirus*, or dire wolves. More probably they were the rarer *Chasmaporthetes*, a relation of the hyena but with a build and dentition more like that of a cheetah.

DAGGERTOOTH (CHAPTER 2) Two beasts may have been known by this name—either *Smilodon*, the classic "sabertoothed tiger," or its slightly smaller relation *Homotherium*. The "biting cat" that killed the large beaver *(Casteroides)* was probably a close ancestor of the puma.

WISANTS (CHAPTER 4) Wisant or wisent is another name for the bison, then a newcomer to these lands and still evidently retaining its forest-dwelling habits. It was only after the end of the Long Winter that its descendants the buffalo spread out across the plains.

HOUNDS OF NIARAD (CHAPTER 9) These are correctly identified as whales. Their eerie songs reverberating through the hulls of small boats can still startle modern crews; they sing chiefly in calm water, though, not while hunting. Also, the description fits no known living breed. The elongated body twice the length of the boat (making it around sixty feet), the long jaws with large wide-spaced teeth, the dermal armor and apparent lack of any dorsal fin might, however, describe a member of the *Archaeoceti*, often called *zeuglodons* after their best-known member. These are an ancient family of whales parallel with, not ancestral to, modern forms, and believed to have been extinct for some millions of years. This would make them a startling anachronism in the relatively recent period of the Chronicles, but it is worth considering that creatures of serpentine shape are not uncommonly sighted at sea even yet.

MAMMUT (CHAPTER 9) The actual name used is *ksalhat*, but the old Russian form mammut has been substituted, as this beast sounds most like a species of woolly mammoth, probably *Mammuthus columbi*. Despite reconstructions showing it on snow-bound tundra, it was almost certainly a forest animal for most of the year. The sole doubt arises from the size of the beast described; some woolly mammoths were no larger than Indian elephants. It could instead have been some long-haired breed of mastodon. Several kinds were common in Brasayhal during the Long Winter, many larger than woolly mammoths, and the tusks of terrifying proportions. Interestingly enough, the Yukaghir tribes who today inhabit what must once have been part of the Ekwesh realm, still name the beast *xolhut*.

THE FORESTS

The coastal and giant redwoods *sequoia sempervirens* and *sequoiadendron giganteum*, seem to have dominated most of the western coastal forests at this period—as indeed they did until very recently. Understandably, therefore, the forests closely resembled those that survive there today, though naturally they lacked introduced species such as eucalyptus, whose fragrance floods modern woodlands. Then, they must have smelled largely of resiny evergreens, because beside the redwoods they had the almost equally gigantic cedars and firs found today, the bristlecone pine and many other kinds of evergreen; deciduous trees were a minority, but a substantial one. In northern areas, however, a kind of tree is described which can only be the so-called dawn redwood, *metasequoia*, an ancient cousin of the giants, and at about sixty feet high relatively small. It must already have been rare; until recently, when specimens were rediscovered in China, it was thought to have been long extinct.

RELIGION

This is one of the hardest subjects to comment on, for although the peoples of Kerys were aware of forces at work in the world, feared some and respected others, they rarely turned to formal worship of either; when they did, it was usually to darker forces. These tendencies seem to have endured in their descendants.

By the time of the Chronicles, though, the settlers in the north were already losing their ancient knowledge of the powers, both favorable and hostile, and the will that lay behind them. That knowledge was absorbed into the animistic beliefs of the newcomers, more comprehensible to a simple peasant society, and relegated to folk legend. For example, the royal banner of the Lost Lands showed Raven flying across the sun, leading men to its light. But this eventually became transmuted to a tale of Raven stealing the sun for mankind, and so it has endured.

In the Southlands greater wisdom was preserved, but it had hardened—or fossilized—into patriotic and civic ritual. To a sophisticated sothran such as Kermorvan an appearance of Raven would be like a statue stepping down off its pedestal, Athena appearing to Pericles.

Common to both countries, though, was a concept of afterlife they called the River. This they saw as a barrier to an afterworld beyond perception or return, except possibly by dark arts. That image may in part derive from the dark regions of tundra and taiga forest that always spread ahead of the Ice, lands crossed by a network of rivers icy with meltwater. For these were the realm and preserve of Taoune, and there the dead were ever to be found.

EKWESH RELIGION

Though a full account of the Ekwesh society, and the strange forces at work within it, belongs in later volumes, some account of their religion should be given here; its blacker side was well known, but Kermorvan had evidently learned something more. In its original form it was the same simple animism as that of the other peoples of their land, but as the Ekwesh grew stronger their religion came to be dominated by the shamans who became powers in the clans second only to the chieftains; in some cases they wielded more real power. Their rites involved dancing to drums and ecstatic, visionary frenzies in which their pronouncements were regarded as oracular. At this stage they still retained some recognition and reverence of the powers, but a new element gradually began to intrude itself: the outright worship of the advancing Ice. This was organized as a kind of secret society or mystery religion among the upper echelons of the clans, to which only the elect and powerful were admitted, and it drastically changed the character of their society.

The cannibalism that made them so greatly loathed and dreaded was apparently an ancient custom, probably encouraged by the dwindling of food supplies as the Ice overran their lands. But originally it had been a funeral rite, intended to honor and perpetuate the dead by absorbing their wisdom and bravery. The new cult made it a rite of debasement and domination, battening on thralls. It fits the pattern of a society being systematically corrupted and turned against its neighbors. And, indeed, it appears that the Ice cult made deliberate use of even greater atrocities in its rituals to create a dark bond among its votaries and heighten their ruthlessness. Similar ideas have been attributed to recent cults, such as thuggee in India and the Anioto and Mau Mau in Africa.

SMITHCRAFT

True smithcraft had a definite religious significance in the Northlands; smith's work was an act of secondary creation linking them to the shaping powers and their creator. Though by the time of the Chronicles it was somewhat taken for granted, it kept a great civic importance. The town smith was a privileged citizen, responsible more to his guild than the town authorities; he was usually the best-educated man in small villages, and through his journeyman's wanderings the most widely traveled. He would marry couples over his anvil, symbolically joining them as the rings he forged for them. Later he would name their children, and in the smaller towns might also give them an elementary education. Most smiths, though, remained little more than smiths, never achieving mastership. Those who did might simply be accomplished craftsmen, like Hjoran, but often they were already wealthy enough to rise above the day-to-day business of smiths, and devote themselves to civic affairs, fine art or even scholarship and natural philosophy; a few individuals, however, turned to personal ambition.

The people of Bryhaine regarded smithcraft as mere superstition, but nonetheless flocked to buy the work of northern smiths in preference to their own. Certainly it had a fixed base of ritual in the introduction of music, verse, pattern and shaping at various stages of the creative process; these were seen as expressing and harnessing the power or talent latent within the smith. Music or verse might come first. Music was generally held to be the more intense influence on the work, but for that reason the less finely controlled; the words gave direction to the intensity. The pattern caught and bound the influence thus expressed, and the completed shaping of the piece gave it the necessary identity.

In the duergar the power of true smithcraft seems to have been more evenly spread than in ordinary men, with fewer troughs and peaks among individuals. That, and the immense reserve of experience maintained in a long-lived and stable society, gave them an advantage. But a truly powerful human smith could often achieve much more, and create work of startling intensity, if only he had the skill.

True smithcraft did not automatically confer skill in working metal, but the greater the skill, the more it was intensified. And such skill there must certainly have been; in the years of the Chronicles, metalworking, especially among the duergar, reached heights that have barely been equaled. The making of Kermorvan's sword, as recounted in Chapter 7, is a fair summing-up of the process by which *bulat* steel was made, the secret of the ancient sword-smiths of Damascus; the oiled-silk patterns and the golden sheen were characteristic. That technique produced a carbon steel, combining elasticity with great strength, that even advanced industrial processes have not matched. The Damascus smiths did not understand how their process achieved this, and neither did modern researchers, until recently. Elof and his duergar master evidently understood it perfectly.

It is worth noting that metalworking long remained something of a separate and mysterious art, even in societies that had lost all memory of true smithcraft. Among the Touareg of North Africa, the smiths form a separate caste, in some ways inferior but respected in others; the curse of a smith is not taken lightly. And in our own society the village smith was a powerful figure in folklore, and especially folk medicine, a "kenning man" by virtue of his profession.

THE CHRONICLES

In Kerbryhaine the recording of history was something of a religious exercise, drawing moral guidance and lessons from the errors of the past, and it was probably some surviving aura of this that caused the Winter Chronicles to be preserved when so much else was lost, numinous things to be copied and recopied even when their meaning had entirely faded.

Although the date they were written cannot now be said for certain, there is no doubt that the world they record is not so very remote. In its vast age the world has endured many long winters, many ages when the polar ice has thrust its crushing fingers outward across warmer lands. But only in the four great glaciations of the most recent, or Quartenary, era can there have been men to record them. There are other indications which may narrow the field further. We have seen that the world of the Winter Chronicles bore a very great likeness to our own; its plants and animals, despite some slight inconsistencies and archaic forms, are recent enough to be recognizable in such of the same habitats as man has spared. Even more striking are the maps in some Chronicles; when we translate them from different mapping conventions and projection techniques, as has been done for the endpaper map, and allow for the greater width of coastal land exposed by the drop in sea level at this time, the resulting coastline is recognizably recent. All these strong similarities suggest the most recent of the four glaciations. Known as the Wurm or Wechsalian, and in America the Wisconsinian, this is generally agreed to have reached its height some eighteen thousand years ago. Its rise was slow, its decline remarkably rapid. And it is at the height of just such a major glaciation that the events of the Book of the Sword occurred.

MICHAEL SCOTT ROHAN was born in Edinburgh, Scotland, and graduated from Oxford with a master's degree in law and legal philosophy, and a great dislike of law. He is the author of several works of nonfiction; one science fiction novel, *Run to the Stars;* and numerous short stories.

THE ANVIL OF ICE begins Mr. Rohan's spectacular fantasy trilogy, *The Winter of the World.* (Watch for *The Forge in the Forest,* second volume in the trilogy, coming next year from Avon Books!) Mr. Rohan writes, "The story has a million roots but derives most from my love of mythology, archaeology and prehistory, and also classical music."

AVONOVA PRESENTS
MASTERS OF FANTASY AND ADVENTURE

SNOW WHITE, BLOOD RED 71875-8/ $4.99 US/ $5.99 CAN
edited by Ellen Datlow and Terri Windling

A SUDDEN WILD MAGIC 71851-0/ $4.99 US/ $5.99 CAN
by Diana Wynne Jones

THE WEALDWIFE'S TALE 71880-4/ $4.99 US/ $5.99 CAN
by Paul Hazel

FLYING TO VALHALLA 71881-2/ $4.99 US/ $5.99 CAN
by Charles Pellegrino

THE GATES OF NOON 71781-2/ $4.99 US/ $5.99 CAN
by Michael Scott Rohan